Battle Dawn

Book Three of the
Chronicles of Arden

First Edition

Shiriluna Nott & SaJa H.

Edited by Karen Robinson of INDIE Books Gone Wild
Proofread by Jennifer Oberth of INDIE Books Gone Wild
Cover Design by Dennis Frohlich

In honor of the lives impacted by the tragedy at Pulse Orlando. For those who were lost. For those who were shattered. For those who are now afraid. Together, we are stronger than hate. Together, we are love. And love always wins.

— Shiriluna Nott & SaJa H

If you would like to receive notifications regarding upcoming releases in the Chronicles of Arden series, please sign up for Shiriluna Nott's mailing list here;
http://www.shirilunanott.com/mailinglist.html

Links to other books in the *Chronicles of Arden* series:

A CALL TO ARMS: BOOK ONE
http://www.amazon.com/dp/B00OK3HUSI

NIGHTFALL: BOOK TWO
http://www.amazon.com/dp/B00X1UTEBW

TABLE OF CONTENTS

The World of Temhara

Teivel

Northern Empire

Dassel

Amsel

Nales

Ostlea

Highmore

Pinnacle Peaks Mountain Range

Beihai

Darkspear Lake

Shiraz

Jacdant Mountain

Terria Lake

Arden

Winterfell

Willowdale

Silver City

Lake Talhador

Shantar

Zio River

Tempist River

Nishila River

Sea of Tiberan

Gulch Bay

Greenbank

Lake Asmar

Raja

Tahir

Anumi River

Galia

Snowy Desert

Gyptia

Lavendel

Tallo Rainforest

Tembo

Nailah

PROLOGUE

A light breeze drifted through a window set high in the bedchamber, but it was neither the frosty air nor the sound of thin flax curtains brushing against the granite walls that roused him. An ominous feeling—a dark foreboding that something was amiss—tore his mind from the drowsy haze of slumber and set his heart pounding within his chest.

Hasain Radek's eyes slid open, and with no small effort, the young lord lifted his head to peer around his room. Moonlight flooded the chamber, illuminating the velvet canopy above and chasing the shadows from even the farthest corners of the room. The hour was late: the length of time just before dawn when Death itself seized the world and only with the climbing sun could life break free.

Hasain rubbed his clammy arms as he sat up. The prostitute by his side shifted in her sleep but didn't wake. Long tendrils of hair framed her naked body, and full, painted lips curled into a smile atop her placid face. Her presence did little to ward off the chill in Hasain's bones and served only as a bitter reminder that his life was in ruins.

The putrid stench of vomit infiltrated his nostrils and brought back hazy memories of the previous night, spent alone and drunken at some rundown tavern. Shameful heat scorched his cheeks. When had he returned here with the prostitute? A mark ago? Several marks ago? His mind, muddled by whiskey, couldn't recall any of it. Then again, nothing in Hasain's life made sense anymore. He'd become a wraith, a shadow of his former self, going through the daily motions without direction or purpose. Would he ever wake from the endless nightmare, or was it his fate to be trapped inside this miserable existence forever?

"Enjoying the fineries in life, are you?"

Hasain's heart stopped. That voice—where had it come from? Was someone else here? Wide-eyed and trembling, he whirled around, trying to find the source of the intrusion. "Who—who's there? Show yourself!"

The silken lilt returned, caressing him as though it were an old friend. Hasain gasped and tried to pull away, but there was no escaping it. The voice came from nowhere and everywhere at the same time.

"You're not at all what I was expecting, Radek's heir. Lying with a whore—vomit puddled over the side of your bed like some common drunk. Were Rishi not already dead, he would surely die of shame to see you now."

The words pierced his heart like a knife. He reeled, rage and despair surging up to fill the gushing wound. "I know who you are! Father warned me about you."

Eloquent cadence dissolved into hard rasps and swelled to envelope the room. *"Oh, he warned you, did he? And what did the dead king tell you of me?"*

Letting out a strangled cry, Hasain pulled the bedsheets tight to his chin but was too terrified to move further. He stole a glance toward the prostitute, and a shudder raced up his spine when he realized she hadn't stirred. The whore remained completely motionless beside him, as if trapped by a spell, the sound of her shallow breaths the only indicator she was even alive.

Frantic eyes darted around the room, but still Hasain couldn't see the entity who had spoken. Yet in the dark recesses of his heart, he *knew*. He couldn't hide from his fate anymore. At last, it was time to face the legacy of the red stone.

Heart hammering in his chest, Hasain replied, "You're him, aren't you? The demon. *Leviticus.*"

Sinister laughter rippled through the room, and then—

The blood drained from Hasain's face when movement near the window caught his eye. His first instinct was to tear his gaze away, but fear held him paralyzed, and he could do nothing but stare in horror as the creature materialized out of thin air before him.

White fabric wrapped seamlessly around alabaster skin, cascading down a slender trunk until the silken material grazed the floor. Auburn locks fell over a sharp nose and fierce eyes. A pair of thin lips perched atop a smooth, pointed chin and were pulled tight into a wicked smile that even the long wisps of hair couldn't fully conceal.

Hasain pressed his back to the wall, feeling nauseated. What right did such a treacherous monster have to take the appearance of a human man?

The room spun as the demon floated soundlessly across the stone floor, stopping not even an arm's length from the foot of the bed. His silver eyes shone in the moonlight, hard, calculating gems.

"I suppose he filled your heart with misgivings about the tormented creature trapped within the stone," the demon hissed.

Repulsion rose to gag Hasain as he watched in utter horror. The demon's lips, they didn't move when it spoke.

"Did he tell you I'm a ruthless schemer who will stop at nothing to have my way?"

Hasain recoiled further. "He said I'm not to trust you! And I don't. I won't listen to you. I won't succumb to your lies."

A cunning leer flicked across the demon's face. *"Bold words, Hasain Radek, but how do you manage them? I can hear your frail, mortal heart hammering away as if to make a grand escape. Is there any of your father in you? You may look like him, but you reek of cowardice."*

Hasain's voice abandoned him. He longed to deny the accusations and proclaim his bravery. But it wasn't true. The demon was right. Hasain wasn't brave or noble like his father. Since the King's death, Hasain's life had spiraled out of control. He was no longer allowed inside the council room, and his privileges had been stripped away. His father's grace wasn't available to shield Hasain from the scorn of the royal councilors, men who had no place for the bastard son of the dead king. His name could grant little more than luxury now, and he'd bitterly resigned himself to the fate of a pampered nobody who would never again have any real influence. He was nothing.

Hasain didn't voice his despair, but his sullen eyes betrayed the anguish he felt inside.

Leviticus descended, looming menacingly above the bed. *"You understand the laws of the stone, do you not?"*

Hasain understood as well as he could. His father's note had detailed at least the most basic principles of dealing with the stone and the prisoner within. Koal, Aodan, and the few others who knew of the demon's existence could also recount what Rishi had told them while he was still alive. None were experts on the matter, but at least Hasain wasn't alone— whether he felt like it or not.

Leviticus didn't hesitate to press his point. *"It's a dark hour for your country. What's your plan of action? Are you going to continue to drink away your youth and good health, or do you intend to do something?"*

"There's nothing I *can* do. It will fall upon Deegan to rectify the actions of Arden's steward."

"Ah, yes. That's right. Despite being the eldest son, the mere fact that you're a bastard prevents you from taking what should be your birthright."

Hasain locked his jaw, refusing to respond to the insult.

"I can help you with that, you know. All of it. The loss of your privileges. The country being in the hands of a madman. You not being in line for the throne. Everything. I can make it all better. You only have to allow me. You only need ask."

Leviticus leaned precariously close, and Hasain scrambled to get away. In his panic, his elbow knocked into the prostitute's shoulder. Still she didn't stir.

Hasain raised his chin defiantly, glaring at the demon. "I will *never* allow you to ruin me! My father was a wise man, and he told me to never listen to your lies!"

Silver eyes flashed dangerously, two shards of lightning in the dark. *"Your father was a fool. I came to him thrice on the day of his demise, and each time he rejected me. I could have pulled him from that deathbed and allowed him to continue his rule. But would he see reason? No! Rishi Radek's pride and stubborn nature were his downfall. Are you going to be the same, Radek's heir?"*

The bile at the back of Hasain's throat made him want to retch. He wished the demon's words were a lie. He longed to be able to say as much—but he couldn't. They might well have been true. His father *had* always been stubborn to a fault. Had the King really had the chance to live on, only to deny the demon's assistance and meet his demise? At what cost had Rishi Radek's pride remained intact? And if he'd known what sort of doom he was leaving Arden to, would he have chosen differently? Wouldn't it have been for the greater good to accept the demon's help?

Even with sinking doubt flooding him, Hasain managed to keep his voice level. "He must have had his reasons. He had great faith in Deegan."

Leviticus sneered. *"As the eldest child, you received the stone and, therefore, the birthright to wield it. His faith should have been in you."*

Hasain shivered. Eldest? Didn't the demon know? Had Rishi somehow managed to keep Kieran a secret? Hasain tucked the information safely away in the back of his mind. Perhaps he could best the creature yet. "I never had reason to question my father's faith in me. I wasn't in line to be king, but he loved and nurtured me just the same. Be gone, demon. I have no use for you."

The unsettling smile that spread across Leviticus' face made every hair on Hasain's body stand on end. Again, the demon chortled. *"With an imbecile on the dead king's throne and a child prince who is years away from receiving his crown, do you really think things won't get any worse? Fine. I suppose you must see for yourself. That is something you've inherited from your father. You know where to find me when you see your error."*

And then he was gone. Hasain gasped. The demon hadn't walked away, nor had he fled through the open window. No. He simply ceased to be there.

Across the chamber, a flash of crimson flickered from atop a chestnut armoire. In the light of the waning moon, Hasain could see the red stone glowing through the keyhole of its box. A shiver ran up his spine as he leapt from his bed, careful to avoid the cold vomit, and raced to shove the shameful secret into a drawer. Maybe if he locked it away, it would be as if the demon had never come to him. He could go on pretending his life wasn't spinning out of control and that his father wasn't dead.

Hasain retracted his hands from the drawer, exhaling with relief when he saw no further sign of the crimson light. Perhaps the entire night would prove to be nothing more than a nightmare.

Somewhere behind him came the sound of rustling linens. The prostitute shifted in the bed, stirring from her entranced slumber. Hasain grew nauseated at the sight of her. He needed a bath. And fresh sheets. And someone needed to get her out of here before sunrise.

He threw open the door of his armoire, reaching for a clean robe— and froze. The haunted, dark eyes of his father stared back from the depths of the closet, eerily silent, unmoving, and unyielding. Hasain tore his gaze away from the portrait. Like the red stone, he kept the painting locked away. He couldn't stand to look at it. He couldn't bear to gaze into his father's eyes. Not while Hasain's life was in such shambles. He slammed the armoire shut as bitter tears spilled down his cheeks.

Unable to stay inside the bedchamber a moment longer, Hasain threw a robe around his shoulders and slipped into the hall. He'd get a servant to take care of the whore and another to prepare a bath for him. He couldn't sleep now anyway.

CHAPTER ONE

Gibben Nemesio pressed his back to the wall to avoid being trampled. A pair of burly sentinels plowed through the corridor, armor-clad with swords swinging from their hips and looking as though they were marching off to battle.

Not today, Gib thought, running fingers through the short, brown curls that crowned his head. *But who knows what tomorrow will bring. We'll all be facing war soon enough.*

Straightening the cloak around his shoulders, he peered once in each direction to ensure no additional soldiers were planning to barge through the narrow hall. The path seemed clear. As he stepped away from the wall, he heard the amused voice of his younger brother.

"You know," Calisto remarked in a reminiscent tone. "You'd think they would've had the insight to make this hall a little wider. I mean, this is the main passageway inside the barracks, after all. How do they expect an entire army to squeeze through the corridor all at once?"

Gib glanced briefly over his shoulder. "We just came on a bad day. Everyone's in a frenzy, getting ready to leave."

The sound of quickening footfalls met Gib's ears, and a moment later, Cal appeared. "You don't think Liza left already, do you?"

"Let's hope not." Gib nudged his brother in the ribs. "Come on. We don't want to miss her. The Two know I'll never be able to find her once the army mobilizes."

The brothers walked side by side until the corridor branched into opposite directions, leaving Gib to rack his memory for which path would take them toward Liza's quarters.

Daya, how can anyone navigate this place? The endless corridors and damn wooden walls all look the same!

Of course, deep down Gib knew that wasn't the case. He merely hadn't spent enough time inside the barracks to know the difference.

And be grateful for that, you lucky bastard. Had you not earned the favor of Seneschal Koal, this would be your home.

"That way," Cal said, pointing to the left.

"How do you know?"

Cal's chestnut-brown eyes sparkled. "Look." He motioned toward

12

the wall. There, practically beneath Gib's nose, an arrow had been sketched onto the faded wood with the words "Women's Quarters" crudely written beside it. A toothy grin spread across Cal's face. "Didn't you learn how to read during *any* of the four years you attended Academy?"

Gib choked back an exasperated laugh. "Oh, hush. I have the right to be out of sorts. Here I am, lost inside the barracks of Silver City like some kind of dolt."

"Do you think getting lost would be a valid excuse for you not to go to war?"

"It would certainly send Koal into a tizzy." Gib chuckled at the thought. "He'd probably order half the Ardenian army to go searching for me if I didn't arrive."

Cal set a hand on Gib's shoulder, his wide beam fading. "Are you *sure* you have to go?"

"You know I do. It's my duty. And besides, all my friends are going. And Seneschal Koal. I can't abandon them."

"I wish I could go with you."

"No. You're too young. King Rishi fought hard to preserve the lives of Arden's youth. Had the old law not been overturned, you *would* have been forced to march. But now the High Council can't demand a man fight until he reaches the age of sixteen."

Cal's jaw stiffened. "They wouldn't have to force me to march, Gib. I could volunteer."

"Absolutely not. Your job is to stay here. Be a student. Learn all you can. With any hope, this war will be done by the first snowfall. I'm going because I must. Liza's going because *she* must. You and Tay have to hold down things here while we're gone, okay?"

Cal hung his head. "Yeah, I guess. I just wanted to help."

"You can help by staying where it's safe." Gib placed one hand onto Cal's shoulder and squeezed gently. "Just knowing that you and Tay are protected here in Silver will give me peace of mind when I'm out there. Now, come on. Let's keep moving. We have to find Liza."

Determined to drop the conversation altogether, Gib focused his attention on the task at hand. Again, he read the sign Cal had pointed out.

All right. To the women's quarters. Since General Morathi insists on segregating women soldiers like they're infected with the plague. Chhaya's bane.

Gib had taken only a single step forward when a tall, dark-haired soldier rounded the corner and the two of them nearly collided. Gib tried to jump out of the way but was a second too slow. He could hear the man let out a testy sigh when the path was momentarily blocked.

The soldier turned a fierce scowl onto Gib, reaching up to smooth the crimson cape rolling down one shoulder. "Watch where you're going, *boy!*"

"S—sorry."

13

As the man strode past, he reached out and gave Gib a nasty shove, sending him stumbling back. Cal placed his hands on Gib's shoulders, steadying him. Both brothers scurried to get out of the way, but the tall soldier was already well past them. The man didn't even spare a backward glance as he stormed down the corridor.

Cal huffed. "What do you think his problem is?"

"Probably worried," Gib replied. "Just like everyone else. Stress brings out the worst in people." Gritting his teeth, he resumed walking.

"He still had no right to push you aside. Doesn't he know you're Seneschal Koal's understudy?"

"Doubtful, Cal. No one really knows who I am here." Gib squinted as he passed by an open window and sudden, bright light flooded the corridor. "And besides, that man was wearing a red cape. That means he's at least a captain. He outranked me."

The wooden floorboards creaked beneath Cal's boots as he ran to catch up. "Didn't Koal used to be a captain?"

"Years ago, yes. Before he ever dreamed of becoming Arden's next seneschal."

"Maybe someday *you'll* be a captain."

"Perhaps. But I really doubt it."

"Maybe someday you'll be a seneschal."

Laughter erupted from Gib's mouth. "Goddesses, no! I don't think I'd ever be able to handle Koal's job."

"It's an entertaining thought though, isn't it? Imagine, Gibben Nemesio, poor farmer from Willowdale, ascending to become the Right Hand of the King."

"Yeah, imagine that."

Gib furrowed his brows as he contemplated Arden's many troubles. Things had only gotten worse since King Rishi Radek's murder, nearly two moonturns ago. Neetra Adelwijn, brother of Seneschal Koal and the newly elected Steward of Arden, was running rampant, determined to undermine or destroy every bit of progress the late king had worked a lifetime to achieve. To make matters worse, Neetra had also managed to win over enough of the High Council to have the votes needed to send the country to war against Shiraz. The scale had tipped in his favor, leaving Seneschal Koal, Dean Marc, and the remaining loyalists to the Radek family scrambling.

Gib didn't know what would happen, but he hardly had time to think about it. He hardly had time to think about anything besides the impending war. His own life seemed one misstep away from complete disarray, though the friendships he'd forged over the three and a half years he'd been living in Silver City remained strong. Kezra Malin-Rai and Nage Nessuno would be marching at his side. Tarquin Aldino, however, had been abruptly ordered—much to his dismay—to oversee production at his father's Armorer's Guild here in Silver. For the foreseeable future.

Gib supposed he should be happy at least one of his friends would remain out of harm's way, except he knew how much Tarquin had wanted to go and how useless he felt having to stay behind.

But Gib couldn't dwell on Tarquin's plight now with far too many other people to be worried about. Zandi Malin-Rai, Gib's new companion, had opted to ride to war, as well as Joel Adelwijn—

Gib's stomach flopped. *Why?* Why did his thoughts *always* come back to Joel?

He'd put forth an honest effort. He'd tried to make amends with his former lover, but their relationship remained frigid at best. They'd agreed to be civil. Joel even wanted them to be friends.

But what kind of friends don't speak for sennights on end? If Joel meant everything he said that night we talked at the Adelwijn estate, why is the warmth zapped from a room every time we're both in it?

Gib didn't know. Only the Goddesses could see what fate lay ahead. For now, all Gib could do was focus on the war. If Joel wanted to repair their broken friendship, it was on him to make the first move. Gib couldn't dedicate any more energy to the cause if Joel wasn't willing to reciprocate.

The narrow corridor again snaked in two separate directions, and Gib paused, trying to recall which path led where.

"Left again," Cal said. "The other hall leads back toward the training courtyard."

Gib peeked around the corner to make certain no angry soldiers stood waiting for him to blunder into their way. Much to his relief, the corridor lay vacant. "Okay, come on. We've gotta be close."

They walked the length of the corridor in silence, Gib leading the way and Cal just behind. At the end of the hall, a lone door stood open. Gib's boggled mind finally cleared as he stopped before the threshold. He remembered the heaving beams above and the unpolished, splintering door from his previous visit. A jolt of hot resentment rushed to his head. Why were the women's quarters in constant disarray? Did the people in charge not care?

No. Of course they don't.

Gib poked his head into the room. "Liza?"

Sitting on a worn mattress near the distant corner of the room, Liza Nemesio glanced up. Her square face brightened, and a second later, she was on her feet and rushing toward the boys. "Gib! Cal! I was worried I wouldn't get a chance to see you before I left."

Liza spread her arms wide and wrapped Gib in a firm embrace. Tufts of her wild, mousy brown hair tickled Gib's nose, but he paid the unruly locks no mind, hugging her tight. "I sent a message this morning that I was coming to see you. Didn't you get it?"

"No. But with the way things have been around here lately, that doesn't surprise me. Everyone is frantic. The note probably got lost somewhere. I'm sorry."

"Hell, it's not like it's your fault," Gib replied, stepping back so he could meet her kind eyes. He remembered, years ago, having to look up when he spoke to his sister, but now, even with his modest stature, he stood taller than her. But only just so. "Where is everyone?"

Liza's face contorted. "Neetra 'pardoned' the women soldiers. He told us we could remain in Silver if we were willing to permanently renounce our positions as soldiers."

Gib's mouth fell open. "He did *what?*"

"It happened just this morning," Liza explained, her voice worn. "Many of the women were afraid. They—they opted out. There weren't many to begin with, and now there are even fewer." She squeezed Gib close. "I'm glad you came. My troop is leaving within the mark. Where's Tayver?"

"Tay couldn't make it," Cal said, rubbing the back of his neck as he wandered closer. "He had to stay and help Master Nireefa finish stitching the tabards the Tailoring Guild was ordered to craft for Arden's army. He asked us to send his regards."

Gib reached into a pocket, his mind still reeling from Liza's news. "I have another note to give you." He pulled the folded parchment free and held it out to her. "It's a reassignment order. Koal signed it last night."

"Reassignment order?" Liza made a face as she snatched the parchment from his hands and unrolled it. "For me?"

Biting his lip, Gib nodded. "If you want to, Koal says he can reassign you. You'd work directly for him, alongside me. You can take this note to your captain. They can't refuse an order from the seneschal."

Liza let out a sharp breath. "Gib—"

"We could be together." Gib could hardly stand to meet his sister's eyes. He'd known there would be a chance Liza would reject the offer, but he had to try. "We'd be able to watch each other's backs this way. And surely the safest place to be is by the seneschal's side."

"Brother," Liza replied, her voice firm. "I appreciate the offer. I really do. But I have to decline. I've been with the same unit for five years, and I'm just now *finally* beginning to earn the respect of my comrades. I can't start over again. And I can't accept Seneschal Koal's charity. He's been so good to you boys, but I'm not and never have been his responsibility. You understand, right?"

Gib stared past Liza, fixing his gaze on the shoddy wall. "If you change your mind, the offer still stands."

"I know. And I promise to check in on you as time permits."

"Right. In an army of ten thousand soldiers, how hard can it be to find one person?"

"I'll just ask for Seneschal Koal. I know you'll be close by."

"I still can't believe Koal is going," Cal remarked. "He's the seneschal of Arden, not the general of Arden's army."

16

"It's custom for the king to march with the army," Gib said.

"But there *isn't* a king right now." Cal, always candid, stated the obvious. "Is that why he's going? Because there's no one else?"

"He's going because Neetra is a coward and won't go himself."

"Seneschal Koal used to be a captain," Liza added. "He's seen combat firsthand. He fought in the Northern War years ago, before we were even born. He's really the better choice to send. Neetra couldn't manage to lead a thirsty horse to a water trough."

Wincing, Gib ran his fingers through his curls. "While I agree with you about Koal's experience on the battlefield being beneficial, having the seneschal absent from the council chamber has the potential to be disastrous. Koal is a voice of reason on the High Council—one of the only ones left, I fear. With him gone, Neetra is going to run Arden into the ground."

Cal snorted. "The new steward is already doing just that, regardless of whether Koal is here or not."

"Unfortunately, you're right." Gib's thoughts wandered to the many things he'd seen and heard in the council chamber over the past two years. The meetings of the past had always been vicious, but since Neetra's election, there was almost no contention to be had. In fact, with the exception of Koal, Marc, and a handful of other councilors still loyal to King Rishi's law, no one disputed *anything* the new steward proposed.

It's almost like the rest of the councilors are mindless sheep. They'll follow any path Neetra chooses, even if he leads Arden straight to war and death.

A sharp voice bellowed from the corridor, cutting through Gib's thoughts. He raised his eyes from the floor even as Liza did the same.

"That's the order to move out," Liza said. She turned penitent eyes toward the two brothers. "I have to go now. Tell Tay I said goodbye. I love you all."

"Be safe, Liza," Cal murmured into the worn fabric of her uniform as they embraced one final time. "We love you, too. And we're so proud of everything you do to keep Arden safe."

Liza pressed a soft kiss to Cal's forehead. "I'm more proud of you boys than you'll ever know. Stay out of trouble while I'm gone." She ruffled his hair and stepped back. Raking the back of one hand across his eyes, Cal nodded in silent agreement.

"I'll find you on the road," Gib said, giving Liza a gentle hug.

Liza trudged to the far side of the room, where a rucksack and leather-bound sword were propped against the wall. She slung the pack over one shoulder and fastened the sheathed weapon to a girdle around her waist. A linen tabard woven around polished leather armor and the golden phoenix of Arden, embroidered into the cloth, glittered in the low light.

"How do I look?" she asked.

A sense of pride mingled with the dread of knowing Liza stood in

17

harm's way. Gib's stomach twisted into a knot. Seeing his sister standing before him, donned in her sentinel uniform with a sword on her hip, suddenly made everything feel *real*. Arden was going to war. Liza would march into battle. *He* would march into battle. Thousands of lives might be lost, including those closest to him.

I have to be brave—for Tayver and Calisto. I can't let them see my fear. They have to believe everything will be all right, even if I don't.

Gib inclined his head. "You look like a true warrior of Arden, and I know you'll defend her with everything you are."

Sunlight filtered into the room through an open window above the workspace, bringing in the fresh scents and sounds of springtime. The fragrance of newly blossomed flowers wafted into the Academy classroom, and the light breeze trickling through carried a songbird's melody, enticing the occupants to stop and listen to the beautiful tune.

Joel Adelwijn, mage of Silver City and son of the seneschal, paused his lecture and let out a deep sigh. Surrounded by such serenity, it was easy to close his eyes and believe he sat in the midst of a lovely garden and not a classroom at all.

And while I'm at it, perhaps I can lie to myself and pretend everything is fine— that I'll wake up tomorrow to just another peaceful spring day.

He wasn't very good at telling lies, however. He never had been.

What was it Gib used to jest about? "Your features are so much better suited for honesty, Joel Adelwijn," or something like that.

He suppressed the urge to frown. It didn't matter. Nothing did anymore. And not even the best liar in Arden could convince him he wasn't about to leave to war.

The sound of someone clearing his throat snapped Joel back to the present. Across the room, Kirk Bhadrayu stood with a small gathering of first-year mage students. The former Imperial made no attempt to hide the concern in his deep green eyes or the downward curl of his lips. "Are you all right?"

Bless him. I don't think Kirk could be uncandid even if he tried, Joel thought with a wistful smile. *He's always worn his heart on his sleeve. I'm so glad I accepted this teaching position with him.*

"I'm fine. I seem to have momentarily lost my train of thought." His grip tightened around the satchel he held in one hand. "Shall we continue?"

Without awaiting a response, he reached into the pouch and pulled out the last remaining runestone. He set it upon a marble pedestal with the half dozen others he'd already retrieved from the bag and did his best to cast away thoughts of warfare and death. He owed it to the students to not become distracted.

Rays of light poured down from the rafters, illuminating the pearly-white stones. Small enough to rest in the center of a palm, each was perfectly oval in shape and smooth as silk, polished from centuries of tumbling in the treacherous waters off Arden's western coast.

Joel motioned toward the pedestal. "Everyone come take a runestone."

The five students trundled to the front of the room, each taking their turn to select a stone.

"So," Kirk picked up where Joel left off, giving him a needed reprieve to collect his thoughts. The two mages were aptly matched, often knowing the other's thoughts even before speaking. Dean Marc had been wise to place them together as trainers. "Can anyone recap yesterday's lesson?"

Inez Adelwijn, the steward's daughter and Joel's cousin, raised a hand. Feisty and quick-witted, she was one of the brightest students in the class, and despite being Neetra's daughter, she was well-liked among her peers and professors. "We learned how to imbue runestones with energy."

"Correct," Kirk replied, praising her with a gentle smile. "And why did we learn how to do this?"

"So we'd be able to utilize the power later. We captured the excess energy inside the stones to call upon in the future when it's needed."

Kirk drew his hands together as he sat on the edge of a desk. "And why is the ability to tap into the power of the runestones important?"

Inez's twin brother, Inan, answered this question. "Because, as mages, our personal energy stores are always finite—so the imbued runestones give us the ability to push past our boundaries if the need arises."

"Very good," Kirk said. "And true. No mage is invincible, even those with extraordinary power. We *all* have limits."

Inan raised his chin proudly, looking every bit like his father but without the arrogance that constantly tarnished Neetra's fair features. They looked so alike it might be easy to fault the young lord for his sire's atrocious acts, but Joel knew better than to judge. Inan's gentle soul was a stark contrast to Neetra's cruel and cold heart.

Inez bumped her brother's elbow. "Showoff."

"What?" Inan made a sour face at her. "Professor Kirk asked a question. I was merely replying."

Joel cleared his throat, redirecting the siblings' attention before their banter could spiral into all out bickering. "Runestones can be beneficial to a mage in other ways, too. Not only can we imbue and hoard power within them, but we can store messages—even memories—as well. Today, we'll be learning about—"

His words were cut short as the heavy wooden door swung open, banging against the wall. Joel exhaled sharply on instinct, and all eyes turned toward the doorway.

Liro Adelwijn, Joel's elder brother and newly elected councilman, sauntered into the room, tendrils of dark hair wisping around a firmly set jaw and the tail of an immaculate robe trailing like a shadow behind his boots.

Joel took an unwilling step back, his stomach rolling. He did his best to remain calm, but his voice came out sounding almost as flustered as he felt. "Liro, what are you doing—"

"Good day, *brother.*" Liro's sleek voice flowed from his mouth like the hiss of a viper. His cold blue eyes flashed around the room, flicking from one person to the next. "I do hope I'm not interrupting anything of importance."

"We're in the middle of a lesson here."

Liro glared down the narrow bridge of his nose at Joel. "Teaching the whimsical drivel of your father, no doubt."

Joel's heart hammered. "He's *your* father, too, Liro, and you should pay him a little more respect. Father raised you to be better than this." When his older brother offered nothing, Joel crossed his arms over his chest. "I'm teaching *mage lessons.* Magical techniques and theories. Nothing more or less. So you can stop throwing accusations—"

"No need to feign innocence, brother. Don't think I'm unaware of the treacherous lies you've been spoon-feeding Arden's youth. The High Council would be most displeased, were they to learn the truth." Liro's eyes flashed with dark intent. "You might find yourself without a job—or worse—subjected to the full weight of the law—as would any accomplices discovered to be in league with you."

Out of the corner of Joel's eye, he saw Kirk flinch and the small group of students exchange worried glances with one another. Whether or not they understood the severity of Liro's threat, Joel couldn't be sure.

Liro can think what he wants, but I'm innocent. And so is Kirk.

At least for now. That could change after they met with Marc later. Joel didn't know the full extent of the dean's plan, but it was safe to assume they'd be privy to information that could threaten their very lives if the wrong people found out what was going on.

Joel hesitated when he saw a very wide-eyed Kirk shaking his head, silently imploring Joel to let the issue rest. Kirk didn't want to be brought into this—and with good reason. Under King Rishi's rule, he'd been allowed to live in Arden, but if Liro or any of his cronies really wanted to, they could have Kirk exiled. Technically, he was still a foreigner. Joel swallowed, pushing down the fear in his chest.

No one is safe anymore, whether they're innocent or not. Kirk will help us, even with the risks involved.

"Is there something I can help you with, Liro?" Joel asked, struggling to keep his voice steady. "Or did you come here only to belittle me? Surely that wouldn't be worth walking all the way from the palace."

Liro's face drew into a haughty smile. "I'm here on business—though I do, as always, enjoy exchanging pleasantries with you. I have orders from Arden's acting ruler."

Joel bit his tongue to keep from saying something he'd no doubt regret later. King Rishi would have rolled over in his grave if he knew Joel's tyrant uncle sat upon the throne, running Arden into the ground.

Not awaiting a response, Liro gestured toward Inan. "Your father is pulling you from Academy."

Inan grew pale. "Wh–what? W–why?"

Joel placed a hand on his young cousin's shoulder. "On what grounds?"

Liro's eyes possessed not a trace of warmth as they focused on his younger brother. "Security precautions. The councilors agree it's inappropriate and potentially hazardous for the son of the steward to continue taking lessons with—*commoners*. I'm here to escort Lordling Inan back to the palace."

An exasperated squeak freed itself from inside Joel's throat as he floundered for something to say. "You can't just barge in and take one of my students in the middle of a lesson! Just because you're on the High Council now doesn't give you the authority."

"Oh, it doesn't?" Liro cocked his head to the side. "Perhaps you'd like to bring your complaint before our uncle. I'm sure Lord Neetra Adelwijn, steward and *ruler* of Arden, would be happy to remind you how little your opinion really matters."

"And what of Inan's schooling? He's a mage! He needs to be properly trained."

"And he will be. By the finest private tutors in the country—the way *all* royalty and young lords should be educated." Liro jeered at Inan. "Worry not, cousin. After today, you'll never again be subjected to taking classes with vagrants and women."

Inan sputtered incoherently. "B–but I don't—I—"

It was his sister who found her voice first. Inez's narrowed, smoldering eyes speared Liro. "This isn't fair. *Inan* should be the one to decide where he takes classes, not Neetra and *certainly not* the High Council."

Liro curled his nose. "It's already been decided."

"Like hell it has! Inan, just say no—"

A vicious snarl leapt from Liro's mouth. "Shut your despicable mouth or I'll *force* it shut!" He lunged forward a pace, and for just a moment, Joel feared he might have to jump between his brother and young cousin. Liro stopped short, however, pointing a finger at Inez. "Trust me when I say that your father would hold no remorse should I show his foolish daughter to her rightful place."

Inez opened her mouth in retort but was interrupted when Inan set a hand on her shoulder. "It's okay," he gasped. "If this is Father's wish, I'll go."

21

Inez's eyes widened. "Inan, no—"

"I don't want any trouble. It's all right. I'll go."

Joel clamped his mouth shut as he watched Inan shuffle toward the door. He wished he could think of something to say—anything to help the boy—but his mind had gone blank. Likewise, Inez remained silent, though Joel could see the hatred burning in her glare. Inan was right. Defying Neetra would only cause more grief for everyone.

Inan kept his eyes on the stone floor as he departed, but Liro lingered in the doorway a moment longer before following. The councilor flashed a dark smile, for a moment looking like an eerie caricature of Koal. It often astonished Joel how his brother and father could look so alike yet be such different people.

"I'm sure I won't see you again before you depart," Liro sneered. "Be safe, brother. If you're to meet your end at war, there's no guarantee for your soul. Best you stay alive and well, rather than risk eternal damnation."

Joel blinked, feeling oddly numb inside. Perhaps he'd grown accustomed to Liro's constant resentment, or the sting of his words had merely dulled after so many years. Whatever the reason, Joel had no desire to fight back. Not this time.

He couldn't help but recall a time, so many years ago, when the two brothers had loved each other. So much time had passed that Joel could no longer remember what had driven them apart. When had things changed? When had Liro become such a monster? Would their relationship ever recover or were they destined to forever be divided?

"I'll send Father your regards," Joel replied in a muted voice. "I'll even be careful to soften the blow. He needn't ride into battle with a heart broken from disappointment."

Liro raised his chin and some fleeting emotion—Pain? Jealousy? It was hard to judge—passed behind his brooding gaze. A moment later, he turned on his heels, saying not a single word more, and stormed from the room. The slam of the door made Joel wince, and the silence that followed was nearly unbearable.

Goddesses know, I've tried to win back his approval, but I can't change who I am. Not for him or anyone else. Is there nothing I can do? Will he never accept me? What if I march to my doom tomorrow? What if this was my last chance to make things right and I failed?

"I *loathe* him," Inez spat, breaking the silence. "Someday he'll get what he deserves. Neetra too."

Her hiss was almost lost beneath the ringing in Joel's ears, and it wasn't until Kirk set a timid hand on the mage's shoulder that he was able to pull himself from his abysmal thoughts. Somber but caring eyes attempted to make contact, but he couldn't muster the courage to meet them.

"Are you okay?" Kirk asked.

Shaking his head, Joel turned his back on Kirk and the remaining students, opting to stare out the window instead. Fear seized his body, tightening around his throat like a noose. Suddenly the idea of the impending war was an overwhelming terror in the forefront of his mind.

Chhaya's bane, is this really happening?

A half wheelturn ago, he'd barely escaped the Northern Empire alive, and even then, not everyone had survived the mission. Joel's dear friend and mentor, Ambassador Cenric Leal, had lost his life that day, leaving a wife and two daughters to pick up the pieces of a broken life without him.

How many Ardenian soldiers would die this time? When the dust cleared, would Joel and countless others become fallen heroes, the subject of tragic tavern stories about the brave soldiers who gave their lives for their country? When the battle ended, would Joel's own mother and siblings be among those left to mourn, to deal with the loss, to endure the pain as Cenric's family had?

Joel could feel the eyes of the students on his back, but he couldn't face them right now. He couldn't face anyone. Surely no one in the world could ever understand what he was going through—save one.

Gib.

A pang of longing rose to mingle with the fear in Joel's stomach.

Gib would understand. If only I could talk to—No, he reminded himself. *Gib's moved on. And I need to do the same. I can't run to him every time I have a problem. I pushed him away, and now I have only myself. Alone forever.*

Kirk cleared his throat. "Joel?"

Refusing to take his blurry, wet eyes from the window, Joel sighed and offered a simple but terse reply. "Sorry, everyone. Class is dismissed for the day."

The breeze blew unseasonably cool against Kezra Malin-Rai's scalp. She ran a hand through her freshly shorn locks, momentarily stunned by the lack of long tresses. Her sister, Tamil, was still staring with a disapproving look. She'd agreed to cut Kezra's unruly hair, but only after three days of coercion and an entire night of blatant threats.

"It suits you." Their elder brother, Zandi, barely glanced up from his saddlebag as he spoke, but Kezra knew his words were for her. Personally she didn't care if the haircut suited her or not, as long as she could see when she met the Shirites in battle.

Tamil sighed. "Mother will have a fit."

"Then don't tell her." Kezra lifted her bag over her shoulder and trudged over to Epona, her golden palfrey. "By the time I get back, it'll have grown past my ears at least. She'll never have to know how short it is now."

"You should go see her one more time before you leave."

Kezra shook her head. Tamil meant well, but another visit to their mother would only bring more tears and fretting. "She doesn't need the heartache."

For a time, no one said anything, and the only sounds were of horses shifting their weight and saddlebags being secured. Kezra bit her lip against the urge to fill the quiet. Perhaps it was cruel not to go see her mother again, but really, what good would it do? Kezra wasn't going to allow Odessa to talk her out of going, and likewise, Zandi wasn't going to be convinced to stay behind—whether his title would allow it or not. A wry smile threatened to spread across Kezra's mouth.

Though I suspect Zandi wouldn't be quite so adamant about going to war if Gib wasn't also making the journey.

"Try to see it through Mother's eyes, Kezra." It seemed Tamil wasn't quite ready to give up. "How hard must it be to watch her eldest son and daughter ride to war? Think of her. Maybe you shouldn't go. The women soldiers have been given the option to stay."

"But that's not what being a soldier's about, love!" Lord Tular Galloway, Tamil's husband, bounded down the front steps with a bag slung over one shoulder. The sun caught his copper hair and fire shone behind dark eyes when they landed on Kezra, imploring her not to grow frustrated with Tamil yet again. "And Kezra's one hell of a soldier."

Tamil reached for him, and Tular closed his larger hands over hers. Kezra found herself turning away from the pair, both for the sake of privacy and so she didn't have to think of the one she wasn't saying such goodbyes to.

Nawaz Arrio's terrible blue eyes flashed in her memory, but Kezra immediately struck the image down. She didn't have time to long for him or indulge in sorrow. What good would it do anyway? She'd chosen her path, and he'd followed the one set before him. He'd keep his title and privilege so long as he did what was expected of him. Hell, his wife was already pregnant with their first child!

Kezra bit her lip. Enough of this. She couldn't afford to think of Nawaz today. Today she had to walk the lonely way she'd chosen. It might not have been the easiest or most popular path, but she'd be damned to turn back now just to make others happy.

Her blood boiled to think of how carelessly the other women soldiers had been dismissed. Just that morning, General Morathi Adeben had pled his case to Neetra and won the approval of the High Council. The female soldiers had been granted "mercy" in this difficult time. Any of them who wished to stay behind only needed say as much and the general would allow it. In return, they'd relinquish their positions as sentinels and find jobs "more suitable" for them. The High Council touted this pardon as an extreme act of kindness on the parts of both Neetra and Morathi, but

Kezra knew better. Women soldiers still weren't being taken seriously. They were seen as disposable. A liability.

Lies!

With a drawn face, Kezra tightened the straps, securing her bag to Epona's saddle. Zandi met her eyes briefly, and she could tell he wanted to say something but refrained. Just behind them, their sister and her husband were still saying their farewells.

Tamil's voice trembled, but all things considered, she was doing a remarkable job keeping her emotions in check. "When you come back, we're going to start a family, right? No more getting around it."

Tular remained as collected as ever. Nothing seemed to ruffle his feathers—a drastic difference from his elder half-brother, Hasain Radek. "I'll be back. And when I am, we'll buy a whole damned orphanage if you want."

"We'll need at least four children. Maybe five or six even. My mother had seven."

Tular raised an eyebrow. "We'll need a maid. And a bigger house."

"I miss you already." Tamil laughed, her fragile voice finally cracking.

Kezra didn't want to watch their exchange but found herself glancing over anyway. Strange warmth blossomed in her chest. She hadn't really gotten to know Tular before he'd married Tamil, and it would be a lie to say Kezra hadn't had some misgivings at first. Tular's aloof manner and the knowledge that he was Hasain's half-brother had made it difficult for Kezra to trust him.

But then, when things went wrong between her and Nawaz, Tular had offered Kezra residence at his estate. And when Zandi hadn't been able to bear their father's drunken tyranny for another moment, Tular granted sanctuary a second time without one word of dissent. How could Kezra not accept Tular as family after he'd bestowed such generosity?

"Harper will be here to keep you company. Make sure to get her moved into the estate as soon as we're gone."

And there he was, at it again. Tular had consented to allow the youngest Malin-Rai sister, Harper, to come live with Tamil in his absence. The formal story was that Tular didn't want his new wife to have to be alone for the duration of war, but Kezra understood the full extent of his generosity. Their father, High Councilor Anders, had been even more insufferable since his promotion. His drinking had gotten worse, and the more he drank, the more *handsy* he became. Harper needed to get out of that house.

Kezra's skin crawled as she fought to suppress memories suitable only for the darkest of nightmares. She refused to think about the past or the horrors inflicted upon her. Not now. Not when she needed to be strong. Shaking her head, Kezra refocused her attention onto her sister.

"Yes, I know." Tamil wiped away a tear. "Harper has promised to help me keep house while I finish the last of my training."

Tular smiled, a rare gesture, and took his wife by the shoulders. "You'll be a midwife when I return. No more understudy lessons for you. That's something to look forward to, isn't it?"

Kezra hated witnessing her sister's tears. War was an ugly thing, ripping families apart, forcing them to lose precious time with one another. If all worked out well, however, and Tular did return safely, Tamil would be able to start the next part of her journey in exactly the way she wanted. She'd be a midwife, have a blossoming family, and have bright prospects all around. Kezra wasn't much for prayers or faith, but if indeed The Two were watching over them, a prayer for Tamil's happiness seemed appropriate.

Zandi cleared his throat softly as he settled into his saddle. "We should be on our way. We don't want the army to leave without us."

"Or do we?" Kezra huffed back at him. Taking hold of her own saddle, she swung onto Epona's back. It was time to go. Past time. Lingering here would only cause more anguish, more pain.

Tular joined them, mounting the third and final horse in the courtyard. Tears streamed down Tamil's face as she returned to the steps of the estate. Raising her emerald eyes, Kezra took a moment to study the vine-encrusted stone walls and tall panes of painted glass, dedicating each detail of the mansion to memory. Only The Two knew when and if she'd ever see it again.

Kezra's gaze fell upon her comrades. Though the weight of the world surely pressed down on them, both sat tall in their saddles—Zandi in his flowing mage robes and Tular in sentinel garb. Neither man offered words, but their eyes sought out Kezra's, and a mutual understanding passed between them. They weren't just leaving Tamil and the estate today. They were leaving their youth and any remaining illusions of innocence. Once they passed through the rusted iron gate, there would be no turning back.

With grim resignation, they departed.

CHAPTER TWO

Prince Didier Adelwijn stared into the empty courtyard below. From his vantage point so high above the ground, he could see tufts of green peeking above the previous year's turf. It seemed impossible that new life was able to find its way through the shriveled grass, yet—against all odds—it somehow had.

The sun was out today, but no warmth reached him up here, locked away in the royal suite. Even as he squinted against the harsh light, Didier felt cold. He *always* felt cold of late.

"Diddy, it's your move."

Diddy blinked, and at once, his attention returned to the board game set before him. "Oh, I'm sorry. I'm a bit distracted."

His younger brother, Deegan, cocked one brow as he observed Diddy. The Crown Prince's shrewd, brown eyes were hauntingly reminiscent of Rishi Radek's, despite the fact that Deegan's soft facial features and straight umber hair had clearly been inherited from their mother's side of the family.

"I can tell," Deegan replied. "Normally you're bad at Senet. Today you're downright *terrible*."

Despite his sour mood, Diddy smiled and countered his brother's latest move. "See if I ever go easy on you again."

From across the sitting room, Princess Gudrin shifted in her seat with an impatient sigh. Their mother, Queen Mother Dahlia, was braiding the little girl's hair. Gudrin, however, had never been one to sit still for long and already seemed to be growing restless.

"Someone's coming down the hall," Gudrin proclaimed. "It sounds like Uncle Koal."

Dahlia laughed, leaning forward to kiss the back of her daughter's head. "There's no way you can hear your uncle all the way down the hall! Besides, council shouldn't be over so soon." Dahlia's troubled eyes darted toward the door, however, and both Diddy and Deegan stiffened, preparing themselves for whatever might come.

Not even an instant later, Aodan Galloway burst through the bedchamber door and headed for the receiving room. His face remained gaunt, as it had been since the king's death. "Someone's comin'. Sounds like Koal." He didn't wait for any of them to respond before going to wait at the main door.

Heart thudding, Diddy climbed to his feet. Deegan turned in his chair, expression meek. No one said or did anything. Even Gudrin stopped fidgeting, her gaze blank as she no doubt focused on listening.

The door slammed open, and Koal's livid voice could be heard a second later. "It takes half a mark just to get here! Do you know how many checkpoints I had to pass through? Not even Rishi was as well guarded as you and Dahlia are now."

"Guarded, my arse," came Aodan's rough reply. "That son of a bitch has me under lock an' key. I can't even piss without him knowing."

Their words subsided while the sounds of Koal putting his boots away and exchanging them for slippers could be heard. Diddy's heart twisted. His father wasn't here to enforce the rule any longer, but still no one wore shoes inside the royal suite.

"So, what was the verdict?" Aodan finally asked. "Why are ya out of council so soon?"

When Koal offered no immediate response, everyone within the suite held their breaths. Diddy's lungs cried for air, but try as he might, he couldn't force his chest to expand. His gaze shifted to his brother, who had gone pale and was visibly trembling. Diddy couldn't imagine what Deegan must be going through. They'd all tried to keep themselves distracted while the fate of their crown prince was decided, but now, with Koal here to presumably deliver the news, there was no point in holding together the façade.

Koal Adelwijn strode through the doorway with Aodan on his tail. Tall and imposing, Koal's presence had always given Diddy a sense of security. But not today. The grimace on his uncle's face made Diddy's heart sink and said more than any words ever could.

Dahlia's eyes were already wet as she stood and reached for her brother. "Koal?"

"I'm sorry," Koal said. "The High Council has spoken. Deegan will ride."

The world spun out from under Diddy's feet. He stumbled forward, knees knocking off each other, and found himself having to lean against the wall for support or risk toppling over. War? His little brother? How could this be happening? He'd already lost his father. He couldn't lose his brother, too. His family was already so broken. How would they go on if another tragedy struck?

Sobs rose to greet his ears as Dahlia collapsed against Koal's shoulder. Gudrin also wailed from her seat on the floor, rubbing both eyes with small, clenched fists, and Deegan sat rigidly on the edge of his chair. Diddy managed to collect himself long enough to place a hand on his brother's arm, offering silent support.

Aodan's face twisted into a reddened mask. "They can't send him! There're no more child soldiers!"

"That's right," gasped Dahlia. "He's only thirteen. He's too young."

Koal remained grim. "Marc and I tried to make that point. We even had some others agree with us, but not enough for the final vote. We couldn't sway Neetra. I'm sorry."

"*Damn him!*" Aodan screeched, kicking over a vase. Diddy jumped as the vessel shattered into a million pieces upon the marble floor. "He'd better pray I never find him alone—"

"Aodan," Koal warned. "My brother has ears everywhere. Don't test your luck."

The bodyguard didn't seem to be listening. He stormed about the suite in a frightening rage. "I'm goin' with you then! Hasain's already volunteered himself, so if Deegan goes too, then that's *it* for Rishi's sons!"

Koal shook his head. "You can't go."

"The hell I can't! I promised I'd protect Rishi's children. He made me *vow*. I have to go."

Aodan's proclamation struck a chord deep in Diddy's heart, and he found himself lost in memory, back in his father's bedchamber as the King lay dying. The hour grew late and all who waited knew the end was imminent. The King's consciousness had been fleeting and inconsistent for some time already, and he'd been sleeping fitfully for a mark or more when it happened.

Rishi opened his eyes and fixed a stern look across the room. Diddy glanced up from his seat at the foot of the bed, startled by how lucid his father seemed to be, so close to the end.

"Aodan," Rishi rasped. "What are you doing?"

Aodan came to the King's bedside, face mottled red and tear-stained. In one hand he carried the small vial, the bottle that was supposed to carry a remedy for influenza but instead had been the vessel used to poison Rishi.

The bodyguard knelt beside the King's prone form, shaking from head to toe, clutching the poison bottle against his chest. "Anywhere ya go, I go, too. It was my vow—"

Rishi lifted a trembling hand and took the vial away. "No. Not now. This time you can't come with me."

"I can! There's enough poison left inside the bottle—"

"No!"

Shouting drained him quickly, and Rishi sunk back into his pillow. For several agonizing moments, his ragged breaths filled the chamber, and everyone gathered around tensed, waiting for the worst, waiting for him to pass beyond their reach.

His stubborn nature didn't allow him to succumb just yet, however. Even as his body failed him, Rishi's eyes remained open and focused on Aodan. "Bird—" Penitence shook the King's ebbing voice. He must have known time grew short. "I still need you, Bird."

Aodan laid his damp face against the quilted bedspread. "What, Rishi? What more can ya ask of me?"

"The children. I need you to watch over them for as long as you can. It's the last command I'm ever going to give you. I have to go. I have no choice. But you stay. Stay here. Promise that you'll protect our family."

Diddy shuddered. No matter how hard he tried to move past his father's death, he always seemed to keep coming back to that day. He should have found a way to stop the poison's spread. He shouldn't have given into despair so quickly. If only he'd been stronger, braver—maybe if he'd kept fighting, his father would still be alive.

"Aodan, see reason." Koal's firm voice tickled the edge of Diddy's consciousness and brought him back to the present. "I don't trust Morathi for a moment. If you go, there'll be a target on your back from day one. Let *me* do this. Let *me* protect Deegan. I stand a better chance of surviving, and you know it."

Aodan paced rapidly back and forth across the room, saying nothing more. Diddy watched, not begrudging the bodyguard for even a moment. Diddy couldn't imagine what it must feel like to be torn between duty and sound logic. How could someone ever make that kind of decision?

Deegan finally broke the impenetrable silence. As he took to his feet, the Crown Prince made tentative eye contact with Aodan. "It makes sense. Uncle Koal is seneschal for a reason. Father trusted him wholly. And so do I. Neetra and his cronies tried to have you thrown out when Father died. They'll try to be rid of you now, too, if the chance arises. Don't give them that chance. Stay here and help us dethrone Neetra."

Aodan crossed the room in nearly a single bound. He went down on one knee, placing his hands on Deegan's shoulders. "It's war, Deegan. There's no promise for yer safety."

Deegan refused to crumble beneath the bodyguard's fierce gaze, a true testament of the young prince's courage. "There's no promise of safety for *any* of us, but Uncle Koal is right. It'll be easier for Neetra and Morathi to get rid of you if you go. Stay here. Keep Mother, Diddy, and Gudrin safe. Help our allies bring down Neetra. I'll be protected with Uncle Koal. I promise."

Aodan rose without another word and stormed over to the window. He kept his back to them, but even without seeing his face, Diddy was certain Aodan wept. Diddy opened his mouth, wanting desperately to reassure the bodyguard that everything would be okay but faltered. What good would such empty words do? Surely they'd bring no comfort. No one could foresee the future. No one person could guarantee Deegan's safety.

Gudrin ran to join Aodan. Despite being nine and entirely too old to be held, she raised her arms, and Aodan swept her up in an instant. He'd carried her for so long, Diddy couldn't imagine what would happen once

Gudrin grew too tall or heavy. Together, princess and bodyguard curled up on the windowsill, consoling one another.

Koal gave his sister one final embrace before turning his attention toward Deegan. "You need to ready yourself. We ride to the gathering field in one mark."

Deegan held his chin high, like their father had always taught them to do. Determination hardened the young prince's face, making him suddenly appear older, wiser. "I'm ready, but I—I don't know what to pack."

Koal offered a hand to his nephew. "I'll help you prepare."

Kirk focused his gaze straight ahead as he walked down the lonely corridor leading to Dean Marc Arrio's office, being sure to keep up with Joel. They moved silently, accompanied by only the sounds of their boots shuffling against the stone floor.

The halls of Academy were barren at this hour, making the space feel even larger. Kirk absently counted the high, painted windows that lined the hall as he passed by each. Light filtered through the glass in a stunning display of rich reds and fluorescent yellows. The vibrant artwork was reminiscent of the motifs from Kirk's native land, but the familiarity did nothing to lift his somber mood. He didn't want to recollect his homeland. He wanted to forget it.

From the moment he'd escaped through that portal, Kirk thought he'd left the dangers of the Northern Empire behind. It had been a fresh beginning, a chance for Kirk and his sister to start anew. His sister *had* started over. Just one moonturn ago, she'd married Roland Korbin's son and moved to the outskirts of Silver City to live on the Korbin manor with her new husband.

Kirk was happy for her. It seemed almost impossible that within the course of a year, she'd gone from being a lowly Imperial servant to a fugitive fleeing the Northern Empire to lady of an estate. Her marriage to an Ardenian man also offered Kenisha an extra level of security. It would be harder for those in power to exile her, should her loyalty to Arden ever be questioned.

Kirk held back a shudder, hoping such fears were unjustified. They'd both sworn themselves to serve their new country. Arden was their home now. They couldn't be forced to leave. They had nowhere to go.

Kirk risked a sideways glance at Joel. "It appears the springtime rains will hold off a bit longer than usual. That should make for easier travel, don't you think?" He hoped his question would pave the way for light conversation, but he knew better than to pine like a foolish child. The unfortunate circumstances around them were difficult to ignore.

Joel didn't immediately answer, choosing to stare ahead at the great, oak door rather than meet Kirk's eyes. The light from above bathed Joel's skin in a rosy glow, but the downward pull of the mage's lips was a clear indicator of his sullen mood.

"It would seem so," Joel replied at length, his tenor voice a pitch lower than normal. "If the fair weather holds through the summer, I'm sure the people can look forward to a bountiful harvest."

"Some good fortune would no doubt lift the country's spirit. Not to mention army morale."

Kirk's attempt at optimism was met with a shrug of indifference. Kirk couldn't fault his friend's detached behavior. Joel was leaving for war, after all. Many of his friends and family were also going. It was surely impossible for him to find anything to be cheerful about. Kirk himself felt guilty that he wasn't going, but when he'd voiced such concerns, Joel had been quick to remind him that *someone* had to remain behind and train Arden's young mage students.

"Indeed." Joel drew to a halt before the office door. "A bit of sunshine never hurt anyone."

Kirk smiled. The conversation, pointless as it might be, was still a welcomed alternative to the uncomfortable quiet that had lingered since they'd departed the classroom.

I don't really care what we talk about as long as I get him to speak. I'll willingly discuss the weather all day long if it means avoiding silent lamentations of warfare and death.

"You say that now," Kirk replied with a chuckle. "But wait until the army tents are filled to the brink with soldiers nursing burn wounds and complaining of sunstroke. The Healers will have their work cut out for them."

"I'll consider it a blessing if a little sunstroke is the worst problem our Healers face."

Kirk winced. "Sorry. I didn't mean to joke—"

"There's nothing to be sorry about." Joel's clipped reply was as chilly as a Midwinter snowstorm. His icy blue eyes passed briefly over Kirk before refocusing on the door. "I know you're trying to skirt the issue, Kirk, but there's no need. We both know the reality of the situation. Tomorrow Arden marches to war. I've accepted it."

Kirk swallowed the lump that had formed in the back of his throat.

Have you really though?

He refrained from asking the question aloud, opting to change the subject altogether. Motioning at the door, Kirk asked, "Is Dean Marc here? Should we knock?"

Joel raised a fist and tapped it three times against the wooden frame. "Guess we'll find out." There was no immediate answer.

He sighed and lowered his hand. "Apparently not. I had hoped we could speak with him before I left."

Kirk wasn't even sure why he was here, but whatever the reason, it had to be something important. True to his elusive nature, Joel had offered no details when he'd asked Kirk to come to the office with him.

"Do you want to wait?" Kirk asked. "Maybe Dean Marc will show up."

Joel cast a worried gaze around. "I'm not sure how long I *can* wait. I still have to pack and report to my father at the gathering field."

"Is it something I can tell the dean for you? I don't mind waiting, if you must go."

A sad smile flicked across Joel's mouth. "Sometimes I believe your heart is almost *too* caring."

Kirk gave the other man an incredulous stare. Too caring? Joel had helped save Kirk and his sister from an existence of misery within the Northern Empire. Kirk owed his very *life* to the Ardenian mage.

Joel leaned against the wall and wrapped his arms loosely around himself. "Thank you for offering, but no. This is something I have to speak to Marc about myself. And before you ask why I wanted you to come, it's because I need you here. There's something I want you to do while I'm gone, but I'm afraid I can't tell you anything more until I make sure Marc is on board with the plan."

Kirk nodded. "I'll gladly help in any way I can. I know I've said it too many times already, but Keni and I really are indebted to you. We owe you our lives."

"And I've reminded you on just as many occasions that without your help, we'd never have made it out of the Northern Empire alive. So that would really make us even, right?" A playful spark flashed behind Joel's eyes, leaving Kirk to wonder if there'd been a time when such moments weren't a rare occurrence. What had Joel been like as a child? Or as a student in Academy? Before all this nonsense with the new steward of Arden and the tragic death of the late King, had there been a time when Joel was happy?

"Fair enough," Kirk replied at length. He raised his chin in a stubborn manner. "Then as a true and loyal friend, any task you ask of me, I'll do my best to see it through."

"Likewise. It means a great deal to me, that even in such dark times, I have someone I can trust."

"I don't know what I'll do while you're gone. With both you and Seneschal Koal leaving and Keni on the outskirts of Silver, I feel as though I'll have no one here I can trust."

"There *are* people you can trust, if you know where to look. Marc is one such person. My father would trust his very life with the dean, as would I. King Rishi confided in him, too. I can only speculate the number of secrets the King entrusted Marc with over the years."

"Your family is close with Dean Marc then?" Kirk asked.

"Mm, yes. Da and Marc have been friends since they were enrolled in Academy together. He's like a second father to me." Joel lowered his voice to a whisper. "Truth be told, I'd trust Marc over certain kin of mine."

Kirk shuddered as the words brought to mind both Liro and Neetra Adelwijn. It was hard to imagine that someone as kind and gentle as Joel could be related by blood to such monsters.

The sound of brisk footsteps stole the attention of both men. Kirk glanced up in time to see a dark figure round the bend in the hall.

Tall and trim, with jet black hair and eyes, Marc Arrio stormed toward the office in long strides. Dressed in an embellished jerkin crafted from fine leather and sporting calf-high boots polished to a sharp shine, he might have been more daunting if Kirk hadn't known Marc to be anything but amiable.

As the dean drew nearer, though, it became apparent that an uncharacteristic scowl contorted his features. Kirk braced himself. Was something wrong?

It could be nothing, he reminded himself. *Marc hasn't exactly been acting normal lately. Ever since the King died—*

"What are you two doing here?" Marc asked as he approached. "Shouldn't you be preparing to leave, Joel?"

"Yes." Hesitation lined Joel's smooth voice. "I need to speak with you before I go. Are you—all right?" He placed a hand on Marc's shoulder, and Kirk became all too aware of the dark bags beneath the dean's eyes.

Marc shook his head. "No. I'm not all right. Neetra called for an emergency council meeting this morning. I'm just returning from there now."

"Emergency council meeting? What for?"

With a sigh, Marc produced a small, golden key and jammed it into the keyhole. The door swung open, accompanied by the groan of rusty hinges. "Come inside."

Marc disappeared into the office with Joel on his heels, but Kirk hesitated in the doorway. Should he follow? Was he privy to whatever the dean was about to say?

Joel waved him forward. "Come on, Kirk. Hurry."

Biting his lower lip, Kirk slunk inside. He cast a wary gaze in Marc's direction, but the dean was paying him no attention whatsoever.

Joel closed the door without being asked and turned wide, frantic eyes onto Marc. "What's going on? What happened in the council chamber?"

Marc slumped down in the plush chair behind his desk, clasping his hands so tightly his knuckles turned white. "Koal and I tried to fight the order. We tried to prevent it. But those bastards, Neetra, Morathi, Anders Malin-Rai—they got exactly what they wanted."

Joel pressed his back against the door. Kirk wondered if he was trying to fall through it. "What did they do?"

Marc shook his head from side to side, as if in a state of disbelief himself. "The High Council has deemed it necessary that a member of the royal family ride with the army. Normally, that responsibility would fall upon the king, but since Arden is without—" Marc paused when his voice wavered and it took several agonizing moments for him to regain his composure. "Since Arden currently has no king, the High Council is instead calling upon a royal prince to go."

"A royal prince? You mean *Deegan*?"

Kirk took a gulp of air only when his burning lungs begged it of him. Crown Prince Deegan was King Rishi's only heir to the throne, and he was being thrown into *combat*? The idea seemed ludicrous. What if something were to happen to the young prince? What if Deegan were killed? What would become of Arden then?

Marc sighed. "I'm afraid so."

"But Hasain is going! He's Rishi's son. He's a Radek. Surely he can represent the royal family."

"You know as well as I that Neetra and his cronies won't allow a bastard to represent Arden, regardless of how qualified Hasain may be."

"Deegan's still a boy! He's too young for war. Not to mention he's the only eligible heir King Rishi has left. They can't send him to die in Shiraz. At least here in the palace, he has some measure of protection."

Marc offered an unconvincing smile. "Your father will keep him safe. Having Deegan there is mostly for show anyway. He'll just be there to inspire the troops and keep morale high. Koal will see to it that Deegan doesn't come within twenty leagues of the enemy."

"Oh? Which enemy? The Shirites or the ones lurking within *our own ranks*?" Joel smashed a fist against the wall. "I know what this is about. They're trying to eradicate the Radek bloodline."

"Joel, I don't think—"

"No, it's the truth and you know it. My uncle will do *anything* to keep the crown for himself, and the wolves on the High Council want things to go back to the way they were before the Radeks came into power. Look at what's happening! First they got rid of Rishi and now Deegan—"

"*Careful*," Marc hissed, and for the first time since entering the office, he glanced at Kirk. "Watch what you say, Joel. We don't know who we can or can't trust."

Kirk recoiled. Got rid of King Rishi? What were they talking about?

"That's actually the reason I came today." Joel moved closer to Kirk. "With my father and so many other allies leaving, you're going to need help, Marc."

"Help with what?"

"Digging up enough incriminating information to dethrone my uncle, of course. If it's as we fear and Neetra truly is trying to discredit or eliminate the Radek bloodline, he *cannot* remain in power. We have to find a way to get him off the throne before it's too late."

35

"It's not that simple," Marc replied. He folded his arms over his chest and let out a huff. "Even if we find enough dirt on Neetra to justify removing his title, do you really think the High Council will vote in our favor when it comes time to elect a new steward? Remember, *they* voted Neetra into power in the first place."

"I know." Joel's delicate voice wavered when he spoke. "But if you can find *any* kind of information to use against Neetra, at least it's something to start with. We'll have to come up with a plan to deal with the others as well."

Marc furrowed his brow. "Yes. Especially your brother. How Liro got voted onto the High Council—it's not right. In the chaos surrounding the King's death—everything fell a little too neatly into place. It was planned. It *had* to be planned."

"The seat should have gone to Hasain," Joel agreed. "Speaking of Liro, he paid Kirk and me a visit earlier. He interrupted our magery lesson and pulled Inan out of class."

"What? Why?"

"Neetra's orders. He thinks Inan should no longer be schooled with commoners, so he's hired private tutors and forbade Inan from stepping foot outside the palace walls."

"If you ask me, it seems like Neetra's trying to mold that boy into what he and the High Council want. Tell me something. If the Radek line were eliminated, who would be next in line for the throne?"

Joel's face pinched. "There isn't anyone else. If they won't allow Hasain or Gudrin to rule, they'd have to elect a new king. Someone from a different bloodline."

"Right. And look how convenient it is that Neetra Adelwijn is already sitting high and mighty as steward, with an heir waiting in the wings."

"Then it's even more crucial that Neetra be dethroned and Deegan kept out of harm's way."

Kirk's head spun in a whirlwind of confusion. He'd been desperately trying to follow the conversation, but the longer he listened, the more perplexed he became. Joel had mentioned in the past how corrupt the High Council of Arden had become, of course—the way the newly elected steward chose to run the country was proof enough of that. But what was this about the Crown Prince being in danger? Were people out to get Prince Deegan? And why did Dean Marc and Joel speak of the late king as though his death wasn't his own doing? Was there more to the story than what the public knew?

Kirk jumped when he felt a hand grip his shoulder. Craning his neck, he found it difficult to breathe when he discovered Joel was staring at him. The mage's sapphire orbs were ablaze, as if some kind of internal battle raged within him.

Kirk's heart thudded to a stop. He'd meant what he said when he'd

36

promised to do anything Joel asked—no matter how perilous the task might be—but was he *really* ready to hear whatever Joel had to say?

"My friend, you saved the lives of my father, my brother, Hasain, NezReth, and me. Without your help, I have no doubt we wouldn't have escaped the Northern Empire. I hate to ask even more of you—"

"You know you can ask anything," Kirk whispered. "I haven't forgotten what you did for Kenisha and me either."

Joel's gaze faltered, falling to the floor. "Marc has already agreed to search for information—anything that can be used against Neetra or his supporters—anything that might help us remove the steward from power. There are others who are willing to help, too, but they are under constant scrutiny, making it quite difficult. With my father, myself, and so many others leaving, Marc will need someone he can trust—someone to help him dig for evidence. Can you do this for me? Can you be Marc's right hand man while I'm gone?"

"Yes," Kirk replied without allowing himself time to think about the possible implications of such a request. "Of course I can."

Marc shifted in his chair. "Joel, are you *sure*? It's a terrible risk, bringing any outsiders into this mess. Are you certain you know his character? Are you certain we can trust him?"

"I've already trusted Kirk with my life once. He won't betray us. You can't do this on your own, Marc."

"And he knows if Neetra gets wind of what we're doing, the repercussions will be—severe?"

Joel opened his mouth to respond, but Kirk beat him to it. "With all due respect, Dean Arrio, the Emperor of the land I came from was so cruel that he forced his own people to battle to the death in an arena—*for sport*—and anyone thought to be plotting against him was tortured and executed without warning or fair trial. I know the consequences of defying those in power, and I *certainly* know danger. I've lived in it my entire life. If Joel thinks I can be of service, I want to help. I came to this country to escape tyranny. If there's *anything* I can do to prevent such heinous acts from happening in Arden, it's worth the risk."

Marc remained quiet in his chair, tapping the cherry armrest with one finger. As Kirk waited with bated breath for an answer, it was as though the world itself had come to a grinding halt. Would Marc accept Kirk's help? And what had he actually agreed to anyway? Would he even be able to help? He was just a mage! He didn't know anything about Ardenian politics or the men who ran the country.

"All right," Marc said at long last. He slumped farther down into the cushion and let out a defeated sigh. His eyes reflected hardships too dark and terrible for Kirk to comprehend. "So be it."

"Thank you," Kirk whispered.

Marc laughed—an eerie, broken sound that sent chills down Kirk's spine. "Don't thank me just yet, Kirk Bhadrayu."

Head down and heart racing, Hasain stormed through the palace halls. He didn't slow to glance at the royal portraits because he still couldn't bear the weight of his father's measured gaze. Even now, when Hasain believed he was doing the only honorable thing left by going to war, he was still certain he didn't deserve Rishi's approval.

Hasain's shoulder was still heavy from the weight of Aodan's hand moments before, and the soft echo of Dahlia's well wishes continued to ring in his ears. They'd sent him off with all the warmth a family could bequeath, yet Hasain still felt utterly alone. It seemed no one could help lift the gloom in his heart.

How much longer would the grief suck all vigor from his soul? Weren't two moonturns spent in mourning enough? Shouldn't the fog of despair inside his head begin to clear by now? This couldn't go on forever, could it? His father was never coming back. But would Hasain? Would he ever be more than a shadow of his former self?

He gritted his teeth.

I have to push past the grief. I have to focus on keeping Deegan safe. It's not fair he should have to ride to war. He's only thirteen, for Daya's sake!

Law mandated the head of the country lead his troops into battle, yet the coward who sat upon the throne had chosen to send his boy-nephew instead. If Neetra had any honor at all, it would be *him* going. Hasain nearly laughed from the absurdity of such a notion. Neetra wouldn't know honor if it jumped up and bit him in the arse. He was too busy trying to strip the remaining Radeks of their power.

Hasain shook his head. Thinking about how much he hated Neetra would do him no good. He needed to pull himself back together, so he made an effort to recall the good things in life he still possessed. There were his fine rooms inside the palace; Neetra hadn't yet attempted to toss Hasain out of his home. The servants still treated him as they always had, when he'd still been the respected son of the King. He had a fiancée, Dame Naida Cordula. She was less than he'd hoped for in a wife, but his father had arranged the courtship himself, before he'd died, and Hasain had not the heart to fight the marriage any longer. Besides, it wasn't as though Kezra had turned to him, even after her fallout with Nawaz. If Hasain couldn't have what he wanted then he'd settle for what his father had provided.

The great stairs came into view ahead, and he smoothed his battle robes without thought. Cut short above the knee, the robes were tailored to allow better movement in combat. Likewise, he would be able to carry a sword with ease. It wasn't typical for a mage to carry such a cumbersome weapon, but Hasain had his doubts as to whether he could hold his ground with magic alone. Frankly, he wasn't sure whether he could hold his own with a sword either. His lack of skill in both magic and weaponry was yet another reminder of his inadequacy.

His father had always tried to convince Hasain to study harder, to hone his magic and finesse his weaponry skills, but instead Hasain focused his time and energy into becoming a politician. The King had also gone above and beyond to ensure his children were trained with a blade, even taking time to schedule private lessons with Weapons Master Roland. If Hasain had even *once* taken the training seriously, perhaps he'd be better prepared now.

Hasain tried not to think anymore, lest he fall further into the pit of self-pity. Thinking would do nothing but slow his footfalls. In a flurry, Hasain bounded down the carpeted steps, more than ready to be out of the palace. But first he had to collect Nawaz so the two of them could ride to the gathering field together.

Just as Hasain's boot hit the bottom step, a piercing voice rose from within the throne room, echoing off the painted ceiling and down the hallway. Hasain curled his nose. Such an offensive shriek could belong to no one else but Neetra Adelwijn himself.

Hasain hesitated at the base of the staircase. He could hardly stomach the idea of having to look upon the man who'd just sent Deegan into danger, but morbid curiosity propelled him forward. Who was the steward so viciously scolding? Holding his breath, Hasain crept closer until he could peer around the corner and into the throne room.

Neetra perched upon the dead king's throne as if he belonged there, pompous, arrogant. Scowling like a rabid dog, he leaned forward, knuckles white as he dug his fingers into the velvet armrests. The target of his fury, Nawaz Arrio, stood limply before his stepfather, eyes downcast and back slouching.

"If you do this, Nawaz Arrio, don't think you can simply come crawling back at war's end— *should you live*—and beg to be reinstated. Your title and my blessing are not so lightly renounced."

Hasain clutched the wall as he eavesdropped. Renounced? What was going on?

Nawaz lifted his reddened face. Dressed in his Healer jerkin with a crossbow strapped to one shoulder, he was prepared to tend wounded soldiers or fight as needed. He'd bravely elected to march for Shiraz even though he could have easily escaped such a fate. Hasain couldn't comprehend why Neetra would have any cause to belittle the young lord.

Nawaz pulled a golden ring from his finger—the crest of the Adelwijn family—and clenched it in his fist. "The title never meant anything, and if I'd ever *once* had your blessing, I wouldn't be doing this."

Heat rose to Hasain's face in an angry wave. Neetra was stripping Nawaz of his title? Why? On what grounds?

Across the throne room, Nawaz's brother and sister stood with their longtime servant, Bailey. Hasain hadn't even noticed them until Inez broke away from the other two and reached for Nawaz with a trembling hand.

"Don't do this," she gasped. "You don't have to go to war. You can stay here with us and be safe."

An indignant growl escaped Neetra's clenched jaw. He issued his daughter a cold glare, but Inez only glowered back at him with equal ferocity. Hasain's spirit dared soar, if only for the moment.

Inez turned back to her brother. "Think of your wife and unborn babe, Nawaz. They need you, too. You still have the ring. Just—"

Nawaz shook his head and stared down at the golden band. "This ring never made him want me. He never accepted me as a son. Truthfully, this changes nothing."

"Well put," Neetra scoffed. "So hand it over and be gone already!"

Inez whirled on her father so quickly Hasain jumped back a step. "Shut your mouth! You're the reason for this! You've driven our family apart!"

Neetra leapt to his feet, his face an ugly red. "Don't you *dare* speak to me in such a way! You forget your place, *girl*. Don't forget, I can take away your title as easily as his!"

Inez reeled back, visibly shaken by Neetra's threat. Her painted lips fell open several times, but it appeared her voice had been stunned away. Bailey swept over to her and wrapped his arms around her shoulders, shielding the young girl from her deranged father.

"Disowning two children in one day, Neetra Adelwijn?" the servant spat. "I should think such conviction would require a spine. Be done with this. Send away the stepson who only ever sought your approval so you may dismiss us as well. We grow nauseated with the sight of you."

Hasain gasped. How could Bailey say such things and not lose his head?

Neetra's face darkened from red to purple, and his clenched fists and bulging eyes were only further testament to his rage. For a moment, Neetra faced Bailey as if he might engage the servant, but ultimately, the steward turned his attention back onto Nawaz.

Pointing a savage finger at his stepson, Neetra's roar reached all corners of the room. *"Choose!"*

Hasain waited breathlessly to see what his friend would do. Thinking back, he couldn't remember a time when Nawaz hadn't been Neetra's stepson. Their relationship had always been strained, but Hasain never imagined it would end like this. Nawaz had done everything Neetra had *ever* asked. He'd gone to Academy to become a Healer, despite having no interest in the profession. He'd married Heidi even though it meant giving up the woman he truly desired. The only thing Nawaz had done wrong was be born someone else's son. Insanity! There truly was no way to please Neetra.

Nawaz lurched forward, face set like stone, and placed the ring at Neetra's feet. Before Hasain even had a chance to process what was happening, it was over.

A hard lump formed in the back of his throat. He'd just watched Nawaz give up his title. He'd just watched his friend's disownment.

Letting out a sob, Inez ran to Nawaz with her arms outstretched. "You'll always be our brother. Come back to us alive and well."

Weeping as openly as Inez, Bailey put his arms around both of them. His voice was muffled by distance, but Hasain could still hear the servant's words. "You're *my* son, if you'd have me. Remember, we love you. Be safe."

Nawaz's shoulders shook as he leaned against his remaining family. Blotchy red pigmentation turned his ears cherry red and seeped down his neck. But he didn't completely lose his composure. Not in front of Neetra.

Neetra picked up the ring and fell back into his seat, ignoring the display in front of him. As he turned the band over in his fingers, the steward's expression remained vapid. If he was celebrating victory, he did so discreetly. Hasain couldn't begin to imagine what was going on inside Neetra's tangled mind.

"Inan, come say goodbye to your brother," Bailey commanded in a brittle voice.

A gasp drew Hasain's attention. Inan had, at some point, wrapped his arms around a pillar and now clung to the marble column as if his life depended on it. The young lord's cheeks shone with tear trails as he glanced toward his father with wide, terrified eyes.

Nawaz shook his head. "No. Stay put, Inan. He values your blind loyalty over your heart."

Inan whispered a meek farewell but didn't move.

Hasain had seen enough. Taking a deep breath, he stepped away from the wall and made his presence known to all inside the throne room. Neetra openly scowled, recoiling into the dead King's chair, and Nawaz rushed to cover his shameful tears.

"Come, Nawaz," Hasain pressed gently. "It's time to leave."

Nawaz nodded, wiping a sleeve across his face. "Yeah. Let's go." He gave Bailey's shoulder one final squeeze and cupped his hands around Inez's face before following Hasain from the room.

Hasain was surprised when Neetra didn't fight for the last word. The silence at their backs helped propel them forward.

CHAPTER THREE

"I can't believe you're leaving."

Tears welled in the corners of Lady Mrifa's eyes, threatening to spill down her powdered cheeks. Standing beside the lady, Heidi Adelwijn sniffled and raised a kerchief to wipe at her own glistening face. Carmen, the youngest of the Adelwijn children, twisted the sleeve of her tunic and stared at her boots. A distraction, no doubt, but of the three women, her composure was undeniably the best.

It took all Joel's strength to keep his own emotions in check as he said farewell to his family. He wasn't ashamed to cry but knew it would be easier for his mother and sisters if he didn't. They didn't need to see how frightened he truly was.

Mrifa threw her arms around Joel's neck so snugly he could barely breathe. "You only just returned from the Northern Empire, and now you're being thrown into danger again. And your father—" She laid her face against his neck, and the tears, at last, did fall.

"I'll be back," Joel reassured her. "And Da too. It's not going to be anything like the Northern Empire, I promise."

Mrifa whimpered, the sound muffled by Joel's long, raven hair. "It's worse than the Northern Empire. It's *war*!"

Joel rubbed her shoulders, trying to bring some small measure of comfort to his grief-stricken mother. "It is war, but Da and I will stay safe. More than likely, the Shirites will tuck their tails and run when they see Arden's army approaching. What good would it do for their unorganized bands of militia to take on an army of our size?"

"Joel's right, Mother," Carmen added. "Arden's army is ten times the size of Shiraz's and *much* more competent. The enemy will be sent running all the way back behind the walls of Tahir. They don't have a leg to stand on against us."

Mrifa finally released her hold on Joel. "Koal said as much." She sighed, taking up a strand of blonde hair and twirling it around one finger. "Forgive me for worrying."

On all accounts, it *did* appear Arden had every advantage going into the campaign. Most of the troops were well trained: a mix of experienced veterans from the Northern War and young sentinels who'd taken lessons with Weapons Master Roland Korbin. Combined with roughly two hundred mages hired to fight and a team of skilled Healers, the size of the army swelled to an impressive ten thousand bodies.

Shiraz's own forces numbered in the hundreds. They had fewer soldiers, fewer mages, and fewer resources. Their militia-styled army, made up of small brigands, was more suited to ambush attacks and small-scale battles. To meet Arden on the open field would spell disaster for them. But none of this did anything to soothe Joel.

The warriors of Shiraz knew their own land better than anyone from Arden ever would. They had lived in the arid wastelands for centuries. They knew how to survive the harsh climate. Arden's forces would have to rely on supply trains for food and fresh water from the Nishika River. If access to either of those sources were disrupted, Shiraz would only need to wait patiently for their enemy to die of thirst or starvation. Stranded beneath the vehement desert sun, it wouldn't take long.

And there was something else, too—a thought so dark it seized Joel's body in terror.

There's a very real possibility Shiraz won't be acting alone. May The Two help us if the Northern Empire gets involved in this war.

He'd been there. He'd sat in that miserable, wicked chamber in Teivel and watched the Dhaki princes sign the treaty with Emperor Lichas Sarpedon. No matter how many times the High Council denied an alliance between Shiraz and the Northern Empire, Joel knew it was true. He'd seen it. Koal had seen it. Even Liro had been present—

And then Liro had the audacity to tell the other councilors there was nothing to worry about—that the treaty had only been an agreement allowing the Empire to utilize Shiraz's trade routes—that Emperor Sarpedon had no interest in joining the campaign against Arden. And Neetra and the other councilors had *believed* him.

Horseshit! How can they be so blind to the truth? Sarpedon has been trying to weasel his way inside Arden for years! And how easy will it be if our military is destroyed? We can't take on Shiraz and the Northern Empire and hope to survive. Why won't my uncle see reason?

He couldn't worry about it right now. Pushing the dark thoughts aside, Joel gave Carmen's shoulder a firm clasp. "You take care of Mother and Heidi while we're gone, okay?"

"I will. And the baby, too," Carmen replied. "Remember, you might be an uncle by the time you return."

Joel cast a forlorn smile at his other sister. Heidi's pregnancy wasn't showing yet, but that did little to ebb the grief she was surely experiencing. It wasn't fair. Heidi and Nawaz were expecting their first child together, yet this pointless war was about to tear the new family apart. There was no telling when or even *if* Nawaz would lay eyes on his child.

Heidi's eyes glistened as Joel embraced her. "Promise you'll look after my husband. Make sure Nawaz stays safe."

"I promise." Joel meant the words wholeheartedly.

Readjusting the rucksack slung across his shoulder, Joel turned away from his family. It was time to go—and none too soon. He couldn't bear to see their tears any longer.

Otos, longtime servant of the Adelwijn estate, held the door as Joel made his exit. The old man nodded, and Joel returned the gesture. Exchanges of words seemed unnecessary. Otos had been attending the family since Joel was a toddler. He'd care for Mrifa and the girls until his dying breath. That went without saying.

In the courtyard, Lady Mrifa's handmaiden, Tabitha, stood waiting beside Joel's horse, an energetic filly named Ivory. Tabitha offered him the reins. "Your horse, m'lord."

Joel ran a hand up the length of Ivory's braided leather bridle, grateful Tabitha had taken the time to saddle her already. "Thank you, Tabitha. Mother will need you inside the estate shortly. This—won't be easy on her."

"Of course, m'lord. I'll go at once. May The Two keep you safe." Tabitha gave a hasty curtsy before dashing toward the house.

As Joel watched her form disappear through the door, he wished to the Goddesses he could forsake his duty to Arden and run back inside too.

I don't want to leave again! It's not fair to them! They're expected to pick up their lives and go on pretending everything's all right when it's not.

Ivory tossed her head and pawed at the cobblestones. Sighing, Joel gave the filly's neck a pat. Her sleek, silver coat matched Joel's mage robe so perfectly he had to pause and take a moment to stare in awe. Surely they'd make an impressive pair on the battlefield: a flash of white lightning galloping across the golden sand dunes of Shiraz. Unfortunately, the imagery, lovely as it was, did nothing to calm his nerves.

"I hope you're ready," Joel whispered, words spoken more as a means to reassure himself than to make conversation with the horse.

Without sparing another backward glance, he led Ivory across the courtyard and through the wrought-iron gate that marked the edge of the Adelwijn property. When Joel closed his hands around the cold metal bars, the rusted hinges squealed as though the estate itself was protesting his departure.

He'd just finished securing his rucksack to the saddle when a timid voice rose above the din of the street, calling to him. "Joel!"

Joel spun around and blinked in confusion. "Kirk?"

The two friends had already said their goodbyes outside Marc's office earlier that day, so it came with great surprise to see the Imperial mage trotting in Joel's direction.

What in the two worlds is Kirk doing here?

Kirk appeared as though he'd run clear across the city. His deep brown hair was a disheveled mess, and his slight chest heaved from overexertion. "Oh, thank the Blessed Son you didn't leave yet!"

"What are you doing here?" Joel asked. "Is something wrong?"

Kirk paused, still trying to catch his breath. "No, no. It's just—I forgot to give this to you earlier." He extended a hand. In his palm rested a small pendant, plated in silver dust and molded into the shape of a soaring bird. "This is for you."

"What is—"

"A falcon."

Joel smiled wistfully and pointed to the heirloom ring on his finger. "The Adelwijn family crest is represented by a falcon."

"Then it's fate you have this." Kirk slipped the pendant into Joel's hand. "The clans of free folk in the North—those who have avoided conquest by the Northern Empire—believe the falcon to be a symbol of protection and good luck. You'll need *both* protection and luck while in Shiraz."

Joel brought the metal token closer, examining it. The craftsmanship was beautiful, with special attention given to detail. Miniscule black and grey beads added texture to the falcon's mighty wings, and a turquoise gem represented each of the bird's eyes. He ran his thumb over the smooth, outer edge of the pendant in admiration. "Where did you get this? It's lovely."

"My mother gave it to me many years ago. She told me it would protect me from harm and lead me to good fortune. I suppose it's done its job so far. I survived childhood in the streets of Teivel and was lucky enough to meet you—but I think you'll need it more than I will now." Kirk reached into a fold in his robe and pulled out a simple chain necklace. On reflex, Joel steadied his hand, watching as Kirk proceeded to loop the silver cord through the pendant. "This way you can wear it around your neck, close to your heart." Kirk's eyes darted to meet Joel's.

Joel was surprised how swiftly warmth rushed to his face. "Kirk, I can't take this. It belongs to you. If something were to happen and it was lost—"

"It's a gift. Please take it."

Joel froze as Kirk's hands closed over his own and gently pushed the trinket toward him. The touch was warm, inviting, reminding Joel just how lonely he was—

No. He shook his head. *I can't afford to let myself get attached to Kirk or anyone else. Not when Arden's on the brink of war. It can bring nothing good. Only heartache.*

Joel slipped the pendant back into Kirk's hand. "I'm sorry. I can't."

With pained resignation, Kirk closed a fist around the rejected gift and drew it close to his chest. Unmasked hurt glazed his eyes, driving Joel to turn away.

You'll thank me for doing this someday. It's better this way. No attachments, no broken hearts.

45

Joel grasped the pommel with trembling fingers. "I should go." He hoisted himself onto Ivory's back. Settling into the saddle, he only managed to lift his face when Kirk approached from the side and handed him the reins.

"Safe travels, Joel Adelwijn." Kirk's deflated voice was barely audible above the clamor of the busy street. "I'll do all I can to assist Dean Marc while you're gone."

Joel swallowed. Had he asked too much of his friend? While Joel was fighting the Shirites, Kirk would be waging a very different kind of war as he and Marc sought to dethrone Neetra. Both missions carried overwhelming risk and—should they fail—severe consequences.

"You stay safe as well," Joel replied, his voice cumbersome as he worked to keep it steady. "My uncle is ruthless. Don't let your guard down, not even for an instant."

A fleeting smile crossed Kirk's lips. He leaned closer, his torso pressing against Ivory's saddle. "Don't worry about me. I survived the Northern Empire, remember? Dean Marc and I will be fine."

For the sake of his sanity, Joel forced himself to believe the words. He *had* to believe things would be all right in the end. Otherwise, what was there left to fight for?

Joel gripped the reins so tightly his knuckles began to go numb. He could feel time growing short. Like sand trickling through an hourglass, it slipped away, leaving him with only one thing left to do—say goodbye.

Joel sat tall in the saddle and cleared his throat. "Farewell."

"Until we see each other again," Kirk replied. "Goodbye."

If. If we see each other again.

Agonizing despair drowned Joel's mind until nothing remained except a dull ache. For the sake of his friend, he should have put on a valiant front, but Joel couldn't bring himself to smile or offer any other such reassurances.

Joel jumped when he felt a hand clasp his forearm. He tried to tear his gaze away, but Kirk's eyes were ablaze with conviction so undeniable they held Joel captivated. Everything else in the world faded away, if only for the moment.

"Joel, we *will* see each other again. I know it."

Joel opened his mouth, but the lump in his throat prevented any words from flowing free. He didn't know what to say. All he knew was that he didn't want to leave.

That decision wasn't his to make. Kirk gave Ivory's rump a firm slap, and the filly leapt into motion. Joel could only cling to the reins as he was carried away.

And I thought the barracks were a madhouse. This is complete and utter chaos.

A cart stacked with supply crates and pulled by two oxen bustled past Gib, the spoked wheels nearly running over his boots. Taking a deep breath, he pulled on Astora's reins and directed the young mare through an opening in the congested war camp. How was he ever going to find Koal in this mess?

All around, men and women scurried like frenzied ants, pitching tents, amassing supplies, and fetching fodder for beasts. Kegs were being loaded onto wagons, the contents sloshing inside as the barrels rolled past. The smell of cheap ale burned Gib's nostrils, and with great dismay, he realized he'd likely have to suffer drinking it for the next several moonturns.

Ah, you've become too privileged, Gibben Nemesio. This is your punishment. Six months of nothing but stale ale and moldy bread.

Gib moved along before he was yelled at for interrupting the flow of traffic. Close by, a swordsmith hovered tirelessly over a grinding wheel, whittling down a pile of swords in need of sharpening. Gib set a hand on his own weapon, still sheathed and tethered to Astora's saddle. The blade was so dull he doubted it could even cut through a sheet of parchment paper, but getting it sharpened would have to wait. He was already tardy enough to warrant a harsh scolding. If he waited around to have his sword attended to, Koal might just flog him. Perhaps, though, the man might know where Gib could find the seneschal.

"Excuse me, sir," Gib called out in a spirited voice. "Can you tell me where I might find the command post? I'm looking for Seneschal Koal—"

The swordsmith never glanced up from his work, but he grunted and flippantly waved a hand. Whether he was showing Gib the right direction or just trying to get him to leave, he couldn't be sure. He didn't dare bother the man a second time and, with a dejected sigh, kept moving.

The air was thick with the smell of smoke, leather, and hay and the sound of yelling soldiers. A sea of faces surrounded him, but he recognized no one. He wished he knew where Liza was. His sister had always been wise beyond her years. Surely she could help him locate the seneschal. Hell, about now he'd even be happy to see Hasain, though the young Radek lord would no doubt ridicule Gib for losing his way.

Then again, maybe he wouldn't, Gib thought with a frown. *Hasain hasn't exactly been himself since King Rishi died.*

The death of a father was not something easily forgotten or brushed aside. Gib knew firsthand how devastating it could be. His own father had been murdered, leaving Gib alone to care for his young siblings and look after the family farm. Hasain's situation was different, of course, but certainly Gib could understand the pain the young lord must be feeling. Hasain would get through it, though. Everyone grieved at their own pace. King Rishi's death was still a fresh, open wound, but in time, Hasain would find a way to stop his bleeding heart. They all would.

"Do my eyes deceive me? Is that you, Gibben Nemesio?"

A sheepish grin flashed across Gib's face. He'd recognize Nage Nessuno's voice anywhere.

Nage stood some twenty paces or so away, flanked by two young women. Dressed in uniform with brown hair trimmed and neatly slicked back, it was hard to imagine this was the same poor boy Gib befriended years ago. Nage had come to that first sentinel training class half-starved, in rags, barefoot, and, like Gib, with nothing to show for himself. It was ironic that now, as they prepared for war, both men had so much worth fighting for.

Even as Gib approached, Nage's attention kept drifting toward his fiancée. Spirited and sharp-tongued, Nia Leal had long since eased her way into their core group of friends—and into Nage's heart. Never before had Gib witnessed Nage so happy, and even with danger imminent, his spirit remained high. Gib envied his friend. What would Gib give to feel a sliver of hope again?

Nage kept one arm draped around Nia's shoulders but offered his opposing hand for a shake. "Finally found your way, eh, Gib?"

"More like stumbled upon it by accident," Gib replied as he slid down from Astora's saddle. He grasped Nage's hand and reserved a bow for the two women. "A pleasure as always, Lady Nia."

Nia's eyes were reddened and moist, but her smile remained genuine. "It's nice to see you again, Gib. I'm not sure if you've met my sister yet."

The other girl, dressed in mottled soldier garb, offered her hand. "Hi. I'm Gara."

Gib *had* met her once before. On the morning Koal, Joel, and the others had left on their mission to the Northern Empire, Gara had accompanied her father, Ambassador Cenric Leal, to the royal courtyard. There, she'd said her farewells—her final farewells. Cenric hadn't made it out of Teivel alive.

She didn't need a reminder of her father's death, so Gib kept his mouth shut about their prior meeting. It hardly mattered anyway. Gara probably had no idea who he was. "Gib Nemesio, understudy of Seneschal Koal. I'm pleased to make your acquaintance."

"Oh, right." Gara's inquisitive hazel eyes met his, and Gib was certain he detected a trace of recognition. "You're Joel Adelwijn's companion. I've heard so much about you."

When they shook hands, Gara's grip was solid. Gib's pa had always said that was a sign of good character.

Gara released his hand and brushed a stray lock of hair away from her heart-shaped face. Her hair was cropped surprisingly short by Ardenian highborn standards. Ladies of the court were expected to grow their tresses long and lavishly, though Gib imagined holding female soldiers to the same standard might be impractical.

"I think it's admirable what Joel and you have done, professing your love publicly like that," Gara continued. "Not to mention brave. You're lucky to have each other."

Gib's cheeks flushed with uncomfortable heat. "Uh, yeah. Joel's a good friend. I am lucky." He searched desperately to change the conversation. "So, uh, are you a sentinel too?"

"I'm with the scouts," Gara replied, her eyes brightening. "I'll be roaming ahead of the army. Should the Shirites have any tricks up their sleeve, *I'll* be the hero riding in to warn your arses to prepare for trouble."

Nia's shoulders drew tight. "Well, let's hope there's neither trouble nor the need for heroics."

Nage reassured his fiancée by rubbing the small of her back. "Don't be worryin' about us. We'll be fine. After all, we got the famous Gibben Nemesio of Willowdale to watch our backs!"

Gib snorted. "Oh, please."

A single tear slipped down Nia's cheek as she leaned against Nage. "I should be going with you. There's a shortage of Healers, and I'm nearly fully trained—"

"No. Think of your mother. She's fallen ill. She needs you here." Nage cupped Nia's face between his roughened hands and wiped away her tears as they fell. "You can't leave her alone. She doesn't have anyone else. You gotta stay. And when I get home, everythin' will go back to normal."

"And we'll be married, yes?"

"The very day I return. I promise."

Gib politely looked away as the couple shared a kiss, while Gara busied herself with tending to the horses.

"Here," she said, offering Gib a pail of water. "For your mare."

Astora had buried her muzzle inside the bucket even before Gib set it onto the ground. "Thanks." He watched the horse drink for several moments before uttering a sigh. "I'm supposed to report to the seneschal, but I have no idea where he is."

Nage kept Nia wrapped in his arms but glanced in Gib's direction. "Command's set up on the north side of the valley. I'd reckon that's where he'd be."

Gib tipped his head back, searching. The sun drifted low in the western sky as it made its steady decline toward the horizon. All too soon, nightfall would be upon them. "All right. I better get going then. I'll come find you later. Save me a ration of food?"

Nage grinned. "Yeah, yeah. And if you happen across Kezra, tell 'er she's late!"

"Kezra Malin-Rai?" Gara asked, her eyes going wide. "Among us women soldiers, her name is almost as renowned as Gibben Nemesio's. She will come, won't she? Despite the High Council's latest decree?"

Gib couldn't help but laugh at the absurd idea of Kezra not showing up. She was perhaps the bravest person he knew. To defy her father—the entire High Council, really—what kind of courage had that taken? Even with the odds stacked against her, she continued to stay one step ahead of adversity. Kezra *always* had a plan of action, and she'd be damned if the men on the High Council stopped her.

"I don't think you have to worry about that. She'll come. If Kezra were lying on her deathbed with the plague, she'd still find a way to be here."

"Aye," Nage said. "Kezra wouldn't miss this for the world."

Gib bid farewell to Nage and the girls and climbed into Astora's saddle. Koal was probably going to skin him alive for being so late, and now that Gib knew where to find his mentor, there were no further excuses to justify his tardiness. Prodding Astora into a brisk trot, Gib went in search of the seneschal.

The bustle from earlier had finally begun to fizzle. Many of the soldiers now congregated around fire pits, preparing their meals and settling in for the night. Boisterous laughter rose as kegs were opened and enjoyed, and the aroma of smoked meats wafted through the war camp, carried by a gentle, crisp breeze.

The mood seemed light, even jovial, but Gib knew better than to assume the soldiers had all forgotten why they were there.

Let them enjoy tonight, for tomorrow the grueling trek begins.

Gib found his way to the command post before even a quarter of a mark passed. He'd been worried he might not know the place when he saw it, but now, all doubt flew from his mind.

On a lonely hill set away from the rest of the camp, an enormous pavilion had been erected. Unlike the simple wedge tents used by the common soldier, this was an elaborate six-sided structure that, at the highest peak, towered above Gib's head. The outside of the tent was dyed in regal Ardenian blue, and each flowing panel was crafted from quality wool Gib guessed could withstand rain, hail, dust, or whatever other elements The Two decided to throw at it. Openly gawking, Gib left Astora hitched to a pole at the base of the hill and approached on foot.

Golden sunlight bounced off the plate armor of two lone sentinels standing watch outside. These were not average soldiers, however; the quality of their flowing, azure capes and the intricate fluting carved into their shining steel chest plates could indicate only one thing. Gib raised an eyebrow. Why were royal guardsmen here, so far away from the palace? Their sole duty was to protect the Radek family. Surely they hadn't been taken from their post and ordered to march in Neetra Adelwijn's contrived war.

Unless there's someone here they're protecting. Chhaya's bane, what if Diddy's here? Or Deegan? Daya, please don't let it be Deegan.

Gib refused to believe the young Crown Prince would be allowed to ride into battle, but Neetra was beyond reasonable. He'd put the Radek heir's life in danger if it meant saving himself the hassle of getting his own hands soiled.

Before Gib had taken more than a single step forward, both guardsmen drew their swords, the sound of steel on leather slicing through the air. Two sets of narrowed eyes glared at Gib through slits in their ornamental helms and neither face held a trace of warmth.

"You there!" one of them barked. "Turn around and go back the way you came."

Gib hesitated. Because he worked so closely with Koal, many of the royal guardsmen inside the palace had memorized Gib's face, and rarely did they give him trouble. Likewise, he recognized most of them, too. These soldiers, however, he had never seen before—and they clearly didn't know him either.

He did his best to keep his voice steady and amicable. "Hello. I'm supposed to meet with Seneschal Koal—"

The guardsman pointed his blade straight at Gib, expression turning from unnerving to downright frightening. "Did I stutter? Only officials are allowed past this point. Get lost!"

"No, wait!" Gib floundered where he stood. "Sorry, I think there's been a misunderstanding—"

"Soldier, I'm warning you to leave. *Now.*"

"I'm not a soldier. I'm Seneschal Koal's understudy. My name's Gib. Gibben Nemes—"

"I don't give a damn who you are. Turn around and go back the way you came! Or do we need to *assist* you?"

Gib's eyes darted up the hill. If only he could make his presence known to Koal. The seneschal could sort this out in an instant. He contemplated making a dash for the tent in hopes of reaching his mentor before the guardsmen caught him. No. That probably wasn't a wise decision.

Gib elicited a groan. "If you won't let me pass, at least get Seneschal Koal to come down here. He'll gladly tell you who I am."

The second guardsman sneered at Gib. "Piss off!"

Defeated and exasperated, Gib locked his jaw and went silent. How was he supposed to meet with Koal if these guards weren't going to give him a chance to explain himself? And *why* were they being so rude?

"Don't worry, Nemesio," a rough voice called out from behind him. "I had both of these dolts in basic sentinel training. Neither of them could strike the broad side of a barn, let alone a moving target."

Gib dared to hope as he craned his head around and saw Weapons Master Roland Korbin sauntering closer.

Dressed in unadorned, practical sparring attire, the master trainer nevertheless looked intimidating. Tall and broad-shouldered, Roland's grizzled face and sharp features complemented his no-nonsense approach, and despite his lowborn upbringing, Roland's fierce presence commanded respect.

Roland kept his somber gaze fixed on the two soldiers as he drew nearer. "Renard Acker and Alden Beasley, how—pray tell—did two bootless slugs like you find your way into such lofty positions when last I knew, you were both supposed to be shoveling the stables as punishment for *thievery and assault?*"

The first guardsman's mouth opened as he smirked, revealing two rows of yellowed teeth. "The general himself appointed us to the Royal Guard. Seems the High Council wanted extra protection for Crown Prince Deegan."

Gib couldn't help but squirm where he stood. So this meant Deegan *was* here after all.

Letting out a disgusted grunt, Roland flung his hands into the air. "I suppose the rigorous training all former members of the Royal Guard had to endure doesn't mean a damn thing now if Neetra is just going to let his dogs do whatever the hell they want."

Gib grimaced. Roland was right. This wasn't how things were supposed to be done. Neetra had taken the throne, and suddenly all laws were being thrown to the wind. The security of Arden's royal family was no laughing matter. Why were two *criminals* being allowed to protect the prince?

Still shaking his head, Roland pushed his way past the two sentinels. "Gib, come with me."

The guards jumped to block him, standing shoulder to shoulder with swords at the ready. "I'm afraid you'll have to turn around, Weapons Master. We have strict orders from General Morathi that *no one* is to disturb the command tent tonight."

Roland froze, his hazel eyes glinting with some disconcerting emotion Gib couldn't name. "I don't take my orders from General Morathi. I'm here at *Seneschal Koal's* command." Gib struggled to breathe as Roland set one hand on the hilt of his sheathed sword, daring the guardsmen to object a second time. "Now move aside and let us pass. Despite what you may think, the seneschal's voice still weighs heavily in this country."

"For now," the guard sneered.

With locked jaws and faces blotched red from anger, the pair of sentinels finally stepped aside. Gib startled when Roland took him by the elbow, silently guiding him forward. He could feel the guardsmen glaring at him but refused to look back.

Roland remained grave as they made their way up the hill. "That lot has no business being part of the Royal Guard. What the hell is going on?"

Gib had a few choice words he wished to say but kept quiet. Roland surely knew the peril Arden faced. Appointing questionable, untrained soldiers with the task of keeping the Crown Prince safe was a horrible idea.

With the King dead and Neetra in control, it was imperative Prince Deegan survive. If anything happened to the only remaining Radek heir, Arden would certainly fall into darkness.

"Are you coming to Shiraz, too, sir?" Gib asked, trotting to keep pace with Roland's longer strides.

"Nay. Just here to deliver a message. And offer assistance on the home front."

Gib didn't have time to ponder Roland's cryptic response, for all too soon, they reached the pavilion. The master held open the loose tent flap, and Gib had to duck briefly when he passed through the entrance.

Shadows bathed the interior of the tent, reaching all corners—from the bare ground to the tent's apex, suspended by spoked poles some three feet above Gib's head. Gib blinked, his eyes slow to adjust to the dark. The only source of light was a lone lantern, set upon a table in the center of the room. Gathered around it were five bodies, the low light illuminating their grim, worried faces.

Koal was first to glance up. Cords of silver dusted the seneschal's dark hair, and the once-telltale age lines around his mouth and eyes were now deep rivets in his fair skin. He'd aged since Gib had first met him, even more so in the past few moonturns. Gib imagined it had to be hard on Koal; Rishi Radek hadn't just been Koal's king. He'd also been a dear friend.

Gib's stomach flopped when he noted Crown Prince Deegan lingering in Koal's shadow. The boy's striking resemblance to his uncle was so undeniable Deegan might well have been Koal's son. But when Deegan raised his face into the light, Gib felt like he was staring into the keen, sharp gaze of the late King. The spark in the Crown Prince's brown eyes irrefutably belonged to Rishi Radek.

"There you are," Koal groaned, scolding Gib with a measured glare. "I was beginning to wonder if I needed to send a search party to retrieve you."

Gib rubbed the back of his blistering neck. "Almost, sir."

Deegan lifted his chin, and if Gib wasn't mistaken, the slightest hint of a devious smile flickered across the prince's mouth. "Welcome, Gibben Nemesio. We're all thankful you've finally arrived. My uncle would have surely been lost without his favorite servant at his side."

Standing on the opposite side of the young prince and looking painfully worn, Hasain curled his nose and gave Deegan a swat on the back of the head. Not even a trace of the young Radek lord's usual smirk played upon his lips, and his dark eyes were hollow. There'd been a time when he, too, would have teased Gib for being late, but Hasain had grown detached since the death of his father. Gib would have gladly welcomed Hasain's typical jeer if it meant things could go back to the way they were.

Gib took the opportunity to bow to Deegan while fishing for a response. "I suppose it would have been smarter of me to ride with someone who knew where they were going, Highness. Despite being in Silver for nearly four years, I still manage to get lost more frequently than I care to admit."

Deegan snorted and motioned for Gib to rise. Out of the corner of Gib's vision, he saw Hasain roll his eyes.

"You could have ridden with me."

Gib's breath caught in his throat at the sound of Joel's silken voice. He'd known the mage was coming, of course, but actually seeing him did little to lessen the jab to Gib's stomach.

Joel stood between Hasain and Tular Galloway, white mage robe standing out against the dark riding attire of his comrades. Somehow, it seemed appropriate. Joel was extraordinary, a precious jewel set upon a pedestal, evocatively beautiful and born to stand out from the crowd. Untouchable. Perhaps it was just as well he and Gib had parted ways. Joel deserved someone equally spectacular—not some misfit farmer pretending to blend in among the elite.

"Yeah," Gib managed to utter, the tension in the room a near tangible entity. "Maybe."

Joel's haunted eyes remained downcast, as if making contact with Gib might destroy him. Gib's cheeks burst with uncomfortable heat. His mouth fell open as he searched for words. He felt like he should say more, but in the moment, speech failed him.

Fortunately, Roland pushed his way into the tent, sufficiently putting an end to the uncomfortable lull. "Chhaya's bane! The war's gonna be over by the time you're done with greetings, Nemesio. Move your arse."

Gib lumbered aside. "Sorry."

"Roland? What are you doing here?" Koal asked.

The Weapons Master let out a groan. "First, I have to ask—what's with the two thugs outside, and *why* are they part of the Royal Guard?"

"Morathi appointed them and half a dozen others after the council meeting this morning."

"That's horseshit. Can't you dismiss them?"

Koal shook his head. "Neetra approved it already. There's nothing I can do."

"Even better I was sent then."

"Sent?" Koal raised an eyebrow. "By who?"

"Your sister." Roland's hawk-like gaze swept across the room until it settled on the young Crown Prince. "Dahlia wanted me to deliver a gift to her son."

All eyes turned to Deegan. The prince stiffened under the scrutiny. It was hard to believe he was a mere boy of thirteen—the same age Gib had been when he first came to Silver City. "What gift has my mother sent, Weapons Master?"

Roland opened his mouth to respond, but a new voice answered first.

"It is I, Radek heir."

54

Gib nearly jumped out of his skin. The enigmatic words cut through the air, sharp as a knife, startling him, along with everyone else. A swirl of white silk flashed within the gloom, and from the corner of Gib's eye, a lone figure materialized. He blinked to be sure he wasn't hallucinating. On the far side of the room, where Gib was *certain* there'd been empty space a moment before, stood the Blessed Mage, Natori.

She stepped forward, the light from the lantern a golden sheen against her mage robes. Insightful, violet eyes regarded the gathered men, and when she bowed to the young prince, Gib caught sight of the slender longsword fastened to her back, resting between her shoulder blades.

At once, memories flooded Gib's mind of blue flame sprouting from the steel as Natori raced through the palace halls. On the night Joel and the others escaped Teivel, Gib had witnessed a glimpse of how formidable the Blessed Mage could be.

Koal was the first to recover from Natori's unexpected arrival. "So, you will accompany the army into Shiraz then?"

"Let me make something very clear, Seneschal," said Natori. "I care naught for Neetra Adelwijn's false war. Nor will I follow orders from the likes of Morathi Adeben. Long ago, I swore an oath to protect the Radek bloodline. I am here to safeguard Prince Deegan. If he goes into enemy territory, then I go as well."

"And NezReth?"

"He will stay with Dahlia and the remaining children."

Koal gave her a curt nod. "Good." His somber gaze shifted briefly toward the prince. "I won't always be able to keep both eyes on my nephew."

"He'll be safe under my watch," Natori assured.

Hasain slipped a hand onto Deegan's shoulder. "We will help. All of us will."

Tular and Joel nodded in unison, and Gib found himself doing the same. He'd long since sworn his loyalty to the Radeks. King Rishi's death wasn't about to change anything. Back on that first day of class, when Diddy had introduced himself, Gib would never have imagined his life would become so intertwined with the royal family. They'd allowed him into their home and, more importantly, their hearts.

There wasn't a thing Gib wouldn't do for them now. He'd protect Deegan like the prince was one of his own brothers. If that meant jeopardizing Gib's own life, then so be it. Safeguarding Arden's future was worth *any* sacrifice, and though no one said the words aloud, Gib knew those gathered felt the same.

Koal motioned toward the map that lay unraveled upon the table. "We'll move out at dawn. The army will travel east until we reach the Nishika. From there, it's a straight shot south along the river into Shiraz." He tapped one finger against the withered parchment, and Gib craned his

55

head to get a better view, even as Roland moved closer to examine the map. "Our scouts have reported that most of the skirmishes are taking place on the border villages of Perth and Ashvale—here and here. With any luck, we can secure Arden's border with minimal losses and be home in three moonturns."

Roland raised an eyebrow. "And if Neetra and Morathi push for a full-scale invasion? What then? What if he demands you take the army all the way to Tahir?"

Silence settled over the room like thick fog. Gib's stomach twisted into knots. It had always been in his nature to hope for the best, but experience told him only a fool wouldn't prepare for the worst. How far would Neetra take this war if securing the border wasn't enough? Would the steward not be happy until every soldier—Shirite and Ardenian alike— lay dead?

Koal finally replied in a voice heavy with burden, "Then we'll *have* to find a way to stop him. Our allies left behind will have their work cut out for them."

Roland leaned forward, giving a firm nod. "Don't concern yourself with Neetra. We'll do whatever we must to get that bastard off the throne. *You* need to watch out for Morathi. He's up to something. I can feel it. Putting his own agents among the Royal Guard to protect Deegan from the Shirites—that's a pile of horseshit! If you ask me, Morathi and his thugs are the bigger threat to the prince."

"I know," Koal lamented. "But there's nothing I can do about it right now. Throwing allegations at Morathi won't solve anything. Neetra would demand proof, and even if I did have any, he might not listen."

Roland snorted. "And what proof would be sufficient for that snake anyway? An Ardenian blade thrust into Deegan's back?"

The master's words sent a queasy wave sweeping over Gib, from his head to his stomach, where it settled like a brick. The general wouldn't truly betray the royal family, would he? King Rishi and Morathi had never seen eye to eye, but to murder the heir in cold blood? No. Gib couldn't believe it.

Deegan took a step back, growing pale. Any trace of the wit he'd displayed moments before faded, and once again he was a boy of thirteen, frightened and unsure. Hasain and Tular moved closer on instinct, and Joel extended one arm, squeezing his young cousin's shoulder. Natori took post behind Deegan, her eyes ever-vigilant within the shadows.

Koal continued to stare at the map, but his gaze was distant and detached. Gib could only speculate what his mentor might be thinking.

Finally, the seneschal lifted his head and with somber eyes scanned the room, looking from face to face until he'd measured them all. "Everything is going to be all right. It has to be."

Gib stood tall, but inside he couldn't have been any more afraid.

CHAPTER FOUR

Arden's army departed at dawn, the rising sun guiding them east. Rolling hills of springtime green impelled them forward, quickening their steps and drawing them away from Silver. In his mind, Gib conjured images of the high, outer city walls, sparkling in radiant morning sunlight and the waters of the mighty Tempist winding their way along Traders Row like the coils of a serpent. The view was surely exquisite, but Gib refused to turn in his saddle and glance back. To lay eyes upon his home would only remind him of all the things he was leaving behind.

For the first half of the day, Gib rode with Deegan's royal escort. This might have been more enjoyable if not for Morathi Adeben also choosing to accompany the party. As Gib followed in silence behind Koal's dappled palfrey, he was all too aware of the general's presence. Slate grey eyes shifted restlessly from one party member to the next—assessing— *calculating.*

At times, Morathi would speak with Koal, but the exchanges were impersonal at best. Morathi's voice matched his formidable appearance: deceptively calm, like a viper waiting for an opportunity to strike. Gib could hardly stand to listen to it.

Worse, though, were the spans of time when the general ceased talking altogether. In those moments, the conversation from the previous evening swelled inside Gib's head, heightening his nerves and bringing him within a fever pitch of complete hysteria. Were Roland and Koal's concerns valid? Was Morathi only waiting for an opening to betray Deegan? The thought of harm coming to the Crown Prince turned Gib's blood to ice.

Koal must have noticed Gib's apprehension. Just after midday, he asked Gib to relay a series of messages to officers near the front line. Although Gib was relieved for the opportunity to get away from Morathi, guilt gnawed at his conscience. He'd sworn to protect the Radek family. What if something happened to Deegan while Gib was off playing the role of messenger boy?

Of course, the chance of that happening right then and there was about as likely as getting struck by lightning on a cloudless day. They weren't even three leagues outside Silver, and here, surrounded by ten thousand armed soldiers, only a fool would attempt to harm Deegan. Besides, Hasain and Tular hadn't left Deegan's side since the previous night, and Natori's unyielding presence couldn't be ignored. No, the prince was safe. For the time being.

Gib found himself riding up and down the line for the next two marks, delivering Koal's orders and collecting reports. As he passed by score after score of unmounted soldiers, trudging along with supplies and armor strapped to their backs, he'd never been more grateful to have Astora. How different would his life have turned out had he never met Joel? It was probable he'd be among the foot soldiers—if he'd even survived this long.

Gib realized with dismay just how painstakingly sluggish the journey to the border was going to be. Less than half of Arden's army was mounted, and even slower than the men who made the trek on foot were the beasts of burden: oxen and mules pulling full carts of food, ale, and weaponry supplies. The animals kicked up dirt in their wake, which soon became a giant plume of dust that burned Gib's eyes and left his throat parched. Was this all he had to look forward to for the next several moonturns? Dust, sweat, and the constant paranoia that Deegan would be attacked?

When he returned to Koal with one last report, the seneschal praised Gib for a job well done and promptly dismissed him again, all but ordering Gib to go find his friends and spend the remainder of the afternoon traveling with them. Gib couldn't muster enough energy to protest.

Four marks later, Gib winced as he threw his leg over Astora's saddle and dismounted for the final time that day. Extending his arms above his head, he tried to work the kink out of his lower back. He hadn't ridden for so long in one stretch since he'd traveled back and forth to the farm in Willowdale.

"Not used to riding much, are you?"

With a smile, Gib glanced over his shoulder, following the sound of his companion's soft voice.

Zandi still perched in his saddle, though his worn face suggested he was also tired. After such a long ride, strands of onyx hair had escaped from beneath his turban, and the heritage mark painted above his brow had faded from rich red to pale pink. He still looked lovely in the warm glow of the setting sun. Orange blazes of light accented his dark features and played about his moving lips.

"I haven't ridden on anything but cobblestone in so long that I'm feeling it too," Zandi admitted, his sharp emerald eyes seizing Gib's attention.

Gib mustered a grin. "We could hobble over to the Healer tent once they get it raised and beg for something for saddle sores."

"No," Zandi chuckled. "When I passed Nawaz earlier he was already complaining about how many blisters he'd have to look at tonight. He might have been right. Look at all of the marchers. They're already tearing off their boots."

Indeed, a great many soldiers were trudging over to the riverbank and readying themselves for a good soak. Gib couldn't say he blamed them, and seeing that he wasn't as bad off as those who'd traveled on foot, he promised himself to hunt twice as hard for firewood when the time came.

Gib rubbed the back of his neck. "I wasn't aware you were on speaking terms with Nawaz, given—circumstances."

Zandi shrugged and finally climbed down from the back of his own horse. He gritted his teeth upon landing, and Gib had to wonder if the mage was in more pain than pride would allow admitting. "He wasn't actually talking to me. I just happened to be within earshot. But I would speak to him, if he had any desire or the need arose. Kezra doesn't say much about Nawaz, but she hasn't placed demands on the rest of us not to interact with him."

"That's good, I suppose. I'd like to hope their friendship could recover one day, but I know how hard it is."

At length, Zandi nodded. "That might be too much to ask. Kezra isn't like you." He paused to take a deep breath, as if politeness obligated him to ask the following question. "How is Joel? Have you seen him lately?"

"Last night and again this morning," Gib replied hastily. He snapped his mouth shut. It seemed unfair that Zandi should always have to be so understanding. Didn't he grow weary of Gib's fumbling reassurances concerning his relationship with Joel? Wasn't Zandi ever jealous?

Gib didn't want to talk about Joel anymore. Zandi deserved as much. "I better go find Koal. I need to check in with him, though I doubt I can be of much help. At this point, I'll probably just get in the way."

"You sell yourself short. Seneschal Koal trusts you. He handpicked you from a sea of other young men who'd *kill* to be in your position. Clearly he must see something in you. You're too modest for your own good."

"Maybe. Or perhaps it's all a clever ruse to make people like me."

Zandi's eyes danced with amusement. "Well, if so, it's working." His hand brushed across Gib's, and for a brief moment, their fingers interlocked. But before Gib could even squeeze Zandi's hand, he'd already pulled away. "I'm going to find Kezra now. I guess I'll see you after you're done meeting with Koal."

"Sure. I'll find you when it's time to eat."

Gib smiled as he watched Zandi disappear into the crowd. Because he was so tall, it took a few minutes for the mage's crimson turban and white robes to become entirely indiscernible.

When at last Gib could no longer see his companion, he sighed and took up Astora's reins. "Come on. Let's find Koal."

The seneschal wasn't difficult to locate. His tent was being raised directly beside General Morathi's. Koal stood away from the bustling workers, engaged in deep conversation with Hasain and Tular.

Gib hesitated. Koal looked busy and hadn't even noticed Gib yet.

I don't want to intrude. Perhaps I'll just come back later.

Before Gib could debate further, a young servant girl approached. Likely a year or two younger than Gib himself, she gawked with bulging eyes before bowing. "Might I take your horse, m'lord?"

Gib waved desperately for her to stand, wondering if this was how Diddy must have felt every time a servant fawned over him. "Oh, for Daya's sake, I'm no lord. And I can feed and tend her myself."

The girl faltered, her mouth falling open as she glanced around, perhaps expecting to be chastised. "Apologies, apprentice of Lord Seneschal Koal. Should this humble servant address you with a different title?"

Heat pooled on Gib's cheeks as he was certain he was embarrassing himself even more than he was confusing the poor servant. "N–no. Gib is fine. Or Gibben, if you must. But I haven't a title."

The girl remained frozen in a half-bow. Exasperated, Gib finally relinquished Astora's reins for lack of knowing how else to fix the situation. "I suppose you can take my horse if you want, but honestly, I don't mind tending her myself."

Immediately, the servant jumped to take command of the reins. "It is my pleasure to serve you, Gibben Nemesio. I'll feed and water your mare and tether her with Lord Seneschal Koal's palfrey."

Gib watched as she led Astora away, wondering if he'd ever learn to accept help from the servants. After nearly four years of living among the highborns of Silver, it seemed silly how much he continued to fumble around the hired help. He supposed some things would never change.

"I presume you'll never have any servants of your own, seeing as you still have trouble letting them do their jobs."

Joel's cool voice startled Gib. He hadn't even noticed the mage approach.

"You're right," Gib replied, surprising himself by how quickly he managed to recover. "If I one day have an estate of my own and fail to maintain its upkeep, it'll be my own fault for buying a house so big."

The demure smile that came to Joel's lips made Gib flounder. How was it that Joel never lost his composure? Even after a full day of travel beneath the unforgiving sun, not one strand of his flowing hair was out of place, nor had his mage robes lost their pristine shine.

Joel quirked a brow. "That would be your logic. Humble to a fault. I'm half-surprised you're not helping collect wood or digging fire pits."

"I planned to, but I, uh, have to check in with Koal first."

"Oh, I see." Joel's smile faded when he glanced in the direction of his father. "You might want to wait."

"Is everything all right? What are they talking about?"

"I'm not sure. I haven't been invited into the conversation myself."

Hasain made sudden eye contact. Gib expected to be ignored—as was the young lord's specialty—so he was shocked when Hasain actually alerted Koal to their presence. Koal's features tightened with indecision before he hastily waved them over. Gib knew the look all too well by now. How many times had he been measured in this exact way right before being sworn to secrecy?

Without a word, he came to a halt by his mentor's side. Koal pressed a finger to his lips, confirming Gib's suspicion that this wasn't a public discussion, nor was it up for debate. As soon as Joel had taken his place next to Hasain, the conversation resumed.

"There's nothing to worry about," Tular said. "Aodan's a fair teacher. I know how to conceal myself. I haven't been discovered yet, have I?"

Koal sighed. "I trust your intentions wholly. It's your execution that concerns me. I mean it, Tular. If Morathi sees *anything* suspicious, he'll report back to Neetra. Your safety isn't all you have to consider. Think of the implications for Deegan, as well as the consequences for both Aodan and Gudrin."

Tular narrowed his eyes. The sudden change in his countenance made Gib shudder. "I'll protect my family. Don't you worry about that, Seneschal."

"*We'll* protect *our* family," Hasain echoed through gritted teeth.

Koal's own expression remained unreadable. "We all have to be on high guard. There's too much at stake."

"Right. It would be a lethal blow to Arden if all of us were to die in one strike."

"Hasain, we don't know for sure that's what's going on here."

"Horseshit. Neetra is delivering us in one neat little package to the Northern Empire's new ally. What power would he have if suddenly there was no Radek heir or seneschal to comply with?"

Koal's severe gaze speared Hasain. "Keep your voice down. You never know who might be eavesdropping on a private conversation."

Hasain inclined his head in the slightest show of a bow, but his face twisted into a grimace. "May we take our leave now? We wish to go see if Deegan is well."

Koal's attention jumped back and forth between the two brothers before settling onto Hasain alone. "You may go, but first—are *you* well, Hasain? You know why I'm asking."

The inquiry seemed innocent enough, but the way Hasain's shoulders went rigid suggested otherwise. All the Radek lord's typical eloquence vanished. "I–I'm fi—is this really the time to ask about—*that?*"

"The perfect time," Koal replied. "Despair and dark times feed all our doubts. You'll tell me if you ever need help."

"I don't need help. Your focus needs to be on Deegan, our *prince*."

The fine hairs on Gib's neck stood on end. What in the two worlds was this about? Whatever it was, it didn't sound like anything good. He locked eyes with Joel, who appeared equally perplexed, but both men knew better than to speak.

Hasain glared, red-faced. He seemed done with the matter, whatever it was. "May I go now?"

Letting out a sigh, Koal waved the young lord off. "Go. But don't think we're through discussing this."

Hasain and Tular hurried away without hesitation.

Koal began to follow on their heels but turned back long enough to address Gib. "Stay here. I'm going to check in on Deegan as well and make sure the defenses surrounding his pavilion are sufficient. I'll return in just a moment."

They stood in well-rehearsed silence, though Gib could barely hold back a snort long enough to ensure the seneschal was out of earshot. He turned skeptical eyes onto Joel. "What the hell was that about? Or am I *supposed* to be flailing around in the dark?"

"I have no idea what Father was getting at with Hasain, but—" Joel's voice trailed off with uncertainty.

Gib let out a sigh. He didn't have the patience for skirting around the issue. Not today. Not after riding from dawn to dusk. "But *what*?"

"But," Joel continued distantly. "I'm beginning to suspect something about Tular. I can't say for sure yet—don't give me that look, Gib! If I'm wrong and I say something, I'll be locked away as a madman. My theory is quite a stretch."

"It can't be any bigger a stretch than mine. You should have read the book Diddy suggested to me last winter."

Joel didn't respond. Instead, he gazed across the field, watching with a bleak expression as the flurry of work continued.

Gib decided not to press the matter further.

So I'm to be left in the dark for a while longer. What else is new?

"I should find a smithy and have my sword looked at."

Blinking, Joel seemed to come out of his daze. He offered an apologetic smile. "I need to go through my supplies as well. I think I'll go to the Healers' pavilion first, though, and see if there's any help I can offer."

"I'm sure they could use assistance dressing blisters."

Joel's lips formed a fragile smile, but laughter must have been beyond him. It didn't matter. Gib would take the smile. Even if the two of them were never true friends again, at least they could continue to converse with one another. Gib didn't know if he could bear losing Joel entirely.

"Well, there's Father," Joel said. "I'll take my leave now."

Gib couldn't think of anything to say, so he simply waved. Father and son passed one another with little more than a mutual nod, and then Koal was standing in the empty space left in Joel's wake.

"How did the ride treat you?" the seneschal asked.

"Apart from the creaking when I climbed down? Not bad. Tomorrow might be worse."

Koal watched with stern attention as the servants finished securing his tent. "Your muscles will be stiff. You could ask the Healers for a remedy tonight. It will help until your body's had time to adjust to the long hours of riding."

"I might do that."

A pregnant pause left them both speechless, and despite the mundane nature of tent-lifting, both men scrutinized the progress being made for lack of words.

Finally, Koal broke the silence with a deep sigh. "How are you doing, Gib? I mean *really* doing? Are you prepared for this campaign?"

Gib chose his words carefully. "As ready as ever, I suppose. If there's a way to better prepare for the possibility of dying or losing my sister or friends, I can't think of it. Tonight I'm going to visit the blacksmith and then see if I can find a sparring partner. I'll brush up on the old drills Roland taught me."

"Still using that old hand-me-down sword, are you?"

"I could have gotten something a little newer but—I chose to leave what money I had with Tay and Cal. They'll need it more than me."

Koal shook his head. "If you were dying of thirst, you'd still send your last drink to those boys. They're lucky to have you."

"They're what I have left. Liza and I might not come back. Tay and Cal need the best chance we can give them. It's that simple."

"They have family, Gib. *You* have family. You're a good and faithful apprentice, but you're more than just that. Mrifa and I consider you our son. You know this, don't you?"

Gib scuffed his foot and tried to think of something to say, but of course, his mind had gone completely blank.

Koal didn't let the silence fester. "War is serious. It needs to be treated with the utmost respect. You'll need a formidable weapon."

The seneschal pivoted and approached a pile of what must have been his belongings. Among the horde sat an elongated crate. Without hesitation, Koal lifted the lid and rummaged through the contents. Even before he turned around carrying a long parcel wrapped in coarse linen, a sneaking suspicion had stolen over Gib.

He opened his mouth to protest, but Koal shot him an uncompromising glare. "Don't try to say no. This is for you."

Dumbstruck, Gib reached for the gift with arms that felt as heavy as iron pillars. "You didn't have to do this. I—I don't know what to say." He fumbled under the added weight of the package, doing his best to undo the twine binding the mysterious gift.

The string finally pulled loose, and the linen fell away. Gib's breath caught in his throat at the sight of a splendid leather sheath, embroidered with crimson ribbon meant to depict dancing flames. His hand passed over the intricate hilt, trembling at the feel of polished dark cherry. The hardwood grip was engraved to resemble a serpent of some sort—no, not a snake. *A dragon.* The twisting dragon of Beihai had an open maw, breathing fire and giving birth to a cross guard shaped like the Ardenian phoenix.

Gib couldn't swallow as he gaped at the striking craftsmanship before him. "A part of our king still reigns."

"You'll have to forgive my lack of imagination," said Koal. "Rishi's sword was the same, with the dragon and phoenix just so. It somehow seemed appropriate."

"A king's sword in the hands of a peasant farmer?"

"This one's a bit shorter."

The sly edge to Koal's voice made Gib want to laugh. "I probably couldn't have lifted his sword even if I tried."

They *did* share a restrained chuckle at that.

Koal rested his upturned palms beneath the sheathed weapon, supporting its weight. "Why don't you try it on for size?"

Gib held his breath but managed to nod. He set one hand around the hilt, grasping coarse shagreen between his fingers, and pulled the blade free of its sheath with the crisp sigh of metal on leather. Koal took the protective casing and stepped away, giving Gib space.

Centering himself, Gib closed his eyes, recalling the teachings of Weapons Master Roland during Gib's first two years in Academy. His shoulders instinctively squared as he took stance, and with a deep exhale, he swept into motion.

The blade cut through the air in clean, efficient lines. Its weight grounded Gib, but it wasn't overly heavy. The sword's length was tailored perfectly to Gib's arm. His balance never wavered once as he held the weapon out straight in front of him and swung it high above his head in one sweeping motion. Gib wondered briefly if perhaps he'd been born with this sword and was only now being reunited. They were two halves of a same whole.

He came to a graceful rest and met his mentor's eyes. "It's perfect."

Koal nodded. "You're going to be fine. There's nothing more I can do for you."

It was strange how grown up Gib suddenly felt, as though receiving the sword had somehow bridged the gap between adolescence and manhood. Yet still a twinge of doubt prowled the edge of his consciousness. When the time came, would he be able to use his newfound weapon? Would he really be able to slay another living man?

"What are you going to name it?"

The question confused Gib. "Name it, sir?"

Koal's mouth curled into a half-smile. "Every valiant weapon needs a suitable name. What will *yours* be known as, Gibben Nemesio?"

Gib shook his head. He didn't know. He'd never been wealthy enough to afford such a glorious weapon. Likewise, he had no idea what sort of name would be appropriate. Gib squeezed his eyes shut. His restless mind wandered, darting aimlessly from one misplaced memory to the next.

But then it settled on one particular instance in time—the King's funeral—when Gib had looked upon Rishi Radek's lifeless body, placed so delicately inside the walls of his tomb, and had promised to do everything he could to keep Arden whole. He'd made a vow. *An oath.*

The name rushed to Gib with undeniable clarity. He opened his eyes. "Oathbinder. For the pledge I swore to protect King Rishi's legacy and his country."

With an approving nod, Koal came forward and wordlessly offered the leather casing. Gib reached for it, lifting Oathbinder high into the darkening sky, and when he did, something caught his eye. Engraved in the high polished steel were words.

"Victory not in death, but in life," he read aloud. "Victory not in persecution, but in justice."

"Something to remember," Koal whispered. "When you're out there, on the field of battle and you begin to think your only purpose is to murder, don't lose yourself, Gib. Those of us who take up a sword for Arden do so to protect her and her people. When you come home, you won't be a killer. You'll be a peacekeeper. I know this of you and will never stop believing it."

Gib couldn't say he understood Koal's advice exactly, but he tucked the wisdom away in the back of his mind anyway. He hoped he wouldn't ever *have* to understand the seneschal's words. He hoped he would never have to kill.

Kirk tapped his fingers on the armrest of Marc's plush office chair. The dean took notice only after what felt like an eternity.

"Sorry for the delay. Otho should be along any moment. Sometimes his work keeps him late."

It wasn't late, only midday, but Kirk's nerves were on edge. Arden's army had departed three days earlier, and with it Joel, one of Kirk's only allies in this strange new world. Now, sitting in this office, with a virtual stranger whom Joel had asked Kirk to place his trust with, he found himself wishing desperately that he could talk to his sister. He hadn't seen Kenisha in what felt like ages.

I must have been out of my mind. If I get myself caught or am betrayed, Keni and I will both face exile or worse. I shouldn't even be here—

The memory of misty blue eyes and a modest smile made Kirk's breath hitch.

No. For Joel, I can do this.

His hand instinctively rose to touch the place where his mother's pendant usually rested against his collar bone. The pendant was with Joel now, though Kirk couldn't know for sure if Joel had yet discovered the token, hidden inside a saddlebag.

May its luck keep him safe. May he return unharmed.

Marc continued to shuffle through paperwork, signing some and discarding others as he tried in vain to reach the bottom of the pile. He appeared to be in no mood for conversation, but Kirk couldn't stand the silence any longer.

"So," Kirk offered gingerly. "This Otho fellow, he seems so different. I can scarcely imagine how he and you know one another. Are you sure we can trust him?"

The sound of Marc's quill scratching across parchment filled the room. Only after he'd set aside the signed document did the dean finally glance up. "I've known Otho since before he could walk. He had a bit of a rough start, that boy—a father who died in combat, an uncle who refused to acknowledge him, and mother who chose hard whiskey over her own son." Marc shook his head in aversion. "Fortunately, Roland took the boy under his care, and Otho's been a good and loyal apprentice for years now. He'll probably take Roland's job someday if the old knave can ever be convinced to retire." Marc chuckled, but his eyes remained grave. "You needn't worry. Otho is loyal to the Radek family, and he's going to help us while Roland is absent tending to matters on his farmstead."

Kirk nodded, hoping the gesture would mask his skepticism. He couldn't help but be suspicious. In his native land, only a fool would place his trust in a stranger. With the exception of Joel and Kenisha, Kirk found it hard to place his trust in *anyone*. And neither of them were here.

A loud knock brought Marc's head up. Without a word, he pushed himself to his feet and went to open the door.

"Otho, come in."

Kirk forced a smile and stood. Otho returned no such warmth, feigned or otherwise. His homely features were set in a hard look of indifference as he crossed the threshold and pointedly ignored Kirk's offered hand.

A shock of indignation stabbed Kirk in the chest, but Marc stepped between them before anything could be said. "Otho Dakheel, this is Kirk Bhadrayu. Kirk, this is Otho."

Kirk lifted his nose. "Oh, we've already met, Dean Marc. At my sister's wedding." He offered his hand a second time, a smug leer spreading across his face.

It was true, the two had met on the day Kenisha had exchanged her vows with the Weapons Master's son. Otho was apparently some sort of adoptive child and understudy to Roland, but it was Kirk's impression that Otho was more a quiet, slinking shadow than a man. Indeed, Kirk probably wouldn't have remembered him at all if not for his eerie amber eyes and unfavorable behavior. To Kirk's knowledge, Otho hadn't once wished Manuel Korbin good fortune or offered the new marriage a blessing—though Kirk did recollect Otho snarling something about the foolishness of marrying an Imperial.

What must he think now? Would he take Kirk's hand?

Beneath the scrutiny of the dean, Otho relented. Their handshake was brief, impersonal, and obviously forced, but Marc talked on as if he hadn't noticed. "All right. You know each other already. Good. That should make working together easier. You both know why you're here, correct?"

Otho got straight to the point. "How do we expose Neetra? He's the steward now. You can bet he's made certain that he's *exceptionally* well-guarded."

"I know. That's why we have insiders working with us, too."

"What insiders?"

Marc waved his hands. "Relax. People we can trust wholly. You'll see."

Kirk's mood only further deflated. The more people who were involved, the bigger the chance of someone slipping up and saying something incriminating. Or what if one of them was caught? "How big is this operation, Dean Marc? How tangled is this web?"

"We're just a small part, Kirk. One thread in the tapestry."

"That's all fine and good, but how do we keep track of where the other threads interweave? If one is plucked, the whole thing could unravel."

"I understand your concern, but I assure you we're being as safe as possible."

"Safety is a relative term. Circumstances being what they are, I have a lot to lose if this goes badly. My sister—"

"We each have our place," Otho grunted, his voice harsh and devoid of empathy. "If you don't like yours, then leave."

Kirk reacted without hesitation—odd, considering how ill at ease he'd been of late. "I will gladly do all I can to help the country which gave Kenisha and me a second chance. Even if it meant draining my magic dry, I would do so willingly. It would be a small price to pay for the future we've been given the chance to have here."

Otho didn't seem convinced. Kirk knew better than to instigate further, but his temper was now sufficiently stoked. He knew what people whispered behind his back. He knew Otho wasn't alone in his distrust. And yes, perhaps if the shoe had been on the other foot, Kirk would feel the same. That only made him angrier.

He turned a piercing glare onto Otho. "And what are *you* doing here anyway? As the Weapons Master's apprentice, I *know* you must be well trained with a sword. Why aren't you out there, marching toward Shiraz with the other *brave* men?"

Icy silence blanketed the room, and the bitter stare Otho countered with made Kirk regret his hasty words, if only a little.

Otho curled his nose. "The army doesn't train itself, Imperial."

"Enough of this!" Marc scolded both of them. "We can't be fighting among ourselves."

Folding arms over chest, Kirk clamped his mouth shut.

Marc is right. We have enough working against us without making enemies of our allies.

He stole a glance at Otho, who had slouched his shoulders and now glared out the window next to where he stood.

Though no one can convince me to place all my trust on the line. Not yet.

Kirk cleared his throat. "What now, Dean Marc?"

"We're waiting for Aodan to arrive."

Aodan Galloway? The Queen Mother's new husband? Unable to still his nervous hands, Kirk straightened the front of his robes. Had he known he'd be meeting a member of the royal family, he would have taken the time to make sure he was presentable for such an occasion.

Kirk ran out of time to worry when a light tap rose from the door.

"That's odd," Marc mused aloud. He sprung from his chair and crossed the room. "Aodan doesn't usually knock." As he pulled the heavy door open, the sound of creaking hinges gave way to surprised, fumbling words. "O–oh. Prince Didier. What brings you here?"

Kirk's head swam.

The prince is here?

"I assume I'm welcome in your office, Dean Marc."

Marc hadn't yet managed to quell his surprise. "Well, of course you're welcome. I just—I wasn't expecting you. Is Aodan coming?"

"Shut the door, please."

Without further questioning, Marc hurried to obey the command.

Prince Didier's demeanor was not entirely friendly as he stepped into the small office. He was a handsome young man, tall and of a medium build, with dark eyes and hair that offset his fair complexion. It was a shame he seemed intent on maintaining a scowl. His father's death must still have been haunting him.

Didier's eyes landed on Kirk. "You are Kirk Bhadrayu, correct?"

"Yes, Highness." Kirk bowed low for good measure. "I'm happy to be at your service."

"And where is—oh, Otho! I nearly didn't see you back there."

Otho gave the barest of bows. "Greetings, Highness."

"My family is grateful to have one as brave as you helping us."

Brave?

Kirk's chest tightened. If Otho was so courageous, then why wasn't he at war with Joel and the others? Surely Weapons Master Roland could handle training recruits by himself. Nothing was honorable about hiding away in the city when healthy, young men were needed in the field.

"Just doing my job," Otho replied, recoiling from the praise.

A smile finally graced the prince's mouth, proving Kirk's theory correct. Didier looked better when he wasn't frowning. "Aodan trusts you. That's no easy task."

"He trusts Roland. I'm just a familiar name."

"You sell yourself short, Otho Dakheel."

Marc coughed, redirecting the conversation. "Diddy, what are you doing here? Is Aodan coming?"

The smile vanished from Didier's lips. He turned somber eyes onto Marc. "Lord Galloway is under tight lock and key of late. As I'm sure you recall, there are those on the High Council who would rather see him exiled. It was easier for me to slip away this afternoon."

The dean's jaw tightened. "Of course. Since Aodan sent you in his stead, does that mean you'll be helping?"

"There's not much I can offer you today, but the near future may yield better results. As Neetra's servant, Bailey has access to the steward's chambers. When opportunity presents itself, he intends to steal a key."

"The key to Neetra's chambers? That's dangerous."

Didier's face hardened with agitation. "Do you have another suggestion, Dean Marc? A better option? Bailey is a grown man. He understands the risk he's taking."

"I know, *Highness*. I only worry for his safety—"

"So long as you refrain from giving him any remedies, I'm sure he'll be perfectly safe."

The sudden chill in the room nearly froze Kirk to the bone. He had no idea what the prince meant, but the hollow desolation that flashed behind Marc's eyes was proof enough that the conversation had tread into forbidden territory. Kirk dared glance sideways at Otho, but the apprentice also appeared to be at a loss.

Marc folded his arms across his chest. "All right. You've made your point, Prince Didier. If that's all, I suppose we'll wait for more news."

"Yes. Someone will be in touch. I suggest you remain alert." Didier pivoted away from Marc and strode toward the door. "I'll show myself out. Kirk, Otho, thank you for meeting with me today." He'd left before either man had a chance to finish bowing.

Kirk winced as the door slammed, leaving nothing but uneasy silence and a plethora of questions behind. What had all of that been about? Kirk wanted so badly to ask Marc, but the dean seemed to be at wit's end.

His skin took on a pallid hue as he slumped into the seat behind his desk. "You two may go. I'll send for you when I have news."

CHAPTER FIVE

Over the next two sennights, Kezra fell into the routine of life while marching. Breakfast came at dawn, and they were on the road before she was even fully awake. Midday meal was taken in the saddle, and they stopped only at dusk for dinner and sleep. Most nights, however, once food had been eaten and personal needs were met, there would be a spare mark or two to enjoy recreational time before the campfires fizzled.

Kezra and the others had taken to sparring on such evenings, as both a means of maintaining contact with each other and a way to loosen their stiff muscles after a long day's ride. Most importantly though, it also helped hone their weaponry skills. And it was something Kezra needed for herself.

Sitting atop Epona's back all day left Kezra's mind to wander, circling over the same damned issues again and again. How many times would she have to rethink her problems before they finally disappeared? She couldn't console her mother or do anything to help her siblings while she was out here. Her father would either get what he deserved or he wouldn't. And Nawaz—Nawaz might as well be a shooting star. No matter how badly Kezra longed for him, he remained entirely out of reach. He'd made his decision and so had she.

Training served as Kezra's release, and it wasn't long before she found herself the unspoken leader of the nightly sparring sessions. Really, she didn't mind. If she was busy correcting posture and re-teaching technique, her own woes could be temporarily pushed aside. So she approached her new role with a willingness that probably shocked all who knew her.

Of their group, it quickly became apparent Gib was in need of the most practice. Kezra feared her friend had perched upon his cozy chair in one too many council meetings. His lack of finesse was proof enough that he'd all but forgotten Roland's lessons from the first two years of Academy.

Nage was better prepared, though the same couldn't be said of Kezra's own brother. When she'd tried to convince Zandi that learning how to swing a sword might prove to be a wise decision, he'd scoffed and assured her his magery skills were quite sufficient enough. Kezra had stormed away in frustration after that. Mages! They were impossible!

Now, a fortnight into their long trek, Kezra raised her sword to counter Gib's attack. Already he was showing improvement, though it wasn't in Kezra's nature to be nurturing. "Come on, Lovely, you can do better than that, can't you?"

Gib kept his own blade close to his torso, but experience told Kezra he'd soon rush her.

"You know," he snorted. "I've spent the past two years sitting through political classes and council meetings. It's reasonable that I've gone a little soft around the edges."

Gib lunged, as expected, and Kezra spun away from him, laughing. "With that cushy job of yours and homemade meals from Lady Mrifa, I'd say you've gone a little soft in the *middle*."

Chuckles arose from their gathered spectators, and Gib's face darkened into a most stunning shade of crimson.

Another misstep and Kezra had Gib's feet out from under him. He landed with an ungraceful thud on his back, eyes as wide as saucers. Their audience clapped at his blunder.

"Ha!" Kezra jeered. "What's your excuse now? Too much riding today?"

"Maybe," Gib groaned. He remained unmoving in the dirt. "Riding makes the knees weak. Keep this up, and you'll make me soft in the head."

"I don't think so, Nemesio. Your skull is pretty thick." Kezra offered a hand and pulled Gib to his feet, noting how good it felt to smile again.

More laughter arose from the crowd. Gib dusted himself off and took a bow, bits of clay and grass ensnared among his mousy curls. "Yeah, yeah. Laugh it up. I'd bet there isn't a single one of you who can stand up to Kezra and fare any better than me!"

Kezra's own face flushed as she gave him a hearty clap on the back. Sometimes she didn't know what she'd do without Gib's friendship. No one else had ever given her such encouragement. No one else had ever made her feel more valid.

It crossed her mind that perhaps it was time for another good, long talk with him. She needed it, even though it was difficult to admit. Gib could be counted on to listen to her woes yet pass no judgment, and his advice always proved to be invaluable.

Yes. They needed to talk. But not tonight. She just wasn't ready to open up quite yet. She would face her emotions in due time, but right now, it was beyond her.

Kezra turned to face the crowd. "All right, who's next?"

Gara Leal was on her feet before anyone else could think to move. She was a wiry wisp of a thing, barely weighing enough to keep from being blown away by the wind. Dressed in mud-brown scouting gear and hair cropped shorter than even Kezra's, Gara barely resembled the pampered dame Kezra knew from court.

"I suppose it's time for my beating." Gara laughed, grinning sheepishly.

Nage, who lounged atop a supply crate, whooped loudly. "If Kezra knocks out all your teeth, *you're* gonna be the one explainin' it to Nia and your ma!"

The look Gara shot him made even Kezra chuckle.

Gara unsheathed her weapon, a flimsy, short blade that reminded Kezra more of an oversized dagger than a true sword. Given Gara's modest stature and her work as a scout, Kezra couldn't say she was surprised.

She still needs to know how to best an opponent, even if she's outmatched. Hell, I've won duels with nothing more than a broken whiskey bottle.

Kezra took stance. She didn't bother offering encouragement or well wishes. Weapons Master Roland had always said such formalities were a waste of words, and Kezra tended to agree.

Both women had just given a nod—the sign for commencement— when a slithering voice drew away Gara's attention.

"Remind me again, Seneschal, why you were in favor of women soldiers?"

Kezra flinched, but she refused to look at the general. Morathi's callous words were terrible enough without actually seeing him.

The sound of Seneschal Koal's exasperated sigh suggested he had just as little tolerance for the general. "I've made the same argument since the topic came upon the council table. Why would we dissuade half the country's population from enlisting?"

"I see. And when a farmer harvests his wheat, half of its weight is the chaff. You don't see the farmer trying to sell the unfit portion as food."

Out of the corner of her eye, Kezra watched Gara tighten her jaw. Kezra's own heart hammered in her chest, stoking her anger. If Morathi weren't the general—if Kezra had any rank or power over him—she'd have told him exactly what she thought of his analogy.

Seneschal Koal came into view even though Kezra had made a point to avert her glare. "This is clearly something you and I are going to have to agree to disagree on. I never have, and never will, see women as useless weight. Weapons Master Roland has had only positive things to say since we allowed women to train as sentinels."

The disgust in Morathi's voice was nearly palpable. "Roland Korbin is a lowborn imbecile. He wouldn't know his arse from a hole in the ground."

Nope. Too far.

Kezra whirled around, setting fierce eyes upon Morathi. "Then you better pray that *imbecile* has trained your army well." The words were out of her mouth before she could stop them.

Stupid!

Kezra bit her lip. How could she be so stupid?

All around, people froze. Nage's mouth hung open. Zandi sat rigidly, cupping one hand over a horrified grimace. Gara's eyes were so wide they might pop right out of their sockets. And Gib—humble, quiet Gib was—*smiling* at her?

His grin reignited the fire Kezra had nearly let gutter. She raised her chin defiantly. So she'd said it. There was no going back now. She might as well embrace the consequences.

"You there, *girl*!" The general's bark made Kezra want to wince, but somehow she managed to stay motionless. "What did you say?"

Her lungs refused to expand. "Kezra Malin-Rai, sir."

"What?"

Kezra took in a gulp of air as she tucked her sword back into its sheath and turned to meet Morathi's glare. "My name is Kezra Malin-Rai, sir."

Menacing grey eyes narrowed into tiny slits. "Soldier, I didn't ask for your name, and you're very soon going to realize that neglecting to answer my questions is the same as refusing an order. It's a dangerous game you play. Now, I suggest you tell me what you said before you were permitted to speak."

Somehow Kezra's voice cooperated with her trembling lips. "I said, 'you'd better hope that imbecile has trained your army well,' sir. It seems illogical the general would allow such a person to train his troops—"

Morathi advanced on her so fast she fell back a step. "No one *asked* you to *think* of *anything*! Your job is to follow orders and die for your country if you fail to defend it. Do you understand?"

Kezra opened her mouth, but nothing came out. All she could think about was the time during her first year of Academy when Liro Adelwijn and Diedrick Lyle had coerced her into the hallway and attempted to force her out of her weaponry classes. The path she'd chosen had never been guaranteed easy, but she'd not shied away from it then, and—The Two help her—she wasn't going to now.

Morathi loomed above her, his rage stifling and terrifying. "Do you understand, *girl*?"

Tears sprang to her eyes, but she wouldn't let them spill over. Not for this son of a bitch.

"She understands, sir."

Kezra blinked when Gib slid a hand onto her shoulder.

"Kezra is one of the smartest and most talented soldiers from my year," Gib went on, his voice calm and steady, an anchor in the rolling sea. "She's also one of the best trained of us and has even been kind enough to help whip me back into shape."

If Morathi had been upset before, he was nothing short of furious now. He shot back to his full, towering height and pivoted on one heel to glare at Koal. "Look! Even your apprentice has forgotten his place!"

Koal nodded, a flicker of mirth gleaming in his eyes. "You may have a point. Despite saving the King's life, Gib still thinks of himself as a peasant. I'd say he's more along the lines of a hero."

"In my day, heroes didn't spar with women."

"The winds are changing," said Koal. "Those days are hopefully gone for good."

Gib's grip tightened against Kezra's tunic. She wished she could muster the courage to raise her eyes. Surely Gib must have been as taken with the seneschal's words as she.

Morathi, however, was fed up. He shook his head, disgust tracing his hard features. "I sincerely hope these changing winds are all you've hoped they'll be, Seneschal. You favor women soldiers so greatly, yet look around—how many of them do you see? What hope will there be for Arden if her army abandons her from fear and cowardice?"

Kezra balled her hands into fists at her side. The general could go to hell! Who did he think he was to denounce the women who'd fought so hard to be taken seriously? Anger rocked her body with so much force she had to lean against Gib to stay on her feet.

Koal's frown deepened. "Let's move on, shall we? We still haven't discussed a plan of action to ensure the safety of our supply train nor the concerns I have with Prince Deegan's protection."

Morathi curled his nose and fixed Kezra with one final, superior glare. "Yes. Finally a topic worth discussing."

Kezra's heart continued to pound as she watched the two men disappear into the crowd. Her jaw and fingers ached from being clenched, but she ignored the pain. Her hands itched to take hold of her sword and throw it right into that bastard's back.

Damn that man. Damn him!

"Don't listen to him," Gib muttered. "Morathi is the worst sort there is."

Kezra knew Gib spoke the truth, but rage had pushed her beyond caring. "But he's right, isn't he? Where *are* the women soldiers, Gib? We were never many, but now we're nearly none."

No one said anything for such a long stretch that Kezra was sure the conversation had ended, until Gib sighed. "You're here. Gara's here. Liza's here, somewhere. You and the others are making history. This is only the beginning. Nothing changes overnight."

Gara cleared her throat. "Gib's right. Slowly, the tides are turning. And you can't fault the women who opted out. No one wants to go to war—"

"No," Kezra growled. Dark, startling rage scorched her veins, turning her insides black. "But the brave have shown up anyway." With nothing left to say, she tore away from Gib. "I've got to go."

"Kezra—"

"No, Gib. Not now! Just stay here. I need to be alone."

Kezra sped away from Gib's outstretched hand, knowing deep down she wasn't being fair. It had crossed even *her* mind to stay behind when Neetra had given them the option. Of course, she'd put the silly idea to rest, but—she'd entertained the thought, hadn't she?

It didn't matter. The brave had come. The general didn't know what he was talking about—and for that matter, Morathi had best learn to watch his foul mouth. If he wasn't careful, someone might one day teach him a lesson. They might even rip that treacherous tongue right out of his mouth. He deserved as much.

Joel worked the metal wedge into the space where the two slabs of wood connected and pushed down with both hands. The lid of the crate lifted away with a loud *pop*.

"Careful of broken glass," Nawaz warned. "Those supplies have been traveling for more than a fortnight. Some of them prob'ly got jostled on the barge."

Joel eyed the contents of his container: four rows of neatly stacked jars, squat in size and each filled with pea-green healing ointment. He raised his face, uttering a chuckle. "Worry not. Your *unlimited* supply of mugwort salve appears to be safe."

"Good," Nawaz replied, not bothering to glance up. He rummaged through a second crate close by. "Not even a moonturn in and we're already running low. Hopefully now that we've reached the Nishika, they'll keep us supplied."

Joel snorted as he hauled the crate to the opposite side of the tent and set it with the containers that had already been checked. "I hope so, too. Morathi would probably face complete mutiny if we suddenly weren't able to treat the soldier's blistering feet."

"The blisters I can handle. But, Chhaya's bane, if I have to look at one more saddle sore—"

Both men shared a laugh as they continued to sort through the supply crates that had been delivered to the makeshift Healers' pavilion a mark earlier.

A gentle breeze rustled the awnings above and carried the scents of fresh grass and roasted wildfowl into the space. Through the open-ended tent, Joel caught a glimpse of the evening sky outside. Bands of red and orange sat low on the horizon, buckling beneath the weight of the growing darkness. The muted voices of dining soldiers hummed in Joel's ears, a collective murmur that was soothing rather than irritating. Somewhere in the distance, he could even hear frogs singing along the riverbank.

The army had been mobilized for just shy of a full moonturn. The rolling hillsides east of Silver City were long behind them, replaced by smooth, flowing grasslands that made for easy travel but offered little variety in view. One sennight ago, they'd reached the fishing village of Davenport, nestled on the edge of Lake Talhador. Joel recalled scarcely being able to contain a gasp at the sight of clear water stretching endlessly into the horizon. Beneath the cloudless sky, the lake sparkled, like it might have been made of diamonds.

After only a day's reprieve to rest and restock, the army had turned due south, following alongside the Nishika River, the vast waterway which would guide them all the way to Arden's southeastern border—and beyond. With regular shipments of wheat, rye, grain, and other vital supplies now being delivered by barge, the army was moving even faster. Koal estimated they'd reach the border within another moonturn. Then things would get interesting.

Joel finished checking the last two remaining crates he'd been assigned before taking a seat on the edge of a nearby cot. Nawaz seemed determined not to quit until every last phial was examined and properly stowed away. At last, the young Healer closed one final lid and took a seat beside Joel.

For some time, they sat in silence, gazing at the tower of sorted crates and admiring the work they'd completed. Joel was almost sad there was no further toil. The longer he busied himself here, the longer he could avoid returning to his own campfire.

"Thanks," Nawaz said at length. "For helping."

Joel shrugged. "You looked like you could use it. Every time I happen upon you, you're up to your elbows in grunt work."

"Eh. I like to stay busy. Keeps my mind from wandering." Nawaz turned in his seat, giving Joel a sideways glance. "*You've* been spending a lot of time at the Healers' pavilion lately. You suddenly rethinking your decision to become a mage?"

"Goddesses, no! Even if I had the Healing gift, I'm afraid my stomach isn't nearly stout enough to handle all that a Healer's job entails. I can't stand the sight of blood."

"Oh, I see. Then I guess you just miss my company too much to stay away, right?" Nawaz waggled his eyebrows.

"No. I mean—" Joel groaned as Nawaz feigned dejection. "Yes, sure. I enjoy our nightly banter. But that's not the reason I'm here." Nawaz didn't press further, but Joel felt compelled to better explain himself. Staring into the dimming light, he let out a troubled sigh. "Riding with Father and the others all day is trying. Coming here is a nice excuse to get away."

Nawaz cocked an eyebrow. "Things still awkward with Gib then, eh?"

Biting his lower lip, Joel shook his head. There was that, yes, but Gib wasn't the only reason Joel had been keeping his distance from the command tent. Nor the main reason.

All this time spent riding had given Joel time to ponder, to think about everything that had happened over the past year. And the thoughts hadn't been pleasant. The carnage of the arena in Teivel, Cenric's murder, King Rishi's death—

And the secret the Radek family seemed so desperate to keep hidden away but each day became more apparent to Joel, no matter how hard he tried to deny it. What if his inclination proved to be true? What if the people closest to him—his own family—had been harboring a lifetime of secrets that until recently, Joel hadn't had an inkling about? How could they lie to him for so long?

"It's not just Gib," Joel managed to fumble out when he realized Nawaz was still awaiting a response. "It's—everything. I don't know how much longer I can grin and bear all the things I've heard and seen over the past few moonturns. I'm feeling a bit overwhelmed."

"I just try to avoid thinking about anything of substance."

"Does it help?"

"No. Not really." Nawaz absently rubbed the bare place on his finger where the Adelwijn crest used to lie.

Joel's own hands sought to busy themselves, and before he realized it, he was touching his own ring. The golden band, encrusted with sapphires and engraved with the Adelwijn coat of arms, shimmered in the low light of the fire, its weight atop Joel's finger a sudden reminder of how fortunate he truly was.

I must be the most ungrateful person in all Arden. Here I am, wallowing in self-pity. At least I have a family that loves me. At least I have a father who's proud to call me his son.

"I'm sorry about what happened between you and my uncle," Joel said, keeping his eyes lowered. "You deserved better than to be treated so unjustly all those years."

Nawaz shifted his weight, frowning. "What's done is done. Gotta keep looking to the future."

Good. Finally, something positive to discuss.

"And what a bright future you have. Just think! When you arrive home, you'll be a father. And, bless The Two, I'll be an uncle!"

"Yeah. There'll be lots of changes. That's for sure."

"You and Heidi will make fine parents. If anything good has come out of this whole mess with Neetra, it's that you won't have to worry about pleasing him anymore. You'll be able to focus on your family and to hell with what my uncle thinks of you. Heidi loves you. My parents love you. Marc loves you. And as for Neetra, he's never been able to requite love to *anyone*—"

"Aye. Unrequited love. Possibly the most heartrending thing in life."

Joel fell silent. There it was, the colossus lounging in the middle of the tent that both of them seemed content to ignore. Nawaz was still pining for Kezra Malin-Rai.

Joel understood. Gods, he understood. Solitude would always be the more appealing option if he couldn't be with the person he loved most. But Nawaz had made the decision to marry, and whether or not he continued to harbor feelings for Kezra, he needed to be a good husband to Heidi now. She deserved as much.

I hope for Nawaz's sanity he's able to move on. I don't think I'll ever be able to stop loving Gib. Not completely.

Joel rose shakily to his feet. The pavilion had become too stifling. He needed fresh air. "I better go. I promised myself that before I went to sleep tonight, I'd charge the satchel of runestones that has been hiding away inside my saddlebags since we left."

Nawaz didn't fight Joel's departure. "Yeah. See you around."

Joel returned to the command tent with a heavy heart. Outside, Hasain and Tular sat with Deegan in front of a roaring campfire, engaged in muted conversation as they took their meal. Blazes of fire cast a faint glow across their faces, warming Deegan's and Hasain's dark eyes and accentuating the swirls of sunset red in Tular's hair.

The aroma of roasted quail and blackened trout beckoned Joel to join them. He almost did—but the doubt tormenting his mind held him back. As he lurked beneath the long shadows of the pavilion, Joel wondered what else in his life might be fallacious. Were there more secrets to be discovered? Were there more lies that hadn't yet been brought to light? Could he even trust his own friends and family anymore? The longer he thought about it, the more betrayed he felt. How deep did the deceit run? Was *anything* he'd been told genuine?

Quiet tittering drew his attention back to the campfire. Deegan was doubled over, trying to contain laughter. Hasain or Tular must have said something funny. As Joel looked on, Tular raised one hand toward the Crown Prince, his eyes bursting with malice—

Visions of the monster inside the arena, slicing a bloody line across Nikodemos' abdomen, snapping the gladiator's neck like it had been a twig, sent a wave of panic surging through Joel's body. Before he knew what he was doing, he'd instinctively pooled magic in his hands, preparing to unleash it in a violent wave. If that *thing* tried to harm his cousin—

Tular clasped Deegan on the back, hollering with laughter. Joel blinked, blood pounding in his head in a deafening squall. Tular hadn't been trying to attack the prince. He was merely playing.

Joel's mouth twisted into a horrified grimace. He stumbled back, the conjured magic sizzling in his palm as he released it back into the air. Tular would never harm Deegan. Joel knew that. But in the moment, terror had clouded his judgment.

Raising one hand to cover his shamed face, Joel retreated further into the shadows.

Stop this nonsense! Has Tular ever given you reason not to trust him? What about Aodan? Gudrin? They might be—different, but that doesn't make them dangerous, does it?

Subtle movement in the darkness drew Joel's attention. Startled, he whirled around, his body once again on full alert. His heart skipped a beat when he realized Blessed Mage Natori was standing not even a full arm's length away. Where had she come from? How long had she been there? If he hadn't been so caught up in his own distress, would he have sensed her presence earlier?

Natori made no indication she saw Joel. She didn't make eye contact, nor did she incline her head in greeting. Shadows blanketed her face and hair, but her violet eyes cut through the night, two lavender orbs against a backdrop of gloom. Joel opened his mouth, though he didn't know what to say. When words failed to form, he found himself following Natori's gaze back toward the blazing fire.

A twig snapped inside the inferno, preluding a deep sigh from the Blessed Mage. Natori's voice came to life, but still she didn't look away from the flames. "Do not be so quick to judge that which you do not understand. Reckless ignorance breeds unwarranted fear. Remember that, before you pass judgment."

Joel floundered where he stood. Did Natori somehow know what he'd almost done? She couldn't *really* know, could she? "Lady—I–I don't understand."

Natori's body remained perfectly motionless, statuesque—except her eyes. They finally shifted away from the campfire, seeking out Joel. "Oh, but I think you do. The creature you saw inside the arena, do you believe it was inherently evil? Was it *truly* monstrous?"

"No." Joel managed to shake his head. "It didn't want to kill those gladiators. It was just trying to defend itself. The real monsters were the men who forced it to fight."

"Some of the most dangerous monsters in this world are *human*, Joel Adelwijn. A good bit of wisdom to remember when you begin to doubt your heart."

Unable to hold the Blessed Mage's gaze any longer, Joel focused his attention onto the dirt beneath his boots. "I—thank you. You've given me much to think about."

"Keep your friends and family close, youngling. In the end, they are all we ever truly have."

With a faint nod, Joel excused himself. He wanted to be alone. He needed space to clear his muddled head. He knew he should probably reflect upon Natori's words, but not tonight. He couldn't handle any more difficult thoughts right now.

Ivory had been tied to a post with several other horses on the far side of the clearing. As Joel approached, her ears perked, but she didn't lift her muzzle from the bucket of water by her feet. Joel scratched the filly's neck for a few moments before rummaging through his saddlebags, stacked neatly beneath the long shadows of the tent. It wasn't long before he found the runestones, heavy and bulging within a burlap sack. Clutching the satchel close to his chest, Joel scanned the vicinity, seeking a quiet place, away from the rest of the world.

Set near the outskirts of the war camp, yet still within view, a fire burned low, its flames barely more than pulsating embers. Abandoned and lonely, it beckoned Joel forward. It was the perfect place to work.

Joel took a seat a safe distance from the fire and made himself comfortable. The red-hot coals licked his face with drowsy heat. The warmth helped soothe his mind and relax his stiff muscles. Setting the satchel in his lap, Joel worked to undo the bit of rope that held the pearly stones inside. There was a good number of them. Joel had packed the stones himself. Even if he couldn't charge all of them in one sitting, the magical toil would keep him busy for the next mark or two.

Charging runestones was one of the more menial tasks a mage had to perform, but given the circumstances, it was exactly the kind of job Joel needed: something to lose himself in until exhaustion rendered him unable to do anything but fall onto his sleeping mat. If he needn't think, he wouldn't have to worry.

Joel pulled the first runestone free and placed it in the palm of his open hand. He took a moment to admire its smooth, rounded edges and iridescent shimmer before closing a fist around the object. Shutting his eyes, Joel centered himself and drew power from the magic ley line that ran parallel to the Nishika. He channeled the raw, untamed energy through his body, harvesting it, molding it, and finally redirecting it into the runestone. The runestone absorbed the energy, soaking up the magic like water into a doily, until it could hold no more. Satisfied, Joel set the stone aside and reached for another.

"H—hello? Joel?"

The newcomer's words jarred Joel out of his meditative state.

Zandi's footfalls fell silently as he stepped within the fading light of the campfire. Hands clasped together at his waist and cheeks dusted red, he kept his face downcast. His emerald eyes, wavering and uncertain, somehow lifted to meet Joel's.

Joel froze. What did Zandi want? They hadn't once spoken since the army mobilized. Hell, they hadn't exchanged words in entire moonturns before the trek even began.

"I was hoping we might have a word," Zandi said.

Joel opened his mouth, but he didn't know what to say. He'd been caught so off-guard he couldn't rally a response.

Zandi didn't allow the silence to grow. "Is now a good time? I can come back if you're—" His eyes flicked toward the satchel. "O–oh, you're charging runestones? May I help?"

Joel clenched his jaw, holding back the urge to curl his nose.

No, he wanted to say. *No, you may not help.*

Proper protocol dictated he should be polite, however, so with a sigh, he motioned for the mage to sit.

Zandi's cheeks darkened further as he kneeled. "Thank you."

Joel nodded curtly and moved the satchel into the empty space separating them, so both he and Zandi could reach it with ease. He didn't want to converse, but for Gib's sake, he'd try to be civil.

Zandi didn't move, save for his fumbling hands. "I'm sure you must hate me."

"I don't hate you, Zandi." Joel bit the inside of his cheek, turning the runestone in his palm from side to side, knowing he should say more but unable to bring himself to.

Crimson flecks of light shone like miniscule mage orbs in Zandi's eyes as he stared into the dying embers of the campfire. "We haven't had an opportunity to speak since—since everything happened, and I just wanted you to know how much respect I have for you—have *always* had for you. It seems so long ago now, the day you stood up and courageously declared your love for another man."

Joel tightened his grip around the runestone. "Nothing more than an idealistic boy making a foolish choice. My actions did little more than bring shame to my family name and give the court something scandalous to gossip about."

"No. You're wrong. What you did gave so many people hope. People like me."

"It doesn't matter. Nothing has changed."

"Change takes time. You mustn't give up."

"Any hope for change died with the King. If you hadn't already noticed, Arden's in the hands of a madman now."

Joel refocused his attention onto the task of charging the runestones and hoped Zandi would do the same. As well-intended as Zandi might be, Joel was in no mood for reminiscing about the past. He didn't want to think about *anything* right now, least of all the country's dire predicament or his doomed romance with Gib.

For a time, they worked without speaking, but the hush didn't last long. Joel had just plucked a fourth runestone from the satchel when Zandi sucked in a jagged breath and squared his shoulders. Joel braced himself.

"I'm sorry for the way things turned out." Zandi's words were gasped more than spoken. "I'd have it be known it was *never* my intention to come between you and Gib. You were gone, and he seemed so lost. I approached Gib with honorable intent. I just wanted to help him, to be a friend. I–I never meant to—fall for him."

Joel ground his teeth.

Don't scream. Breathe. Just breathe.

"The cracks in our foundation already existed. You had little to do with the actual crumbling. Our fate was sealed the moment I made the decision to step through that portal."

"I'm sorry. Truly." Zandi's voice wavered, thick with desperation. "If it's any consolation, I *do* love Gib. I'd never hurt him. And even if you and I are never friends, I hope the two of you can one day reconcile—"

Joel had heard enough. His voice clipped as he interrupted the other man. "Not to be rude, but I'm really in no mood for company right now. Can you please just leave? I'd rather be alone."

Zandi averted his eyes and folded his arms across his stomach, a barrier between them. "I'll go. I just—had to speak my mind. And now that I have, I'll take my leave." He clambered to his feet and gave a quick bow. His hands trembled as he deliberately turned his back to Joel. "Farewell, Lord Adelwijn."

Joel watched the mage depart. Guilt mingled with relief, creating turbulent waves of emotion that tumbled in his stomach. He pushed the feelings aside. He couldn't dedicate thought or energy to Zandi's wants right now, not when more pressing issues already burdened Joel's mind. What had Zandi expected would happen anyway? That they'd have a friendly chat and suddenly everything would be all right? Nothing could ever be so simple.

Joel stared at the tiny runestone, still nestled within the curves of his palm. Weariness stole the vigor from his body, and he found it suddenly difficult to keep his arm steady. But he couldn't stop now. The thought of returning to his sleeping quarters, of lying idle and unable to sleep and allowing his mind to wander, was unbearable.

So Joel plunged back into his work, remaining beside the campfire long after the last cinders had turned into lifeless obsidian shards. He pushed himself past weariness and exhaustion, refusing to stop. By the time he reached the bottom of the satchel, delirium fogged his mind, but the hazy nothingness it provided was blissful. Tomorrow, there'd be hell to pay for his expenditure of energy, but right now, he couldn't have cared less.

Joel pawed clumsily through the bag one last time, making certain he'd left no uncharged stones behind. In his search, his fingertips brushed against cold metal. He blinked in surprise.

What in the two worlds?

Taking the unknown object into his grasp, Joel pulled his hand from the satchel.

Moonlight illuminated the fine outer edges of a pendant, decorated by tiny colored beads and shaped like a soaring bird. Two turquoise eyes made from gems gazed at him, and a chain rope spilled from the trinket like silver tail feathers.

At first, Joel didn't know what he was staring at, but then, at once, a bolt of clarity shot through the mist and he remembered. Kirk's falcon pendant! The one he'd tried to gift Joel as he'd been preparing to leave—but Joel had refused to take it. So how had the trinket wound up in the bottom of the runestone satchel?

Joel took the silver chain between his thumb and forefinger. The pendant dangled in the night air, free from its prison at long last. As it swayed, the smooth metal glistened, and for a moment, the falcon truly appeared to be alive, fluttering on the breeze.

Kirk's words, spoken so long ago, echoed in Joel's ears. *"It's fate you have it. Here, take it. You'll need both protection and luck in Shiraz. We will see each other again. I know it."*

A deep calm settled over him. How the pendant had found its way to him suddenly didn't matter. It was here now. And right now, in his hopelessness, he desperately needed something to hold onto.

Joel slipped the chain around his neck, adjusting the pendant so it rested against his collarbone. The weight of the falcon was a reminder of the protection the trinket provided—and Kirk's promise that everything would be all right.

CHAPTER SIX

"**I**s that it?"

"Yes. The village of Perth."

Gib peered down the gentle slope at the settlement below. Dust rose from the unpaved streets, lingering in the static air. From his vantage point atop Astora, he could see shoddy houses, packed tightly together and topped with sparse thatching that glowed yellow in the harsh sunlight. A barrier of jagged, wood beams surrounded the village.

"Reminds me of Willowdale during a drought," Gib said with a reminiscent sigh.

Koal sat tall in his saddle, his palfrey so close its wide flank brushed against Astora's shoulder. The seneschal's expression remained grim as he followed Gib's gaze. "The people of the south are a tough lot. I imagine they'd have to be to survive such an unforgiving climate."

Gib shook his head in disbelief. "I don't know how *anyone* could live out here. How do they grow any crops with the heat ready to scorch everything it touches?"

"You're asking *me*? You're the one who grew up on a farm."

"Good point." Gib laughed.

Joel, whose silver filly pawed the ground restlessly on the opposite side of Koal, raked a hand across his damp brow. "Are we just going to sit here staring at the village all day, or will we actually go inside at some point?"

Joel's long locks lay flat against his neck, and the sleeves of his white robe clung to his arms instead of flowing freely around him as they should. He looked more like a drowned cat than a man—a lovely drowned cat, of course.

"Patience," Koal replied, flashing a sour glimpse in his son's direction. "We're awaiting Deegan and the general."

"I'm here!"

Gib turned in time to see Deegan hoist himself into his saddle. With a nudge to the belly, the Crown Prince prodded his horse forward, leaving his sentries—Tular, Hasain, and Blessed Mage Natori—scrambling to catch up. A mischievous grin stole across Deegan's face as he pulled to a halt beside his cousin.

Joel openly scowled at the prince. "Dare I ask why *you* are in such high spirits?"

"Aren't you?" Deegan countered. "Finally, a moment's reprieve from riding! *Ye gods*, I don't want to even *look* at another saddle for at least a full sennight."

"It could have been worse." Joel chided the young prince in the same fashion his own mother might have, were she there. "What if you had to walk the entire way with the ground troops?"

Gib held back a chuckle, but he couldn't fault Deegan's enthusiasm. Traveling from dawn until dusk for two straight moonturns had become a grueling nightmare, taxing on both mind and body. Reaching Perth, which sat along Arden's southeastern border, meant there would finally be a chance to rest and recoup. And then—who knew what the army's next move would be.

Gib cleared his throat, catching Koal's attention once again. "How long do you reckon we'll stay here?"

"No way of knowing for sure. We'll need to meet with the village officials, assess the situation across the border, and send a report to the High Council—things that might very well take a bit of time." The age lines surrounding Koal's mouth pulled his entire face downward. "Though I wouldn't get too comfortable if I were you."

Again, Gib's eyes flicked toward the village. "I suspect comfort will be hard to come by here."

"Do you think we'll be treated to a great feast tonight?" Deegan asked. "I'd love a proper bath and a warm bed to sleep in."

Gib bit his inner cheek. He sometimes forgot Deegan had lived a *very* sheltered life and really had no idea how difficult life outside the palace could be.

Koal coughed politely. "Don't get your hopes up."

Tular was considerably less gracious. Spearing the prince with incredulous eyes, he leaned over the side of his saddle and knocked his elbow against Deegan's. "Have you taken a minute to *look* at the place? You'll be lucky if they can even offer you moldy bread! This isn't the royal palace in Silver."

Hasain snorted. "This isn't even a hovel along Silver's outskirts."

The tops of Deegan's ears flushed red. "I know it's not the same as the palace. I—just thought that–that—" Dark eyes shifted toward Koal, silently pleading for support. When none was offered, Deegan groaned and hung his head. "*Fine*. Stale bread for dinner it is then. For the sixtieth bloody day in a row."

For several moments, the party observed the village without speaking. The voices of conversing soldiers and the sounds of tent stakes being pounded into the earth rose behind them. Gib's skin felt as though it were being seared beneath the midday sun, but he refused to voice his complaints aloud. Things could have been worse. He could be assembling tents or digging latrine pits.

Tular raised a hand, shielding his eyes against the glare of the sun. "Looks like there's a gathering in the town square. They're expecting us. What are we waiting for?"

Gib squinted. How in the two worlds could Tular see so far away? When Gib attempted to make out anything beyond the thatched rooftops, the buildings and dirt streets all blurred together in a mass of drab.

"We're waiting on Morathi," Koal explained for a second time. "Then we go."

Hasain folded his arms across his chest. "Well, where is he? It's bad form, keeping both the Crown Prince and seneschal waiting."

"Enough whining! Here he comes now."

Gib grimaced and turned in his saddle to see for himself.

General Morathi rode through the war camp in a flurry of plate armor and pompous arrogance, a half-dozen underlings running on foot beside his hulking stallion. The tail of the general's cape cascaded behind him like the coils of a crimson viper—not an unjustified analogy. The man *was* a snake. Gib found his nose curling in disgust as he maneuvered Astora farther down the line so Morathi could ride beside Koal.

As the general came within earshot, Gib could hear callous orders being given. "No excuses. I expect this camp to be fully up and operational by the time I return. Have I made myself clear, soldier?"

"But, sir!" one of the pages gasped as he dashed to keep up. Beads of sweat poured down his reddened face. "Half the army is ill with heat exhaustion!"

Morathi waved off the man's concerns. "Well, good. It's about damn time the Healers actually had something to do. Send the afflicted men to the pavilion for a remedy and then get them back to work."

The page sputtered. "Perhaps camp should be assembled in the evening, sir. The Healers have advised the men to rest—"

"And there will be plenty of time to rest, *after* the camp is erected." Morathi gave his horse a sharp jab in the flank. The beast lurched forward, nearly trampling one of the underlings who hovered a bit too close. "I'll discuss it no more. See to it that my demands are met, or I'll make sure you're held personally responsible."

The page locked his jaw. "Yes, sir."

Morathi dismissed the remaining underlings with a flick of his wrist and, as Gib predicted, took post beside Koal. The general's icy gaze passed over each of the gathered party members, but—also predictably—he chose to acknowledge only Koal and Deegan.

"Highness. Seneschal." The cool words dripped from his lips, leaving Gib to wonder if Morathi even knew *how* to be kind. Was he capable of empathy? Or joy? Gib couldn't recall a time when he'd seen the man smile or heard anything other than hatred being spewed from his mouth.

Koal, always a diplomat, overlooked the general's foul mood. Gib imagined his mentor had become jaded after so many years sitting next to the man on the High Council. Unraveling one gloved hand from his horse's reins, Koal motioned ahead. "Shall we?"

Morathi merely grunted in response and with another kick to his warsteed's haunches, began the descent toward the gates of Perth. A plume of dust sprayed into the air behind the horse's gait, stinging Gib's face and leaving his throat raw. Deegan huffed, and Gib glimpsed the young prince rolling his eyes as the rest of the party pushed forward.

They descended the slope in single file. Arid flatlands stretched for leagues in every direction, a vast, sprawling carpet of dirt and gravel. With the exception of the Nishika's azure water snaking its way into the horizon, Gib couldn't spot a single patch of verdant color. Any grass that had managed to sprout quickly withered into stringy, brown tufts beneath the oppressive sun. Gib wondered how long it'd been since the countryside had last seen rain.

As they closed in on the village, the horrendous condition of Perth's outer wall couldn't be ignored. Gib examined the ramshackle structure with growing apprehension. Not only were many of the wood beams rotted or broken, but entire gaps between staves left the settlement exposed and vulnerable to attack. One section of the wall even showed signs of having been set afire, the wood planks charred to a black crisp. Gib thought to point it out to Koal but realized the seneschal was already scrutinizing the damage with a wary eye.

Fifty counts later, they had passed through the open gate leading into the village. A handful of protectors—men in scant leather armor and bearing only spears for weapons—let them through without question. Inside, crudely constructed wattle and daub houses were so tightly packed together that once again, the party was forced into single file as they navigated through the narrow streets. Gib found himself bringing up the rear. He took the opportunity to get a good look around.

Though considerably larger than Willowdale, Perth was only a fraction the size of Davenport, and the entire village would probably have fit onto the Academy grounds of Silver City with room to spare. Stout, coarse-haired boar and a colorful variety of chickens patrolled the dirt streets, free ranging and unguarded. Gib supposed there was really no need to pen them. After all, even if the beasts wandered beyond the wall, there really wasn't anywhere for them to go.

The stench of human sweat and animal droppings filled Gib's nostrils, offensive and putrid, but it was a reminder of his own humble beginnings. Living among the highborns of Silver, it was all too easy to forget the world from which he'd come. Shaking his head, Gib swore never to dismiss his past. He was *proud* of his heritage. The enduring strength of the simple folk had helped shape the man he was today.

The farther inside the party trekked, the more people they encountered. Gib's heart ached at the sight of the villagers, dressed in ragged clothing with dirt matted into their hair. The inescapable dust plastered their faces, masks of grime upon their sun-worn skin. Some continued to go about their daily routines while others stopped what they were doing to gape at the newcomers. Gib felt for them. He knew, at least on some level, the struggles they faced. He wished he could do something for them. Ahead, Gib caught Deegan glancing around from atop his palfrey, eyes large and brows sitting high on his forehead. Did he see now? Did he finally understand?

As Tular foretold, a sizable group of villagers was gathered in the town square. Gib pulled Astora to a stop behind Koal just as a balding man with a large nose and friendly disposition separated himself from the crowd. He wore a black doublet over frayed trousers, sturdy, high-quality fabric but faded to a dull grey and worn from years of sun exposure.

"Greetings, milords!" the man said with a sweeping bow. "My name is Cormag Barclay, mayor and overlord of Perth."

Koal inclined his head and proceeded with introductions. "Greetings, mayor. I am Lord Koal Adelwijn, Seneschal of Arden. These are Crown Prince Deegan Radek, heir to the throne; Lord General Morathi Adeben; Lordlings Hasain Radek, Tular Galloway, and Joel Adelwijn; my apprentice, Gibben Nemesio of Willowdale; and Lady Mage Natori."

The mayor's deep-set eyes broadened, the creases lining his face stretching wide. He couldn't have been any older than Koal, but living under such unforgiving conditions had done him no favors. Again, he stooped forward. "It's an honor to be in the presence of such renowned men. And to have Arden's future king in my village—well, I never thought I'd see *that* day! Whatever you may need, Highness, ask it of me. I am most humbly at your service."

Deegan motioned for Cormag to rise before he could babble further. "Thank you for welcoming us so graciously to Perth, Lord Barclay. It's good to be here."

Cormag soaked up the prince's praise like a sponge. "Please, allow us to tend and stable your beasts, and I will show you to your quarters." He waved a hand, and almost immediately, villagers rushed forward to take the horses.

Gib dismounted and handed Astora's reins to a young girl with curly black hair and rosebud lips. She flashed him a sultry smile, and Gib blushed as he stammered out a thanks.

They left the town square behind, traveling on foot toward the far side of the settlement. Cormag led the way, conversing with Koal and Morathi as he waddled along. Deegan stuck close to Koal's side, listening attentively.

"It's been a rough start to the summer," Cormag said, wiping away the perspiration that sat atop his bare head. "We don't get much for rain, as you can probably imagine. But in all my years, I've never seen a dry stretch last so long. Bless The Two that the Nishika is still flowing healthily. Don't know what we'd do if the river dried up."

"Has there been any trouble from across the border?" Koal inquired.

"Not a stirring from the Shirites in three moonturns now, milord."

"Three moonturns?" Koal raised a brow. "Your rampart appears to have been recently attacked. The fire damage—"

"Aye. Happened a few cycles ago. A Shiraz brigade shot the wall with blazing arrows. I suspect they were trying to raid our livestock. Perth's defenses held, but we lost four men that night. That makes a dozen defenders slain since the turn of the wheel. Good lads, all of them. May their souls make safe across The Veil."

Morathi's thin lips pulled into a scowl. "Perth was attacked three moon cycles ago, and you haven't yet repaired the village fortifications? Mayor, I must question your ability to lead. Mending that wall should have been your highest priority. Should Perth fall into the hands of heathens, the blame will rest solely on *you*. The High Council would be most displeased to hear news of Arden losing ground to enemy scum."

"Apologies, milord." Cormag's face had gone an ugly, blotchy red. "We did the best we could with what resources we had. Timber is in limited supply, and with my able-bodied defenders now numbering around twenty, I couldn't risk sending a foraging expedition north." He licked his lips, eyes shifting nervously to Koal. "We—did send word to Silver City, asking the High Council for assistance, but a response was never received."

Gib exchanged knowing glances with Joel. If Arden's welfare was left solely in Neetra's hands, anyone who wasn't highborn would starve to death before Deegan could claim his crown. Neetra just didn't care.

Morathi clearly had no plans of responding, so—per usual—the task of making amends fell unto Koal. His tone was sincere as he addressed the mayor. "Now it is *I* who must apologize. The influenza outbreak last winter and the persistent drought in the south have created a backlog of petitions in the council chamber. I've repeatedly encouraged the councilors to address these appeals, but I'm afraid the war on Shiraz has taken priority."

"It wasn't my intent to place blame, Lord Seneschal," replied Cormag. "These are trying times for all, with the country being without a king." He paused then, and sorrow lingered in his gaze as he turned toward Deegan. "Here in Perth, news of the late King's passing was met with great remorse. Condolences to your family, Highness."

"Thank you," Deegan replied frailly.

Ahead, what had to be the mayor's manor came into view. An unkempt courtyard of shriveled grass gave way to high, stone walls that stood out against the surrounding cottages. Gib would have been impressed had he not spent the past four years living inside the Adelwijn estate. In comparison, Cormag's manor was crude, even homely. Gib nearly laughed at his own musings.

Oh, how jaded you've become, Gibben Nemesio.

Cormag ushered them through a rickety gate. "Please, come inside."

Passing through a thick slab of timber that served as the front door, the mayor led them down a corridor that opened into a great hall meant for parties and other social gatherings. The room was sparsely furnished; one lengthy table made from coarse ironwood sat in the center of the space atop a shabby red carpet. The stone walls were cold and bare—Lady Mrifa would have surely gone into a tizzy at the sight, demanding fine paintings and tapestries be hung—and the extravagance Gib had grown accustomed to was absent, replaced by stony practicality.

"You'll find two bedchambers at the end of the hall," explained Cormag. He motioned down a second corridor across the room. "If you find you need additional quarters, my wife and I can set up cots in the study so you may also have our bed."

Koal dismissed the offer with a shake of his head. "You needn't do that. Two chambers will be sufficient."

With a firm nod, Cormag set a hand on the tabletop. "I've ordered a boar be slain so you may feast tonight. This hall is yours to use as a command post while you're here. I employ no servants, but you'll find the villagers ready and willing to assist you, should you need help. Anything you may require, don't hesitate to ask."

"Do you have a map?" Koal asked.

"Of course, milord. I keep a map of Arden in my study. I'll fetch it now." Cormag bowed and left the room.

Gib took a seat at the table only after the others had. With Hasain and Koal on either side, he felt like a dwarf sitting between giants.

"While we're here, we should help them rebuild the wall," Deegan said. "We should also assign a group of soldiers to stay in Perth, to train the villagers so they can better defend themselves."

Morathi issued a crass snort. "And take valuable manpower from our army? In the middle of a campaign, nonetheless? No offense, *Highness*, but I believe it's best the logistics of warfare be left to grown men."

Deegan raised his chin, as stubborn and defiant as King Rishi had ever been. "Correct me if I'm wrong, *General*, but under the old draft law you and my uncle fought so hard to retain, would I not be considered grown?"

Gib's mouth fell open, caught somewhere between gaping in horror and an inane grin.

Careful, Deegan.

"Duty and compassion command me to aid these people," Deegan continued without pause. "I won't abandon Perth to an unknown fate."

Morathi's face darkened with rage, and his large hands twitched like he might want to settle them around Deegan's neck. Natori and Tular watched the movement with wary eyes.

Before the general had time to voice a response, Cormag whisked back into the room, a sheet of rolled parchment nestled in the crook of his arm. "This here is the most detailed account I possess of Arden's eastern and southern provinces."

He spread the map wide across the tabletop. Gib reached to hold one end in place while Joel took the other.

"Here we are." Koal placed his index finger on a blot of ink near the center of the map. "And this must be Ashvale." He moved the same digit two inches lower.

"Aye," Cormag confirmed.

"And the bridge?"

Cormag tapped the parchment. "Sits not even three dozen furlongs north of the hamlet. Kaleth's Crossing is the only bridge within a hundred leagues in either direction. When your army proceeds into enemy territory, you'll want to cross the river there."

Koal's face hardened, but he didn't look up from the map. "*If* the army proceeds. You claim there have been no recent skirmishes in Perth. If that holds true elsewhere, I see no reason why we can't focus our attention on strengthening security along our border."

Morathi scowled so viciously he might have passed for a snarling dog. "We're ten thousand soldiers strong, well-fed, armed, and only twelve leagues outside Shiraz. *Now* is the most opportune time to attack. And once we've obliterated every hovel between here and Tahir, they'll dare not set foot on Ardenian soil ever again."

"I will *not* endorse reckless violence," Koal said through gritted teeth. "Not if a peaceful solution exists."

Morathi slammed a fist on the table. "So you'd have us lie belly up, waiting for those savages to cut out our throats? *Foolish!* We must be the first to act."

"That decision lies with the High Council. I will send them my report."

Morathi's eyes gleamed dangerously. "Yes. And I will send mine."

Shaking his head, Koal turned back to Cormag, who was terrified and sweating. "Lord Barclay, have any recent reports of trouble come out of Ashvale?"

"No, milord." The mayor paused, licking his lips. "That is, no news at all has come, I'm afraid."

Koal's shoulders tensed. "No news? You mean you haven't had *any* contact with the village? How long?"

92

"Not in three sennights now, Seneschal. We sent a rider. Must be going on a fortnight now since he left. Ashvale is only a two-day trek by horseback. He should have returned days ago."

Gib's stomach flopped. Did this mean something was wrong? Was Ashvale in some kind of trouble? What other explanation could there be?

Koal did a good job masking his concern, but Gib wasn't fooled. He could see apprehension written in the lines across his mentor's face.

How serious is this?

A smirk flickered on Morathi's mouth. "Rethinking your stance yet, Seneschal?"

Koal sighed, but Gib could tell he was anxious. "Let's not rush to any conclusions. We don't know if anything is actually wrong. We'll send a party to Ashvale. If anything is amiss, we'll know in four days' time. In the meantime, there are reports to write and a war camp to oversee."

Morathi gave a firm nod. "Very well. I'll have a troop assembled and ready to leave for Ashvale within a mark." He pushed his chair away and rose. "Mayor Barclay, fetch my horse." Not awaiting a response, Morathi stormed down the long corridor, leaving Cormag to chase behind the trail of the general's cape.

Koal looked around the room. "Deegan, I want you to stay here while I compile my report. I suppose the rest of you are free to go, if you wish. We'll assemble here on the eventide."

"I'm staying with Deegan," Hasain replied at once. Tular echoed his brother's words with a simple nod. Natori didn't need to say anything. Gib knew she wouldn't leave. She hadn't once left Deegan's side since departing Silver.

"Is there anything you need me to do, sir?" Gib asked.

"No. Go be with your friends. I imagine they could use some help around camp."

"You're probably right." Gib climbed to his feet. "Guess I'll be back in time for dinner."

Koal chuckled. "I *know* you wouldn't miss *that*."

Joel stood as well. "I doubt I'll be of any use here, so I'm going to the Healers' pavilion. It's likely Nawaz will have chores for me."

Gib followed behind Joel as they left the manor and went back into the blazing afternoon heat. Thick, dry air sat heavy on the ground, making it hard to take a deep breath. Gib shielded his eyes from the sun and grimaced. A breeze would have been nice, anything to chase the stale air away.

Morathi was nowhere to be seen, though he'd departed only moments before. Gib held back the urge to roll his eyes, certain the general had ridden back to the war camp at a full gallop, eager to escape the "deplorable hovel."

"Shall we go find the horses?" Joel asked.

Gib nodded. "I could see the roof of the stable from the town square."

"Good. You lead the way."

They walked in silence, content to observe the village and its inhabitants and therefore avoid conversation with one another.

The townsfolk bustled about their lives as if the summer heat didn't faze them. Then again, maybe it didn't. After all, they'd spent their entire existences surviving these wastelands. Maybe the visitors from the north were the odd ones here, sweating like cattle and falling ill to sunstroke.

"Does it remind you of Willowdale?" Joel asked at length.

"Willowdale wasn't so dusty," Gib replied, winning a soft chuckle from the mage.

"I guess I never truly understood how hard life was for you. I'm sorry."

"It wasn't all bad. Honestly, I miss it sometimes."

"Really?"

Gib brushed damp curls off his forehead. "I miss the simplicity. Life was hard, yes, but we never had time for cutthroat politics or devising schemes to overthrow our foes. Everyone helped one another without expecting anything in return. I guess that's what I miss most."

"I imagine I'd miss that, too."

They found the stables easily; surrounded by wattle and daub huts on either side, the large, open-sided structure was hard to miss. A youngling scurried to fetch Astora and Ivory. At first, it startled Gib to see a child so small had been trusted to oversee the horses, but then he remembered how fast children in poor communities were expected to grow up. Hadn't he himself been left in charge of an entire farmstead at the age of twelve?

As they waited for their horses' tack to be assembled, Gib leaned against the broad-planked gate and allowed his mind to wander.

So we've reached Perth. Now what? How long will it be before we learn our fate? If there's been trouble in Ashvale, will we invade Shiraz?

He dared seek out Joel's gaze. "What do you suppose the High Council's decision will be, when they read Koal's and Morathi's reports?"

"I really don't know. Father has his supporters on the council, but so does the general. It's no secret Neetra and the new High Councilor have both aligned with him—not to mention my own brother. It won't take much to convince them the only solution is to invade Shiraz."

"Horseshit. They're just going to get Ardenian soldiers killed for no reason."

"I agree. Let's hope no other villages along the border have reported recent attacks. It's the only chance we have of the High Council siding with Father. If the Shirites have pulled back, then *maybe* we can avoid this war altogether." Joel's frown deepened. "I must admit, I'm a little concerned about Ashvale though. Did you see the look on Mayor Barclay's face? He's worried. I could tell."

"Do you think Ashvale is in trouble?"

"I suppose we'll know once the scouting party returns. Pray to The Two there's just been a miscommunication, or else my uncle will have his way."

"The fact that our fate lies in Neetra's hands makes me ill."

A remorseful smile flashed across Joel's face, but any response he might have had died on his lips as the stable girl returned, leading the horses through the open gate. It was almost comical the way she commanded the two beasts; had either mare decided to fuss, surely the child wouldn't be able to maintain control over them.

"Yer horses, milords," she said, curtsying and handing over the reins. "I fed and watered 'em and gave 'em a good brushin' m'self."

"Thank you." Joel fished through a pocket inside his robe and pulled out three silver coins. "Here, for your kind service."

The girl's eyes went wide. "M–milord, I–I–can't—"

Joel practically had to shove the coinage into her tiny hand to get the girl to take it. "I insist."

She gaped down at the silvers, mouth hanging open in shock for several moments, before reality finally seemed to settle. Letting out an elated gasp, the youngling all but threw herself at Joel's feet. "Thank ye, milord! Thank ye!"

"No, thank you."

Gib stared fondly at his former companion.

Bless his heart. He has absolutely no idea. He doesn't know how much he just changed that poor girl's life.

The two men climbed into their saddles and began the trek back up the hill. Already, tents loomed against the horizon and supply wagons were being unloaded. On the outskirts of the encampment, soldiers with buckets tromped to and from the banks of the Nishika, collecting water for horses and cooking. More foraged for tinder; Gib imagined they'd have to settle for brushwood and dried reeds. He hadn't seen more than a handful of *actual* trees within leagues of here.

Near the camp's center stood the Healers' pavilion, its cerulean apex reaching toward the cloudless sky. The brightly painted canvas was easily discernible, surrounded by the drab shades of the other tents—as was intended. If a soldier suffered an injury, finding the pavilion swiftly was imperative.

Joel directed his filly toward it. "I'm going to help the Healers. I suppose I'll see you for dinner, if Nawaz doesn't have me sorting salves all night. Enjoy the company of your friends."

Gib bit the inside of his lip. "Yeah. I'll see you later. Tell Nawaz I said hello."

They parted ways, leaving Gib to roam the encampment in search of his friends.

95

He stumbled across them along the camp's eastern edge. Kezra and Nage were both hard at work raising a tent, while Zandi tended the fire pit nearby.

"All right, I'm here!" Gib announced as he slid from Astora's saddle.

Kezra raised her face. Beads of sweat glistened on her forehead, and her dampened sentinel uniform clung to her body like a second skin. "Typical. You show up *after* all the hard labor has already been done."

"Hey, I'm sorry," Gib groaned, leading Astora to a pole where the other horses had already been bound. "Koal asked me to ride into Perth, alongside Morathi and the prince. I came back as soon as I was dismissed."

Dust flew up around Nage's boots as he pounded the last tent post into the ground. "How did that go?"

"About how you might imagine," Gib replied. He looped Astora's reins around the pole, twisting the braided leather strap into a loose knot. "We met with the mayor. Morathi insulted him, and Koal had to scramble to make amends. Same story, different day."

Zandi flashed a grin, though he didn't glance up from the fire. "Have we even left Silver? You're complaining just the same as you do after returning from any given council meeting."

"Apparently it doesn't matter how far I go," Gib muttered under his breath. "I can't escape that damn chamber." Kezra wordlessly offered him a wineskin and he took a long drink. The warm, bitter water was unsatisfying but helped moisten his throat. "Thanks," he croaked, before passing the wineskin onto Nage. "Where's Gara?"

"You just missed her." Nage tipped his head back and took a swig from the container. "She had to go on patrol duty. Morathi's orders—something about a scouting mission."

And just like that, Gib's mood deflated again. "Ashvale," he said without thinking.

"What's that?"

Gib could have kicked himself in the arse. Why? *Why* had he even brought it up? As if his friends needed more to worry about. Why couldn't he keep his fat mouth shut for once in his life?

He scrambled for something to say. "Oh, uh, nothing. I just overheard Koal and Morathi saying they were going to send soldiers there."

Nage's brow creased. Damn it. He was already concerned. "Nothing bad, I hope?"

Gib twisted his hands together, busying himself. "Uh, no? I mean, I don't know. I don't think so. They didn't really say much else about the matter." He could feel Kezra's glare without even looking at her. Gib held back the urge to groan. He *knew* he was a bad liar. Of course they didn't believe him.

He made a point to turn his back to Nage and Kezra and, instead, focused his attention on Zandi. If Gib couldn't fool his friends, he could at least pretend they weren't standing there judging him. "Is there anything I can do to help?"

"As a matter of fact—" Zandi's emerald eyes sparkled as he tossed an empty bucket at Gib's feet. "Go fill that. We need water for cooking."

Gib took the pail without a single complaint and trudged toward the riverbank. He would gladly haul water until dusk if it kept him from having to explain what he'd overheard.

By the time Gib reached the edge of the Nishika, however, he'd all but convinced himself he was overreacting. Yes, the fact that no one had heard from Ashvale in entire sennights was troubling, but it wasn't cause for panic just yet. There were a dozen logical explanations why Ashvale wasn't returning correspondences that had nothing to do with a possible Shiraz attack. Koal had been right to send a scouting party, but it didn't necessarily mean the soldiers were walking into disaster.

Gib set the gnarled wooden bucket into the river, watching as murky water flooded its interior.

For the love of The Two, calm down. You can fret when you have actual reason to.

"Gib?"

His head shot up. He'd recognize his sister's gentle voice anywhere.

Liza stood on the ridge of the riverbank, looking valiant in leather armor and knee-high riding boots. Rebellious, frizzled curls escaped the ponytail at the nape of her neck and dust glazed her square face. Despite it all, she smiled as brightly as ever. Gib couldn't recall a time when his sister had allowed an ill-favored circumstance to deter her spirit. Even when their father died—at their family's darkest hour—she'd never lost hope for a better tomorrow.

"Hello, stranger," Liza teased. She trotted forward, loose gravel catching her boots and causing her to waver just slightly as she closed the space between them. "I must have just missed you. Your friends said you'd gone to fetch water."

Gib hoisted the bucket into an upright position and set it by his feet. "Liza! I was going to find you later, I swear. But Koal asked me to ride into Perth, and then my friends needed help—"

"Relax. I'm not here to give a scolding. I have something for you." Without further elaboration, she pulled a small object, wrapped and hidden by coarse linen, from behind her back and offered it to Gib.

"What is—?" Gib's eyebrows knitted as he pushed aside the fabric, revealing the Adelwijn family's copy of *Tales of Fae*. He recognized the frayed binding and faded cover from the many nights he'd spent reading from the book. "I don't understand. How did you get this?"

Liza shrugged. "I found it. Cal must have slipped it into my pack when you two paid me a visit in the barracks. You know him. He probably thought we would find comfort in reading from it."

"As if either of us has time to read out here."

"I've stumbled my way through a few of the stories here and there, as time permits. I think you should have it now though. The Two only know the next time I'll see you."

Gib cradled the book against his chest and bit his tongue. He knew Liza understood his duties must come first, but it didn't make him feel better about the fact he'd *barely* seen her since the army's mobilization. "I'm a horrible brother. I'm sorry."

"Stop it. I know you're busy."

"I could still make time to see you!"

Liza cocked her head to one side. "Really? When? You're the seneschal's understudy, for Daya's sake! Give yourself a little slack."

"But you're *family*, Liza. Family should always come before duty. I don't want you and the boys to think I've abandoned you."

"There's nothing you could ever do to make me think that. Tay, Cal, and I—we know how much you love us. Don't *ever* doubt that. The four of us might go days, sennights—hell, even entire moonturns—without being together, but that doesn't matter. Love doesn't just wither away and die. The boys and I know that, and I know you do, too."

It took Gib every ounce of strength he possessed to will his voice not to tremble. "You're right. I *do* know. But you can't blame me for always wanting to do more. I'm stubborn to a fault."

Liza chuckled. "You get that from Da. He was the same. He wouldn't pause to think about himself until everyone around him was taken care of."

Sudden and crushing grief tugged at Gib's heart. "He was a good man."

"Aye. He was. And so are you." Chestnut eyes twinkling alongside her smile, Liza reached out and clasped Gib's shoulder. Her touch was firm, reassuring. "I know I've already said it until I'm blue in the face, but Ma and Da really would be proud of the man you've grown into."

Gib didn't know what to say, so he merely nodded.

For a time, they stood side by side, both staring aimlessly at the far riverbank. Flecks of sunlight danced across the blue-green waters, beautiful and serene, reminding Gib of his childhood. Had the rugged landscape instead been draped in grass, he and Liza could almost be standing along the bank of the Tempist River, in the fields behind the farm.

Memories of splashing through the shallow water after a long day's work warmed Gib's heart. He could still hear Tayver and Calisto's gleeful laughter as they played hide and seek among the reeds. Liza lounged beneath the shade of the old willow tree where both of their parents had been laid to rest, a fishing pole in hand. She always caught a good bucketful of fish from that spot, enough for all of them to eat until their bellies were bursting. Perhaps such luck meant their Ma and Da were still watching over them, in some small measure.

"I came to say goodbye. I'm going to be gone for a few days."

The words pulled Gib back to the present. His brow creased as he turned to face Liza. "Goodbye? What do you mean?"

"My troop has volunteered to accompany a scouting party to the village of Ashvale. I'll be gone at least four days, possibly more. I just wanted to let you know, so you aren't running circuits around camp looking for me."

"N–no," Gib blurted, his chest and lungs seizing. "You *can't* go."

"Why not? What's wrong?"

Gib took Liza's hand before he knew what he was doing. "I just—it's a feeling I have. The mayor was talking about how Ashvale had gone dark. There's been no word from the village in entire sennights now. The mayor even sent a messenger, and he didn't come back. You could be riding into trouble! Please, stay here."

"We were forewarned to be on guard. You have every right to be concerned, but please, try not to worry. I won't be going in there blind and unarmed. And *if* we do run into trouble, believe me, we're well trained. My troop has been stationed on the eastern border before. We spent half a wheelturn fending off Shirite raids outside Winterdell, remember?"

Gib shook his head, unwilling to accept her words. "I can talk to Koal. He can make it so you don't have to go—"

"No. Gib, this was *my* decision. *I* volunteered. *I* want to go. You're not the only person in Arden willing to defend her."

Gib tried to swallow, but his mouth had gone dry. He wanted to fight her decision, to somehow force her to stay behind or to argue with her until she changed her mind—but he knew she wouldn't. Liza was just as determined as he. Stubborn to a fault.

"All right, fine," Gib heard himself say. His voice sounded foreign in his ears. "You're right. I can't force you to stay, and it's selfish to ask you to choose the coward's way out. Just—just promise me you'll be careful. Stay alert out there, and if anything happens—"

Before he could speak another word, Liza pulled him into an embrace. "I promise. I'll remain vigilant. Everything will be fine, you'll see."

Gib hugged her fiercely. "I love you, Liza."

One of Liza's hands rested atop his head, stroking his curls. "And I you." She released him, holding him by the shoulders at arm's length. A faint smile played on her lips. "And when I return, you *must* formally introduce me to your new catch. That Zandi Malin-Rai is quite lovely to look at."

Gib could feel his cheeks burning. "I–uh–if you want to."

99

"Of course I want to," Liza replied. Her left eye twitched in what was perhaps a subtle wink.

Gib took the water bucket in one hand while gripping *Tales of Fae* in the other. "Take care of yourself out there. I'll try to hold things down here while you're gone."

"You always do, Gib. Always."

Liza squeezed his shoulder one final time. Her grip was firm and steady, like Gib remembered their father's to be. It gave Gib the hope he so desperately needed. Liza was right. Everything would be fine. They'd made it this far together. Luck, fate, or perhaps even the will of The Two had allowed them to survive until this point. Surely they wouldn't be abandoned now—would they?

CHAPTER SEVEN

Kirk forced himself not to sneer when Otho came into view down the corridor—quite a distance down, to be exact. It would seem none of the students in the hall dared get too close to him. Indeed, they all went out of their way to give the homely man a wide berth. Otho either didn't notice or didn't care as he remained steadfast at his post beside Dean Marc's office door.

Kirk thought to offer a greeting as he stopped beside Otho but opted against it when Otho didn't even grace Kirk with a glance of acknowledgement.

Fine, Kirk thought, scowling. *Two can play this game.*

Leaning against the wall, he folded his arms across his chest and waited in silence. Clearly the Weapons Master's assistant hadn't taken it upon himself to learn any *manners* since they'd last crossed paths.

Nearly two moonturns had come and gone since Marc had held that first meeting. Kirk had begun to wonder if the entire thing had been a dream or something his ever-present paranoia had conjured up. Both Prince Didier and the dean had insisted the time to act against Neetra would be soon, yet Kirk hadn't heard a single word on the matter since. As the sennights turned into fortnights and then entire moonturns passed by, it seemed probable Marc and the others had chosen to move forward without Kirk. Perhaps entrusting the Imperial mage was too much of a risk for them to take, despite Joel's assurance that Kirk was an ally.

Kirk begrudgingly accepted it. He'd known trust would be hard-earned because of his former ties to the Northern Empire. He'd known making a life for himself in Arden would be an uphill battle. But he hadn't anticipated the *loneliness*. With Joel gone to war and Kenisha outside Silver, he had no one else to talk to.

So when the hastily-scribbled message from Marc had arrived just after dawn that morning, Kirk almost hadn't believed his eyes. *Meet me at my office before the midday bell tolls* was all the note had read, with Marc's signature scratched into the parchment beneath.

Kirk's first inclination was that the dean needed to discuss something Academy related. This couldn't have anything to do with Neetra, could it? They'd obviously found Kirk unsuitable to be privy to such information.

Though, with Otho Dakheel also present, what else could this meeting really be about?

They stood in silence for what felt like forever. The midday bell rang, the singsong sound reverberating off the vaulted marble ceiling. Finally, when the melody had ceased and they stood alone in the abandoned hall, Kirk couldn't take it anymore.

He sighed and glanced over at Otho. "Are we guarding the door?"

Otho openly aired his disdain. "He's not here yet. Door's locked."

"Are we early?"

"No. He's late."

Kirk chewed on his bottom lip, caught between the urge to further ignore Otho and the need to validate himself. Why did Otho insist on treating Kirk like he was some kind of deviant? He had every intention of making Arden his new home, and he'd be damned if some ill-mannered weaponry apprentice was going to make him feel unworthy.

Luckily, Kirk didn't have to suffer Otho's company alone for much longer. Marc rounded the corner and hurried down the corridor toward the two young men.

The dean's face was grim as he approached, and he didn't waste time with formalities. "All right, good. You're both here. We're probably not going to get a better chance than this. Follow me."

Kirk's heart raced when the trio entered the royal palace half a mark later.

Marc didn't bring them through the main entrance. The door they used was modest in both height and stature and was guarded by only a single man donned in plate armor. Marc said not a word, and the sentinel allowed him to pass through with nothing more than a hasty nod, leaving Kirk to wonder if this was normal protocol. Surely it couldn't be. He'd lived inside the Imperial grounds in Teivel for nearly half his life and *never* were people allowed to come and go without thorough questioning. Was this all part of the "chance" Marc had cryptically mentioned?

"Stay close," Marc warned, motioning for Kirk and Otho to follow.

Kirk had no complaints with the order. He hadn't been inside the palace since he'd first come through the portal, and he had no intentions of becoming lost now. If he were separated from Marc and Otho, he'd *never* be able to come up with a plausible explanation as to why he was there. He'd probably be thrown into the dungeons, or worse.

Marc directed them down one narrow hallway after another. The darkness seeping from within the corridors made Kirk leery. Every room, hall, and courtyard in Teivel had always been illuminated by mage-orbs. He wasn't used to creeping around in the shadows.

"Where are we going?" Otho finally asked.

Marc hesitated, slowing so Otho and Kirk could catch up. He kept glancing around wildly, as if he might be expecting an ambush at any given moment. "We're going to the council room. Come on. I'll explain more once we're inside."

Marc continued to guide them, often peering around corners before stepping fully into the corridor. Kirk held his breath and tried to keep his footfalls light. What might happen if they were caught? He hoped Marc had a good excuse as to why he and two underlings were sneaking around the palace should someone stumble upon them.

They ascended a steep, spiraling stairwell, the dean leading the way and Kirk bringing up the rear. He was nearly out of breath by the time he set foot on the floor above. Marc drew to a halt only after a few paces. A polished wood door barred the way, and they could go no further.

"This leads into the gallery above the council room." Marc's hand went around the brass handle, and leaning his shoulder against the bulky hardwood, he pushed the door open.

Otho cocked an eyebrow. "Should have been locked."

Marc motioned for the underlings to go through first. "There are still *some* royal guardsmen who are loyal to the King."

Kirk's breath caught as he passed beneath the doorframe and into the room beyond. If someone had told him a wheelturn ago he'd be sneaking into the chambers of Arden's High Council, he would have laughed aloud and called them mad.

The chamber inside was murky and encumbered by shadow, though had the heavy curtains lining the gallery been drawn open, the entire space might have been bright and inviting. A stale scent hung in the air, like the smell of an old chest filled with linen and mothballs. Three rows of chairs smothered in worn velvet were arranged into a crescent and overlooked an oversized roundtable below.

Kirk swallowed. So this was the place where Arden's laws were forged.

Marc turned his back long enough to secure the door. "All right. We need to do this as quickly as possible. There's no council meeting scheduled today, but that doesn't mean we have time to dawdle."

"You still haven't informed us *why* we're here," Kirk said, following behind Marc as he trudged down the carpeted steps leading from the gallery to the chamber's base. Kirk could hear Otho's light footfalls at his back.

Marc waited until they'd reached the bottom floor to respond. "Before Koal left, he mentioned Neetra's election. If we can find some kind of proof that it was rigged—"

"Would it be enough to get him off the throne?" Otho asked darkly.

Marc met each of the underlings with a troubled gaze. "I—I don't know."

Otho let out a groan and shook his head. "Everyone knows the seneschal *should* be on the throne until Deegan is old enough to rule. Why was a vote even needed?"

"Because something isn't right. That's what we have to try to figure out."

Kirk shifted his weight from one foot to the other. "You don't sound very sure of this plan."

"I'm not. But Koal is my friend, and he's asked me to do this for him. I'm *not* going to fail another friend."

Kirk couldn't imagine what Marc meant by that but didn't have time to ponder. The dean pulled a crate of files out from a shelf beneath the table and passed it to Kirk. A moment later, he handed a second box to Otho and kept a third for himself.

"I'm not sure what's in any of these, so we're just going to have to divvy them up and go through all of it." Marc set his own crate onto the table with a sigh. "Diedrick Lyle—the High Council's Records Keeper—is in charge of documentation, and he doesn't tend to divulge where he files everything away."

Otho snorted. "Lyle is a known supporter of the new steward. What's to say he hasn't conveniently made anything pertaining to the election 'disappear' already?"

"That thought *has* crossed my mind," Marc admitted. "But it's still worth looking."

They set to work in silence. Kirk emptied his crate and leafed through his assigned stack of paperwork, taking pains to make sure everything stayed in its proper order. Neetra couldn't suspect what they were doing. Kirk's heart continued to hammer in his chest, no matter how many times he told himself to calm down.

Most of the documents he passed over were of trivial nature: tax receipts, rejected petitions, and other documents Kirk barely understood. He set them aside and dug deeper into the crate. Still he found nothing. As the minutes flew by, Kirk began to doubt *any* of them would find useful information. Perhaps Diedrick Lyle had indeed purged all records of the election. Had they risked their safety sneaking into this chamber all for nothing?

Otho cleared his throat. "Marc. Election ballots." He waved a handful of loose parchment slips in the air.

The dean stepped around the table and came to stand over Otho's shoulder. His face darkened as he read through the paperwork. "It was so close."

Kirk crept closer, examining the documents for himself. His heart dropped to the pit of his stomach. "Seneschal Koal lost by one."

"One vote is all it takes. But now with Liro on the High Council, we've lost the numbers advantage completely. Neetra knew full well his brother was his only *real* competition. I'm sure he bought off or bribed everyone else to vote for him. But without proof, our hands are tied."

"Were there any swing voters?" Kirk asked. "People who normally voted with the seneschal but went against him that time? Can you tell who cast which ballot?"

"The vote was supposed to remain confidential, but let me see." Marc silently went through each of the thirteen pages, scrutinizing them with a critical eye. At last, he fished one from the pile and held it close to his face. "I'm pretty sure this one belongs to Joaquin Aldino—his handwriting is so flowery and all. He typically voted with us. Though lately, he's been voting alongside the likes of Anders and Liro."

"Could you interrogate him? Ask him if he voted for Neetra instead of Koal?"

"I don't know. Joaquin is usually pretty laid back, but he might start asking difficult questions if I go to him."

Kirk nodded. That made sense. Perhaps they could search for evidence of this Joaquin Aldino being bought off before the vote took place.

A noise from the hall caused all three men to freeze. Beyond the closed door, footsteps rapidly approached, and Kirk could hear two voices snarling back and forth.

"*Put everything back!*" Marc hissed, scrambling to gather the scattered parchment.

Kirk's heart pounded as he threw his pile of paperwork back into the crate and shoved it beneath the table. His thoughts leapt to his sister on her new husband's farm with so little protection. If he were caught, would Kenisha also stand to be punished?

The voices in the hall were growing louder.

"Where do we go?" Kirk squealed.

Marc spun around in a panicked circle. "Into the gallery! Hurry!"

They raced up the steps in single file. Kirk made for the door at the back of the gallery, but Marc waved his hands in the air, motioning for them to hide behind the last row of chairs. The sound of a key scraping through a lock below confirmed there was no time to make a dash for safety. Not without being caught. Kirk dove to the floor beside Marc and Otho just as the main chamber door flew open. The bang of wood against stone helped conceal Kirk's gasp.

His mind whirled with a thousand terrible questions.

What if we've been betrayed? What if someone is here to arrest us? Will they interrogate us first or just kill us? Are they looking for us right now?

A furious voice cut through the air. "Steward, you promised swift change and thus far you've yet to deliver on that promise. Others on the High Council grow restless alongside me. You must know I'm not the only one who is displeased."

Steward? Steward Neetra?

Kirk bit his lip. He wanted to peek around the chair, but his frozen limbs refused to cooperate. All he could do was stare at the dirty floor ahead and listen.

"I'm in full control of the situation, High Councilor," a second man replied. "Change doesn't happen overnight. I'm only one man, and now I have a war to oversee as well."

The first man's seething voice filled all corners of the chamber. "This war is part of the problem. Shiraz wouldn't even be a concern if you'd already signed the agreement with—"

"*That* cannot happen while Deegan remains in line for the throne and Koal continues to sit on the council."

Chairs scraped across the stone floor below as the two men sat at the table. Kirk did his best not to squirm. Were they getting out the crates? Would they notice the files had been pawed through?

"Well, out with it already, Neetra! What of Morathi's latest report?"

"I received word the army will approach the border any day now. It would seem they're on schedule, despite the added burden of the women who turned down the pardon."

"An embarrassment to our country! We had an agreement the women soldiers wouldn't march. They'll only weaken our ranks and provide opportunity for the enemy to strike us down."

Neetra let out a sniveling groan. "There wasn't time to have the law overturned. You know as well as I do, Anders. I did what I could, given time constraints, by offering the pardon."

"Morathi is livid. His humiliation will come at a high cost."

"Morathi has his own charges to worry about while he's gone. If he wants the threat of Radek rule eliminated then he knows what must be done."

"No easy task with your brother underfoot! For all your promises of swift action, your weakness still shows through so long as Koal remains seneschal."

Neetra took his time responding. "There is a specific plan of action. There always has been. Upsetting the plan now could have harsh repercussions. There's only so much I can do without Koal figuring it out, and if that happens, we run the risk of him rallying the outlier councilors. Like it or not, he still holds a certain amount of power in this chamber."

"Then maybe we need to alter our course of action. Arden is in chaos! Soon all the women will be in power and men will be running around in skirts. The lowborns will make the laws and respectable lords will be forced out of their homes! There'll be no order. You have to do something!"

Kirk clamped his mouth shut to avoid voicing indignation. Beside him, Marc rolled his eyes, and when his somber gaze met Kirk's, the young mage could tell the dean shared Kirk's sentiment. He had heard stories,

106

mostly from Joel, about this High Councilor Anders Malin-Rai, and apparently every word of it was true.

A small opening between the chair legs afforded Kirk a glimpse of the men below. Neetra scowled and stuck his pointed nose into the air. "You worry too much. It just so happens that I have my advisers looking over the laws now. Surely there will be something in there to correct all of this trouble Rishi Radek introduced."

Anders slammed a fist on the tabletop. "That idiot *changed* the laws! He didn't simply look the other way—"

"I tell you, your fretting is for naught. Soon there'll be secrets coming to light which will discredit Radek for good. The dead king's monsters will be his undoing. Once the people of Arden know how badly they've all been deceived, there'll be no fighting the move to go back to our old ways—before the crown was ever placed on a foreign head."

Kirk dared glance at his comrades. What did Neetra mean? What secrets had the King been keeping?

Otho's furrowed brow indicated confusion, but Marc's face had gone alabaster white. Kirk reached for the dean without thinking, only to be scolded by a single shake of the head.

"In the meantime," Neetra said, "keep me informed about what the councilors disapprove of most, and I'll see that arrangements are made to sate them."

Anders pushed his chair away from the table. "Fine. I have to go now anyway. I still haven't had time to clear all of my things from my office at Academy."

"Yes, yes. Go get your belongings so no one will know how much whiskey you required to get through a day of teaching."

"Don't preach to me, Neetra Adelwijn. I'm no fool. Your monsters could be your undoing just as easily as Radek's will be his."

Neetra leapt to his feet and rushed to catch Anders. Kirk couldn't see the Steward's face, but his stride suggested nothing less than fury. A moment later the door slammed shut and the key rasped for a second time. Neetra's shrill yell could be heard echoing down the outer corridor as the two men retreated.

Kirk exhaled. Was it possible he'd been holding his breath throughout the entire encounter? His lungs burned as though they were engulfed in flames, and his stomach felt knotted and unsettled. But at least he was safe. For the moment, they hadn't been caught.

Otho was the first to move, all but jumping to his feet. "What the hell was *that* about?"

Kirk set one hand on the chair ahead as he rose, using the object to steady his shaking knees. "What were they talking about? What secrets was the King keeping?"

Marc refused to meet either of the underling's expectant gazes. In four strides, he'd reached the balcony door and was ushering Kirk and Otho through. "We have to go to the royal suite. *Now.*"

A stiff breeze blew from the courtyard below. Diddy lifted his nose to the air, a frown tugging at the corner of his mouth. Did he smell smoke or was his troubled mind playing tricks on him again? A deep foreboding had taken up permanent residence in his heart, and he could no longer discern whether the frequent harbingers of doom were real or merely figments of his imagination.

"Ya ever smile anymore?"

Diddy jumped, startled, and spun around to face his stealthy guest. "Aodan! You nearly stopped my heart. Were you spying on me?" He tried to laugh at his own joke but couldn't muster the strength.

Aodan sat upon the marble railing and swung both legs over the edge, allowing his boots to dangle precariously. The overcast sky threw shadows across the bodyguard's grave features and sought to dampen the smoldering embers in his single eye, but the stubborn set of his jaw proved he wasn't ready to quit fighting just yet—but he looked so damned tired.

"Yer on *my* balcony. Trespassing, really."

"I'll smile when you do. Father would want you to smile again."

"Diddy," Aodan warned. "Stop."

Diddy clenched both hands around the stone balustrade and glared into the royal courtyard far below. "So this is it, then? Are we never going to speak of him again? Are we simply going to pretend he never existed?"

Letting out a groan, Aodan turned his back to Diddy. The pair lapsed into angry silence for a time, neither man willing to apologize first, until Diddy's anger lost its bitter edge and he finally conceded.

"I'm sorry. I didn't mean to push you. It's just that—don't you ever miss him?"

Aodan whipped around so fast Diddy reached for the bodyguard, fearing he might fall to his death, despite the impossibility of such a thing. The pain etched across his weary face made Diddy recoil. Had he pushed Aodan too far this time?

"Do I *ever miss him*?" Aodan threw his hands into the air. "*I'm* the one who failed him! And now look at what's happening! That clown's on the throne, and Deegan's in the direct path of harm. Not to mention so are Koal, Hasain, and Tular! And all the while, I'm trapped here in this stone cage. So much fer my vows! I might as well be *dead.*"

"Don't say such things! Mother and Gudrin need you—especially Guddy. What would she do without you? Aodan, we love you. You know that, don't you?"

"Aye. A bunch of fools, the lot of you."

Diddy's response was cut short when Gudrin scampered onto the balcony.

"Marc's here!" the princess chirped. "NezReth is letting him in!"

Aodan was on his feet and rushing through the open doorway before Diddy could even get his scattered thoughts together. Pushing down feelings of dread, he hoped against hope for good news. Perhaps Marc had found something useful to use against Neetra. Maybe they wouldn't have to take the next—and much more risky—step. Absently, Diddy slipped a hand into his pocket, clenching the cold, iron key within.

"Come on!" Gudrin yanked so hard on his arm Diddy swore he heard his elbow pop. "Let's go."

"Guddy," he scolded without any real conviction. "Be careful."

Gudrin gazed up at him with large, remorseful eyes, and with a sigh, Diddy patted her shoulder, unable to truly be upset. It wasn't her fault she often forgot her own strength. She was only a little girl, after all. Diddy couldn't imagine what it must be like to have to hide all the time.

Beyond the terrace, Diddy heard the thump of a door closing as, presumably, Marc was ushered inside. Voices spoke back and forth in the receiving room. Diddy couldn't make out Marc's words, but the dean's tone suggested urgency.

Gudrin tilted her head to one side, listening. "Something about Neetra. Something bad."

Diddy took a deep breath, preparing himself for the worst, and together, he and Gudrin went to see what news their ally had brought.

Inside the suite, both NezReth and Aodan stood before a *very* flustered Marc. The dean's disheveled hair and pallid complexion seemed proof enough that something was wrong. Diddy's thoughts immediately flew to his younger brother, hundreds of leagues away by now. Had Marc received news about Deegan? Had something happened to him?

"I'm telling you," Marc gasped. "This is serious. I didn't have time to leave them behind!"

Them?

Diddy blinked as he noticed for the first time that Marc's underlings, Kirk and Otho, stood just inside the door. Instinctively, his grip tightened around Gudrin's hand. What were they doing here? Surely they weren't trusted wholly yet—especially the Imperial mage. Had Marc gone completely mad? Why had he brought them here?

"This is a most serious breach of protocol, Marc," NezReth said. "Your underlings shouldn't be here."

"They're our allies, NezReth. Kirk helped you escape Teivel, and we've all known Otho since he was a child. Besides, they overheard the exact same thing as I. They just don't understand the full implication. There's no reason not to trust them."

"Aye?" Aodan strode back and forth across the suite, never once taking his fierce gaze off Marc. "Because it's not like anything suspicious has come to pass since the arrival of the Imperial."

"Joel entrusted Kirk to me. *Joel Adelwijn.* You know him as well as I do."

Aodan's voice climbed higher. "Joel is a whelp, barely outgrown his milk teeth. I have no question about Joel's heart, but his judgment is lacking."

"Enough." It was Dahlia who finally put an end to the argument. She sat upon a lounge near the back of the suite, barely more than a shadow herself. Diddy often worried for her. His mother's health had been on a steady decline since the King's death.

"They're already here," the Queen Mother continued. "They've already passed through the checkpoints. Will it not look more suspicious if they leave on their own, and so soon? As it is, Neetra will surely pay us a visit later, anyway, to inquire about our company, so let's make this meeting worth the scrutiny, shall we?"

Letting out a frustrated huff, Aodan slumped down onto the lounge beside Dahlia, but Diddy remained unconvinced. He watched the two underlings with a shrewd eye. They hadn't even bothered to remove their boots by the door. Proper form told him to stay quiet, but he so badly wanted to speak up and demand they follow the rules.

"All right," Aodan said, folding his arms over his chest. "Out with it then. Why are ya here?"

Marc's hands trembled as he spoke. "There was an opportunity today to get into the empty council room. The three of us snuck inside and went through the documentation kept there, looking for anything that might help us prove Neetra's election was rigged."

Dahlia's voice lifted. "Any luck?" It was the first time Diddy could recall his mother sounding optimistic since Rishi's death.

Marc waved a hand, dismissing—and likely dashing—her hope. "Some, but that's not what this is about. While we were there, Neetra and Anders Malin-Rai came into the chamber. We weren't caught. We managed to put everything back and hide up in the balcony before they got the door unlocked, but we overheard some troubling news."

Marc hesitated, almost as if it pained him to continue, but Dahlia pressed him for more. "Tell us what you heard, Marc."

"Anders was complaining that there are men on the council who are displeased with Neetra for not making radical change happen sooner. He said Neetra was going to have hell to pay if he couldn't get the results the others were looking for. And that's when Neetra said something along the lines of "Morathi has his own charges. If he doesn't want a Radek to rule then he needs to take action.""

Aodan recoiled as if he'd just received a slap across the face. "*What?*"

"There's more. He also said something like, "the dead king's monsters will be his undoing. When everyone knows how badly the country has been deceived by the Radek bloodline, the people will embrace a new ruler." I think Neetra means to discredit Rishi. It sounds like he knows more than he should."

Diddy's heart pounded as he clutched his sister's hand. Did Neetra suspect the truth? Their family secrets had always been wrapped tight, but there were never any guarantees someone wouldn't figure everything out, no matter how careful they tried to be.

In the window, Dahlia gasped. Aodan held her against his shoulder. "What do we do now? We can't just let the bastard take the next step!"

NezReth had already crossed the suite and was pulling parchment and ink from inside a writing desk. "Koal needs to be notified. Immediately. He will keep Deegan safe."

"That's not good enough!" Aodan jumped to his feet once more, pacing as frantically as a captive animal. "I should just go out there with 'em. I could be there in two days, maybe less depending on how far they've gotten."

"You can't do it, Aodan," Marc protested. "They're close to the border. You'd be exhausted. And you'd have no reason to be there—no logical excuse for how you arrived so quickly without being ported. Morathi would report back to Neetra. They'd know something was amiss, and he'd send someone after you. You'd be too tired to defend yourself, let alone Deegan and the others. You'd only be putting them at greater risk."

"I can't just sit here on my arse and do nothing!"

"You can't go."

Aodan growled, a low, dreadful sound that filled the entire room. Diddy braced himself. Aodan wouldn't forsake his secret now, would he?

Out of the corner of his eye, Diddy watched the Imperial mage draw a sharp breath and back clumsily toward the door. Otho grasped the empty space at his waist where a hilt would lie, had he been carrying a sword. Diddy's heart ached within his chest. Was this all there was left for his family? Suspicion? Distrust? Hatred?

Marc waved both hands in the air. "Calm down, Aodan. Look, I'm just trying to help you. You have to trust me."

Diddy bit his lip and could feel Gudrin's hand tremble beneath his own. Both siblings knew even before Aodan lost his tentative grip on control that Marc had pushed the bodyguard too far.

Crimson from head to toe, Aodan whirled toward Marc, pointing savagely at the dean. "Rishi trusted you too! He trusted you right up until ya helped him for the final time! I don't know how much more of your *help* this family or country can stand!"

"Aodan!" Dahlia gasped.

If Aodan heard her, he pretended he hadn't. Diddy was glad for it.

His mother meant well, but it was high time someone said the truth, wasn't it? For all of Marc's good intentions, he fell terribly short when it came to actually being helpful.

The dean looked like he might curl up and die right then and there—and it would have been a lie to say Diddy didn't enjoy the possibility at all. A part of him knew, deep down, Marc had never intended to hurt Rishi, but intentions aside, the king was dead because of Marc's lapse in judgment.

Marc stared into the distance, as if he could see something the others couldn't, and a tear slipped down his cheek without hindrance. "You know I didn't mean for anything to happen to Rishi, don't you? I would *never* intentionally harm him."

Aodan's expression twisted back and forth between rage and sorrow. "Intentional or not, ya killed him. He *trusted* you and you *failed* him!"

"I've apologized. I've said it over and over again until I'm blue in the face. I can't take back what happened. Don't you know I wish I could? I wish *every day* I could go back to that moment and realize what was in the vial before I gave it to him. It should have been a remedy for the flu. I don't know how—"

"It doesn't matter how! It was your job to check the damned thing before ya gave it to him!"

"*I know!*" Tears streamed down Marc's cheeks. "I know I failed him! I know no amount of apologizing can ever undo what I've done but *please*—Aodan, we were friends once. We're still friends, aren't we?"

Aodan's hands balled into fists. "No, we're not *friends*! How can ya even ask? What makes ya think I could ever forgive something like this? I can't pretend everything's goin' to be all right! Nothing will ever be all right again."

The bodyguard stormed into the deeper recesses of the suite, and Gudrin released Diddy's hand to give chase. A wave of conflicting emotions washed over him. He didn't know how to feel. Victory because someone had finally voiced what he'd wanted to for so long? Shame for not saying it himself? Or sorrow? His father never would have wanted them to be fighting so viciously among themselves.

Dahlia approached Marc with open arms. He didn't fight the embrace, collapsing against her shoulder.

More irrational anger stole over Diddy. His mother and Marc looked wrong together. He couldn't stomach the thought of it.

"He's in pain, Marc," Dahlia murmured. Diddy could only just make out her words. "Don't think he's truly so angry with you."

Marc shook his head. "I can't fix this. I'm trying, but I just can't. Koal should be here. He could make everything right."

"Koal has always depended on your help. You have a job to do while he's gone."

"What if I can't do it? What if I make things worse?"

"I have faith in you. I know you can do this. Koal trusts you. Rishi trusted you, too. What happened could have been blamed on anyone."

Diddy knew her words were the truth, even if he didn't want to hear it. Deep in his heart, in the place he was desperately trying to ignore until the pain lessened, he knew Marc wasn't really at fault. The dean had been framed. He'd been a victim, the same as Rishi. It just seemed easier to be angry than to face the truth.

Marc wiped a palm across his damp cheeks, looking haggard and defeated. "What else would you have me do?"

Diddy slipped a hand into his pocket. The key inside felt unnaturally heavy, a burden no one should have to bear. Bailey had managed to sneak it to the royal suite earlier that day. Aodan refused to even touch it, claiming he didn't want the steward's stench to rub off on him.

With his arm outstretched, Diddy crossed the room. "Bailey left this for you."

Tears ran dry and were forgotten the instant the key switched hands. Marc turned the object over in his fingers, examining it narrowly. "Is this—?"

"Neetra's. Yes." Diddy risked a quick glance at Kirk and Otho. He still wasn't sure whether or not he could trust them, but perhaps this would be an opportunity for them to prove their loyalty. "While my uncle is in council, perhaps you can have your underlings comb through his things. If he's hiding something, there's a good chance you'll find it there."

Otho made a sour face and crossed his arms over his chest. "Neetra's quarters will be well guarded. A key won't do us any good if we can't even get to the door to use it. How do you propose we get around his sentries?"

An artful smile crept upon Diddy's face. "I'll show you."

113

CHAPTER EIGHT

The tree must have fallen recently. Small leaves clung to its spindly branches, still alive but beginning to curl, showing the first telltale signs of withering.

Liza Nemesio slid from her saddle and approached the dying tree. Burls jutted out along the downed shaft like bubbles made from wood, but even so, the gnarled trunk would still make for a better seat than the ground. She let Lilly's reins loose. The mare had been trained not to wander, and Liza rarely worried about the horse spooking anymore. In her advancing age, there wasn't a whole lot that could startle the old girl.

Pulling a ration of dried meat and crackers from within her bag, Liza flopped down and began to eat. Lilly nibbled at the leaves nearby, silver tail swishing back and forth behind her as she, too, enjoyed a reprieve from traveling.

The troop had stopped for a quick rest to water the horses and scarf down their midday meals. They were on schedule so that, by evening, they'd be housed and fed in Ashvale. Liza couldn't deny she was excited at the prospect. Maybe she'd even get a real bed. She couldn't remember the last time she'd slept on anything besides a mat.

Ah, in Ostlea we had cots. Still not the same as a bed, though, and horribly drafty.

Liza ripped a morsel of meat free from the larger chunk and popped it into her mouth.

Either way, I don't think sleep would have come any easier. Not with our fingers and toes turning into icicles. The cold was more dangerous than anything coming down from Nales.

Here in the south, a nasty bout of sunstroke stood just as likely a chance of killing a person as a Shirite brigand. Liza's troop had faced both already. They'd spent an entire wheelturn in Winterdell, the northernmost township on Arden's eastern border, in the shadows beneath the Pinnacles, where the summer heat scorched the ground and the winters were cold enough to freeze limbs solid. They'd lost two men to the elements, and another two when the Shirites had attacked Winterdell's ramparts. Liza hadn't told her brothers about it, though none of them ever asked either. She was glad for it. She didn't want them worrying about her. She worried enough for the entire family.

Liza wished above all else that her brothers remained out of harm's reach, but it was a futile dream. The boys were growing up. Even now, Gib waited with the rest of the army in Perth, protected for the moment, but only a dozen leagues from Shiraz. Tayver and Calisto were in Silver, yet both were young men in their own right. Once, it'd been her responsibility to shelter them from the many evils of the world. Now she could only watch as they made their own way. The feeling was bittersweet.

Appetite suddenly gone, Liza stowed away the rest of her meal and set her rucksack aside. With a heavy sigh, she leaned back, pressing her palms against the downed tree for balance. Coarse, rigid bark stung her calloused fingers, as though the tree, doomed as it was, continued to fight for its life. Liza found herself staring down at it with remorseful eyes.

The ancient ironwood had likely seen better days, days of amity and prosperity, before bloodshed ravaged the countryside. Steadfast in its vigil over the land, it had surely watched villages rise and crumble and people live and die. It saw the shattering of peace—the beginning of the war. Now, with its severed trunk lying flat against the earth and roots torn from the soil, it likely wouldn't see the end.

Liza's stomach twisted into knots.

With any luck, our fate won't be the same. Hopefully we will see the end of this war.

Brisk footsteps caught her attention, pulling her back to the present. Liza lifted her face and smiled at the newcomer: a young, reedy girl with expressive hazel eyes and hair that was sheared close to her skull. She was one of the scouts, not a member of the longstanding troop. Liza didn't know her name, and even though they'd been traveling together since the previous afternoon, they hadn't spoken before now.

"You're Gib's sister, aren't you?" the girl asked.

Liza began to rise, but the girl motioned for her to remain seated, so Liza extended one hand for a shake instead. "That's right. I'm Liza Nemesio."

"Well met. I'm Gara Leal. My sister's fiancé, Nage Nessuno, is Gib's friend from Academy."

"Oh, right." Liza scooted farther down the log, allowing room for Gara to sit. "Please, have a seat if you'd like."

A smile spread across Gara's round face as she plopped down. "You and Gib look so much alike that I just *knew* you had to be the sister he talks about all the time."

Liza chuckled. "My three brothers and I *all* look alike. The same damn unruly curls cursed the whole lot of us. A gift from our mother."

"My sister and I both take after our father. When I cut my hair short, Da jokingly said looking at me was like staring into a mirror—" Gara paused as her bottom lip quivered. She quickly turned her face away. "Sorry. He was killed this past winter. It's still hard to speak of him."

115

A terrible ache seized Liza's heart. She knew all too well what the young girl must have been going through. "My deepest condolences to you and yours. My own father died unexpectedly several wheelturns ago, so I understand."

"I know. Gib told me." Gara raised her face. Her tiny hands continued to tremble in her lap, but for the most part, she seemed to have recomposed herself. "He and I talk sometimes, when we've stopped for the evening. I could be in the worst mood, yet he somehow always manages to make me feel better. Now I know why his friends speak so highly of him. He's been a lot of help these past two moonturns."

"That's Gib. Always helping. He's possibly the most selfless person I know."

"His is such an inspiring story. To come from where he did, to beat the odds and find himself in Seneschal Koal's good favor. You must be very proud of him."

"I am. I can't ever say it enough."

Liza smiled sadly, wishing her parents were here to see them now. The boys had been too young to remember their mother, but Liza remembered. She remembered her mother's sweet voice as she comforted Liza during a storm, or the time when she'd scraped an elbow falling from a fencepost and her mother had cradled Liza while she cried. Without a doubt, Holda's gentle heart and forgiving soul had been passed onto the children. Liza could see it in the boys and even in herself. Their blind bravery and stubborn streak, though, came from their father. A part of Jakeob Nemesio would always survive so long as the family kept fighting for what they believed in.

What might their parents say, now that the children were grown? Surely they'd be proud of Gib graduating from Academy. They'd likely praise Tayver's talent for sewing and be happy to see how well Calisto could read.

Liza frowned. Would they be proud of her? She'd done all she could to provide for the family. She'd raised the boys as best as she knew how. She'd tried to teach them the lessons of their parents: that hard work and determination would always be rewarded and love was greater than any amount of gold. She'd given her brothers the best chance she could.

Her heart panged. She would have given anything in that moment just to know if she'd made her parents proud.

Gara hopped to her feet. "Well, I better go. Rocelin and I are going to scout ahead. We'll make sure there's a hot meal waiting for you in Ashvale when you arrive."

"How much farther do you think we have?"

"Not far at all, according to the map. You should be passing over the bridge at Kaleth's Crossing within a mark. Ashvale's a league away once you're across the Nishika."

"That's good to hear."

Gara gave a little bow. "It was a pleasure to finally meet you, Liza Nemesio."

The scout began to leave, but as she passed, Liza's sisterly instinct got the best of her. Her hand shot out to grab Gara's forearm. "Hey, stay careful out there. Be on the lookout for trouble."

Brushing a hand over the sheath fastened at her waist, Gara nodded stiffly. "I will."

Liza waited until Gara's slight form disappeared beyond the rest of the soldiers before taking hold of Lilly's reins. "Come on, old girl. Let's get you a drink before we have to leave."

She led the mare toward the riverbank. Lilly followed at her side like an obedient puppy, ears flicking forward as the soft trickle of running water reached them. A moment later, she tossed her head like a rowdy yearling and trotted the last few steps to the river's edge. Liza chuckled, watching Lilly all but bury her face in the clear water.

Liza stroked the horse's silver neck as she drank, reflecting on all they had been through together. Lilly had been a good and loyal steed over the years. Together, they'd traveled to all corners of Arden. But Lilly was getting old. She deserved to spend her remaining years grazing happily in a pasture, not risking life and limb on the battlefield. Liza wished she could keep Lilly by her side forever, but it just wasn't fair to the horse.

When we return to Silver, I'll find you a wonderful home, Liza promised.

She gave the mare's shoulder a pat and then said aloud, "We'll get through this last mission and then you can rest. Daya knows you deserve it, old girl."

Lilly raised her head, as though she might be considering Liza's words, but then her nostrils flared and her round eyes shot toward the far side of the river. Liza instinctively reached for her sword, still tethered to Lilly's saddle.

With eyes narrowed against the blinding afternoon sun, she searched for what might have caught Lilly's attention but could see nothing. Just an endless sea of dirt and dried grass. Her hand slipped from the gilded hilt.

Odd. What could have startled her?

"Ay-up, Liza!" a chipper voice called from over her shoulder.

Liza pivoted. "Daya, Brim! Don't sneak up on me like that!"

Her good friend and fellow soldier, Brimsley, trotted closer, grinning like a fiend. He waved a wineskin at her. "Thirsty?"

"A little early in the day to be drinking hard liquor, don't you think?"

Brim arched one bushy eyebrow. "Do you take me for a fool? The captain would have my head if he caught me gettin' drunk on duty. It's water, I swear."

Liza took the leather canteen, though she sniffed its contents before taking a drink. Brim was known to be a bit of a prankster. Liza had no intention of falling for one of his wiles now.

This time, he hadn't been joking. Cool, fresh water brought needed relief to her dry tongue and parched lips. With a sigh, she returned the container. "Thanks. I needed that."

Brim nodded as he raised the wineskin to his own mouth and took a long swig. "We're gettin' ready to head out soon. The scouts say the bridge ain't too far from here."

Liza watched Lilly out of the corner of one eye. Whatever had held the mare enthralled moments before must have passed, for Lilly's attention had already drifted. She now nibbled at the sparse reeds that grew in the shallow water, tail swishing back and forth as though nothing had even happened. A bit of the tension left Liza's shoulders. It must have been nothing—a bird or insect or even a blade of grass blowing in the wind.

"Captain Brishen's requestin' a word with you." Brim waggled his brows, smiling slyly. "Maybe it's something to do with a certain promotion someone's been deservin'."

"Oh, stop. There are plenty of people who deserve it other than I."

"You need to stop being so modest, my friend. There ain't anyone else in this troop who's as dedicated. *You* deserve to be captain."

Liza shook her head. It was no secret Captain Brishen was planning his retirement, but true to Liza's humble nature, she refused to think she had any chance of succeeding him. Despite being allowed into the military, she'd yet to hear of *any* women earning a promotion within the ranks. Especially a rank as lofty as captain.

"You really think this country is ready for such a thing? A woman, wearing the red cape of the captain and giving orders to men?"

Brim shrugged. "Ready or not, the moment's upon us." Liza shot him a skeptical glance, to which Brim only chuckled and added, "Just you wait an' see. You're destined for greatness, Liza Nemesio!"

Liza's mouth twitched upward, dangerously close to something that resembled a smile. Whether or not she was "destined" for a promotion, she appreciated Brimsley's enthusiasm and his support.

Liza found Captain Brishen near the outskirts of the encampment. He perched atop a saddlebag, using it as a cushion to rest upon as he ate his midday meal. Mage Yama, a former professor at Academy who'd been reassigned to travel with the troop around the same time as Liza, stood beside the captain. His long, snowy hair matched the hue of his mage robes perfectly. Likewise, Captain Brishen's silver uniform seemed like it had been tailored to complement his greying beard and hair, though Liza knew the man was far too practical to be concerned with such a thing.

The two men conversed in muted voices but quieted when Liza's shadow fell across them. Liza inclined her head, hoping she wasn't interrupting anything important. "I don't mean to impose, but you wanted to see me, sir?"

For a pause, neither man said anything, but then Yama bowed hastily to the captain and excused himself. "I'll give the order to move out, Captain."

In a whirl of white robes and flowing hair, he departed. Liza couldn't be sure, but she thought the mage might have even winked at her as he passed by.

Captain Brishen beckoned with one calloused hand for her to approach. "Liza Nemesio, I was hoping you and I might have a word."

She gained no insight from his impeccably neutral words. Captain Brishen had always been difficult to read. Even now, as his sharp eyes studied her, Liza had no inkling what he might be thinking. He would have made an excellent politician, had he not joined Arden's military.

"Yes, sir," she replied, shuffling closer. "Of course we can."

"Good. Very good. Tell me, how are you?"

Liza blinked. That seemed an odd question. "Fair enough, sir, given that we're at war. It's different than being stationed in one place, but I think I've adjusted as well as can be expected. We all have."

"Aye, we have." The captain chuckled. "I don't think I've spent this much time in a saddle since the Northern War. And back then, in my youth, I didn't have to worry so much about creaking bones and swollen feet. I suspect you were too young to remember much of the Northern War, aye?"

"I wasn't even born yet, sir. My parents wouldn't get married for another two years after the war ended. They told me stories though, of course. My father lost his elder brother. He would have been about the age I am now when he died."

"I, too, had a brother fall during the war. Two years younger than I. He wasn't even drafted like so many unlucky men. The brave fool volunteered." Captain Brishen shook his head. "He didn't even survive a full moonturn on the front."

The story hit home. If anything happened to Gib, Liza didn't know what she'd ever do. Struggling to keep her voice steady, she let out a sigh. "My little brother is with the army in Perth."

"I'm sorry to hear that. I know not a single soul who doesn't have stakes in this war, whether they themselves have been called to arms or a loved one has. No one's immune to it. No one can escape it. You must be worried about your brother."

"Every waking moment, sir," Liza answered honestly. "I don't fear for my own safety nearly as much as I do his."

"I wish I could tell you it gets easier, but it doesn't."

"I've been suspecting that's the case for some time now. But really, is anything in life ever easy? I'm no stranger to adversity, and neither is my brother. Our family's been through a lot. We've seen our share of hardships and heartbreak, but we've always managed to pull through. Strife is a two-sided blade, after all. It can break a person down, yes, but it can also make them stronger. If we'd never known struggle, we wouldn't have the strength to make it through this war now."

"Such wisdom from one so young. You continue to impress, Liza Nemesio."

The captain ran his fingers through his grey hair, and it dawned on Liza just how much he'd aged since she'd first joined the troop. His hair had been a rusty brown back then, with only the slightest peppering at his temples. It seemed ironic that he'd grown so old, yet Liza often felt like the same, timid youth from years past. Had so much time really gone by?

Captain Brishen measured Liza with astute eyes. "What are your plans after this war is done? After your tenure is over? Are you going to leave the military?"

"And do what?"

"Perhaps you'd like to get married? Have children?"

Liza held back the urge to laugh. "I've never been one to fit into societal molds. And truth be told, I don't think I'd make a very good housewife. I know how to swing a sword, repair armor, and assemble horse tack. What good would any of those skills do me in the kitchen? I'm more suited for a soldier's life. It's what I know."

"Aye, but is it what you *want*? You joined the army out of necessity because you had no other choice. It was a means to provide for your family. Now that your brothers are grown—able to care for themselves—what keeps you here?"

Liza took her time responding. She'd never dedicated much thought to *why* she stayed; it was just something in her heart Liza felt was right. A feeling of duty and of pride.

At last, she said, "What keeps me here, sir? Loyalty to Arden, I suppose. The desire to protect the people I love and defend those whose names I don't even know. Justice for my father. A sense of pride. Not every man or woman is courageous enough to risk their life for their country. I've found myself in good company, amongst the bravest of the brave. Being a sentinel of Arden is an honor, a privilege, and I'll continue to fight for her until age rends me unable or death takes me."

Captain Brishen nodded with approval. "Spoken like a true warrior." With no small effort, he climbed to his feet, his right leg stiff and sluggish to bend. He hoisted the saddlebag he'd been using as a cushion into his arms and made a point to turn his back as he secured the sack to his white palfrey's saddle. "I'm ashamed to admit I had my doubts when King Rishi passed the law allowing women into our ranks. I believed they didn't have the strength to wield a weapon nor the ability to keep their wits about them in the heat of battle. You, of course, proved me a fool."

"Not a fool, sir. Naïve, perhaps, but never a fool."

"No need to mince words. The truth is clear. I was wrong."

"You weren't alone in your assumptions. Many felt the same as you." Liza winced and then added, "Many still do."

An artful grin crept onto Captain Brishen's lips. "I'd say anyone who doubts a woman's ability to fight should be forced to spend a wheelturn on the border with one like you. I dare say their opinion would change rather swiftly."

Liza didn't know what to say, so she simply smiled.

Clearing his throat, the captain turned fully around. Sharp, gauging eyes fixed onto Liza, and she held her breath, knowing whatever he planned to say next would be important.

"Perhaps it's time for another first—something to *really* give our good steward Neetra Adelwijn reason to whine about."

Behind them, Yama's crisp voice raised above the din as he relayed the order to move out. Liza could hear the bustle as men hastily gathered their belongings and climbed into their saddles.

Captain Brishen must have also heard, but he didn't budge. "As you're probably well aware by now, this campaign is to be my last. After the war, I have every intention of returning to Silver and never leaving again, living out my remaining days lounging on velvet pillows, with Healers doting on me and good wine and food only a cook's order away. I dare say I deserve as much, after thirty-five years of service."

Liza laughed. "You do, sir."

"Of course, that leaves my post vacant. And I've never been much for politics. I *could* save myself a headache and let General Morathi fill the position after I'm gone—"

Liza's grip tightened around Lilly's braided reins. If the decision was left to the general, she wouldn't only miss an opportunity for a promotion—she'd likely be at risk of losing her job completely. The Two only knew what kind of arrogant dog Morathi would appoint. Liza bit her tongue, suppressing the urge to voice her opinion aloud.

"But," Captain Brishen continued, "truth be told, I never cared for the man. He would likely assign one of his pompous underlings, fresh out of Academy—someone with no inkling of battle and no respect for my men. No. I can't, in good conscience, allow that to happen." A defiant spark twinkled in his eyes. "Besides, I've known who I want to name as my successor for some time now."

"O–oh, sir?"

The captain crossed the space between them in a matter of seconds. Large, rough hands settled on Liza's shoulders, the weight nearly crushing her. "You, Liza. You will replace me."

Even though she'd been informed Brishen might choose her, the news still hit her like a club to the head. Liza's immediate reaction was to

121

refuse. He couldn't be serious. She wasn't cut out for something like this! Yes, she enjoyed being a soldier—she was even good at her job—but she couldn't *lead* others. Could she?

Liza struggled to form coherent words against her trembling lips. "But I—*me*, sir? Are you sure—"

"Before you start making excuses as to why you think you *can't* do the job, why don't you consider all the reasons you *can*? Tenacity, candor, wit—not to mention unwavering patience and loyalty—these are all qualities you possess that will serve you well. I've watched you step up and take the lead before, like you were born for the job. I haven't come to this decision lightly, and more so, I'm not just picking you as a means to ruffle feathers on the High Council. You really are the best suited, Liza."

"There will be resistance, sir. The law allowing women to serve in the military is still so new. One of us being promoted to captain is unprecedented."

"The men in our troop respect you. They'll follow your lead. As for the rest, they'll all too soon see how wrong they were to underestimate you."

Liza couldn't quite meet his gaze. "Do you really believe that, sir?"

"Aye. I do." Captain Brishen smiled slyly. "It appears you're out of excuses, so do me a favor—drop the modesty and accept my offer."

"I—" Liza's mouth fell open as she tried to come up with something to say, but she could think of no valid arguments to make. The captain spoke the truth. She *was* worthy. She *did* deserve the promotion. Yes, by accepting, she'd be welcoming adversity with open arms. General Morathi would protest, and likely the High Council, too. She'd never be free of the criticism or the blind animosity.

But nothing in life worth fighting for came easy. Hadn't her parents taught her as much? If she wanted the world to change then she had to stand up and seize this opportunity.

Swallowing her fears, Liza nodded stiffly. "All right, sir. I'll do it. I accept."

There. She'd said it. No going back.

"Very good. I think you've made the right decision. I'll make the announcement to the troop tonight. For now, we best get our arses into our saddles before they leave us behind."

Liza snickered. "I'd rather that *not* happen, sir." Grinning, she grasped the pommel of her saddle and prepared to swing onto Lilly's back. "Navigation in unknown lands is best left to the scouts—"

Suddenly, Lilly balked, the first indication something was wrong.

Liza barely had time to register that before a rogue shadow flicked across the ground—and then another—four, five, a dozen. Her head shot up.

What in the—

And then all hell broke loose. Liza gasped, staring in wide-eyed horror as a shower of arrows rained down onto the troop.

"*Ambush!*" Captain Brishen hollered, diving for his shield. "We're under attack!"

Liza instinctively reached for her own weapon, pulling the sword free from its sheath. An arrow whizzed past her face, so close she could feel the cold air graze her cheek. A second shaft skidded through the dirt beneath Lilly's hooves. The mare reared, letting out a frightened whicker, while Liza fumbled to unclasp her shield from Lilly's saddle. A terrible melody of angry screams rang in her ears—the sounds of her comrades wailing in pain as they were struck by arrows.

The shield finally slipped free. Liza clutched the metal slab against her body and whirled around, getting her first look at the enemy. Her blood ran cold.

Goddesses, help us.

Shirite fighters swarmed the opposing riverbank like a hive of angry wasps, their enraged battle cries filling the air. Bowmen two rows thick kneeled at the cusp of the hill, releasing one deadly volley of arrows after another. Even more soldiers massed behind them, waving cutlasses and sharpened pikes above their heads. Liza couldn't count them all.

"To me!" Captain Brishen shouted above the tumult. "Soldiers, to me!"

Liza dashed to his side without hesitation, hearing the telltale tick of arrows as they pelted her shield. The rest of the troop—those still able—were also fighting to make their way to the captain. Liza's stomach churned when she realized they were stumbling over the bodies of their fallen comrades.

Mage Yama reached Liza and Captain Brishen first. One sleeve of the mage's robe was shredded, and crimson blood seeped from a gash beneath the silver fabric, but he didn't even seem to notice. Hazy light engulfed his gnarled, outstretched hands, and even as Liza watched, some of the enemy arrows exploded into balls of cerulean flame, disintegrating in the air before they could reach their targets. *Some.* But not all. Not every arrow could be stopped.

"They have a mage with them," Yama hissed as he crouched between Liza and the captain. "The damn mage cloaked their approach!"

Blood roared in Liza's ears; she could barely decipher the mage's words above the noise. Cloaked? By some kind of magic?

Captain Brishen peered through a tiny gap between his shield and Liza's. "Only one?"

"Yes," Yama replied. "He's in the back. I can feel his magic, but I can't target him. He's too well protected. I've shielded our forces against his attacks, but deflecting any more arrows will drain my energy even faster—"

The captain gritted his teeth. "You worry about the mage and leave the archers to us."

More Ardenian soldiers were rallying now, lifting their shields to create a blockade against the enemy onslaught. Liza caught sight of Brimsley farther down the line. His mouth drew into a grimace as he worked to span a crossbow. Three other men were also pulling back the strings on their bows. Liza wished like hell she had a ranged weapon.

"Shoot the archers!" Captain Brishen bellowed. "Bring them down!"

Brim took aim. His arrow shot off like a lightning bolt, whizzing across the Nishika. A shriek arose from the Shirite horde, and one of the enemy bowmen crumpled to the ground. Brim dropped to one knee, already reloading his crossbow. Another soldier darted above the barricade to take Brim's place. He, too, fired into the enemy line, and a second Shirite slumped forward, hands grasping at his spurting throat.

The enemy answered with a volley of their own, but now that the Ardenian soldiers were in formation, the arrows were mostly ineffective; the majority bounced harmlessly off the shield wall and skidded into the dirt. Arden's arrows, however, were finding their targets. With every round fired, more Shirite archers dropped, writhing and bleeding on the ground. Their final, gurgling screams made Liza shudder. How many of her own men lay dead or dying behind her?

The Shirites must have realized they'd lost the element of surprise. Already they seemed to be changing tactics. The bowmen fell back, outranging Arden's crossbows, and the more heavily-armored foot soldiers ran forward. Brim shot one down, two, and three—but for every man who collapsed, more jumped to fill the empty space.

We're outnumbered. So terribly outnumbered.

Hopelessness tore at Liza's chest, but she refused to give in to despair.

She watched in horror as the Shirite footmen rushed into the Nishika. Their iron helmets and weapon points gleamed as they splashed through the waist-deep water, surging with deadly precision toward the Ardenian side of the river.

Captain Brishen readied his sword. "Prepare to engage!"

Liza crouched low, every muscle afire. Adrenaline pumped through her veins, thrumming in her head and sending electric tingles from her toes all the way to her fingertips. Around her, soldiers chanted, their rallying cry one and the same. *"For Arden! For Arden!"*

Liza lifted her own voice, joining them. A fire like none she'd ever known flared inside her, consuming her fear and invigorating her spirit. Live or die, she was ready to fight.

The Shirites had reached the shoreline. Water sloshed in their boots as they climbed, closer and closer. They were moments away, almost near enough to touch. Setting sights on the closest, Liza pulled back her sword and braced herself.

For Arden, and for my brothers!

In a blaze of steel and angry grunts, her blade crashed against the enemy's. The impact rattled her to the core, rocking her back several paces.

Liza scrambled sideways, barely avoiding a second blow, but already she was adjusting to her opponent's larger frame and weight.

The broad-shouldered footman stood at least a head taller than she, but Liza was far from helpless. She'd spent her entire career sparring against men twice her size. She just had to outsmart him.

Letting out a savage growl, Liza flung her shield at the man's face. The metal rim hit him square in the jaw. A wail erupted from his mouth as his bottom lip busted open, and on instinct, he cupped the oozing gash with his free hand. His eyes flitted away from Liza for only a split second—and she took full advantage of it.

In one clean sweep, Liza ran her sword through the weak armor just beneath the footman's arm. He went to his knees, flailing, screeching in pain. When Liza pulled the sword free of him, blood painted the blade crimson.

She pivoted away, a second Shirite already pushing over the crest of the hill and barreling toward her. This man was smaller, quicker, and likely just as nimble as Liza. They circled one another, a dance of deadly blades. Shield and weapon poised, Liza waited for him to make the first move.

The soldier lunged—he *was* fast—and Liza twisted just out of reach of his cutlass. She brought her sword down in a fury, catching him between the shoulder blades as he teetered past. Not a killing blow, but sufficient enough to disable him. Liza darted away, seeking another opponent.

The battle raged around her. Grunts, shouts, and guttering moans of agony filled her ears. Already, bodies scattered the riverbank, motionless, bloodied corpses in the dirt, Ardenian and Shirite alike. The sight only flamed Liza's bloodlust.

A wisp of red fabric flashed past the edge of her vision. Captain Brishen appeared beside her, his satin cape swirling as he engaged nearly a dozen enemy fighters. Gone was the aging man Liza had spoken to earlier. This man she barely recognized. Like a predator, he danced across the battlefield, movements precise and blows swift. With each strike of his sword, another enemy dropped to the ground.

Liza fell into place at his side, guarding his back even as he wordlessly did the same for her. Out of the corner of one eye, Liza saw Brim, bloodied but still fighting, and somewhere behind her, Liza could hear the crackle of lightning as Yama engaged the Shirite mage. United, their strength knew no limit. Together, they stood a chance.

Hope rekindled in Liza's heart.

We can overcome this! We can survive! I will live to see my brothers again—

And then Captain Brishen went down. One moment he'd been fighting, and in the next, he slumped to the dirt, grasping at the enemy blade now protruding from his throat. His mouth fell open, a silent scream upon his lips, his eyes wide and all pupil. One trembling, blood-soaked hand fumbled in vain to dislodge the weapon. The other hand valiantly gripped the hilt of his own sword. Even as he lay dying, the captain wasn't ready to give up.

Liza leapt to protect him, but she reacted a second too late. The Shirites had already caught the scent of fallen blood, and now they went in for the killing blow. With one adroit strike across the throat, Captain Brishen's troubles were over.

A cry tore loose from Liza's mouth.

No!

Tears stung at her eyes, but the sorrow was swiftly consumed by unbridled and terrifying rage, shaking her straight to the core and momentarily stealing her breath away. And then icy shock settled over her. She lunged forward, screaming, sword clashing against the closest enemy.

Battle trance seized hold of her body and numbed her mind until nothing was left but the primal urge to slay. Slash. Pivot. Slice. Dodge. Liza went through the motions like a puppet on strings. Lunge. Slam. Dash. She didn't think. She didn't feel. She simply reacted.

The Shirite soldiers were closing in around her. She couldn't see Brim anymore, and the sounds of Yama's magic had become lost to the drone of foreign shouts. She was alone, drowning in a sea of enemy greens and reds. Where were her comrades? Were none left?

Liza let out a moan as her shield was knocked away. She groped for it, but the metal wedge rolled out of her reach. She clutched her sword, now her only means of defense against the horde, and fought on. Pain shot up her leg and then across her side as blows landed in rapid succession against her leather armor, but she didn't stop. She refused to.

Keep fighting. Don't stop. Don't give up.

She cut down another man. And then another. An enemy shield slammed against the side of her face, the impact leaving her seeing stars. Hot blood trickled down her cheek and weariness racked her body, but still she didn't stop. The thought of leaving her brothers alone kept her afloat.

Don't give up. The boys still need you!

A sharp pressure burst between her shoulder blades and through her chest. Pain lanced her body, the agony like nothing she'd felt before. Liza gasped. She couldn't breathe! Why couldn't she get any air?

Her hands instinctively shot to her sternum, where a rigid edge jutted through a break in her armor. She ran a hand over the protrusion, shuddering when hot, thick liquid smeared her fingertips. Somewhere in the back of her muddled conscience, Liza knew what it was and why she should be terrified, but her mind and body had both gone numb.

Shadows clouded her vision. Liza blinked, an attempt to fend against the darkness, but she was so damned tired—and the ground beneath her was so very soft, cradling her body like a warm embrace, tempting her to sleep. She couldn't recall when she'd laid down, but suddenly it didn't matter.

Time slowed to a crawl. Had a moment passed or an eternity? She was supposed to be doing something, only she no longer knew what. Somewhere in the distance were voices—shouting, perhaps? No. Not shouting. Laughing. It was her brothers, calling for her to come play.

The boys were young again as they dashed toward her without a care in the world, and Liza smiled, happy to see them. Their tiny, outstretched hands beckoned for her, soothing and inviting. With a heavy sigh, Liza set her cheek against the sand, and her eyes fluttered shut as she broke free of the world and raced off to join them.

CHAPTER NINE

"*H*asain."

The voice came slithering out of the darkness like the hiss of a viper. Hasain's eyes burst open, woken from a restless, tormented slumber. He was certain something had just brushed against his foot, but when he glanced into the shadows, he could see nothing.

The forms of his sleeping comrades stood out against the bedchamber walls, but none of them appeared to be awake. Even Deegan's bodyguard, who'd been assigned to sit post by the door, slouched upon his stool with his chin tucked to his chest. Light snores lifted around his motionless body.

Sneering, Hasain rolled onto his side. Useless. The men Morathi had assigned were completely useless. Closing his eyes, Hasain tried to will himself back to sleep.

"*Hasain Radek.*"

Hasain sat up, gasping for air. Something had just touched his face. He was sure of it. He looked around wildly. Was someone playing a trick?

Tular, the most likely culprit, lay asleep on the floor beside Joel. Deegan was tucked safely in the innermost corner of the room, with Koal and Natori propped against the wall on either side of the young prince's bed. Not one of them stirred. It couldn't have been any of Hasain's comrades who'd touched him. But then who—

"*You know who I am.*"

A shudder ran down Hasain's spine as the world shrank away, leaving him terrified and vulnerable. He couldn't hear the guard's faint snoring. He couldn't even see the pinpricks of starlight through the worn curtains above. He was alone in the dark, alone with the demon.

"*The hour grows late. Will you still deny me?*"

The lilting voice floated around Hasain, jumping from place to place, but even though he couldn't see the demon, Hasain knew the treacherous being was in the room. The tiny, rigid hairs on his arms told him as much.

"*How stubborn are you? Are you waiting for it to happen?*"

Hasain knew better than to engage the demon, but he couldn't stop himself. "Waiting for *what* to happen? What do you know?"

"*I have a difficult time believing you really are this naïve, Radek's heir.*"

Shadows churned in the air, thickening, taking form. Hasain choked back a cry, watching in horror as the demon materialized before his eyes.

The Demon Leviticus looked human—*almost*. But the pair of silver eyes, glowing like some kind of deranged beast, and smooth, alabaster skin that lacked any true pigmentation betrayed the creature for what he really was.

Leviticus floated around the room, as light as a seed on the breeze, and long wisps of rich auburn flowed freely around his shoulders. Cold laughter trickled down the walls, making Hasain shiver where he sat.

In one graceful swoop, the demon glided to the floor, coming to rest within an arm's length of Deegan's prone form. Leviticus lifted one slender hand, as if he meant to touch the Crown Prince.

Hasain leapt to his feet, sword in hand, and pointed at the demon. "Get away from my brother!"

He all but screeched the words, yet inside the chamber, no one stirred.

A treacherous smile spread across the demon's face. *"Ah! Now there's a bit of your sire showing through. Rishi was always clever when he had his head about him, but one small push and—"* Leviticus cackled, taunting Hasain. *"That fiery temper almost got him killed more than once."*

"Shut your mouth! Stop talking about him! My father was a good and wise king. He had the courage to deny you. You don't deserve to address him so lightly!"

"Wise king or not, Rishi Radek was no saint." Leviticus paused, sweeping the room with a shrewd eye. His gaze lingered on Natori. *"Where's her counterpart? He's not dead, is he?"*

"Of course he's not! Why do you care?"

"They're most powerful when together. Why aren't both of your precious 'Blessed Mages' here with your Crown Prince?"

Hasain hesitated. This had to be some kind of trick. The demon was clever. Why did he care about the Blessed Mages? Was he searching for information that could bring harm to Deegan?

Hasain shook his head, refusing to answer. "That is none of your concern."

Leviticus narrowed his eyes. *"Still determined to die, I see. It would seem the entirety of Arden truly is run by idiots."*

"For the moment perhaps. But he'll be dethroned soon."

"Ah, yes, the buffoon playing the part of a king. How do you live with yourself? Have you no courage to uphold your father's honor? I've seen this Neetra Adelwijn. Surely even you could best him in hand-to-hand combat."

"There are laws in place. I can't just slay the man and claim the throne!"

"No? But isn't that precisely how mortals gain their power? Whoever has the bigger army, whoever commands the most respect, whoever is the most feared, takes what he desires. Humanity has built its empires on such methodology. Why should you be any different?"

"Because I'm a Radek, not a barbarian!"

"*You're a coward. Time marches forward, Hasain. It halts for no one. Whether you act or not, the future will come to pass. The fate of your family is still uncertain, but know this—should you live and they die, you'll have only yourself to blame. Will you be able to live with yourself if you stand by and do nothing?*"

Hasain lowered his sword, the blade suddenly too heavy to hold upright. His mind whirled as he tried to think of something to say. What *could* he say? He wasn't clever enough to outwit Leviticus. He could feel it in his heart. Why had his father entrusted him with the red stone? He wasn't strong or brave enough for this. Rishi had been wrong to place his faith in such a fool.

Hasain swallowed down the hard lump in his throat. The demon was right. He *was* a coward. His father would have been disgusted to see him now. "Go away. Leave me alone."

Leviticus flashed one final leer, revealing two rows of white, pointed teeth. "*Very well. If you insist. Let's hope the rest of your family's bravery exceeds your own. They'll need it if they're to survive.*" Eliciting one final guffaw, the demon ghosted a hand across Deegan's forehead.

Hasain cried out in protest. "Don't touch him!" Enraged, he lunged at the wicked creature—

—and sat up on the lounge for the second time that night.

Hasain fought to bring his ragged breaths under control as he looked around. Everything appeared undisturbed. Joel and Tular lay precisely as they had a moment before. Likewise, Koal and Natori still slept with their backs to the wall, and Deegan shifted restlessly in his bed. Had it all been nothing but a horrible dream?

With trembling hands, Hasain reached into the deep pocket of his robe. The weight of the stone within terrified him. He shuddered. Was the stone pulsating between his fingers, or was it merely his mind slipping away from him?

Whether or not the demon's visit had been imagined, sleep was leagues away now. Hasain stood, wobbling as he picked his way around the others, being careful not to wake them. He paused at the door, and for a moment he considered backhanding the guard who was meant to be standing watch. Instead, he opted to slip past the snoozing sentinel, down the corridor, and through the front door. It wasn't worth the spectacle that would surely ensue, and Hasain didn't feel like explaining to the others why he was awake.

Tepid, dry air washed over Hasain as he stepped outside. When he opened his mouth to take a breath, tiny grains of sand tickled the back of his throat. The dust in the south never seemed to settle, not even in the dead of night. His hands went to his belt, finding the leather bladder he kept fastened there. Lifting it to his parched lips, he groaned when only the slightest amount of water trickled forth. Chhaya's bane. He'd meant to refill the damn thing earlier.

Hasain peered across the courtyard, encroached by shadow. The village well was only just out of sight. It would take but a moment to walk there. He could refill his wineskin and be back before anyone realized he was missing.

The red stone sat heavily in his pocket, its weight ever-present and crushing upon Hasain's soul. His fingers twitched with the sudden urge to be rid of the wretched thing altogether. Surely if he dropped the stone into the well, it would sink to the bottom. The demon couldn't plague Hasain if he was no longer in possession of the stone, could it?

Hasain dipped one hand inside his pocket, fingers brushing over the rigid edges of the stone as he debated. He could throw the thing away and be done with it here and now. But what if someone else discovered it moonturns—even years—later? The stone's fate was bound to the Radek bloodline. Would it somehow find its way back to him, even if Hasain cast it away? Would he even be *able* to get rid of it? In all the years Rishi had been in possession of the stone, he hadn't seemed to be able to escape the demon within. Perhaps Hasain was a fool to believe he could so easily be done with the creature.

The manor door creaked behind him.

"Hasain?" Deegan's soft voice called. "Is that you?"

Hasain yanked his hand free of his pocket. "What are you doing out here?"

The Crown Prince stepped away from the door, rubbing at his sleepy eyes. In the moonlight, Hasain could just make out his brother's ruffled umber hair and dimpled cheeks. "I could ask *you* the same thing," Deegan replied, one eyebrow ticking as he moved closer.

Hasain flinched. Deegan hadn't seen him fidgeting with the stone, had he? "I couldn't sleep. I was thirsty. And that room was too damn hot." It was the truth, somewhat.

"It's *always* hot here in the south." Deegan paused when he reached Hasain's side, staring beyond the courtyard into the dark village. A rebellious yawn escaped his mouth, and he pressed a hand against his lips in an attempt to stifle it. "I wish we could sneak to the river and go for a swim. But if Koal found out where we'd been, he'd have both of us flogged."

"He'd probably do the honors himself." Hasain let out a weary sigh. "You shouldn't be out here. Where's your guard?"

"Asleep on his stool. You know that."

Hasain did his best to ignore the jab of sorrow in his gut. Deegan's sly smile was so reminiscent of their father's it sometimes hurt to behold. "You need to stay safe. You shouldn't be sneaking around without a proper escort."

"There's no safe place and you know it. Neetra sent me here in the hope of getting rid of me for good."

"We'll protect you. You don't have to worry."

"Don't try to spoon feed me sweet lies. I'm not a child anymore."

"I'm not lying." Hasain pointed back toward the manor. "You *know* there isn't a single person in that chamber who wouldn't take death's blow for you."

Deegan swallowed and turned his face away, like he might be ashamed to meet Hasain's gaze. "I don't want any of you to do that."

"I know, but that doesn't change anything. We've all chosen to come with you. You're our beloved prince, and Arden is our home. We're here to protect you and, therefore, her."

Moonlight filtered down from the cloudless sky. In the faint glow, Deegan's eyes glistened. He raked a sleeve across his cheek and looked up at Hasain. "What if I'm not worth protecting? I–I've never been to war before. I haven't ridden into battle. I've taken weaponry lessons with Weapons Master Roland, but it's not the same as facing a real enemy who means to kill me. What if I can't do it? What if I run away? What if I end up being the same kind of coward as Neetra?"

"You are no such thing, Deegan. You're not a coward, and you're certainly *nothing* like Neetra."

"But I–I'm afraid. I wish I were brave like Father always was."

Hasain willed his voice to remain steady. "You're braver than you realize. *Just* like Father. Your heart is the same as his. I can see it. Someday, you're going to make a good, honorable king."

Deegan cast a troubled gaze to the ground. "If I live that long."

Hasain clenched his hands as rash anger shook him to the core. It wasn't fair. Deegan shouldn't have to be worrying about whether or not he would live to see another sunrise. He was just a boy, for Daya's sake. This was far more than any thirteen-year-old should have to bear.

"You *will* live." Hasain set a hand on his brother's small shoulder. "You can trust me when I say that. I'd *never* allow harm to come to you. Whatever it takes, I swear I'll keep you safe."

"I know."

Hasain stared into the darkness, lost in thought. The distant song of crickets and the gentle trickle of the Nishika did little to cast away his apprehension.

He'd meant what he said. He would do all he could to keep his little brother safe. But was his best really good enough? Would he actually be able to protect Deegan when it came down to it? Hasain's weakness had already shown through since the King's death. He'd all but failed his father. He *couldn't* fail Deegan, too.

Hasain touched the outside of the pocket where the red stone lay. He could almost hear the demon's silken voice in his head. *"Should you live and they die, you'll have only yourself to blame. Will you be able to live with yourself if you stand by and do nothing?"*

132

No. Deegan needed to live, by *any* means necessary. Hasain's hand dropped limply to his side. He wouldn't attempt to cast the demon away just yet. Just in case—Hasain hated himself for even contemplating the idea of calling upon the creature for help, but if it meant the difference between his brother living and dying, how could anyone fault him?

Deegan looked up, his eyes free of tears, and the emotions he'd displayed moments before buried beneath a perfectly placed mask. "I think we need to go back inside now. They're waiting for us."

Hasain glanced over his shoulder. Just inside the open door, two sets of eyes peered through the darkness. Natori and Tular stood like living statues, with arms folded over their chests and mouths set in thin lines. It seemed Deegan hadn't escaped unnoticed after all.

Hasain gave his brother a nudge on the arm. "Come on then, let's go."

Deegan nodded grudgingly.

"A little late for a stroll in the courtyard, don't you think?" Natori asked as the two brothers slunk through the door.

Tular cuffed the back of Deegan's head and reserved a narrow glare for Hasain. "*Neither* of you should be wandering around alone. What were you thinking?"

Hasain shrugged, feigning indifference. He couldn't explain himself. He couldn't tell them the real reason sleep evaded him or why he'd increasingly been seeking out solitude these past moonturns.

"We were just talking," Deegan explained. "I couldn't sleep. I saw Hasain leave and just wanted a moment of fresh air. Sorry."

Tular let out a snort. "You'll *really* be sorry if Koal wakes up. Now come on, back into bed, scamp, before your absence is noticed."

With a resigned sigh, Deegan pushed past them and disappeared into the dark corridor. Tular followed at the young prince's heels.

Natori shifted her attention toward Hasain. "We should *all* return to bed. Sleep deprivation won't do us any favors. Now, more than ever, we need to keep our wits about us."

"You're right, of course," Hasain replied. "It's already past midnight, and dawn comes early in the south."

"These last few moonturns have been difficult. It is unfair that such heavy burdens have been placed onto your family, but you are not alone. None of you are. If ever you seek counsel, know that I am here for you."

Hasain lowered his eyes. He didn't want to talk about this, not with her or Koal or anyone else. They didn't know what he was going through. Not really anyway. "I'm of no importance. I'm only the bastard son of a dead king. Deegan is the one who needs counsel. He's the heir—Arden's future. Your focus should always be on *his* protection."

"You sell yourself short, Hasain. You may never be the ruler of Arden, but your father trusted you nonetheless. You *are* important, and so is your given task. You must not take it lightly—"

133

Before Natori could finish speaking, Tular suddenly reappeared from the inner depths of the manor. Without a word, he pulled his sword free of its sheath and went to stand by the open door.

Hasain blinked in surprise. "Tular? What is it? What's wrong?"

The younger brother demanded silence with a wave of his hand. "Something's happening out there."

Natori raised her own blade without hesitation, the ethereal inscriptions running along the steel flaring with brilliant shades of sapphire and indigo, and rushed to join Tular in the entryway. Together, they formed a daunting pair.

Heart pounding in his ears, Hasain pressed his back to the wall and listened. Only silence met his ears, but then again, Tular's hearing was exceptional in comparison. Just because Hasain couldn't hear anything didn't mean there wasn't reason for alarm.

"Footsteps," Tular grunted. "Heading this way."

Hasain had to remind himself to breathe. "In the middle of the night?"

Timid fingertips brushed over his arm just then and he jerked his head around, half-expecting to see the demon's nauseating leer staring back at him. But no—it was only Deegan.

Hasain touched the prince's shoulder. "Keep behind me." It was ironic how steady his voice remained despite the nerves roiling inside his body.

The night was so still Hasain could have heard a pin drop. No one dared move. No one even dared breathe. And then—

Natori's grip tightened around the hilt of her sword. "I hear it now, too."

"I don't—" Hasain began to reply, but he fell silent when the telltale *thud, thud, thud* of boots slamming against dirt met his ears. Someone was approaching, and fast.

A lone figure materialized from within the shadows, just outside the manor gate. Hasain couldn't make out any specific features through the gloom, but he could hear the ragged breathing clear across the courtyard.

"Halt!" Natori demanded. "Who goes there?"

"Help! I need help!" a high, terrified voice gasped. "Please!"

Natori didn't budge. Her blade flared even brighter. "Stay where you are. State your name and your reason for being here."

"I—I'm Gara Leal. I'm a scout in Arden's army. I must speak to the seneschal immediately! Something h–has happened!"

Hasain stepped around both Natori and Tular and rushed into the courtyard. "It's all right. I know her. She's Ambassador Cenric's daughter."

Gara's eyes widened with recognition as Hasain neared, and she took a shaky step forward. Her grip on the iron fencing was so tight her knuckles had gone white. "Hasain? Hasain Radek, you know me! Please, I need to see Seneschal Koal right away!"

Without hesitation, Hasain unlatched the gate and motioned for Gara to follow. "Come with me. I'll take you inside."

Gara swayed as she lurched forward, leaving Hasain to wonder if she really had been holding onto the fence because she couldn't stand on her own. He grabbed her arm without thinking.

Gara leaned against him. "M—my horse collapsed at the gate. I had to run. I—I came as fast as I could."

A shudder rocked Hasain's body. What had happened? Why was she so scared and exhausted? Was the army under attack? He wanted to ask so badly.

"Show her to the great hall," Natori said, stepping aside so Hasain could lead Gara through the doorway.

Tular stowed away his sword. "I'll rouse Koal."

"Please hurry," Gara rasped.

Hasain all but had to carry Gara into the great hall. She clutched him like her life depended on it, her willowy body shaking against his. A sharp, acrid scent clung to her leather scouting gear, so pungent it almost made Hasain choke. Why did she reek of smoke and ash?

Hasain fumbled to pull one of the chairs away from the table. "Here, sit."

Gara slumped down wordlessly. She didn't give thanks, but Hasain didn't fault her for it. At this point, he worried she might be too exhausted even to speak.

Deegan was already going around the room, lighting candelabras along the wall. The sudden illumination chased away the shadows and stung Hasain's eyes. His breath hitched when he got his first real look at Gara.

Her cropped hair stuck out in every direction, as frazzled and wild as her eyes, and her complexion was so pasty it bordered on translucent. Dirt smeared Gara's face and uniform. If Hasain didn't know better, he might have assumed she'd been rolling around on the ground. The scout swayed deliriously in her seat, and Hasain rushed to steady her. Was she going to faint?

Natori squatted beside Gara, taking up one of her hands and pinching the skin just beneath the knuckles. "She's dehydrated. She needs water."

"Here," Deegan called from across the room. He retrieved the water basin from the mantle and brought it to Gara.

"Thank you, Highness," Gara managed to respond. "I—I'm sorry. I should have bowed—"

She began to rise, but Deegan shook his head. "No, it's fine. Stay seated." He dipped a ladle into the bowl and then carefully placed it into Gara's hand. "Drink."

By the time she'd swallowed a third helping, the color had begun to return to her cheeks. "Thank you. That helped."

Hasain removed his hand from Gara's back. Questions churned in his head, burning like parched tinder on a pyre. He opened his mouth, meaning to press Gara for answers, but the sound of quickening footfalls in the hall caught his ear.

Hasain glanced up just as Tular and Koal swept into the room. Joel followed, though he opted to linger in the entranceway, wringing his hands. His frown deepened when he caught sight of Gara, surely begging to ask the very same questions as everyone else.

Koal scanned the chamber with fierce determination, wasting no time with introductions or formalities. He didn't even question why Hasain and Deegan were out of bed. Crossing the room in five long strides, the seneschal set both hands on the tabletop and leaned forward. His eyes locked with Gara's. "Tell me everything, Leal. From the beginning."

Gara nodded. "Y–yes, sir." Exhaling slowly, she squeezed her eyes shut. When she opened them again, she seemed better able to maintain Koal's gaze. "I'm a scout in Arden's army, and I volunteered to accompany the expedition sent to Ashvale three days past. Everything was going as planned. We were making good time. There wasn't a sniff of trouble. Just this afternoon, we were only a dozen furlongs shy of reaching Kaleth's Crossing. The troop stopped for a reprieve, and at the orders of Captain Brishen, one of the other scouts and I rode on ahead. We intended to reach Ashvale and let the villagers know we were coming, but when we arrived— there was nothing left. Ashvale was burnt to the ground—completely destroyed. And the villagers—they were dead. Men, women, children. All of them slain. They—they'd been gutted, sir. Gutted and hung on stakes."

Hasain couldn't recall when he'd backed away, but he found himself with his shoulders pressed to the wall. He gripped the cold stone with both hands, feeling nauseated and light-headed. Someone was speaking to him nearby—Joel—but Hasain couldn't hear anything above the rush of blood in his ears.

Ashvale was gone? At the hands of the Shirites? And all those innocent lives, gone. Murdered in cold blood. What would this mean for Arden? Surely any attempt to avoid open war was now futile. As soon as Neetra learned about this—

"That's not all," Gara said. Her chest heaved with every word. Whatever resolve she'd managed to conjure was already slipping away. "Rocelin and I rode as fast as we could. We knew we had to warn the troop, but—but when we got there—*we were too late.* They'd been ambushed. Th–there were tracks all along the riverbank leading into the water. The enemy must have attacked them from the far side. I don't know—"

Koal waved a hand. "How many are injured? Healers will need to be dispatched immediately."

"No," Gara croaked, shaking her head. "It's no use."

Time came to a screeching halt. No one moved. No one spoke. Not even Koal. Hasain held his breath, waiting—waiting for the inevitable.

Choking back a sob, Gara hung her head. "They—they're dead. We checked. We tried to—but they—I'm sorry—" In the faint candlelight, Hasain caught the glimmer of a teardrop as it slid down the scout's dirty cheek.

Joel managed to find his voice first. His eyes were impossibly large and imploring as he twisted his trembling hands together. "The entire troop, Gara? All of them? Are they *all* dead?"

Gara gave a reluctant nod, the only indication she'd heard Joel's words at all. "We returned as quickly as the horses would carry us. Rocelin's mare collapsed a league back. He told me to keep going. I rode as fast as I could—"

Gara rambled on, but Hasain wasn't listening anymore. His attention shifted to Joel, who had turned on his heels and was making a dash for the doorway.

Hasain scrambled into the hall after him. "Joel! Where are you going?"

Joel didn't slow his pace or glance back. "I have to go."

"What are you talking about? We're supposed to be protecting Deegan. And what if Koal needs us?"

"I don't *care* about any of that right now! I have to find Gib! He needs to know about this!"

"Gib? Why? Can't it wait until morning?"

Joel lurched to a stop so swiftly Hasain all but collided with him. "No. It can't wait until morning." Wrapping his arms around himself, Joel turned around. The devastation in the mage's eyes was nearly too much to endure. "I have to be the one who tells him."

Hasain could feel the blood drain from his face, like sand escaping an hourglass. His stomach clenched into knots. "Tell him what?"

Joel rushed to wipe away the tears that clung to his lashes before they could spill, and a strangled whimper clawed its way free of his throat, a grief-stricken, hopeless sound that chilled Hasain to the core.

Silence. Complete and utter silence.

And then Joel's breathless words lifted from within the shadows. "I have to be the one to tell him his sister is dead."

It is said death does not discriminate. Of every creature in existence, mortal and immortal alike, they all make the same voyage in death. All souls must cross The Veil.

When the Goddesses Daya and Chhaya broke free from the Void of Nothing, they created three realms. Temhara, the mortal world and the world which humanity calls their home. The Otherealm, the place where Their firstborn Children live. And then, beyond The Veil, lies Eternity. This final realm is not a world, but the place where all souls go when their lives have reached their end.

In Temhara, the cycle of life and death is unending, for nature balances the realm, and the creatures there are bound by its law. The immortal Children of the Otherealm follow no such law. Their bodies neither wither nor fall to disease. They linger on forever unless they are killed or choose to cross The Veil and into Eternity of their own free will.

Now it was, in the beginning, that The Veil was left unattended, for The Two, even in all Their wisdom, could not foresee the future. But when the Blessed Son of Light began His Great War against humanity, He watched as, one by one, his brothers and sisters fell, and the Blessed Son was overcome with grief. For once a soul crosses The Veil, they cannot return. Or so it was believed.

It happened that one Child among the Blessed Son's army learned a way to See across The Veil. And he Saw the souls of the fallen Children inside Eternity and that the gate lay unattended. So he passed unhindered into Eternity and collected his brethren. He brought them back to the Otherealm so they might continue the fight against humanity.

Daya and Chhaya saw what this Child had done and They were angry, for They had decreed no soul who crosses into Eternity should be allowed reentrance to the realms of the living without Their permission. Thus, Daya and Chhaya appointed a guardian to watch over The Veil so never again could such travesty occur.

The Gatekeeper is the overseer of Eternity and the keeper of Death. He is the final authority on who shall pass. Even the Blessed Son of Light Himself cannot command the Gatekeeper on matters of The Veil. He holds eternal vigil at His post, never leaving and always watching.

There will come a time when all souls must face the Gatekeeper. It will do no good to lie to Him or hope for escape, for He is always there. And there He will remain, until the day when His soul alone is left in the mortal realm. And then He, too, will cross into Eternity, and The Veil will fall for the last time.

Gib gently closed *Tales of Fae* and set it into his lap. Sighing, he ran his fingers along the frayed binding and sent silent thanks to Calisto for having the insight to slip the book into Liza's pack. His heart twisted a little less painfully while he was still able to hold a piece of home in his hands.

It was odd to recollect a time when reading wasn't the comfort it was now. Not so long ago, Gib had only known the basics of the written word. He hadn't had time to read on the farm. And what would a farmer ever need to read and write for anyway? Signing his name was the most he ever thought he'd need to know. Liza had been so proud to learn he'd become a strong reader. The pain in his heart came back.

Where was Liza now? Was she safe? Gib's stomach rolled. He should have found a way to go to Ashvale with her. She'd refused to stay, but he could have gone.

138

"If you need to talk, I'd have you know I'm here." Zandi's voice was soft in Gib's ear. The mage had been sitting beside Gib all evening, only moving as the fire needed to be stoked.

"I know," Gib replied. "I just—don't have much to say right now."

"I don't think I'd have much to say if I were in your place either."

Zandi continued to brush his long, ebony hair. He'd washed it earlier, and it was nearly dry now. Gib thought to offer to help braid the locks before they could become an unruly mass, but he didn't know for sure just how Zandi's hair had to be put up under his turban. It was probably best not to draw attention anyway. There were already certain soldiers who looked at the two of them in a way Gib didn't like. Zandi, for the most part, pretended not to notice, but Gib was in no mood to tolerate idle hatred. His nerves were raw and his hand quick to fly to the hilt of his sword.

Gib gazed up at the stars, wondering—hoping, really—Liza could see them, too, wherever she was. The fire crackled in his ears. It might have been serene if not for the worry in his heart.

Kezra let out a sigh as she sat down next to Zandi. She had a large piece of crimson fabric slung over one arm. "Ready to put your hair up, m'lady?"

Zandi scoffed at his sister's slight. "Well, we can't both go breaking our mother's heart, can we? One of us has to maintain tradition."

"Spare me the shaming. I cut my hair because I'm a soldier. You've kept yours long because you're vain."

"Who says you have to keep your hair long?" Nage asked from across the fire. He reached into a saddlebag by his feet and tossed a ration of wrapped bread to Gib. "You should eat somethin'."

Gib balked. "I'm not hungry."

"Liar."

"Well, you don't have to—"

"But I did."

"Chhaya's bane! I'm not a child."

Nage smirked. "Well, you're shorter than me. So close enough. *Eat.*"

"*Fine.*" Gib chewed angrily on the loaf and watched Kezra pull her brother's hair into a tight ponytail.

"Our mother hails from Shantar, Nage," she said as she worked. "There are several different temples there, all with diverse beliefs."

"Like here in Arden, how some people worship the Blessed Son and others worship Daya and Chhaya?" Nage asked.

Kezra twisted the ponytail onto the top of Zandi's head and secured it with a pin. "Right. My grandfather married a woman from outside his religion. Neither of them gave up their beliefs entirely nor forced the other to. So my mother was raised to believe some of both."

Nage chuckled. "That's not confusing or anything."

Kezra's smile was brief but bright. "Not at all. Anyway, according to my grandfather's faith, followers are expected to keep their hair long. It's a show of piety and dedication to the Creator."

Nage listened with undivided attention. "So it's a way of staying right with your god."

"Ha! I suppose, but Brother Dearest likes men and ale a little too much to 'stay right' with this god."

Zandi laughed and kicked sand at her. "And you're too mouthy!"

"I never claimed loyalty to any god." Kezra slapped Zandi's shoulder as she unraveled the sheet of fabric. "Sit up straight."

"So, the heritage mark," Nage said, motioning toward his forehead. "Is that part of your grandfather's religion too?"

With well-rehearsed precision, Kezra wrapped the turban around her brother's head. "It comes from our grandmother's faith. It's a symbol of inner strength and reflection—a third eye, if you will. It's painted onto the brow in hopes of being aware not only through the eyes but through the mind as well. It's a call for wisdom."

Nage folded his arms across his chest. "There are some fools on the High Council who could use one'a those. A little wisdom might do 'em good."

Zandi clapped a hand over his mouth. "My father amongst them."

Gib tried to laugh along with the others, but his mind kept wandering back to the dark places it tended to go when he was stressed or worried. He hoped that wherever Liza was, she was also using her head. Perhaps her own personal wisdom would be enough to keep her safe. And if not, maybe The Two—or whoever might be out there—could guide her as well. A bit of extra help never hurt.

Kezra groaned as she checked to make sure the turban was secure. "Anders doesn't deserve a mark. It would probably burn a hole in his head."

"The better to allow the wisdom to flow in," Zandi muttered.

Kezra, Nage, and Zandi broke down into fits of laughter, and Gib found it difficult not to share in their mirth this time. The corner of his mouth curled up, and a moment later, a chuckle broke free. Soon he was doubled over with the rest of them, cackling and gasping for air.

He was laughing so hard he almost didn't hear a timid voice calling to him from the edge of the encampment.

"Gib?"

Gib's heart sank. What was Joel doing here? And at this late hour?

Joel stood just within the glow of the fire. The flames flickered across his face and made his eyes come alive. But something was wrong. Joel's face was drawn tight and pale. *Far* too pale. And he was twisting his hands together in a most unsettling manner.

Gib was on his feet and rushing over to the mage before the others even realized they were no longer alone. "Joel?"

"Can you come with me please?" Joel kept his voice steady, but his misty eyes seemed determined to betray him.

"Everythin' all right?" Nage called out. Kezra and Zandi were also watching somberly.

"I need—I need to speak with him for a moment."

Gib could feel the blood seeping from his face. "W–what is it? What's wrong?"

Joel's eyes darted feverishly to the ground, to the raging fire, and to the spangled sky above, anywhere other than Gib. "Something has happened."

The world was a blur, spinning around him. "Tell me."

Joel opened his mouth but could only utter a broken gasp.

In desperation, Gib grabbed the mage's forearm. *"Tell me!"* He didn't mean to scream, but terrible dread like nothing he'd ever felt before was surging through his veins. He had no control over himself.

Before Gib could say another word, Joel had taken hold of his hands, which was just as well. Gib teetered where he stood. "Gib, it—it's about the mission to Ashvale. I have some bad news."

Gib knew. He knew before the words even had to be said. "Is Liza all right? Is she hurt?"

Joel shook his head. His grip tightened around Gib's hands. "I'm afraid it's worse than that."

Oh gods. No. Not this. No!

Gib slumped to his knees. His legs simply wouldn't hold him. His entire body trembled. "Is—is she—*dead?*"

Joel fell to the ground, clutching Gib. Tears streamed down his cheeks. "Gib, I'm sorry. I'm so sorry."

Pain. Horrible, agonizing pain. It shot through Gib's core like ice shards and an inferno both at the same time. It hurt so much he couldn't scream. He couldn't even cry.

No. Not Liza. Not my sister.

Joel's lips were moving, but Gib couldn't hear over the rush in his ears. He moaned deep in his throat. The agony of his own bereavement pressed down on his soul, choking him. He couldn't breathe. Doubling forward, the contents of his stomach spewed from his mouth in one violent retch after another.

She can't be gone. She was just here. I just talked to her. I just hugged her. This isn't real!

But it was real. Joel's muted sobs, ringing in Gib's ears like a terrible death hymn, all but confirmed it.

Gib staggered to his feet, but his body was so racked with hurt he couldn't manage to stay upright. He crashed to the dirt in a heap. The world tumbled around him in a blur, and his vision darkened. Gib closed his eyes, praying the darkness would sweep him away.

CHAPTER TEN

Five days. Five horrific days.

Joel pressed his fingers against his throbbing temples and tried to recompose himself. He was supposed to be writing a letter to his mother and sisters. Word of the attack had surely reached Silver by now, and Joel wanted to assure his family back home that he and Koal were all right. Joel considered himself lucky. Not everyone could pen such comforting letters.

Joel's stomach flopped unmercifully. Five days. Five days since Liza's death. Had Gib sent word to his brothers yet? Or would telling them now only make matters worse?

With a shaking hand, Joel set the quill down and glanced over at his father. "The worst part is not knowing what I should be doing for him, Da."

Koal made a grim face but didn't look away from the map in front of him. The army was set to move out at dawn, and he was busy charting the next day's trek. The destruction of Ashvale and the attack on the Ardenian soldiers had been the excuses Neetra and Morathi were waiting for. The decree had arrived by carrier pigeon only marks earlier, with orders from the High Council to proceed. Arden was to invade Shiraz. Joel had never known the High Council to agree so quickly on anything.

"He knows we're here for him," Koal replied at length. "He may just need space."

Joel knew he shouldn't keep pestering his father, especially when the seneschal was so busy, but he couldn't help himself. "I only wish to let him know I care. Everything is so complicated though. We're not as—close as we once were."

Koal nodded. His expression was sincere when he finally raised his eyes. "It's not easy to go back to being friends once you've been more. I'm sorry I don't have any answers for you."

Joel didn't push any further. Koal was a good man, and a compassionate father, but emotional guidance had always been left to Mrifa. Joel would just have to deal with his feelings on his own.

Silence arose as they each went back to their tasks. Sunlight trickled through the single glass pane that Mayor Barclay's great hall offered, but the room still felt stuffy and cramped. Joel did his best to focus on his letter, though his mind kept drifting elsewhere and everywhere: from Gib's despair, to the dangerous journey that lay ahead, to concerns about Deegan and the rest of the royal family. So many different worries pressed down on Joel's chest all at once time that for a time, he believed he might collapse beneath the weight.

It was a miracle he was able to finish writing at all. He had just folded the parchment into a neat square when Mayor Barclay appeared in the doorway. "Lord Joel Adelwijn, you have a guest waiting at the front door."

Joel's heart leapt into his throat. "Gibben Nemesio?"

"No, milord. A Lord Zandi Malin-Rai. He has requested to speak with you."

If it had been possible for Joel to deflate into a puddle on the floor, he would have. Didn't Zandi have better things he could be doing? Like *comforting Gib?* The flash of resentment that such a thought brought about made Joel's cheeks shamefully warm, but he didn't care. "I don't wish to see him. Show him out. You may tell him I'm busy——"

Koal cleared his throat. "Perhaps you should go. I can take care of everything here."

Joel turned such a sour look onto his father that Koal recoiled. Joel instantly wished he could take it back. He knew he was being unfair, even silly. With a deep sigh, he conceded. "Very well. I'll speak to him."

Joel excused himself from the table and swept into the narrow corridor. What could Zandi possibly want now? Their last attempt at civilized conversation had all but ended in disaster, but for Gib's sake, Joel was willing to hear Zandi out.

One more time.

Zandi waited just inside the entranceway. He looked awful. His typically handsome face was gaunt, and his eyes lacked any shine at all, save for the tears collecting in the corners. He frowned down at his boots, not lifting his gaze until Joel was but an arm's length away.

"What is it?" Joel asked.

"Could we go outside?" Zandi croaked. "Please?"

Icy concern turned Joel's tongue to clay. He couldn't find a single word to say but reached for the door.

The sun blazed down outside, perched high in the cloudless blue sky. A light breeze rustled through Joel's onyx hair and carried the fresh scent of water from the Nishika. The wind licked Joel's skin, tempering the sun's heat. The day was beautiful—a beautiful *lie*.

Zandi kept his back to Joel as he stared into the unkempt courtyard. "I know you don't want to talk to me, but I didn't know who else to go to. I thought maybe Kezra but—it has to be you. I'm sure of it."

Joel flinched. "What do you need to tell me?"

"He's going to bury her sword. It's all they were able to—bring back. And it's all he has left of her. He's alone. I tried to stay with him. I've never dug a hole in my life, but I would help if I could—but he sent me away."

143

Joel took no pleasure in watching Zandi's shoulders tremble as he spoke. Perhaps at one time—maybe even moments before—Joel would have enjoyed the other man's strife, but this—this was about Gib.

"He's stubborn," Joel replied in as collected a voice as he could muster. "And hurt. Don't worry that his rejection means anything more than that."

Zandi wiped his face on his long sleeve. "I suppose. But I don't know if it's good for him to be alone right now. He might listen to you, or even let you stay with him. He shouldn't have to do this by himself."

Joel bit his bottom lip. Zandi was right, of course. Gib might be hurt—he might be scared and angry—but damn him. He shouldn't have to feel alone in his grief.

Joel had laid a hand on Zandi's shoulder before he even realized he was doing it. "I'll go to him. But just know, if I stay, it will only be because I'm as stubborn as he."

Zandi didn't say anything. He merely nodded and gestured for Joel to go.

The ground was so packed that Gib struggled to get his shovel through the crust. Even once he managed to break the shell, the fine dirt beneath crumbled and blew away on the breeze—right into his face. Gib cursed at the sky and kept digging.

He'd picked this spot because of all the places he'd seen around Perth, this one was the most like the farm. A single tree had set its roots here long ago and somehow beaten the odds. It wasn't anything like the hearty maples that grew along the field back home. The ugly, gnarled trunk and spiny branches that supported only a handful of browning leaves left much to be desired. But it was still a tree—the only tree Gib could find.

Gib's mother and father had been buried at the foot of a great willow that overlooked the farm. The plan, back when Gib was young, was that the four children would one day be laid to rest there, too. A family. Together forever.

Stupid. The whimsical reverie of a fool.

His eyes stung. It must have been the sand. He'd already cried himself dry.

Gib stabbed the shovel into the ground and stormed several paces away. He refused to look at Liza's sword, the only piece of her recovered. If he indulged himself and refused to see it, he could pretend she wasn't gone. He might just be digging a hole beneath a withered tree. It didn't have to be a memorial. It didn't have to be her grave.

He cried out and kicked the tree's trunk for lack of anything better to do. Lies! All lies! Liza was *dead!* She was gone, buried inside a communal grave with her fallen comrades somewhere in the barren wastelands. Nothing he could say or do would bring her back.

Gib finally glanced over at the sword, still wrapped in linen and propped against the tree trunk where Nawaz had left it earlier.

"It was still in her hands," the Healer had said to him. "She went down a warrior, a hero. We laid her to rest with the rest of her troop. They're across The Veil now."

Gib had sent Nawaz away, just as he had done Zandi. It seemed foolish now. He'd never felt so vulnerable and alone. If only Tayver and Calisto were here. Gib shook from head to toe. What was he going to tell them? Should he send notice of Liza's passing? Or would they then worry all the more for him? Perhaps he should let them continue to believe Liza was alive and well. Which was crueler? How was *anyone* supposed to make these kinds of decisions?

Gib sank to the ground beside the sword. The tree offered little shade, but he didn't care. He didn't care about anything anymore. He lost track of how long he sat there, chest heaving and eyes burning.

A wineskin dropped beside him with a loud *thud*. "Pushing people away doesn't work, Gib."

Gib refused to look up, even when Joel's shadow fell across him. "Isn't that exactly what *you* did?"

"Yes. That's how I know."

"I don't want to talk right now."

"Then don't. I'll just sit with you. And when you're ready, I'll help you if you'd like."

"I don't want anyone here!" Gib didn't know where the words were coming from. Just moments before, he'd been scolding himself for shooing Zandi and Nawaz away.

"I won't talk if you don't want me to," Joel replied, his tone poised— the voice of an envoy. "I won't even force you to drink the water I brought. But I'm not going to leave because whether you like it or not, you're *not* alone."

Gib couldn't rightfully name the emotion pounding in his veins. The pressure in his gut wanted to vent upward and spew out his mouth. He wondered, briefly, if screaming might help. Would the unbearable tension inside go away if he poured it all out? He'd more likely be thrown into an asylum for his troubles, and perhaps that was the best place for him. Maybe he'd somehow become entirely disconnected from reality. This was just a nightmare. He was only digging a ditch. And maybe Liza was only sleeping.

Wretched sobbing met his ears, and it took a long while for Gib to realize *he* was the one crying. He opened his mouth, and his shattered heart fell out, piece by brittle piece.

"It wasn't supposed to be like this! She chose to be a soldier! She did this so the boys and I would be safe! So no one else would end up like Pa!

145

We'd go seasons at a time without hearing from her and that was okay because she *always* came back! Well, where the hell is she *now*? How can she still be our hero if she's buried under the damned ground in the middle of nowhere? How is she going to still be with us from across The Veil?"

His lungs quit there. They were probably too torn up from the splintered shards of his heart. Gib gasped for air and dropped his head to his knees. His own desperate sobs carried on for so long he nearly forgot he wasn't alone.

But then he felt Joel's arms slip around his shoulders, and Gib collapsed into the embrace, crying shamelessly. Joel held him close, uttering gentle hushes and kind words. By the time Gib had bled himself dry and his voice ached from overuse, he'd fallen completely onto his side. Joel draped an arm over him, silently stroking Gib's curls and squeezing him with tender care.

Time passed strangely. They might have been there an entire age, the war they'd been marching to a long forgotten footnote in history. Or maybe they'd been there only a moment, just long enough to take a single breath. Gib had no way of knowing for sure.

At last, Gib wiped his face and sat upright, getting his first proper look at Joel since he'd arrived.

His friend was tired, pale, and *beautiful* as always. Joel had always worn his exhaustion as if it were fine silk.

Gentle eyes met Gib, looking him over. "Are you all right?"

"No," Gib replied.

"Good. At least you're not lying to me."

"What's the point? You'd know if I was."

Joel smiled faintly. "I would. Now, you should drink some water."

Gib didn't fight the command and raised the wineskin. Cool, clean water trickled forth, bringing his raw throat needed relief. He replaced the cork and handed the wineskin to Joel. "Did Nawaz send you?"

"No. Was he here?"

"He—he brought Liza's sword to me." Gib motioned toward the wrapped parcel. "If Nawaz didn't tell you, then how did you know to look for me here?"

"Zandi." Joel paused, perhaps to give Gib a chance to recover from his shock. "He's worried about you. He said you pushed him away. But he wanted to be sure you weren't alone."

Gib's cheeks burned with shame. He'd have to apologize later. Zandi didn't deserve to be treated like an outsider. The fact that he'd even gone so far as to fetch Joel was proof Zandi cared deeply. "It wasn't him. I really did want to be alone. It's just—I'm confused. I've never felt so lost in my life."

"We're here for you. *I'm* here for you. I wish I could tell you everything is going to be okay, but—"

146

"It's already too late for that, isn't it? Our king is dead. Arden is at Neetra's mercy. We're set to invade Shiraz on the morrow. Liza's—gone. How, Joel? How do we continue to hope?"

"What else do we have left? We have to keep hope alive, or all of this is for naught."

Gib let out a drawn sigh. "I can't think of anything to hope for."

Joel opened his mouth to reply, but it was a new voice—not Joel's—that spoke first.

"I hope for a sunny day when we get back to Silver." Nage trudged toward them, a shovel slung across his shoulders like a yoke. "Nia deserves a good day when we get married."

Kezra followed in Nage's shadow and met Gib's dropped jaw with stern, unyielding eyes. "You really didn't think we wouldn't find you?"

Looking up at her, with a shovel likewise in hand, Gib's heart spasmed. And then he lost control for the second time that afternoon. Though he had no more tears to shed, he sobbed just the same.

Kezra knelt down and took Gib into her arms. "There's still hope, Gib. That idiot can't keep the throne forever. There *will* be peace. And then your brothers will never have to dread losing another part of their family again."

Her words resonated deep inside Gib's soul. It was true. It *had* to be true. He couldn't give up now. He'd made an oath to see Arden through the darkness.

Liza had fallen before she could see the new day, but though Gib loved her and would miss her terribly, he couldn't follow her. He *would* see Neetra cast off Arden's throne. He *would* return to his brothers. And he *wouldn't* succumb to despair.

With renewed strength, Gib stood and took his shovel into his hands once more. It was time for farewells, and it was time to move forward.

CHAPTER ELEVEN

"Are you sure this is where we're supposed to wait?" Kirk picked at the frayed edge of his sleeve as a means to keep his hands busy. "What if we're in the wrong place?"

Otho let out a gruff sigh. He stood with his back propped against the wall and arms folded over his stout chest. The faded grey tunic he wore did his complexion no favors, though Kirk imagined that, dressed in the same ragged clothing, his own face looked equally washed out.

"This looks like a kitchen to me," Otho finally replied. He motioned sourly toward the towering shelf of pots on the opposite side of the room. "Spending all your time in that comfy Imperial palace, you may not know."

Kirk rolled his eyes and went from playing with his sleeve to rubbing the back of his neck. The coarse wool of the servant's garb irritated his skin and brought back memories of the days when he'd lived on the streets of Teivel, unaware of such luxuries as the silk robes he frequently wore now.

Pursing his lips, Kirk fought the urge to tell Otho exactly how inaccurate his preconceived notions really were.

It's a waste of breath. His opinion won't change. I'll always be the deceitful, pampered foreigner to him.

"Marc said someone would meet us. Where are they?"

"They'll be here," Otho sneered. "Stop fidgeting."

Kirk dropped his hands like a scolded child and forced them to stay idle at his sides. "I'm sorry. It's just—we've been standing here for a quarter-mark already. My nerves are through the roof."

Otho seemed content to scowl at the floor and pretend Kirk wasn't there at all, so with a grudging sigh, Kirk let the conversation fade. As predicted, unpleasant silence rose to fill the void. Kirk wished Joel were here instead. He missed his friend terribly. Really though, anyone other than Otho would do right about now. Why Marc had ever thought it was a good idea for the two of them to work together was beyond Kirk's comprehension.

The mid-morning sun shone down through a single window. The shutters were drawn back, letting in the scent of blooming flowers. A melodious birdsong tickled Kirk's ears, and he was almost certain he heard the swish of horsetails, drifting in from the stables on a light breeze.

The palace kitchen lay abandoned at this hour. Breakfast had long since been served and cleaned up, and it was too early yet for the cooks to begin preparations for dinner. Even so, the aroma of baked bread and cod chowder lingered in the air. Kirk's stomach gurgled in protest. He'd been too worked up to eat a proper meal earlier, and now he was facing the consequences.

Otho scraped a boot across the planked floor. If the apprentice was nervous, he certainly didn't act it. If anything, he appeared bored. "You still have the key?"

With a curt nod, Kirk touched the outside of his pocket where the key was safely tucked away. Marc had passed it off earlier, along with the pair of servant uniforms. The garb had been used to infiltrate the palace. The key was to unlock Neetra's door.

The High Council would be meeting any moment now. Marc had promised it would be a *long* session. Today was the day Kirk and Otho planned to sneak inside Neetra's chambers. It was as good an opportunity as they were ever going to get.

Kirk squirmed, unable to stay still. *I must be completely out of my mind. We're going to get caught. Or lost. I'm not sure which is worse.* He cast a sideways glance at Otho, wishing that—for once—the apprentice might offer encouragement. *Ha. Fish will sooner learn how to walk on land! Why couldn't Joel have stayed behind instead? He and I work so well together. And he's kind and generous—not to mention better to look at.*

Bristling, Kirk tried to clear his mind. It wasn't typically in his nature to be so vindictive. He supposed stress could turn even the most level-headed person hostile.

The patter of clogs against the floor caught Kirk's attention. He sucked in a deep breath and raised his face in time to see a middle-aged woman slip into the room. She wore her silver-flecked ruby hair in a loose bun at the nape of her neck and a soiled apron around her trim waist.

The woman spoke before Kirk could even open his mouth. "Are you Marc's boys?"

Otho answered with a firm nod. "Yes."

"Come on then." She motioned for them to follow. "I'll show you where to go."

She led the way through the kitchen and into a smaller area Kirk imagined must be a storage room. Shelves packed tight with jars of herbs and spices lined one wall, and on the other hung ladles, carving knives, and other cooking utensils Kirk couldn't put a name to.

The red-headed woman crossed to the far side of the chamber and kicked aside a tattered rug that covered one section of the floor. Kirk stared for a moment before he realized a trapdoor was hidden beneath.

"Here's the way in then," the woman said. She leaned down, clutching a small, rusted metal lever. When she yanked on it, the wooden hatch lifted

149

away from the surrounding floor. Darkness seeped out through an ominous hole below.

Kirk swallowed the lump in his throat. "We're supposed to go down there?"

"It's perfectly safe. Only dark. I trust you know where to go from here?"

Maybe. That depends on how reliable Prince Didier's directions end up being.

"We'll be all right." Kirk bowed his head. "Thank you, lady."

He approached the trapdoor like a skittish horse. Every corner of his sane mind screamed against going down there, but it was far too late to turn back. Gripping the edges of the opening, he lowered one leg into the dark, floundering until his boot met solid grounding. He shifted his foot around, testing the surface. A ladder rung.

Carefully, slowly, Kirk lowered himself into the hole. Water squished beneath his boots as he passed the final rung and stepped onto solid ground. He couldn't see a damned thing. Afraid to move, he shuffled aside only because Otho was already halfway down the ladder.

Light from above filtered down, the only source of illumination to be had. And then Kirk heard the woman whisper a hasty "good luck" and the trapdoor snapped shut. There came a strange, sweeping sound—perhaps the woman smoothing the rug back into its proper place—and then brisk footfalls as she retreated from the room. Kirk and Otho were left in silence nearly as thick as the dark.

"A light, mage-boy," Otho said at last.

Right. Of course. Kirk turned his palm upright and called energy to his fingertips. Magic pooled in his hand, swirling, solidifying, and finally taking form as a glowing cerulean sphere. Kirk released the orb into the air, where it hovered above his shoulder.

Kirk blinked, getting his first decent look around. They appeared to be in some kind of cellar. Cobwebs spanned the ceiling, draped like silk nets, and water trickled down cold stone walls. A moldy, stale odor filled the space. The smell, combined with the narrow space, made Kirk's skin crawl. His mind immediately jumped to horrid thoughts of the ceiling suddenly collapsing, leaving him to suffocate and die beneath a pile of rubble.

"What's wrong with you?"

Kirk tried to calm his labored breaths. "Sorry. This brings back memories of the night I escaped Teivel. My sister led us—Joel, Seneschal Koal, and the others—through the catacombs. Part of the ceiling caved. We almost lost our lives in there."

The light of the mage-orb reflected off Otho's amber eyes. For once, they weren't criticizing. "Come on. The sooner we get there, the sooner we get out."

They made their way along the narrow path, the mage-orb fluttering above and chasing away the shadows. This passage was one of many that, together, formed a sprawling network of hidden corridors within the royal palace. Centuries before, such paths had been used by the servants as a means to get to and fro swiftly. Time caused memory to fade, however, and now very few people knew of the network at all. Prince Didier knew only because King Rishi had once shown the passages to all the royal children, should the need to escape undetected ever arise. In dark times like these, Kirk imagined it was a good bit of wisdom to keep tucked away, just in case.

A crumbling stairwell loomed ahead. Kirk kept his footfalls light as he hurried to the top. "It's hard to imagine this passageway was once used daily by the servants. How long do you think it's been since anyone's been through here?"

Otho shrugged, keeping several paces ahead. "Don't know."

Kirk resigned himself to bitter silence and focused on the sound of his boots slapping against the stone pavers. Prince Didier had described the way they needed to go in as much detail as he could recall. It was now up to Kirk and Otho to make it there. Many of the corridors were in crumbles, some even impassable. But the route that would lead them straight to Neetra's suite was open, at least to Prince Didier's knowledge.

I guess we'll find out soon.

They went down one corridor after another. Kirk recited the directions over and over in his mind as he followed behind Otho.

A right turn here. Then there should be a stairwell. Ah, there it is. Now left. Take the second doorway, not the first. Or was it the first?

Otho seemed to remember, so Kirk let the apprentice lead. They entered a corridor that must have been positioned against the outer face of the palace, for traces of light filtered in through crevasses in the stonework. Kirk went over to the wall and peeked through one of the cracks.

"See anything?"

"Daylight," Kirk replied. "And blue sky."

"We must be on the third floor by now. Getting close."

"Do you think we'll actually find anything inside Neetra's chambers?" Kirk hated the idea of risking his life for naught. And besides that, Marc, Joel, and the entire royal family were counting on them. They *couldn't* come up empty-handed.

Otho merely shrugged, his disposition unreadable. "Let's keep moving."

They walked in silence after that. Otho made damn certain to stay three strides ahead, and Kirk didn't have the heart to make another attempt at conversation anyway.

It doesn't matter. We don't have to like each other. When this mission is over, I'll never have to see him again. And once Joel is back, I'll have someone to talk to. I just need to get through this.

Otho stopped abruptly in front of a wooden door, and Kirk hurried the last few paces to catch up with the apprentice. "Is this the door that we're—"

"Quiet," Otho hissed. He tugged on the rusted iron handle, and with a light creak, the door glided open. Leaning through the opening, he peered from side to side before turning back to Kirk. "Looks clear in there. But there'll be sentries in the hall."

Kirk nodded, apprehension twirling in his gut, and followed Otho through the door. Both men had to duck as they passed beneath the low frame. When Kirk reached back to close the door, he was surprised to see that on this side, limestone had been cleverly placed to cover the wooden planks. Only the keenest eye would ever be able to tell the door wasn't just part of the surrounding wall.

Kirk glanced around the tiny, windowless room. They appeared to be in some kind of storage closet. Shelves with linen sheets and towels lined the walls, and a musty scent lingered in the air.

Otho crossed to the opposite end of the closet. He set one ear against the door there, listening, and silently mouthed the word "guards."

Kirk tiptoed closer. The space was cramped; he would have preferred not to stand so close to Otho, and Otho likely felt the same way, but there was little to be done about it. Kirk ignored the urge to curl his nose.

"In the corridor?" he whispered.

Otho shook his head like he might be unsure, so Kirk closed his eyes, centered himself, and invoked mage-sight.

He Saw the life forces around him—the frightened scarlet flicker of a mouse as it scurried along the baseboards, the serene azure of a spider, slumbering upon its web in the rafters. He could even See his own yellow energy, blazing and apprehensive, and Otho's, a poised, collected deep green.

Kirk didn't linger there but moved his attention beyond the door. Tendrils of his consciousness spread out in every direction, probing the surrounding corridors. There, two halls over, ambled a pair of royal sentinels. His magic brushed over them, searching for any signs of suspicion or alarm. They were alert, but Kirk could detect nothing that would suggest they thought anything was amiss.

Kirk's eyes fluttered open as he withdrew his magic. "The hall is clear, but we have to be quick. There's a patrol nearby. I'm sure they keep a close eye on Neetra's door—"

"The key." Otho's hand went around the brass door handle. "Have it ready."

Fumbling with fingers that suddenly didn't wish to cooperate, Kirk reached into his pocket and pulled out the key. He dangled it beneath Otho's nose, just to prove the object hadn't been lost. The gesture was met with an icy glare.

Kirk braced himself as Otho tugged on the handle, easing the door open. The apprentice stuck his head into the hall, looking right and then left. And then he slipped silently through the doorway, motioning with one hand for Kirk to follow.

This is it. No turning back now.

Kirk held his breath and stepped beyond the safety of the closet. The gloomy hall outside lay empty. The lack of sunlight and general coldness of the space seemed a suitable domain for someone as unpleasant as Neetra Adelwijn. Candelabras lined both sides of the carpeted marble floor and cast faint illumination onto the golden trim of a grand, embellished door, not even fifteen paces from where Kirk and Otho stood. It was one of the only other doors in this hall and the most extravagant. It *had* to belong to the steward.

Kirk turned back long enough to ensure the storage room door was shut. Somewhere in the distance, he could hear the muted voices of the royal guardsmen, conversing with each other. Were they headed this way? Kirk had half a mind to whisk back into the closet. No. He couldn't do that. Not with so many people counting on him.

Otho's footfalls were silent as he made his way to Neetra's door. Kirk followed, his heart thumping so persistently within his chest he felt like he might keel over dead at any moment. He handed the key to Otho. At this point, Kirk questioned whether he would have been able to still his trembling hands long enough to get the blasted thing into the keyhole anyway.

For a few, agonizing moments, Otho turned the key, wiggling it one way and then the other. Kirk bit his lip. What if it was the wrong key? Or what if Neetra had suspected the key had been stolen and he'd replaced the lock? What if this entire mission was all in vain? What if—

The lock clicked, like wonderful music ringing in Kirk's ears, and then the door glided open. Otho pushed it just wide enough for both men to slip inside. The voices in the adjacent corridor were growing louder. Kirk could now hear the telltale sound of heavy boots scraping against the floor, closer and closer. The guards were coming.

Without risking a glance over his shoulder, Kirk dove into the suite, hoping beyond hope he hadn't been spotted. Otho eased the door shut and then quickly locked it from the inside. They both stepped away, listening, waiting. Kirk didn't even dare breathe.

Seconds passed. Then moments. And finally, after what felt like an eternity, Otho's rigid shoulders deflated. "They've passed by."

Kirk reached out with his magic, just to be sure. The sentinels had indeed moved on. Delicately, he probed their minds for any trace of alarm but found no evidence of it. He sighed with relief. "They didn't see us. We're okay."

"For now. Don't get too comfortable."

Turning around, Kirk got his first real look at the suite. The drawn curtains allowed little sunlight to come inside, though there was enough light to see. Tapestries and paintings depicting extravagant feasts and Ardenian high society hung from the walls, alongside beautiful dishes that had probably never been used. Decorative vases and other splendid trinkets lined a shelf in the far corner, and every piece of cherrywood furniture was draped with such lavish fabrics Kirk would have been scared to sit upon any of it.

But for all the luxury the suite offered, it didn't feel like a home. There were no family portraits or sentimental treasures, nothing to personalize the space. Just the same, cold overindulgence was everywhere Kirk looked: a fancy dollhouse, but not a place to live.

"There's nothing here," Otho sneered. "Just all of Neetra's useless shit."

Kirk motioned toward a doorway that must have led deeper into the suite. "Let's check in there. He must have *some* place he keeps personal belongings."

The inner room was much like the first: more fine furniture, more trinkets, more luxury, more, more, more. Kirk curled his nose. The contents of this one chamber could garner enough gold to feed a small country. Why did Neetra insist on keeping so many *things*? And why were there so many paintings of great ballroom dances yet not a single portrait of his family? Of his children?

"Check there," Otho said, jabbing a finger in the direction of a bulky writing desk that sat beneath the window. "I'll look in the bedchamber."

Otho disappeared into the darker recesses of the suite, leaving Kirk to inspect the desk alone. A scant amount of parchment paper was stacked on top. He took up the top sheet, being careful not to accidentally knock over a nearby inkwell. They couldn't leave any evidence they'd been here.

The first document was a wedding invitation from one Lord Diedrick Lyle, celebrating the marriage of his daughter. Kirk quickly skimmed the page and set it aside. The second document he tried was a petition for a wage increase from Neetra's estate staff, which the steward had denied. Kirk read through that one in more detail, but while Neetra's injustice toward the servants was unsavory, it wasn't *illegal*. Kirk moved onto the third and final document, which appeared to be some kind of progress report from Inan's private tutor. Kirk rolled his eyes as he read it, recalling the day when Liro Adelwijn had barged into the magery lesson and pulled Inan from Academy against the lordling's will.

With a sigh, Kirk set the report with the other documents he'd already perused. Nothing. There was nothing here to use against Neetra.

Otho's stealthy footsteps announced his return from the bedchamber. "Didn't find anything. You?"

Kirk shook his head as he organized the documents sitting atop the desk in the exact way he'd found them. "Nothing yet."

"Did you look *inside* the desk?"

"I'm getting to it," Kirk replied through gritted teeth, doing his best to ignore the other man's condescending tone. He pulled on the brass handle. The drawer didn't budge. *Oh, for the love of The Two.* "It's locked."

Otho let out a groan and crept closer. "He's hiding *something* if he's gone through the trouble of locking it."

Kirk's fingers traced the outline of the keyhole. "There has to be a key around here somewhere."

"Could be a million different places. Or in Neetra's pocket, for all we know." All but shoving Kirk aside, Otho went down on one knee before the desk, studying the drawer with a shrewd eye. Reaching into his pocket, he took out the key they'd used to enter the suite and jammed it against the keyhole. It was no use. The key didn't fit. Otho spat a curse. "I'll just bust the damn thing open if I have to—"

"You will do no such thing! If you break the desk, he'll *certainly* know someone was here!"

"I didn't come all this way to leave empty handed!"

Kirk desperately looked about the room. He refused to accept Otho might have a valid point. It could take marks—marks they didn't have to spare—to stumble upon a cleverly hidden key. Or worse, they could search all afternoon only to learn Neetra kept the key with him. Then what? This was their only chance. They had to find a way into that desk.

His gaze lingered on a vase that sat upon the windowsill. Its silver shimmer brought back memories of the fine dishes Matron Antonina would bring out for special occasions at the orphanage. She kept them locked away in the pantry the majority of the year, along with everything else of value. Of course, many of the children managed to get inside away. She always hid the pantry key in the most obvious places...

I wonder.

Kirk reached for the vase without thinking, turning the vessel onto its side. A bolt of elation shot through him when he heard something rattling within. He gave the vase a shake and a moment later, a tiny key fell into his palm.

Otho stared, dumbfounded. "How did you know—?"

Kirk set the vase back onto the sill. "Educated guess. At the orphanage, the mistress kept the food pantry locked. But we quickly learned she always hid the key within reach of the door. We'd often snatch the key and sneak inside for a snack. Sometimes, it was the only meal we'd get that day."

"Orphanage?"

Kirk smiled cryptically as he slipped the discovered key into the keyhole. "You'll find there is still much you don't know about me, Otho Dahkeel."

The weaponry apprentice fell silent. Whether he was reflecting on Kirk's words or merely had nothing more to say, Kirk couldn't be sure. At

155

the very least, perhaps Otho would stop harassing him about being a "pampered Imperial."

None of that mattered now though. They had a job to do and limited time. Breath trapped somewhere between his chest and throat, Kirk tugged on the drawer. This time, it slid open with ease. And it was stacked with parchment.

"Well, I'll be damned," Otho muttered.

"We'll split the stack," Kirk said, handing part of the pile to Otho. "It'll be faster to go through that way. Remember, we're looking for anything odd, anything that could possibly incriminate him."

Kirk settled down on the rug with his allotted half and sifted through the parchment.

There's something in here. I can feel it. Blessed Son, please let there be something.

The first cluster of papers he inspected were all bundled together. Kirk carefully undid the twine around them and spread what appeared to be a collection of letters across the floor. He picked up the first one; the parchment was so worn Kirk worried he might accidentally rip it in two, and time had lightened the ink from rich black to a faded, mustard brown. Kirk had to hold the paper close to his face to read the pale words.

Lord Neetra Adelwijn,

I arrived in Amsel this afternoon. The flowers alongside the streets were in bloom. After so long away, I'd forgotten how late spring arrives here. It would have been a beautiful homecoming if not for the sorrow in my heart. Perhaps it is a suitable punishment that I was sent back to Nales after failing to please you. I'll forever regret we were unable to resolve our differences—if not for our own happiness, then for that of the children. Nawaz is not your flesh and blood, but he is a sweet boy, and I know if you allow it, he will love you as a father. I pray you will love him the same as Inan and Inez. Please write at your earliest convenience.

Your loving wife,
Lady Giselle

Kirk frowned. Letters from Neetra's wife? This all felt too personal to be reading, but he picked up the second letter in the bunch anyway.

Lord Neetra Adelwijn,

Six moonturns have passed since I last wrote, yet I've received no word from you. I hope all is well and that the children are healthy. I miss them dearly. I understand you are a busy man, but if you would be so kind as to tell Nawaz his mother loves him, it would bring joy to my lonely heart. I trust you'll send correspondence soon.

Your devoted wife,
Lady Giselle

Kirk skimmed the rest, some dozen or so letters. As time advanced, the tone of each grew more desperate, more hopeless. Had Neetra never responded to any? That poor woman! What kind of monster could force a mother to abandon her children and then never allow contact with them again?

Kirk shook his head in disgust and picked up the final letter in the bundle. This one was penned recently. Neither parchment nor ink had lost any of its shine. The writing style was different from the others as well. Kirk read it with more attention.

Lord High Councilor Neetra Adelwijn,

I regretfully am writing to inform you that my sister, Lady Giselle Dagrun-Adelwijn, has crossed The Veil. By the time the Healers discovered the fever, it was too late to save her. She will be laid to rest beside our loving father and mother, inside the Dagrun family tomb. In her will, Giselle has requested her estate in Amsel be sold and all proceeds be divided equally among her three children, whom she loved with all her heart. Please respond at your earliest convenience so further arrangements can be made.

My greatest condolences,
Lothar Dagrun, Overlord of Dassel

"You find something?" Otho asked.

Kirk shook his head. He imagined he must have been making a horrified expression. "Nothing of use to us, at least I don't think. Were you aware that Neetra's wife is *dead?*"

"No. But for as much as anyone's ever seen her, I wasn't sure she even existed."

"Should I tell Dean Marc?"

"Can't hurt. There must be a reason why Neetra hid it from everyone."

Otho's attention drifted back to the document in hand, and the way his brows elevated suggested confusion.

Kirk cleared his throat. "Did *you* find something?"

"Birthing records."

"Neetra's children?"

"No." Otho's frown deepened. "Princess Gudrin and Tular Galloway's."

"Why would Neetra have those?"

"Don't know."

Kirk chewed his bottom lip, mind spiraling as he tried to find some sort of connection. "Well, we know he's trying to discredit the Radek family. Is there anything in Princess Gudrin's file of—*sensitive* content?"

Otho was silent as he skimmed the first page. "No. Just 'minor but

157

expected complications' after the princess was born. It's noted Marc oversaw the birth. We could ask him about it."

"That seems odd. Isn't birthing babes typically the job of a midwife?"

Otho flipped to the second page. "It is odd. But Marc was always the King's personal Healer. I guess the royal family trusted him over a midwife."

"Does Dean Marc even know how to birth a baby?"

"How in hell would I know?"

Kirk took a deep breath and pressed politely, "I only mean to say this doesn't seem to add up. And what about the other record? The one belonging to Tular Galloway. Isn't he the son of the Queen Mother's new husband?"

"Right. Aodan Galloway."

"Well, why would Neetra have his records?"

Otho brought the second paper to his face, examining it more thoroughly. "Huh. Says here Marc oversaw Tular's birth as well."

"Is Tular's mother someone important?"

"Just a palace servant. But she's also Hasain Radek's mother."

"The King's bastard son?"

"Right."

Kirk felt dirty for even asking, but—"So both the King and his bodyguard had—*relations* with the same—"

"Careful," Otho warned.

"I'm just trying to figure out why Neetra would have two seemingly unrelated birthing records hidden away inside his desk."

Unless they're not unrelated at all.

Kirk squirmed uncomfortably. "What if Princess Gudrin's parentage isn't what they claim? I mean, that day in the royal suite, you heard just as well as I did the way they all spoke about secrets and discrediting the King."

Otho speared Kirk with a glare that confirmed he'd treaded into forbidden territory. "I think you're just grasping at straws now. And frankly, it's none of our damn business."

"But you can't deny the possibility."

"Would it really matter? The princess was never in line for the throne. If it could somehow be proven the King wasn't her father, nothing would come of it. She'd be declared a bastard and life would go on. Why would Neetra go through all this trouble if it wouldn't prevent Prince Deegan from claiming the crown?"

Kirk crossed his arms over his chest and gave Otho a scathing look. "*Fine.* I'll let it go—for now. Let's keep looking."

"Yeah, so we can get the hell out of here."

"Yes, and you can go back to skulking under your bridge and eating small children."

Kirk winced. He hadn't really meant to say that aloud. Otho might have actually grinned as he went back to rummaging. It was the first time Kirk could recall seeing the weaponry apprentice smile.

"Now *here's* something," Otho said suddenly, snatching up a new file. "Looks like Neetra made a *generous* donation to the Armorer's Guild a few moonturns back, 'round the same time he was elected steward. Funny coincidence, that."

"Isn't it normal for guilds to have noble patronage?"

"It is, but remember which councilor Marc said has been voting out of character?"

Kirk reflected for a moment. "Lord Aldino?"

"Joaquin Aldino," Otho confirmed. "Head of Silver City's Armorer's Guild."

Kirk sucked in a sharp breath as the realization dawned on him, but he was quick to play the role of skeptic. "It's wartime. With thousands of soldiers to supply, it makes sense the guild would need extra funding."

"Maybe, but something smells fishy about this."

"If the donation *was* meant as a bribe, it would be difficult to prove unless we can trace the funds—or somehow convince Lord Aldino to admit to it himself."

Otho laughed. "Good luck with that."

Hope wavering, Kirk's hand instinctively went to the place where his mother's pendant usually rested against his throat, but it wasn't there. It was with Joel. *Joel.* He was counting on them.

In the distance, the midday bell began to toll. The melody was soft and lulling yet an insistent reminder they were in a race against time.

Otho's gaze grew darker as he glanced toward the window. "We need to hurry. No telling when Neetra will be back. Keep looking."

Kirk tried to focus on the stack of parchment, but his thoughts kept leaping from one dreadful place to another. As he'd expected, this mission was proving to be much more involved than either Marc or Joel had initially alluded to. Just how deep did Neetra Adelwijn's deceit really run? Even if they could prove he'd done wrong, had he already gained enough power that such allegations wouldn't matter? And what of the royal family? Yes, Joel and Marc trusted them wholly, but could Kirk? What was it they were so intent on hiding? How tangled was this web of lies? Kirk was beginning to wonder if he even *wanted* to further unravel the truth.

As he flipped through the parchment, sunlight caught a fleck of gold, drawing Kirk's attention. Knitting his eyebrows, the mage sifted through the pile with more care, until he found the source of the radiance. A folded document stood out from the others, not only by the fine vellum it had been crafted from, but also the blotch of golden wax pressed into its center. The seal, even broken as it was, was chillingly familiar. Kirk's stomach churned as he brought the document to his face for a closer inspection.

Oh gods, please don't let it be—

159

He sucked in a sharp breath as his darkest fears were confirmed. Imprinted into the waxen seal and glistening like a whetted dagger's edge, was the image of the Imperial dragon. The sight sent a bolt of terror straight through Kirk's heart.

No. Not the Empire. Not here.

Somehow, even though his fumbling hands weren't cooperating, he managed to unfold the document. Rich black ink flowed across the parchment, but Kirk skimmed past the words. His eyes were immediately drawn to the signature at the bottom: *Lord Adrian Titus, Archmage of Teivel.*

Kirk dropped the correspondence as though it had just scalded him. Maybe it had. Seeing his former master's name just about stopped his heart. Suddenly unable to breathe, Kirk let out a gasp and plopped onto his backside. What had he just discovered? Why was the Archmage writing to Neetra? Arden wasn't supposed to be in contact with the Northern Empire. The Empire had tried to murder Arden's envoys.

"*Damn it!* Kirk? What is it?"

How long had Otho been speaking?

Kirk was still in a fog, but he collected the scattered remnants of his mind enough to respond. "I—it's—it's a letter of correspondence. From the Archmage of Teivel."

Otho's eyes bulged. "Teivel? The *Empire?*"

"Y–yes." Kirk reached for the parchment once again, taking it into his shaking hands, and closed his eyes, a means to stop the room from whirling and also to prepare himself.

Blessed Son of Light, don't let it be an alliance. Please not that. Not here. Arden is doomed if Neetra treats with the Empire.

"Come on," Otho groaned. "What's it say?"

Kirk's chest deflated as he finally released all the air trapped inside his lungs. Nodding, he opened his eyes.

"To Lord Neetra Adelwijn," Kirk read aloud. "As always, it gives His Grace, Emperor Lichas Sarpedon, ruler of all the North and favored by the Blessed Son of Light Himself, great pleasure to receive your correspondence. Let me be the first to assure you that you need not worry about retaliation from our great Empire, now that the true enemy—Rishi Radek—is dead. However, justice still awaits his traitorous Right Hand, who had the audacity to accept the hospitality of His Grace—to dine from his table, to make false promises of comradery—all the while plotting his murder. It dissatisfies His Grace to learn that Koal Adelwijn has not yet had to answer for his crimes. Are you not the head of state? The seneschal should have been prosecuted the moment Rishi Radek met his demise.

"There is also the issue of the heir. Deegan Radek is a mere child, but do not underestimate him, nor how far those loyal to the Radek family will go to protect him. Deegan needs to be disposed of swiftly—as do his cohorts—if you wish to retain the crown and stay in the favor of the Northern Empire.

"You have done well by ensuring both seneschal and prince have gone to war. But His Grace prefers nothing be left to chance. I cannot divulge further now, but rest well tonight knowing that neither seneschal nor heir will return to Arden. The sands of Shiraz will consume them, along with all who are foolish enough to come to their defense. This I guarantee.

"With no Radek heir, and without the seneschal's lies to convince them otherwise, the people of Arden will embrace your leadership. You will soon be king, and the marriage of your son and Princess Claudia Sarpedon will be the beginning of a promising alliance between Arden and the Northern Empire. The plan is in motion. Very soon we will all reap the fruit of victory."

Kirk placed the letter on top of the others and dropped both hands to his sides. He parted his lips but couldn't find his voice, so he sat there, feeling numb and disconnected. This couldn't be real. None of this was real. He blinked, shuddering when the letter didn't disappear. It perched atop its pedestal of parchment, the golden dragon seal gleaming.

Angry tears welled in Kirk's eyes. He glared through blurry eyes down at his hands. This was madness! He'd risked his life to flee the Empire, and now Neetra was finalizing an *alliance* with them? And what was this about Seneschal Koal and Crown Prince Deegan? Neetra had already alluded to the fact that General Morathi would do anything he could to see the heir killed, but this sounded worse than anyone had anticipated. *Much* worse. The seneschal and prince could be in horrible danger if the Empire was plotting their demise. And Joel! Joel was out there with them. He could be at risk as well. Gods, the entire Ardenian army would be!

"Seems we won't be returning to Marc empty-handed after all," Otho said with a scowl. He had picked up the letter and was scrutinizing it for himself.

"This—is—this can't—"

Damn it! Why can't I speak?

Kirk let out a frustrated groan, swallowed, and tried again. "Crown Prince Deegan—Seneschal Koal—Joel—their very lives may be in jeopardy! Oh gods, this can't be happening! What are we going to do?"

"All right, calm down. Now's no time to lose your head. It's still a long walk back to Marc's office."

"But someone has to stop this! All of it! Arden can't align with the Empire! You think things are bad here now? Just wait until Sarpedon dispatches his 'diplomats' and suddenly we're all being crushed beneath Imperial tyranny. What will we do?"

Otho was already gathering the scattered parchment and reorganizing it. "I'll tell you what we're doing. You're going to take a deep breath, pull yourself together, and *we'll* put everything back the way we found it. And then get the hell out of here."

"And go wait for Marc to be out of council, right?" Kirk implored, rising to his feet. He didn't know how he managed the feat with the way his knees were shaking.

"Right."

"Marc will know what to do, won't he?"

Otho's hands stopped sorting, and he glanced up. The frown on his mouth was almost as unnerving as the Imperial message. "I don't know. But if the dirt we found today isn't enough to get that bastard off the throne, nothing will be."

Kirk didn't say anything aloud, but his thoughts were dark.

If we don't hurry, there may not be anyone left alive to contest Neetra's coronation.

CHAPTER TWELVE

Kezra couldn't help but notice how thin Gib had gotten. Sitting just within the glow of the campfire, shadows collected in the dips of his hollowed cheeks and sunken eyes. He looked as though he hadn't slept in ages.

With a sigh, Kezra set aside her sword and pocketed the whetstone she'd been using to sharpen the blade. Her own heart wasn't up for merriment or chatter, but Gib was her friend, so she felt compelled to engage him. "How are you feeling?"

True to his nature, as soon as Gib realized he was under scrutiny, his mouth curled into a half-hearted smile. His eyes gave up his lie when they refused to sparkle. Kezra's heart twisted. She hated seeing him so lost.

"I'm not sick, if that's what you're asking," he replied.

"You know damned well what I'm asking."

Kezra didn't bother to mince words. They might have left Liza's tribute in Perth, but Gib still carried the weight of his sister's death. Kezra worried, now that they'd crossed Shiraz's border ten days ago. At any given moment, they could find themselves standing face to face with the enemy. Gib needed to keep his head about him lest he lose it entirely. Perhaps she was being too harsh, but Kezra couldn't think of any other way to get through to him.

Gib winced. He refused to even look at her. "Everything hurts. I'm so tired and sore it's hard to focus on anything. Koal tries to talk to me, and I can't remember what he says. Zandi wants to spend time together, and I don't have anything to say. I don't know what's wrong with me."

Your heart is still healing, Kezra thought, though she'd never say the words aloud. She knew Gib would shut down if she did, so she settled for saying, "This is going to take time. And riding to battle is hard on anyone. I'm going to have calluses on my arse until my hair goes white."

Gib chuckled, but only just. "Yes, and when I'm lying on my deathbed, I'll *still* be finding sand in unfortunate places." He stopped there, his faint smile falling away.

Gods, he looked like he was going to weep. He probably needed to, but Kezra didn't know what to do for him right now. His pride wouldn't allow him to cry in front of the soldiers. But she would push him again, when they next had a moment alone. If she pushed enough, he might get the grief out of his system before they went into battle. The thought of Gib being so scattered while facing the enemy made Kezra's stomach knot.

"The boat's a'comin'!" some imbecile shouted, and both Kezra and Gib raised their faces toward the riverbank. In the distance, Kezra could just make out the outline of the Ardenian barge against the darkening horizon.

"'Ay!" the man yelled again. "E'ryone! The boat's 'ere!"

Kezra rolled her eyes. The fool might as well announce it firsthand to the Shirite scouts, who were sure to be watching the encampment this very moment. While the idiot was at it, he could let them know that not only was there food aboard, but medicines and other vital supplies. Maybe Shiraz could even make some fine torches with the women soldiers' sponge moss and linen strips.

"Keep your damned voice down!"

Kezra shuddered, not at the reprimand itself, but at who gave it. She hadn't realized Nawaz was so close.

He stood beneath the awnings of the Healers' pavilion, watching the approaching vessel with a shrewd eye. Even in the waning daylight, his blue jerkin stood out against the din of leather and mail armor. The polished crossbow he'd possessed since Kezra could remember was strapped to his back; now that the army had ventured into enemy lands, he never seemed to be without it.

Despite herself, Kezra wished she was close enough to see his eyes. Of all his features, they alone haunted her the most. They were what kept her awake at night, restless and hurting. His eyes had always been so *damned* beautiful.

Stop. Just stop.

Cheeks burning, she turned away. There was no reason to dwell on what she'd never again have.

Gib's scrutiny was as heavy and unyielding as her own. "How about you? How're you feeling?"

A spike of raw emotion speared her innards. Is this how Gib felt when she tried to talk to him about Liza? Kezra knew if she opened up, if she spoke, she might very well lose her precarious grip on control. She couldn't speak rationally about Nawaz. Not now and perhaps never again.

Gib seemed to understand. He sighed deeply, his gaze distant. "Perhaps the real war isn't even the one against Shiraz. Maybe the real war is the one being fought inside ourselves every day."

"Then I'm tired of war. Bone weary."

Gib nodded his agreement but said nothing more. Kezra could tell her friend's thoughts had shifted inward again. It was just as well. She didn't feel like talking either.

Out of the corner of her eye, she watched Nawaz take a torch into one hand and make his way toward the riverbank. The barge glided through the tranquil waters. Kezra squinted, barely able to see the forms of the crewmen on deck through the gloom.

Gib climbed to his feet with a sigh. "I'm gonna go make sure Koal doesn't need me for anything else tonight." He placed a hand on Kezra's shoulder as he passed by. "You'll be okay until I return, right?"

Kezra swatted his hand away. "I don't know how I'll manage without you."

Gib might have grinned, but he'd turned and left before she could get a good look at his face.

Her attention returned to the river. For a time she watched the barge as it floated closer, until it finally came to rest just offshore and anchors were dropped into the water.

Nawaz was already ordering soldiers to help unload the barge. The men on deck were silent as they lowered the gangplank. It was odd that none of them seemed particularly worried about the potential difficulty of unloading the vessel in the dark. Why weren't they lighting any torches?

Kezra's hands twitched as the little hairs on the back of her neck stood on end. She'd slipped her fingers around the hilt of her sword before she even realized it.

"Hey Kez." Nage tromped up beside her, a bundle of tinder stacked in his wiry arms. "Where'd Gib get off to?"

"Went to find the seneschal," Kezra replied absently, keeping her eyes on the barge.

A chuckle rumbled in Nage's chest as he added a few scraps of bramble to the fire. "Typical. He always goes runnin' off when there's work to do. What about your brother? He go to see the seneschal, too?" Nage wiggled his eyebrows.

Kezra snorted. "No. He's on patrol duty with Gara tonight."

"Ah, that's right. Lucky them." Nage nodded in the direction of the river. "So much for relaxin'. I reckon we'll be haulin' cargo 'til the wee marks. Hope they got mugwort salve this time. You don't even wanna know where I've been findin' blisters lately."

Any other time Kezra would have laughed along with him, but not now. An indiscernible grunt rolled off her tongue, but she refused to tear her gaze away from the riverbank. Nawaz was helping a group of soldiers secure the gangplank in the sand so the supplies on the barge could be unloaded. He called out a greeting to the crewmen on deck, but something wasn't right. Why weren't they answering him? Kezra's grip tightened around her sword and she stood up.

Nage's brow furrowed. "What is it? Somethin' wrong?"

The words had barely left his lips when a commotion erupted behind them.

"*Shiraz brigade!*" someone roared. "*They're attacking the camp's west side!*"

165

For a moment, all who were gathered froze, uncertain if this was some kind of crude prank or even one of Morathi's premeditated drills. But then a horn began to blare, and everyone knew this was neither ruse nor exercise. This was real.

All around, soldiers unsheathed their weapons and went running. The men who'd been helping Nawaz dropped the gangplank into place and followed the others, leaving the Healer alone on the riverbank. Kezra's heart thudded in her ears, but she didn't move.

"C'mon!" Nage said, scrambling to his feet. "Let's go!"

The hand that wasn't clutching her blade shot out, grabbing Nage's sleeve. "Wait."

"B–but—" Nage sputtered. "We need to help!"

Kezra held her ground. It was treason for a soldier to not follow an order, but something wasn't right here. She didn't know *how* she knew, but she did. Weapons Master Roland had always said to trust one's own intuition. So she did now.

It was just her and Nage and Nawaz left standing on the bank. Everyone else had gone running. And that's when the second attack came.

The crewmen on the barge raised their voices in a unified, bloodthirsty war cry, and Kezra knew the truth instantaneously. These weren't Ardenian crewmen at all. They were Shirite fighters, and this entire thing was a trap.

Kezra's body flew into motion. She dashed forward, reaching Nawaz's side before he'd even gotten the first bolt spanned into his crossbow. His wide, horrified eyes met hers briefly, but they had no time for words.

Cold steel flashed in the moonlight as cutlasses were waved in the air. The glint nearly blinded Kezra. She could hear Nage behind her, screaming for help. She opened her own mouth to yell as well but abandoned the effort a moment later. The Shirite fighters were already filing onto the gangplank, surging toward her.

She didn't dare take her eyes off the enemy, but she heard the snap of Nawaz's crossbow, and the Shirite leading the onslaught crashed into the water, an arrow lodged deep in his throat. It was a small victory but not enough. Two dozen more Shirites were still barreling at them.

"Kezra!" Nawaz's panicked voice rang in her ears, but she wasn't listening. If she could slay just *one* of them before the others cut her down, she'd be content. She wouldn't run, and she wouldn't die without a fight. She only hoped help arrived before Nawaz or Nage suffered the same fate.

With predatory eyes, Kezra targeted one of the fighters, a man who was neither tall nor broad, indistinguishable in every way except for the bright colors of his native garb peeking through the stolen Ardenian armor.

"You," she said, deathly calm, as if she were selecting a sparring partner.

166

He came at her, but hesitantly. His lack of finesse was already apparent. He wasn't trained, not like Kezra. With a heave, she swung her sword, catching him in the arm, cutting the limb straight to the bone. Blood seeped from the ugly gash. He howled and swung clumsily with his own weapon, but Kezra sidestepped and avoided the blow.

She tried not to think about the fact that he was probably younger than even her, that he was someone's son, someone's sibling, someone's beloved. She couldn't think about any of that, lest it destroy her.

His pilfered breastplate fit him poorly. Kezra saw her opportunity. Through gritted teeth, Kezra let out a growl and thrust her sword at him. The sound the blade made as it sank into the man's chest was nauseating, but less so than the throaty wail that followed. He collapsed, bleeding and gasping, and only the fog of battle trance kept Kezra from vomiting.

She gagged as she pulled her sword free of him. No amount of training could have prepared her for this. Not for taking a life. She didn't feel valiant. She felt like a murderer. Maybe she wasn't suited for war after all. Maybe she did deserve to die.

No. Focus.

Kezra whirled around, expecting at any moment to be overrun by the other Shirite fighters. But they were running away from her, up the riverbank and farther into the camp. With a confused cry, she gave chase. Why weren't they trying to kill her? Why were they running away? What were they—

Sudden and scorching heat seared Kezra's face as a nearby tent erupted in a violent plume of flames. Blinded by the explosion, she staggered back. Her skin felt like it was melting off her skull. She couldn't see anything.

"They have a Firestarter!" someone gasped. It might have been Nawaz, but Kezra's ears were ringing so deafeningly she couldn't be certain.

A Firestarter?

Kezra squinted against the burning smoke. Through the haze, the enemy brigade moved together. Those with weapons had formed a barrier around one man, hooded and draped in dark clothing. Fire spewed from his fingers and down his wrists, as though his arms themselves were living torches.

Daya, help us.

More flames. More excruciating heat. Another tent burning.

Shouts rose above the hiss of mage-fire. Ardenian soldiers were beginning to reappear now, but it might already be too late. The entire camp could be reduced to ash by the time the Shirite Firestarter was thwarted.

"They're heading toward the pavilion!" Nawaz howled. He crouched across the clearing, firing off one quarrel after another. "Cut them down! Don't let them ransack our supplies!"

In the midst of the inferno, Kezra's blood turned ice cold.

Oh gods, he's right. Dammit, they're not trying to kill us. They're trying to take out our medicine and food!

Soldiers rushed the Shirites, slashing at them, doing anything to slow their progression. A handful of enemy fighters had already fallen to Nawaz's deadly bolts, but the rest were fiercely protecting the Firestarter, all too willing to sacrifice themselves so his devastation could continue a few moments longer—and a few moments was all he needed.

The Firestarter waved one glowing hand, and the tent just beside the Healers' pavilion exploded, consumed in flame like it was made from dry tinder. Soldiers scattered like ants, trying to escape the blaze. Some of them were on fire, too. Their tortured screams filled the air.

Kezra let out a strangled cry, caught somewhere between rage and horror, and threw herself back into the fray. Steel clashed against steel, ringing in her ears and all the way to her core. She swung her sword, cutting through the enemy horde. Blood sprayed around her in every direction— enemy blood, but also that of her fellow soldiers.

A burning globule whizzed by, so close it grazed her cheek. The stench of scorched hair and flesh filled her nostrils. Whether it was her own or that of her fallen comrades, Kezra didn't know. Her head hurt like hell, and she could feel something hot and thick trickling down the side of her face, but she didn't stop. She *couldn't* stop. She had to get to that mage.

Ahead, the Firestarter stood directly in front of the pavilion with his hands placed against the cerulean canvas. Strange, foreign words rolled off his tongue. Kezra didn't understand the incantation, but she understood the meaning. This was it, the final stand. Any instant he was going to ignite the tent and every scrap of medicine and food the army had would be destroyed. Kezra's heart sank into the pit of her stomach. She wasn't close enough. She couldn't reach him. But maybe someone else could—

She craned her head around. "Nawaz! Nawaz, take out the Firestarter!"

Nawaz already had his crossbow pointed at the enemy mage. People ran around him, crossing his line of sight again and again, but his fierce eyes never wavered from the Firestarter. Motionless, like a predator on the hunt, he crouched and waited for an opportunity to strike.

Kezra cut down another fighter standing in her way, and as the man rolled aside, she saw a narrow path open to the Firestarter, not wide enough for her to make a run at him, but more than enough for one of Nawaz's quarrels.

"Now!" she shrieked. "Shoot him!"

Nawaz's finger hovered over the trigger, and vehement electricity gushed through Kezra's veins. She'd never known him to miss a mark he set for himself.

Do it. Take the bastard out.

A wild, triumphant grin spread across her face—

But the swish of his bolt sailing through the air never came. And the muffled gasp that filled her ears didn't belong to the Firestarter but to Nawaz.

Kezra looked back, horrified, as a lone Shiraz fighter jumped from the shadows and collided with Nawaz. The Healer managed to get his crossbow between himself and the enemy's blade, but the impact sent him teetering backward. The Shirite came at him a second time, cutlass aimed at Nawaz's chest. Kezra screamed as the two men went down in a tangle of flailing limbs and angry grunts, rolling down the riverbank and disappearing from view.

No! No! No!

She started to run toward the place she'd seen him go down, but a sudden impact from behind sent her spiraling facedown in the dirt. Heat licked her shoulders, and the sizzle of scorching canvas filled her ears. Her vision darkened and then went completely black.

When Kezra's eyes fluttered open, someone was violently shaking her arm.

"Kezra? Wake up! Kezra!"

Nage. She barely recognized his voice, frantic as it was.

Kezra rolled onto her back. Had she blacked out? And for how long? The sky above was a red sea of chaos, rippling with smoke and fire. Blinking, she tried to clear her stinging eyes and fuzzy head. People raced around her, shouting and carrying buckets of water that sloshed and muddied the ground. What was going on? Where were the Shirites? Was the fight over? Had the enemy been slain? Her chest constricted. Nawaz! Where was Nawaz? Was he all right?

She sat up so fast it made her dizzy. "W–what happened?"

Nage let out a relieved sigh. "Oh, thank The Two, you're okay." He took Kezra by the wrists and pulled her to her feet. "C'mon, we gotta get water! That damn Firestarter just about torched everythin' before we took him out."

Oh no.

"The medicine? The food?"

"All the medicine and most of the food. They set the damn boat afire, too! We're tryin' to save what's left of the grain. Our mages got a shield protecting it, but we gotta stop the fire from spreadin'."

Kezra dared look for herself. The Healers' pavilion lay in ruins, engulfed in smoke and flames. Soldiers were tossing water onto the charred exterior, but Kezra knew the contents inside were utterly destroyed. The army's medicine. Their food. The fodder for their beasts. All of it, *gone*. They were stranded in the middle of the desert with *nothing*.

She should have cared, but in the moment, a single, terrible reality had pushed all other worries aside. Nawaz. She'd seen him go down. He could be dead.

169

Her eyes wildly scanned the ruined camp. So many colors surrounded her: orange flames blanketing drab brown tents, thick black smoke rising into the night sky, scattered embers glowing red beneath unmoving bodies—but not a trace of blue. She couldn't see his blue jerkin anywhere.

Tears stung Kezra's eyes as hope faded. Where was he? Where was Nawaz?

Gib wandered in the direction of the command tent. Koal probably had no need for him—the seneschal would likely dismiss Gib with a terse word and flick of the hand—but it was the only excuse Gib's mind, muddled as it was, had been able to conjure.

Kezra meant well, he knew, but he just couldn't face her right now—not when his grief was still so fresh. He also knew she and the others were there for him, that all he needed to do was ask and they'd willingly embrace Gib's burdens as though his troubles were theirs too. He loved and appreciated the support, but sometimes, like now, he just wanted to wallow in his misery. Alone.

Liza's death was still a constant ache, like an open wound that refused to mend itself. Three sennights had come and gone, and still the pain hadn't lessened. Gib wondered if perhaps it never would. Would her death, like their father's, haunt him forever?

Gib nodded absently at the two guardsmen standing at attention near the command post. Originally members of King Rishi's Royal Guard, these men knew Gib and weren't prone to heckling him. The same couldn't be said for some of the dogs Morathi had appointed to "protect" Deegan. Gib could barely contain the urge to roll his eyes at the thought.

"Evening, Gibben," one of the guardsmen called out. He waved a gloved hand in greeting. The ornate embroidery stitched into the golden fabric glimmered with each movement. Tay would have appreciated such fine tailoring.

Gib's heart bled anew. Why must everything remind him of Liza's death? He still hadn't written to Tayver and Calisto, and now that the army had crossed into enemy territory, there wouldn't be an opportunity. He would have to tell the boys about Liza's fate in person, when—and *if*—Gib returned to Silver.

Daya, give me strength on that day.

He knew it was his responsibility, but for the love of The Two, he didn't want to be the one to have to break their hearts.

"Is Seneschal Koal here?" Gib asked.

"Aye. In council with the general, last we were informed."

Gib thanked him and kept walking—meandering, really. If anyone happened to be watching, they'd surely conclude he'd lost his way. The pointed apex of the command tent towered ahead, a dark blot against the eventide sky. Too close. He would arrive sooner than he wanted.

I should have walked the camp perimeter a few times before coming here. Maybe it would have given me time to get my head on straight. Chhaya's bane, how am I ever going to fight in this state of mind?

His hand slipped to Oathbinder's shagreen hilt, fastened to his belt. He carried the sword with him always, for protection and because it was a constant reminder of his vow—that he would put aside his fears, his doubts, and his grief—to defend Arden.

Truth be told, he needed the reminder. Desperately, at times. Some days, the vow was the only thing that held his mind intact. Sorrow and doubt occupied so much space in his heart it had become easy to forget what he was even supposed to be fighting for.

"Gib? What are you doing back here?"

Gib blinked and tore his eyes away from his boots. Joel's voice, despite its delicacy, still managed to startle him.

Joel sat upon an overturned bucket just outside the reach of the campfire's dancing flames. Prince Deegan and Tular lounged close by, and all three men were patching various bits of armor that had fallen into disrepair.

Gib shuffled closer. "Hi. Uh, is Koal here?"

"He's inside. With Morathi." Joel's serene expression faltered as he gestured toward the tent. "Why? Is something wrong?"

"N–no. Nothing's wrong. I just wanted to check in with him before I settled down for the night."

"Oh." A bit of the tension left Joel's shoulders. "Well, you'd best wait out here then. You know how Morathi is. He doesn't like the underlings around while he's discussing strategy."

Gib curled his nose and caught Tular doing the same. Quite frankly, Gib didn't care what Morathi did or didn't like. But waiting outside was certainly a better option than having to stand tight-lipped, listening to the general's filth. Gib wasn't sure how much longer he could stomach Morathi. His presence alone made Gib's skin crawl.

And when he opens his mouth and spews hatred—Daya, how does Koal not go mad?

Joel retrieved a second pail and plopped it down beside his own. "Here. Sit."

"You can help us patch armor." Deegan snickered.

"Is that a suggestion or a command, Highness?" Gib asked, bowing to the prince.

Deegan made a face. "Stop. You don't have to do that here." He tapped the place where his circlet usually lay atop his dark hair. "See? No crown. Uncle Koal insisted I take it off, to keep the enemy guessing. No crown means I'm off duty."

Gib snorted as he took a seat. "I don't think it works that way. Crown or no, you're still our prince."

Deegan's cheeks puckered when he smirked. "You're probably right. Father hated wearing his crown, but taking it off never seemed to help him get a moment's rest either. Hasain once told me that when Father first became king, he was summoned so frequently to the council chamber that he resorted to sleeping in his formalwear."

Gib shook his head slowly. "I imagine that couldn't be very comfortable."

"More comfortable than sleeping in armor," Tular muttered, his nimble fingers making quick work of a needle as he pieced a torn brigandine back together.

"That I would agree with." Gib laughed.

How anyone could possibly grow accustomed to eating, sleeping, and essentially *living* in armor while trekking through the desert was beyond Gib's comprehension. The leather and mail cuirasses worn by Arden's soldiers were miserably hot, and the linen undergarments beneath only made the heat even *more* intolerable. The only relief from the blasted armor came when it was time to bathe, and even then, they were rushed along before the moment could truly be enjoyed. It was just too dangerous to be caught defenseless. A soldier without his armor was likely a dead soldier.

"And then we have our precious little mages over there," Tular continued, nodding in Joel's direction. "Complaining about the heat in their flowy, silken robes. Ha! Spare me your woes."

Joel narrowed his eyes at the red-headed lord. "I don't recall voicing a complaint. At least not aloud."

"Maybe not you. But Hasain does. I swear to The Two, the next time he starts whining, I'm gonna knock his teeth down the back of his throat."

Deegan kept his eyes on his busied hands but didn't bother containing his laughter. "I mean, this *is* Hasain we're talking about. Would you really expect anything less from our brother?"

"No, I guess not."

Gib's eyes explored the clearing. "Speaking of Hasain, where is he?"

Again, Deegan chuckled. "He wasn't very enthusiastic about the idea of mending armor with us, so Uncle Koal sent him to fetch water."

"Alone? Are you—are you sure that's a good idea, given how—how many—uh—"

"Given how many people want my family *dead?*" Deegan said what everyone else was already thinking. "No, it's probably not a good idea, but if we're unsafe in the middle of the Ardenian army, then I suppose it's only a matter of time before Hasain and I both meet our doom."

Joel's hand shot up to cover a horrified grimace. "*Deegan!* Don't say such things! You're safe. Hasain's safe. Nothing is going to happen to either of you."

172

The prince merely shrugged and went back to his work, looking entirely crestfallen. He said nothing more, so no one else around the campfire did either.

Gib winced. He hadn't meant to put everyone in a bad mood.

Nice going, imbecile. Way to drag everyone else down into misery with you.

Joel touched Gib's shoulder then, startling him. He glanced up with guilty eyes, expecting to be scolded. Instead, Joel sighed heavily and asked, "How have you been? I feel like it's been forever since we last spoke."

Gib shifted in his seat. "What do you mean? We rode side by side just this morning."

"You *know* what I mean." The sharp edge to Joel's voice made Gib flinch, but a moment later, the mage's expression had already softened. "We haven't had a *real* talk since Perth. Things haven't been easy for any of us, most of all you. How are you holding up? Have you written to Tayver and Calisto?"

If anyone else had asked, Gib would have gotten defensive, even angry. But this was Joel, and the rules could always bend for him.

"I couldn't," Gib blurted out. A wave of untamable emotion washed over him, eroding his resolve and finally settling in the pit of his stomach like a boulder. *Don't cry.* "I couldn't write to them." *Do not cry.* "I couldn't bring myself to do it."

Joel's grip helped center Gib and brought him back from the cusp of the abyss. "Perhaps it's best you tell them in person anyhow. There will be time to grieve properly once you're home. Tayver and Calisto will need you, more than you probably realize."

Across the fire, Tular and Deegan kept their eyes respectfully low, diligently working, pretending not to listen.

Gib glared into the night. "Liza needed me, too, and I failed her."

"You did no such thing."

"I should have gone with her."

"If you had, your brothers would be sending *two* siblings across The Veil instead of one."

"Maybe not. Maybe I could have saved her. And even if I couldn't, it'd be better to die trying than to live with the guilt of knowing I should have done more."

Joel went quiet for a long time, and his face remained so still it was difficult to guess what he might be thinking. Finally, he said, "I think it's normal, when we lose someone dear, to have such thoughts. I often wonder if there was something I could have done to save Cenric. The better part of a year has passed, and at times, the guilt is still unbearable. That night in Teivel, he took a volley of arrows for me. He died so I could live. Did I ever tell you that?"

Gib shook his head. No. Joel hadn't said much about the late ambassador's death at all. "I'm sorry." He hoped that was enough. He didn't know what else to say.

Joel's eyes locked with Gib's. Impossibly blue and boundless, they were also open, the most genuine Gib could remember seeing them in a very long time. The remorse trapped within those sapphire orbs all but shattered Gib's soul.

"And I'm sorry, too." Joel's voice was a deep murmur, like water trickling through ancient stones. "For Liza and—everything else. When this war is over, I'd much like to finally share my grief with someone. Perhaps you'll feel the same way."

"Perhaps," Gib replied. His heart began to race. What was this fluttering in his chest? "And perhaps we can try again to mend our friendship—"

His words were lost when a horn blared in the distance. The sound pierced the night, toppling the serenity and sending it spiraling into chaos.

Gib sucked in a jagged breath and reached for Oathbinder. The call could mean only one thing.

"Draw your sword, Deegan," Tular said, already on his feet.

The young prince did as he was told, unsheathing his blade with trembling hands. "What's going on? What's that noise?"

"An attack, prince," Natori's collected voice lifted above the din of shouts and pounding boots. As deft as a shadow, she swept across the clearing and took post at Deegan's side. The runes on the Blessed Mage's ethereal sword flickered, bathing her dusky skin in brilliant shades of blue.

Gib jumped, startled. Where had she come from? Or had she been here the entire time?

The horn continued to wail, and now a second joined with the first.

Natori ushered Deegan toward the command tent. "Inside. Now."

She reached for the tent flap just as Morathi and Koal flew through the opening. Gib took a reluctant step back. In all the years he'd known them, he'd never seen the two men look more *terrifying*. Towering and fierce with narrowed eyes and gleaming weapon points, the sight of the seneschal and general standing side by side would surely be enough to send the entire Shiraz army running in fear.

"What's going on?" Koal demanded.

"We don't know yet," Joel said. "We heard the horn and—" He paused, the sound of heavy footfalls drawing his attention.

Deegan let out a relieved cry. "Hasain!"

All eyes turned as the Radek lord stumbled into the firelight. Ghostly pale with dark hair flying in every direction, Hasain looked like he'd been running from a ghoul. Gib braced himself.

Hasain trudged closer, inhaling sharply, gasping for air. "The men are saying Shirite riders are attacking!"

"*Dammit*," Koal spat through gritted teeth. "Where? Do you know where?"

"T–they said the western side of the encampment."

174

Morathi stomped forward, looming over Hasain, his steel grey eyes gleaming madly. "How many, *boy*?" he demanded. "How large is the enemy force?"

"I–I don't know." Hasain shrank beneath the weight of the general's glare. "I don't know anything else."

"Foreign scum. They're too cowardly to fight on the open battlefield, so *this* is what they resort to?" Morathi marched over to where his hulking warhorse was being restrained by a page. The general snatched away the reins and snarled at the boy, "Go! Spread the order! All able-bodied soldiers to the western front. Tell them to take no prisoners. If the enemy tries to run, our men are to chase them down and slay them."

"Yes, sir," the page uttered and scampered off.

Calling hastily for a servant to fetch his own horse, Koal turned a stern gaze onto Deegan. "You will stay inside until I return. Understood?"

Deegan's wide eyes were imploring. "Uncle, I can help."

"Not this time, Deegan."

"But I'm not afraid to fight—"

"I know you're not." Koal squeezed the prince's shoulder. "And when the time comes, I have no doubt you'll fight as valiantly as your father ever did. But now isn't that time. I promised I would protect you. I *won't* throw you into unnecessary danger."

Tears clung to Deegan's eyelashes, but with a stiff nod, he finally relented. He ducked as he crossed the threshold and went into the tent. Hasain followed on his younger brother's heels, and within moments both of their forms were swallowed by the shadows.

Koal motioned for Gib and Tular. "I want both of you to stay here with Deegan as well." He leaned in closer, lowering his voice to a mere whisper. Gib strained to hear the words. "No one goes inside that tent— even if they say I sent them. Do I make myself clear?"

"Of course, sir," Gib replied, shuddering.

Morathi huffed impatiently and swung atop his stallion. "Seneschal, I must insist we get to the front."

"*No one.*" Koal's eyes flicked toward the general, and Gib suddenly understood. What better time for Morathi's henchmen to make a move against Deegan than in the midst of an attack?

"Father," Joel called.

Gib's stomach flopped when he noticed the mage had gone to the hitching post where the rest of the horses were tethered and was now returning with his silver mare.

"I'm going with you," Joel stated firmly. "You'll need mages."

At that, Morathi twisted in his saddle. "A valid point." His unnerving gaze landed on Natori, still standing within the mouth of the tent. "The seneschal speaks highly of you, she-mage, though I've yet to see any such exceptionality myself. Why not join us in battle now and prove your skill to all?"

175

Gib's grip tightened around Oathbinder's hilt, wishing instead that it was Morathi's neck. That son of a horse's arse was *purposely* egging her on!

Unperturbed, Natori smiled mockingly. She waved her sword between herself and Morathi. "If it is my skill you doubt, *General*, I can give you a demonstration. Now."

Morathi bared his teeth, his disdain palpable. "The threat to the Crown Prince is right in front of us, yet even now you refuse to act?"

"You're right about one thing, General," Natori replied darkly. Her eyes were so narrow Gib could no longer see their color. "The threat *is* right in front of us—and you may rest assured that when the viper chooses to strike, I will spare it no mercy."

With that, she turned her back and swept into the tent. Gib wanted to cheer.

Morathi's face had gone so red he might burst at any moment. He glared over at Koal. "Insubordinate bitch! I could have her hung for such a crime."

Koal was as stone-faced as a statue. "Try it. Lady Natori has served Arden's ruling family for decades. I'd say calling her loyalty into question is a truer offense."

The general squared his broad shoulders, reminiscent of a giant cat preparing to pounce. Gib instinctively stepped closer to Koal, Oathbinder held at the ready. He could feel Tular at his back. No doubt the soldier was also prepared for any eventuality. Joel watched from his saddle, soft features drawn tight and the glow of magic resting atop his palms.

Go on. Try something, you treacherous bastard.

But Morathi was no fool. He sneered so hard it looked more like a snarl, but he didn't otherwise move, except to raise his flaring nose into the air.

"I trust you'll be along when you've finished coddling the prince," he jeered at Koal and, without awaiting a response, gave his warhorse a jab in the ribs. The beast leapt into motion. The long trail of the general's cape was the last part of him to disappear from view.

Tular made a noise. It sounded like a growl, low and guttural. "Say the word, Koal. Just say the word, and I will end that son of a bitch so swiftly he won't have time to beg for mercy." The conviction in his words was enough to assure Gib that the red-headed lord could and *would* do it.

Koal, however, shook his head. "No, Tular. There are many things worth dying for, but killing him isn't one of them."

"If I die for it, it would be the best damn thing I'll ever do."

"No. *Think*, Tular. Think of Aodan and Gudrin's safety, if not for your own. If you die, you jeopardize their lives, too. Neetra is already onto them. Your corpse would be all the proof he needs."

A servant came forward then with Koal's horse and held the palfrey steady while he mounted. Koal settled into the saddle, casting a final look down at Tular and Gib. "Go inside. Stay with Deegan until I return."

Gib watched from within the command tent as Koal rode away. Joel hesitated for only a moment before following his father. Gib wanted to call out to the mage, to tell him to be careful, but he was already gone, lost to the darkness.

The pair of royal guardsmen Gib passed earlier moved closer, taking post just outside the tent. Soldiers ran past, shouting orders to make for the battlefront, but the guards remained steadfast in their vigil. Like Natori, they were bound to the royal family and would never leave Deegan's side. Gib stayed just inside the entranceway, where he could still have a clear view of the happenings outside. He trusted the guardsmen, but another set of watchful eyes couldn't hurt.

"I should have gone with them." Deegan twisted his hands as he paced around the tent. The lanterns Koal and Morathi—in their haste to leave—must have left blazing cast dim light onto the prince's contorted face. "I shouldn't be hiding away like some spineless whelp. I'm the crown prince."

"You're a child," Hasain said.

"Just because *you're* afraid, Hasain—"

"I'm not afraid!"

"Enough," Natori interjected. "We're staying here because Seneschal Koal commanded it, not for lack of valor."

Both brothers fell silent, and for a time, the only sounds were that of the skirmish, somewhere to the west. Gib tried not to worry about his friends and which of them might be out there battling the Shirites, but such thoughts plagued his restless mind whether he wanted them to or not. He could only hope the fight would end swiftly. He couldn't bear the thought of losing anyone else.

"I apologize," Deegan said at long last. "You're one of the bravest people I know."

"And I was wrong to call you a child," replied Hasain. "I'm sorry."

Gib heard the patter of boots, and then Deegan appeared beside him. Together, they stared into the night.

"How many Shirites do you think there are?" Deegan asked.

Gib answered honestly. "Hard to say. My friend Gara, who's a scout, told me that bands of mounted militia have been following us since we crossed the border."

"Do they have the numbers to challenge our army?"

"No. They've all been small groups. Enemy scouts, in all probability. I'm sure they are reporting back to their war council, just as our scouts do."

Deegan went back to pacing, and Gib couldn't help but be reminded of all the times he'd watched King Rishi do the same.

"Why are they attacking if there's no hope they can beat us?" the prince finally asked.

Tular let out a grunt. His astute eyes followed the prince's every movement. "That's a damn good question. Fifty men against ten thousand? It's a suicide mission. I can't imagine why they'd think it's a good idea to engage us."

"Unless they know something we don't," Natori said ominously.

The tiny hairs on the back of Gib's arms stood on end. What could she mean by *that*?

A moment later, he had an answer.

A flash of light in the distance caught Gib's attention. He turned, meaning to see what had caused such a blinding flare—and that's when the first ear-splintering crackle reached him. He jumped back, nearly dropping Oathbinder into the dirt.

So loud. The sound was deafening, like a nest of hissing vipers trapped inside his skull.

"What was that?" Deegan asked amid a chorus of gasps. "Was that lightning?"

"No," Natori rasped. She and Hasain had both gone rigid. "Magic. Enemy magic."

A second flash lit the night, followed by a second thunderous roar.

Gib flew through the parted canvas, Tular and Hasain at his heels. Tendrils of fire reached toward the sky, turning the navy clouds blood red. The horizon was an inferno fueled by burning tents.

Gib could feel the blood draining from his face. "What's going on?"

"Mage-fire," Hasain choked. "They're burning the encampment!"

"B–but I thought the Shirites were attacking the western flank. That's not—that's—"

Gib reeled.

Shit. Shit, shit, shit!

He'd just come from that direction. That's where he'd left Kezra. And Nawaz. And that's where—

Tular uttered the horrible truth first. "They're hitting the Healers' pavilion. They're destroying our supplies!"

Another cluster of tents went up in flames. People were wailing for help. It took every ounce of discipline Gib possessed to stay put. "We need to do something!"

"No, Gib," warned Hasain. "We can't leave Deegan."

Gib let out a frustrated cry, but he knew Hasain was right. Koal had made them swear they'd stay. The seneschal was counting on them. *Deegan* was counting on them.

So he waited, waited and watched as flames consumed one tent after another. Screams filled the night, but Gib could do nothing. He couldn't help them: not Koal, not Joel, not Kezra, nor Zandi, Nage, Nawaz, or Gara. He could do nothing for them except beg The Two for their safety.

Every moment that passed felt like an eternity, and the longer Gib waited, the more convinced he became that time had somehow halted entirely. Was he trapped in some kind of alternative reality? Would he ever escape it?

Finally, Hasain made a sound, perhaps a whimper. He'd had his eyes squeezed shut for some time, but now he opened them. "I don't feel the foreign magic now. It's gone. I think—I think the enemy's been slain."

"Look!" Tular pointed at the smoldering skyline. "The fire's not spreading anymore. They must have gotten it contained."

Gib looked and saw Tular spoke the truth. Black smoke billowed against the sky, but the flames were guttering. The sight should have made him jump with joy, but it didn't. He couldn't celebrate until he knew his friends were safe and the food and medicine stores were intact. How would he survive if either had been destroyed? How would *anyone* survive?

The canvas rustled at Gib's back, and Deegan peeked outside. "Is–is it over? Is the danger gone?"

Tular and Hasain exchanged somber glances. Gib knew what they were thinking. He knew because his thoughts were the same.

Was the skirmish over? Yes. Was the danger gone? *That* remained to be seen. When the fires were doused and the smoke had cleared, they might discover their doom awaited them in the ashes.

Smoke billowed all around, invading Kezra's lungs and coating her tongue with bitter ash. It didn't matter. Vague noises and frantic voices calling out crackled in her ears but never came to settle in her mind. It didn't matter. Stepping over lifeless bodies, her fuzzy eyes noted some were Ardenian and some were not. It didn't matter.

The Healers' pavilion lay in ruins, scorched and collapsing onto itself. Only small sections of cerulean canvas still stood, haphazardly, to defy the attack it had undergone. She bit the inside of her cheek until the taste of copper mixed with the soot. It didn't matter. It didn't matter. *It didn't matter!*

A strangled cry vented between her chest and throat. Where was he? She'd seen him go down near here. Even in the darkness, she should be able to see the bright blue of his Healer's jerkin.

Where is he?

Soldiers and Healers moved through the ruined war camp, tending the wounded and collecting the dead, but Kezra could only think of one. She refused to worry for Zandi, for Gib, for all her friends. They were all fine. They *had* to be. She couldn't possibly lose Nawaz *and* them both.

"Lookin' for someone?"

Kezra spun on one heel, sword raised and ready to slay whatever creature it was that *dared* sound like him. She choked on a gasp as the moonlight caught the shine of azure eyes and a wide, toothy grin. Could it be—Yes.

179

Yes!

Nawaz watched her from within the remnants of the pavilion. Uniform marred with blood and dark hair tousled wildly about his alabaster face, he was a god, standing inside his broken temple of chaos.

Kezra reeled. He should be *dead*. She'd seen him go down. Yet here he was. Blood pooled around a gash to his left sleeve, but the grip on his crossbow was white-knuckled. He was alive. Alive, and as strong as he'd ever been.

Heart hammering, she flew at him, sword in one hand and the other clenched into a tight ball. "You son of a bitch! I thought you were dead!"

She swung her fist, wanting nothing more than to take out that lewd grin once and for all. How *dare* he frighten her like that? How *dare* he allow her to believe he was *gone?*

He caught her fist before she could reach him, ensnaring it in one large, calloused hand. His grip was vice-like and scorching hot. Kezra choked back a gasp. She'd forgotten how fast he could be.

"No," he rasped into her ear.

Nawaz leaned over her, blue fire roaring behind his crazed orbs, more beautiful and terrifying than she'd ever known possible. And she could tell from the husk in his voice that he wasn't himself just yet, that he was still the wild beast war demanded him to be.

Kezra thought to yank away, but already he was pulling her closer. She opened her mouth to lift a complaint, and his closed over hers.

And that was it. The emotions she'd been stifling, pushing down for moonturns, trying so desperately to ignore, exploded within her, drowning all sense of clarity and reducing her to the most primitive form. She was an animal, as feral and aching as he. A moan tore free from Kezra's throat as she flung her sword aside and melted into his arms.

He tasted of ash, of rage, and of longing. His hands were on her, all over her, and now the longing blazed in her as well. Some feeble sense of dread brushed the edge of Kezra's faltering sanity, but she shoved it aside. She knew they weren't supposed to be doing this, but—why? They could both die tomorrow. Was it so selfish to have what they so fervently desired now?

Nawaz pushed her down into the tangled mess of what used to be the Healers' pavilion. Kezra's hands clawed at him and his clawed at her. She yanked and ripped until she could find skin beneath his ruined jerkin. He was filthy and on fire. So was she. They'd always balanced one another before, opposites in every imaginable way, but now they were the same, both aching. Two flames burning together.

Smoke hung in the air, thick like fog. It wafted into Joel's nostrils and made his eyes water. It covered his clothing, dulling the white fabric to shoddy grey. There was no escaping it.

His hands were shaking. He looked down at them. He barely recognized his own fingertips, dirty and blanketed with ash.

Somewhere behind him, his father's voice clashed with that of General Morathi's. Joel blinked, trying to focus on the words, but his mind was as hazy as the encampment. His jaw ached from the tight clench he held, and his weary limbs screamed for reprieve, but he couldn't rest now. He couldn't even entertain the thought of it.

The skirmish had ended over a mark ago, and the cleanup effort was well underway. Soldiers and Healers alike were collecting the bodies of the fallen and tending to the wounded. Casualties on the Ardenian side were light. *None* of the enemies survived. But the Shirites had still won. They'd won in the biggest way possible.

"What would you have us do instead, Seneschal? Would you rather we slowly starve to death?"

Joel winced. The words weren't directed at him, but Morathi's accusation stung, regardless.

What *were* they going to do? The Healers' pavilion was gone, burnt to the ground, all of its contents destroyed. Even worse, the majority of the army's grain stores had also been incinerated. In a matter of moments, the enemy Firestarter had infiltrated the heart of the Ardenian war camp and taken out their two most precious commodities. Not even the barge was spared. Its blackened husk now rested at the bottom of the river.

They were alone—ten thousand soldiers, stranded in the middle of the desert.

Daya, help us.

Joel's eyes wandered around the clearing. Koal and Morathi debated within light of the campfire. Deegan pressed close to the seneschal, while Natori and the prince's royal guardsmen watched diligently from the shadows of the command tent. Other soldiers lingered nearby, awaiting orders or merely hoping to overhear good news. Their demoralized faces and hollow eyes made Joel's stomach flop.

"Pillaging is no light decision," Koal said, keeping a rigid hand on Deegan's shoulder. "If we go into the homes of the innocent and start taking from them, *they* will have reason to hate us, too."

Morathi had been storming back and forth before the fire, but as Koal finished speaking, the general stopped dead in his tracks and whirled around. "*The innocent?* Do you have *any* idea where we are? There are *no* innocents in Shiraz!"

Joel glanced down at Gib, who shifted nervously. He sat on a bucket, the same one he'd been resting on before the skirmish broke out. His complexion was noticeably paler than was typical, and his hands were shaking in his lap. He didn't say a word, but his desperate eyes kept scanning the faces of the gathered soldiers. He was looking for his friends, and for his companion.

Joel let out a sigh, equally worried. He hadn't seen Nawaz since before the attack.

He's busy helping the wounded. That's why he isn't here yet.

Joel couldn't contemplate the alternative without growing faint. What if Nawaz were dead? What if Heidi were left a widow, and their unborn child brought into the world without a father?

No. He's alive. He has to be.

"The village-folk in this region never asked to be part of this war," said Koal.

Morathi's voice climbed higher. "Those heathens invited themselves into this conflict when they decided to bury their heads in the sand while their leaders crossed our border and slaughtered our people. I say guilty by association!"

Murmurs of accession arose from the crowd. The tension in Joel's jaw pulled tighter. This wasn't boding well. The majority of the soldiers seemed to be *agreeing* with Morathi.

Without warning, Gib clambered to his feet.

"Gib?" Joel reached with one hand, but Gib was already making his way across the clearing.

Two people met him halfway there. One was Gara; Joel recognized her cropped hair and dappled scouting gear. Her uniform was soiled and torn in several places, but otherwise it seemed she'd made it through the skirmish unscathed.

She had an arm hooked around Zandi's back, helping support the mage as he limped along. He clutched one blood-stained hand to his chest and his handsome face was twisted in a pained grimace.

Gib's own expression flitted back and forth between relief and concern. He put a hand on Zandi's arm. "Are you all right? Here, let me see your hand."

"I'm fine. It's nothing, just a little scrape. H–have you seen Kezra?"

"Not yet. I'm sure she's okay."

Zandi went rigid, his eyes widening. "I have to find her." He struggled against Gara's hold. "Let me go!"

Gara only tightened her grip. "You need to rest. You're exhausted."

"B–but I have to find my sister!"

"*I* will go look for Kezra and Nage both," Gara said firmly. "You're going to pass out if you don't sit down."

Gib supported Zandi from the opposite side. "Come sit down. Please? Kezra will kill us if she finds out we let you go wandering off in this state."

Zandi fought half-heartedly but allowed them to lead him. Gib pulled

182

the overturned pail closer, and the mage slumped down onto it. Tears rolled down his pale cheeks faster than he could wipe them away.

"We came here to annihilate the threat to Arden!" Morathi's voice boomed above all other sounds.

Koal sneered, an expression uncharacteristic of him. "So you'd raid goat herders and farmers? These people hardly have the means to feed themselves, let alone a foreign army."

"These *people* are all the same! Dirty, savage, demon worshippers. Arden would be safer if we wiped *all* of them off the map."

"I won't allow for the slaughter of innocents. This is *not* Arden's way."

Zandi suddenly sat up straight, inhaling sharply, and Joel's attention wavered from the debate.

A familiar figure materialized out of the gloom and, upon seeing Zandi, raced toward him.

Joel put a hand to his mouth. Kezra! She *was* alive!

Kezra met her brother with open arms, and he fell against her bosom, sobbing quietly. "I thought—I thought the worst. I thought you were dead."

"I'm all right," Kezra replied, stroking his long hair. She glanced up at Gib and Gara. Her eyes might have even been misty, or perhaps only Joel's were. "Nage is okay, too. He was helping put out the fires when I last saw him."

Gara let out a deep sigh. "Thank The Two."

"What about Nawaz?" Joel blurted, unable to contain his apprehension any longer. He knew Kezra and the Healer were at odds, but that didn't matter right now. He *had* to know that Nawaz was safe. "He was at the pavilion before the attack. Did you see him?"

Kezra's shoulders tensed, and the smile on her lips faded. "Nawaz? He—he's—" Her cheeks first went pale and then darkened to a horrible, blotchy red. Why wouldn't she raise her eyes? Why wouldn't she look at him?

Blood rushed through Joel's ears. He could feel the world spinning out of control. "Oh, gods. He's not—not—is he—?"

"I'm okay, Joel."

Joel whirled toward the familiar voice. "Nawaz!"

The Healer trudged forward from much the same direction Kezra had. His jerkin was stained with dried blood, but he didn't appear to be injured. The blood might not even have been his.

Joel reached for Nawaz without thinking, touching one of his tattered sleeves. "I was so worried."

Nawaz flinched, the first sign that all wasn't well. His deflated eyes darted once toward Kezra, but then he turned his back to her and his broad shoulders sagged. Ashen cheeks flushed into a blaze of crimson.

"J–Joel," he stuttered with a heaving chest.

Joel took the Healer's hand and squeezed gently. What had stolen the life from Nawaz's gaze? What horrors had he seen out there that could reduce him to a shade of his former self?

"Stand with me," Joel whispered. Whatever Nawaz was struggling with, he needed someone to ground him. "It's going to be all right. You're not hurt, are you?"

Nawaz hung his head but couldn't conceal the tremble along his bottom lip. "No. I'm fine."

Joel wanted to press his friend for more, but the argument by the fire had escalated. Swallowing uneasily, he listened.

"We should have focused our efforts on stabilizing the border," Koal said. "We never should have *crossed* it."

Morathi's face twisted into a fierce scowl. "We crossed because the lost souls of Ashvale and the brave soldiers who fell at Kaleth's Crossing deserve *justice!*"

Spirited shouts arose from the crowd.

"There's no justice to be had if one reckless decision leads to the deaths of ten thousand soldiers. Without food for the men and beasts, we won't be able to sustain ourselves all the way to Tahir—and you can bet your arse the raiders won't allow any more barges to arrive. Look, we're three sennights from the border. If the army turns back now, it can reach Perth before losses begin to mount."

"You'd have us run like dogs? You'd let the Shirite savages *win?*"

"There is no path to victory for us now—"

"Like *hell* there isn't." Morathi turned his back to Koal, addressing the gathered soldiers directly. "We mustn't fault the seneschal for wanting to tuck tail and run. After all, it's what he's used to. For *years*, he served a spineless ruler who was content to roll belly-up and allow our enemies to ransack our borders without reprimand!"

"General—"

"But no longer! Arden's new leader will not watch idly while our country is terrorized by heathens, and neither will I. As Seneschal Koal is well aware, as commander of the army, *I* have the final word in all matters of warfare, and I've made my decision. *We march on!*"

Joel held his breath. Why were the soldiers cheering? Had they already forgotten that men like Morathi and Neetra were the reason the army was in this dire situation to begin with?

Morathi raised both hands into the air. "I say it's time the world knows Arden is a force to be reckoned with! I say it's time Shiraz answers for its crimes! I say we pillage and plunder our way straight to Tahir's gates and let those dirty heathens know the *true* meaning of terror! What say you, soldiers of Arden? Are you with me?"

A deafening roar of cheers and clapping hands answered his call.

Joel watched in disbelief. Lies! Why were they listening to the general's lies?

184

He looked to his father for direction, but Koal had fallen back, putting himself between Deegan and the wild crowd. Natori laid a palm over the hilt of her sword, and Tular and Hasain, consciously or not, closed tightly around the prince.

A new terror seized Joel's body. *Oh, gods. Deegan.* The army wouldn't turn on Deegan, would it?

Morathi smiled, sickeningly smug, as the soldiers chanted his name. No one seemed to pay any attention as Arden's Crown Prince was escorted inside the command tent. Joel stared, face contorted by revulsion. This couldn't be real! This couldn't be happening! Had the army really just sided with Morathi?

Nawaz's grip tightened around Joel's fingers. "Come on, Joel. We should go, too."

Joel allowed himself to be led away—away from the insanity, away from the madness. He couldn't allow himself to think any of this was real. If he did, the tiny speck of hope he clung to would surely slip through his fingers and be lost forever.

CHAPTER THIRTEEN

"Kirk. Otho. Come inside."

The ominous undertone in Marc's words didn't sit well in Kirk's stomach.

Kirk stepped into the dean's office behind Otho and closed the door. He wiped a strand of damp hair out of his face, wishing he had a change of clothing. The midsummer heat was downright oppressive, and he'd run all the way from the far side of the building to get here. Now his sweaty robes were clinging to his arms in a most unbecoming way.

Marc sat in the windowsill, looking as scattered as the loose parchment strewn across his desk. He stared through the glass pane into the Academy courtyard like he was watching a battle play out before his eyes.

Kirk took a tentative step. "You wanted to see us?"

"Have a seat."

Swallowing the lump in his throat, Kirk lowered himself into one of the two chairs meant for guests. Otho claimed the other.

Marc was silent for some time, as if something outside the window held him spellbound. His vacant gaze suggested he stared at nothing, however. Kirk knew the look; the dean's thoughts were deep, and most likely dark.

Marc finally rose and went to sit behind his desk. Clasping his white-knuckled fingers together, he leaned against the hardwood, as though he suddenly couldn't find the strength to stay upright by his own accord. His shoulders sagged. "I received news. There's been an attack."

The shock of the words sent Kirk leaping to his feet. "*What? * Where? Wh—"

"Sit. *Down.*"

Kirk flopped back into the chair. His ears thudded along with his heart. He couldn't breathe.

Marc closed his eyes, exhaling deeply. It seemed he, too, was struggling to maintain his composure. "I only know what I was told at council yesterday. A small number of Shiraz invaders overthrew one of our supply barges on route to deliver supplies and then used the vessel to infiltrate Arden's war camp. They destroyed the majority of the army's food and medicine and left half the encampment in ruins."

Otho's amber eyes were uncharacteristically wide. "Were there casualties? How many soldiers did we lose?"

Kirk cringed. He didn't want to know.

"Casualties were—light. Crown Prince Deegan and Koal are both safe."

"What about Joel?" Kirk couldn't resist asking. "Joel's safe, too, right?"

Marc hesitated, and Kirk could tell the dean was uncertain. "Joel has a good head on his shoulders. I'm sure he's all right."

Irrational resentment stole Kirk's voice away, but truly he wasn't angry at Marc, only scared because there was no way of knowing for sure. *Joel is fine. He has to be.*

"Judging by the letter you found in Neetra's suite," Marc went on, "this *could* be the doing of the Empire."

Otho nodded in agreement, but Kirk remained unconvinced.

He thought back to the correspondence from Adrian Titus. "I don't mean to sound skeptical, but I don't think so. The Empire wouldn't have stopped after destroying just the food. It was clear in the letter that Sarpedon wanted *all* opposition to an Imperial alliance annihilated. They would have gone after Prince Deegan and the seneschal directly. They wouldn't have left any chance of the heir's survival, nor Seneschal Koal's."

"What will the army do now?" Otho asked. "Surely they must turn back."

Marc grimaced. "Morathi's given the order to march on. The High Council, of course, voted in favor of the general's decision."

A shudder raced up Kirk's spine. "Are they mad? What if the Shirites sink the *next* barge that tries to reach Arden's troops? What then? They'll be even farther from safety, with no food, and no way for aid to reach them."

"There will be no more ships venturing into enemy territory. The council won't risk losing another. Neetra already sent word to freeze all future consignments. The army will have to pillage."

Kirk threw his hands into the air. "So they'll arrive at Tahir's gates weak, hungry, and completely demoralized *and* will probably be walking straight into a trap devised by the Northern Empire. Isn't there anything we can do? Why can't we send a message to Seneschal Koal? There's still time to warn him—"

"Even if we *do* send a message, there's no guarantee it will ever reach Koal," Marc replied, rubbing at his temples.

"Right," Otho snorted. "And you can bet your arse Neetra's got his cronies intercepting every pigeon from here to the border. If he finds out we know more than we should, he'll be storming our doors before we can blink. We'll all be hanging from the gallows and Seneschal Koal will be none the wiser."

"We have to do *something!*" Kirk protested.

Marc shuffled through the parchment atop his desk, as if half-heartedly attempting to organize it. "Our friends on the front are beyond our reach. We have to trust Koal's experience and judgment. If anyone can get them out of a dire predicament, it's him."

Kirk bit his tongue to keep from lashing out. Did Marc not understand how ruthless Lichas Sarpedon was? Yes, by the grace of the Blessed Son—or dumb luck—Kirk and the others had escaped Teivel, but a half-starved, unprepared Ardenian army would be no match for the might of the Northern Empire. Sarpedon would make *damn* certain of it. He'd hit Arden hard and without mercy. Even Seneschal Koal wouldn't be able to escape this time.

Otho folded his arms over his chest. "What's our next move? What can we do to help from here?"

"I don't know. I just don't know anymore. I've already asked far more of you both than I ever should have. I feel like we're up against a bigger force than Koal or I or anyone else ever imagined."

Kirk's heart began to hammer painfully in his chest. Marc wasn't giving up, was he? "But all the information we found inside Neetra's suite—"

"—is invaluable, but not exactly useful at this time."

"But he's scheming with Arden's enemies! He's plotting to overthrow the Radek line! There must be *someone* you can go to—someone you can tell."

"Who, Kirk? *Who?* Koal's at war. Deegan's gone, and even if he wasn't, he's powerless anyway. And the rest of the royal family? They're *prisoners* inside their own palace. Neetra has swayed the majority of the councilors to his side. He's bought off everyone else and even placed his own agents among the Royal Guard. Now he's spreading mistrust and lies about the Radek family, and the worst part is that people are *listening* to him." Marc squeezed his eyes shut. "Koal is relying on me to hold things down inside the council chamber, but I'm only one man. He was always the unifier, not me. I—I don't know what to do." Marc's voice cracked, on the verge of shattering entirely. He squeezed his eyes shut. "I should have checked it. Why didn't I check it? None of this would have happened! Why didn't I check the damn vial?"

Kirk didn't have any answers. He only had questions. Questions he *never* got explanations for. Would Marc ever entrust him enough to divulge more than cryptic allusions? Hadn't he proven himself loyal by now?

Kirk glanced over at Otho and could tell the weaponry apprentice wanted to know just as badly. And why shouldn't he? They'd both risked their lives for Arden, and neither of them even knew *why*. They deserved answers. Now.

Kirk cleared his throat and asked bluntly, "King Rishi was murdered, wasn't he?"

Marc's eyes popped open and he stared, bewildered, across the desk. Kirk held his breath. So did Otho. Neither man dared breathe until a response was given. Would the dean finally reveal the truth? Would he finally tell them what had really happened to the King?

Silence swelled, filling the room, but at last Marc slumped in his seat and nodded once. "He was poisoned. The healing remedy that was meant to ebb influenza symptoms was tampered with before it was given to him. He drank it without knowing, and by the time we figured out it was poisoned, it was—too late to save him."

The news should have surprised Kirk more than it did, but he'd been suspecting it for moonturns already. "So that day Otho and I went with you to the royal suite, the talk about the vial you gave him, that was it? That was the poison?"

"Yes. I gave it to him without checking it again. It's my fault the King is dead."

"You didn't do it on purpose—"

"It doesn't matter. I still *killed* him! I was framed like a chump. And then to save my worthless arse, Rishi ordered us to make his death look like a suicide. For all the help I've given, I might as well be dead, too. I should have just turned myself in. Maybe none of this would have happened if I had."

Kirk reached across the desk and laid a hand on Marc's forearm. "Or maybe events would have played out in exactly the same way, except the royal family would now be without one of their most fiercely loyal allies. I haven't been here for long, and I don't know very many people, but even *I* can see how much you do to help your friends. They'd be lost without you."

Marc shook his head, blurry-eyed. "Aodan was right. I failed Rishi. And now I'm failing what's left of his broken family."

Kirk didn't know what to say, so he squeezed the dean's arm, hoping the gesture would be enough to show Marc he wasn't alone.

"Who did it?" Otho asked darkly. "Who meddled with the remedy? You know, don't you?"

Marc's face contorted, but he didn't look up. "We have a pretty good idea who was behind it."

A horrified squeak escaped Kirk's mouth. "Was it Neetra?"

Otho curled his nose. "Neetra's too much of a coward to do anything himself, but I'm guessing he gave the order."

"Yes," Marc rasped. Kirk could feel the dean shudder. "There are dangerous men walking among us."

Kirk's skin crawled as he stared out the window, trying to collect his scattered thoughts. Contemplating the King's death wouldn't do any good right now. Right now they needed solutions for the mess left behind. Marc seemed at wit's end, ready to accept defeat, but Kirk had learned from years of surviving on Teivel's streets never to give up.

"There has to be more we can do. What about Councilor Aldino? I think it's pretty safe to say he's been bought off. Otho and I more or less found proof of it inside Neetra's office."

"I already looked into it," Marc said. "Recordkeeping of financial contributions to any of Silver's guilds are available to the public. The Adelwijns *did* make a considerable donation to the Armorer's Guild, but there's no evidence of the funds going anywhere than where they were intended. I don't think Joaquin pocketed any of it for himself."

"He's guilty! I just know it. If only we could get him to confess—"

"Why would he? Joaquin's a little daft, but he's not a complete idiot. I'm not sure why he voted for Neetra to be steward in the first place, but turning on him now that he's in control of the High Council would almost certainly have severe repercussions. Joaquin has much he could lose."

"What if we offered him amnesty in return for the truth? And protection?"

Marc barked a broken laugh at that. "Protection? We couldn't even keep the *King* safe."

"There must be a way." Kirk allowed the silence to fester for several moments before he pressed on. "In the Empire, highborn society was laden with scandal. I see no reason why that wouldn't hold true in Arden as well. You say Lord Aldino has much he can lose. Maybe we can take advantage of that."

Marc raised a brow. "What are you suggesting exactly?"

"Blackmail," Otho muttered, and Kirk nodded in agreement.

"Problem is, we'd need something worth blackmailing him over," Marc replied. "Over the years, I've been privy to some of the more *interesting* gossip at court—probably one of the reasons Koal and Rishi tolerated me for so long—and I'm telling you, I have *nothing* on Joaquin. No secrets, no dirt, nothing."

Kirk gave the dean an incredulous stare. "There must be *something*."

"Not that I can recall. The man's practically a saint. He's always been a good sort, and in the past he typically voted in favor of the King. The fact that Joaquin is now one of Neetra's most staunch supporters is almost unfathomable."

"Well, clearly he's changed. The jingle of golden coins must have been too tempting for him to pass up. Neetra paid him off. It's the only explanation."

Marc rubbed the back of his neck. "Maybe. But I asked around, and there are no indications the Aldino family is in any kind of financial distress. It just doesn't make any sense. Why would Joaquin completely abandon his principles for something he doesn't even need?"

"The lure of money turns many a good man into a monster."

Otho, who'd been quietly listening, shifted restlessly in his chair. "Maybe it wasn't about money. Look, we sure as hell know what Neetra's capable of. If he was brazen enough to arrange the King's murder, what's to say he didn't use fear tactics against Joaquin?"

Marc rapped his spidery fingers against the desktop as he considered. "That's not a bad theory, actually. It's no secret Joaquin is devoted to his family. He loves his wife and children. I'm sure he'd do just about anything to keep them safe."

"Like swear loyalty to a tyrant," Otho muttered. "I also find it peculiar that not one of Joaquin's three sons went to war. The whole lot of them are of age. Two of them are even trained for combat. The youngest, Tarquin, was in Roland's advanced weaponry class just last fall. I remember him going on about how he wanted to be a captain someday. Seems odd that he didn't march to Shiraz."

"Aye," Marc said. "Tarquin was enlisted, but his father convinced him at the last moment to stay behind and help oversee production at the armory."

Otho's eyes narrowed. "Convinced—or *ordered* him?"

Kirk pressed his hands to his aching temples. This was all too much information to process. He felt overwhelmed, like he was slowly drowning. "Neetra could have threatened to send all three boys to the front. Maybe he promised their safety in return for Lord Aldino's support."

"Anything's possible." Marc sighed wearily, his age-lined face drawing tight. "We can speculate all we want, but there's no way of knowing for sure. Joaquin's not going to talk, especially if it means putting his family in jeopardy. It's a lost cause. *All of this* is a lost cause."

The midday bell rang, and Marc closed his eyes, as if mesmerized by the steady resonation. Or perhaps he was just tired—tired and ready to give up. Kirk could hardly shake the gloom from his own bones. He wished there was something more he could do. He felt so helpless.

The bells grew softer, and soon the airy melody faded altogether. Marc rose and went over to the window. Clasping his hands behind his back, he stared bleakly into the courtyard once again. "I think we're done here for today. You two can leave."

"But—" Kirk protested.

"I'll summon you if I receive any news out of Shiraz."

"But—"

"C'mon," Otho said. "Let's go." He closed a hand around Kirk's arm and guided him toward the door. Kirk was too upset to fight against it.

Once they were in the hall, however, the shock had time to wear off. Kirk balled his hands, anger swelling so rapidly it might burst forth from his skin.

"Well *I'm* not ready to give up!" he spat. The words echoed down the length of the empty corridor.

Otho turned away from the door. "Who said anything about giving up?"

"Couldn't you see it in his eyes? Marc is completely defeated. He's not even trying anymore!"

A sly smile briefly softened Otho's homely features. "Has anyone ever told you that you really need to calm down?"

"I—" Kirk pursed his lips. Keni did. All the time. He groaned. "Maybe."

"Maybe you should start listening to them."

Kirk huffed and began to walk away. If Otho thought for a second he was going to have a good laugh at Kirk's expense—

"I might have an idea."

The burning anger subsided just slightly. Kirk stopped, despite his better judgment, and glanced over his shoulder. "What kind of idea?"

Otho trotted to catch up. "Meet me at the Rose Bouquet tavern tomorrow after sundown."

"You think drinking ourselves into a stupor is going to help rectify Arden?"

"Do you want answers or not?"

"Y–yes."

"Then meet me there. And *don't* be late."

Gib could recall, in vivid detail, the fear of the crops not pulling through. He remembered lying awake at night, listening, waiting, and praying for the rains to come. Because if it didn't rain, the seeds wouldn't take. And if the seeds didn't take, the crop wouldn't grow. No crop meant little food in the winter. Little food in the winter meant he and the boys would be outside, rummaging for roots in the snow, worried about when their next meager meal would come, and Gib fearing Tay and Cal might not see the next spring.

He never let the boys despair the way he did though. He was too stubborn to allow hope to fade from their eyes. Even when their father had died—in the family's darkest moment—the gut-wrenching, mind-numbing terror that cost Gib so many a good night's sleep had never once lined Tay's and Cal's young faces. Gib had vowed his brothers would never know true fear, and so they hadn't.

But these people, the peasants of Shiraz, they knew. Fear governed every aspect of their lives. The slouch of their shoulders wasn't that of a young boy thrown too early into manhood, but of people who, for countless generations, had been born with *nothing*. They had no glimmer in their eyes—not even in the eyes of their children. Bone thin, living in naught but rags, and oppressed by their own rulers and foreign conquerors alike, their desolate, sunken faces would haunt Gib forever. He was sure of it. These people hadn't lost hope. They'd never known it to begin with.

Gib wasn't sure how long he wandered aimlessly through decrepit shacks that, together, made up what could scarcely be called a village, but when he did finally glance up, he was surprised to see a familiar figure just ahead.

Kezra leaned against a crumbling fence, staring with dull eyes across the settlement. She'd been scarce of late, withdrawn and often hostile, but she was his friend, so Gib approached, despite fear of dismissal. His stomach tightened as he neared. She looked almost as ragged as the Shirite villagers. Were the moonturns of endless marching beginning to dampen even Kezra's tenacious spirit?

Gib opened his mouth, meaning to greet her, but what spilled forth sounded more like a snide taunt. "Don't you have orders to pillage?"

Kezra folded her arms defiantly over her chest. "Pillage what? Their mud bricks? This village is the same as the others. There's nothing new to be found here."

Gib tried to swallow against his sand-dry mouth and followed Kezra's gaze.

She was right, of course. The village—more of a drab smudge among the dunes—*was* like every other they'd passed through. The same mud huts and reed roofs baked in the sun. The same scrawny goats scavenged for tufts of dead grass. The same tired, meek people hung back with lifeless eyes and broken spirits as their meager possessions were dumped out and gone through, and the best of everything was pilfered. They didn't even protest. Not a single one of them.

"When did we become the monsters?" Gib asked, wiping at his damp eyes. "They'll tell their children stories of the Ardenian oppressors who stole their food and left them for dead."

"If they survive to tell stories."

"This is outrageous. Morathi *knows* what he's doing. How can he leave these people like this?"

"He doesn't care." Kezra's voice was a hollow husk of what it used to be. "No one cares. The monsters from the bedtime tales are real. And they are roaming among our own ranks."

Again, Gib raked a sleeve across his face, watching as soldiers broke through rickety stick fences and pushed their way into huts. The entire scene was eerily quiet: no protests, no cries, just deathly silence.

Kezra shoved a wineskin at him. "Here. Drink. And no more tears. You could die of such a thing out here."

"So now I'm not even allowed empathy?" Gib took a swig, nearly retching as stale, lukewarm water touched his tongue. Corking the canteen, he handed it back to Kezra. "What if we really *are* monsters?"

"You're not a monster. You know the difference between right and wrong. And someday you're going to sit on the High Council and make *fair* laws. Arden will be better off for having you."

"The Shirites aren't 'better off' for having me here. Or any of us."

"I know. But we can't stop the general from giving his commands. We can, however, choose not to follow them."

Gib glanced around, petrified someone might overhear such bold insubordination. "Kezra—"

She raised her chin defiantly. "I'd rather be whipped. I won't kill these people, Gib, because that's *exactly* what we're doing by taking their belongings. This war has already driven me to do deplorable things. I'm no saint, but I'll be *damned* if I'm going to let Morathi turn me into a monster like the rest of them." She came away from the fence, almost unrecognizable in her fury. "Tell me, Gib. Who'd even care if that murdering bastard ended up dead?"

Gib took a terrified step backward. "I don't know. But, Kezra, please don't do anything foolish."

Kezra's eyes remained dark, but her rigid stance loosened. "Don't worry. Like I said, I'll be damned if I let him make the choice for me." She backed off. "I'm going to water the horses."

"Kezra—"

"Don't worry. I'll stay out of trouble. You do the same."

Gib watched her go until he could no longer distinguish her armor from the other soldiers. In more ways than one, he felt as though he was slowly watching his best friend slip away. Was she going to be all right? After war's end, would there be anything left of the Kezra he'd grown to cherish?

Gib wrapped his arms around himself and went to find Koal.

Gib found his mentor near the edge of the settlement. Flanked by Hasain and Deegan, Koal sat in his saddle, observing with silent fury as a group of soldiers emptied a goat pen. An elderly man crouched with two small children just outside the fence. He murmured consolations into their hair, but as each bleating goat was carried past, the younglings pointed and cried hysterically. Tears flowed down their faces, leaving streaks on their cheeks where the dirt had been washed away.

More men were forcing their way into nearby huts and coming out with their spoils. Animals were thrown into crates and taken away. Food and medicine were stacked into wagons and hauled off. Everything else was dumped into the soil. Some of the villagers distanced themselves as their belongings were sacked by the foreign invaders. Others merely sat where they were and cried.

Gib's neck burned as he slunk over to Koal. He'd never felt more ashamed in his life. This wasn't Arden's way. This was the act of tyrants.

Deegan sat rigidly with both hands clutching his reins. "What will the villagers feed their children? After we're gone, will Tahir send aid? The soldiers are taking everything."

"I'm sorry," Koal replied. "I don't have any answers for you. And I don't have the authority to stop this madness."

The young prince clapped a hand over his mouth and looked away. "Father would never allow such injustice to take place beneath Arden's banner."

"Koal," Hasain said quietly, turning in his saddle. "Deegan shouldn't have to see this."

Koal shook his head. "No. Cruel as it is, Deegan *needs* to see this. A good king must witness the darkest side of humanity if he wishes to be a truly compassionate ruler."

"You're right, uncle," Deegan said. Sniffling, he raised his chin. "I won't forget this day. And when I'm king, those responsible will be held accountable for such injustice." His dark eyes were pained as he watched the soldiers pillage, but he didn't look away again.

Neither did Gib. Staring into the hopeless gazes of the peasants all but shattered his soul, but he refused to turn his head. He refused to pretend he didn't see them.

Anger surged inside him, flooding his veins and causing his head to pound. He welcomed it—harnessed it. The rage only fueled his determination. Someday things would change, and men like Morathi and Neetra would pay for what they had done.

A moment passed, or it might have been entire marks for all Gib knew, when a scuffle broke out between a pair of soldiers and one of the villagers. A woman stumbled from within a hut, gripping a bundled sack and trying desperately to keep it away from the men who pursued her.

She tore across the clearing, screaming and sobbing. The soldiers overtook her in no time, however, and grabbed her willowy arms.

"All right, hand it over," one of them said, reaching for the sack.

The woman howled and clutched her bundle more tightly. Jumbled pleas tumbled from her mouth. Gib didn't understand the words, but the poor woman's desperation was clear enough.

"Stop!" Deegan cried. "Leave her alone!"

The command was lost beneath the peasant woman's terrified wails. She struggled against her captors as they tried to rip the sack out of her hands.

"I said stop! Let her go!"

This time, the soldiers heard Deegan's words. They froze, turning with bulging eyes and gaping mouths, but didn't release their hold on the young woman's arms.

Koal brought his horse within a pace of where the men stood, looming above them. "Is *this* how you address your prince?"

"No, sir! We were just followin' commands!"

"Please, Prince Deegan, forgive us!"

The sound of horse hooves pounding against the dirt caught Gib's attention. His stomach flipped at the sight of the general's grey stallion weaving through the crowd. He, along with everyone else in the vicinity, must have overheard the scuffle.

"What the hell is going on here?" Morathi demanded as he rode closer. His lofty gaze passed over each of them before settling on the besieged woman. "What does she have?"

"We don't know yet, sir," one of the soldiers replied.

"Well, take it from her and find out!"

"We were tryin', sir, but—but—"

Koal squared his shoulders. "The Crown Prince gave a command."

"Oh, did he now?" Morathi glared down the wide bridge of his nose at Deegan. "And what was your command, *Highness*?"

All eyes fell onto Arden's heir. Even the Shirite woman had stopped struggling against her captors and was now watching the prince.

Deegan hesitated, looking to Koal for direction. The seneschal nodded, so the prince said gingerly, "I–I said to leave this woman alone."

"And *why* would you do that?" Morathi scolded the Crown Prince like he was a pauper child. "She's clearly stealing something. Look at the sack she carries."

"She can't steal what's rightfully hers. And what can such a small satchel hold anyway? Grain for a single soldier for a handful of days?"

"Or a blade meant to stab the clueless child heir to our throne!"

Deegan paled and flinched away.

Point made, Morathi steered his horse over to the woman. She screeched as he reached down and snatched the bundle out of her arms. The woman bawled, clawing at the general's cape and pleading in her native tongue. With a callous sneer, Morathi kicked her in the abdomen. The blow nearly sent the woman to her knees.

"Let's see what she was so determined to hide," he snarled as he sat upright in his saddle.

He tore open the sack—

—and visibly startled when a baby began to wail.

Gib couldn't breathe. A child? *That's* what she'd been safeguarding?

"Chhaya's bane!" Koal hissed, his face twisting in horror. "She was only trying to protect her infant. For Daya's sake, give the child back!"

Morathi shoved the baby back at the woman. "She can keep the miserable sand rat until it withers in the sun for all I care."

Cradling the infant's dark head, the woman fled to a nearby hut, where a group of older children embraced her. The family held each other, sobbing, and then disappeared inside.

"Back to work!" Morathi barked at the gaping bystanders. "Take everything you can find. And do not pity these savages, for we will find no such pity when we reach Tahir's gates."

196

Dust flew into their faces as the general's stallion galloped off.

Gib tried to get his jagged breaths under control. Morathi might as well have given the order to slay the villagers. Perhaps it would even have been the merciful thing to do, rather than leave them to slowly waste away.

The truth was a black smear on Gib's heart. They were going to die—the goat-herding children, the frail elderly man, the young mother and her too-thin infant—all of them. And here he was, standing and doing nothing to prevent it. Even if Gib survived the war, he might not be able to live with himself when the dust settled.

"What's to become of them, uncle?" Deegan asked, his voice brittle, like it might shatter at any moment.

The seneschal looked on with cloudy eyes. "I don't know, Deegan. I'm sorry."

Gib wiped away a rebellious tear. There were far too many sorrows to count this day. And The Two only knew how many more were yet to come.

The merry music drifting through the open windows should have lifted Kirk's spirit, but instead, it only made him furious. How could these people laugh, knowing their Crown Prince and seneschal were at war? How could they celebrate, when any day now Arden's army would march into battle? Wasn't anyone worried? Did no one care?

Patrons of Silver City's most renowned tavern gathered on the steps, overflowing from within the crowded building and into the darkness outside. A tepid breeze carried their boisterous voices and the scent of ale to where Kirk waited on the opposite side of the street.

It was well past sundown. A crescent moon already hung high in the cloudless sky, spreading crystalline illumination over the cobblestones. The eventide bells had long since quieted, and the vendors who made a living selling their wares along Traders Row had vanished marks ago. Further down the alley, a lamplighter moved to and fro, setting oil lanterns ablaze. Kirk watched curiously, wondering if all streets inside Silver were brightened by fire each night. Surely the poorer districts couldn't afford to waste the oil.

Letting out an agitated sigh, Kirk tapped his fingers against the stone wall at his back. Where in the two worlds was Otho? The apprentice said he'd be there after sundown.

Well, the damn sun is nowhere to be seen. Did he forget? Or just decide not to show up? I swear to the Blessed Son, if this is some kind of cruel prank—

"Hey."

Kirk whirled around. "*Daya*, Otho! I didn't even hear you approach."

197

Shadows played upon the dips of Otho's washed out face as he came within a pace of where Kirk stood. Otho smiled mockingly. "Maybe you should pay better attention then."

"Or maybe you should announce yourself sooner, like any civilized person would."

The smile widened into a toothy grin. "Bad day? You usually play nice longer than this."

"You're late. I've been waiting for a mark already."

"Well, here I am." Otho's tawny-colored eyes gleamed with amusement. "Ready to go inside?"

"I think I have a right to know why we're here. You still haven't told me."

"You'll see. C'mon."

Before Kirk could raise a protest, Otho turned on his heels and walked away. Grudgingly, Kirk followed at the apprentice's back.

The Rose Bouquet tavern was, as Kirk had predicted, packed full. They seated themselves in the back corner, away from the music, dancing, and pipe smoke, at one of the only unoccupied tables. No sooner were their backsides planted did a tavern wench hurry over carrying a platter of sloshing tankards.

"Ale, m'lords?" she asked.

Kirk started to decline. "Oh, no. I'm not here to drink—"

"Two," Otho said, glaring. He laid two copper coins on the table, and the wench left a pair of mugs behind in exchange. Otho shoved one of the vessels toward Kirk. "Are you *trying* to draw attention?"

Locking his jaw, Kirk pulled the tankard closer. He hated having to admit Otho might have a point. Taking a tentative sip from the iron stein, Kirk cast a gaze around the room. "Is it always so crowded?"

"Every night."

Kirk scrutinized the patrons more closely. He found it curious how varied they were. In Teivel, nobility would never be seen mingling with lowborns, but here, such rules didn't seem to apply. Men dressed in finery laughed alongside those in naught but rags.

"Vagrants are allowed inside? They aren't told to leave?"

"Not unless they're thieves. Anyone with money is welcome."

"Things are so different here. In my homeland, the wealthy and lowborns never interacted in such a way."

"It's mostly like that everywhere else in Silver. But not here at the Rose Bouquet. And not at Academy so much anymore either, thanks to men like Seneschal Koal and the King pushing for equality." Otho took a drink from his mug. "Of course, now that the *rat* is sitting on the throne, who knows how long it will be before everything they worked for comes crumbling down."

Kirk nodded solemnly. He'd be damned if he stood by idly and watched Neetra invite Imperial darkness into Arden. "So, are you going to tell me why we're here? Or were you just seeking the pleasure of my company?"

One of Otho's thin eyebrows sprang higher than the other. "Don't flatter yourself, Imperial. This is business." His gaze shifted past Kirk. "You see that man over there? The one with blond hair?"

Kirk craned his head around, searching the room. With so many people crammed into the space, picking one man out from the crowd should have presented a challenge, but almost immediately a tuft of platinum hair drew Kirk's attention.

The man sat inside a booth, his only company a half-emptied pitcher of ale. Turned as he was, Kirk couldn't see the man's face, though judging by the fine quality of his velvet doublet, he was no doubt some kind of lord. As Kirk watched, the man lifted a mug to his mouth and took a long swig.

"Who is he?"

"That's Tarquin Aldino," Otho said. "The youngest son of—"

"Lord Joaquin Aldino!" Kirk exclaimed.

"Right. He's become a frequent visitor here of late."

"Does he always come alone?"

"Yeah, at least every time I've seen him. All his friends went to war."

"Do you think—can we talk to him?"

Otho strummed nimble fingers against the side of his tankard. "He's typically pretty uptight, being highborn and all. At least that's how he was in Roland's class. But a few rounds of ale can loosen up even the loftiest men."

Kirk gave the apprentice a dubious look. "You think if he's sloshed enough, he'll answer questions about his father?"

"Maybe, but I'm not taking any chances. I'm gonna make damn certain he talks." Otho's fingers dipped into a pocket hidden on the underside of his cloak and plucked out a tiny flask. He set it down on the table. A colorless liquid rippled within the crystal vial.

Kirk scrutinized the vessel with narrowed eyes. "*What* is *that?*"

"A very special Healer's remedy from the pavilion. One drop relaxes the body, making the patient forget their sorrows. An entire vial poured into, say, a mug of ale will get them to reveal their darkest, most precious secrets."

"Do you really think this is the best course of action? To tamper with someone's drink? Especially given what we just learned about the death of the—you know who."

Otho rolled his eyes. "We're not killing anyone here, but if you'd rather go on moaning and whining about not finding the truth—" He started to tuck the flask back into its hiding place. "—I can leave."

Kirk groaned. "*Fine.* I suppose so long as it won't harm the man."

Otho smirked victoriously, and Kirk resisted the urge to clobber the other man aside the head. Why did he have to be so infuriating? This was no way for sophisticated people to behave. But—

I promised Joel I'd help. If this is the only way, then so be it. It's very well possible this Tarquin fellow is hiding information about his father. If he knows anything, we need to find out.

Kirk glanced guiltily over at the young Aldino lord again. "Do you suppose we should go over there now?"

"Let him get through his pitcher." A chuckle rumbled in Otho's stout chest. "We can bring him a new one when it's empty."

Kirk tried to relax by listening to the quartet of musicians playing on stage. Even the cheery music couldn't lift his mood. Patrons laughed and danced, beckoning him to join, but he couldn't. Try as he might, Kirk couldn't ease the tension in his shoulders nor the blot of darkness across his heart. Far too much was at stake to indulge in life's simple pleasures.

His gaze shifted restlessly around the tavern, from the ancient wood beams that spanned the ceiling to the great stone hearth that was the cornerstone of the building. The flames danced so vigorously within the pit that the heat they emitted could be felt clear across the room. People congregated near the fire and around the bar, where tavern wenches rushed to refill tankards and serve steaming stew.

His eyes kept drifting back to Tarquin. Kirk watched the young lord take long swallows from the pitcher. He hadn't moved once, but Kirk still worried the lordling might stumble to his feet and make for the door at any time.

"Relax," Otho grunted, rummaging through his cloak again. "He's not gonna leave anytime soon."

He placed another coin onto the table, and a server girl brought a fresh tankard almost immediately. Otho twisted the stopper and poured the contents of the vial into the ale. He muttered under his breath, "Maybe *you* should drink this instead of the Aldino loon."

Kirk glared indignantly. "I'm afraid it wouldn't work on me. I don't have any secrets to divulge."

"I don't care about your secrets. I just wish you'd calm down, for Daya's sake."

Kirk pursed his lips against the urge to say something he might later regret. Arguing with the apprentice would only be counterproductive. They were on the same side after all.

"All right," Otho said after a pause. "He's probably as drunk as he's gonna get without becoming completely incoherent. He probably won't give a rat's arse if we strike up a conversation now. Are you ready?"

"Will this work? Does he even know you?"

"A little. I mean, from Roland's classes and all. Just follow my lead. If he asks, you're my—*distant* relative."

Kirk snorted as he stood. "What? Is being friends simply too much of a stretch?"

Otho took up his half-empty tankard in one hand and the one meant for Tarquin in the other. "Yes."

They crossed the room, faster than Kirk would have wished. He still wasn't sure what to say to this stranger or if he should even say anything at all. He hoped Otho could manage to be personable for once in his life. Otherwise, this wouldn't work. Drunk or not, Tarquin would suspect something if they failed to deliver a convincing performance.

Otho slowed as he neared the booth and feigned surprise when he came to a full stop beside it. "Tarquin Aldino? Is that you?"

The young lord raised his wobbly head. He blinked once, twice. Finally, a trace of recognition flashed behind his blurry eyes. "Otho Dahkeel, what brings you to the Rose t'night? Shouldn't you be training tha troops?"

"Not at this late mark," Otho replied, his square face tightening into a smile. The gesture was clearly forced, but if Tarquin's slurred speech was any indication of his state of mind, then he was beyond noticing.

"Ah," Tarquin said. "Well, I s'pose Roland's gotta let the trainees rest sometime. He never took it easy on me an' my friends though. In basic training, he had us out doing drills in a blizzard. A blizzard!"

"I remember."

"Yeah, I s'pose you assistants got to suffer in the snow alongside us, didn't you?" Laughing, Tarquin waved a floppy arm at Kirk. "Who's your friend?"

Kirk offered his hand for a shake. "Kirk Bhadrayu. Nice to meet you."

"Bhadrayu. Bhadrayu." Tarquin's eyebrows pinched as he tried to place the name. "Huh. And here I thought my family knew just about ev'ryone in the city."

"I'm a newcomer to Silver," Kirk said.

"Ah, that explains your strange accent. Where do you hail from originally?"

"Uh—" Kirk floundered. Blessed Son, he hadn't thought of any of this beforehand. "I'm from—the north."

"Wolfpine," Otho said quickly. "Up on the edge of the Pinnacles."

"Oh." Tarquin's eyes widened, and he chuckled. "I definitely don't know many people from *that* far away."

"Yes, it is quite some distance. Almost a completely different country." Kirk summoned his best attempt at a smile. "Do you mind if we join you, Lord Tarquin? I'm afraid Otho isn't much of a conversationalist."

Tarquin shrugged. "Can't say my company'll be any better, but sure, have a seat." The pink tinge of a blush touched his cheeks as he eyed the empty pitcher by his elbow. "I was just about to order more ale. Maybe not a whole pitcher this time."

Otho didn't miss a beat. He plopped the tainted tankard onto the table and slid it closer to the young lord. "Here. On me."

Kirk sat down, holding his breath while he waited to see if Tarquin would accept the bait. What if he didn't? What would they do then?

"Thanks." Flashing a sheepish grin, Tarquin took the mug into his hands. When he lifted the vessel to his mouth, his grip was so unsteady a bit of ale dribbled over the side. "I always knew you were kinder than you let on in the training arena. I get it though. You gotta be tough to keep tha trainees on their toes."

Otho shrugged. "I suppose."

"Don't worry." Tarquin took a sip and then a second. "Your secret's safe with me."

Kirk watched the lordling drink. How long would it take for the remedy's effects to take hold? Would Tarquin have to finish the entire tankard? What if he drank only half of it?

The silence stretched. Tarquin rapped his fingers against the table, looking bored, and Otho was making no effort to engage with him. Kirk couldn't stand it anymore.

He cleared his throat. "Everyone talks of Weapons Master Roland like he's a slave driver. I can't say I understand. I've only had pleasant exchanges with him."

Tarquin cackled. "An' just how many of Master Roland's classes have *you* taken, Kirk Bhadrayu?"

"Well, none."

Tarquin leaned across the table—swaying from the small effort—and waggled a finger at Kirk. "I suspect you'd change your tune if you had."

"Perhaps you're right. What about you, Lord Tarquin? How many weaponry classes have you taken?"

Tarquin paused, counting and recounting on his fingers.

"Eh, four, I think," he finally said.

"He also had private lessons with Prince Didier," Otho remarked quietly.

Kirk sat back in his seat. "You trained with a prince? Now *that's* a true honor! You must be exceptionally gifted with a sword."

Tarquin's ears and neck were now as red as his face. "Yeah. It was during my first year at Academy. Prince Diddy and I are—were—friends."

"Were friends? Are you not anymore?"

"I mean, I s'pose we still are. It's just, you know, with the ways things have been going over at the palace lately—" Tarquin drank again, as if deliberately trying to drown an unpleasant recollection. When he set the tankard down again, Kirk saw it was nearly empty. "I haven't gotten to see much of Diddy. I haven't gotten to see much of *anyone*. This damn war—" His voice cracked there, and he fell quiet.

Kirk's thoughts drifted to Joel. Always to Joel. "I understand. It's hard to maintain friendships during wartime. We watch our closest allies march bravely into the sunrise, and we're left wondering if they'll ever return."

Tarquin blinked. His eyes watered. "This war's taken *all* my friends away from me."

Otho made deliberate eye contact with Kirk and nodded once. He understood. The remedy was working.

He pressed on, testing the waters gently. "Why didn't you go with them?"

"I wanted to, but—my father—he begged me to stay. I told him it was a dishonor not to go, especially since I'd been training for this for years. He said terrible things would happen—that I wouldn't come back. I thought he was just scared. I insisted on going. I told him it was my duty to Arden." Tarquin wiped at his blotchy face. "Right up until the army was getting ready to leave, I had full intentions of marching with them."

"So what changed?" Otho asked. "Why didn't you go?"

"My father had a decree signed by the steward, placing me in charge of production at the guild. It doesn't even make any sense! My elder brother's been overseeing the armory for years! He's gonna take over when Father steps down. I don't know why they made me—but it was an order. I was forced into staying, even though I wanted to go. I made a promise I'd defend Arden, an' I couldn't even keep it. I had to watch my friends leave—and now I'll probably never see them again. Why'd he do this? Why'd he force me to stay behind?"

Tarquin's voice had become desperate, and patrons were glancing in his direction. Kirk grimaced. The conversation was drawing too much attention.

He called upon a dampening enchantment. It had been one of the first spells he'd learned when he became an apprentice. Subtle and undetectable to the ungifted, any words spoken would be muffled and indiscernible to those outside its barrier. Working quickly, Kirk weaved the spell, draping magic above and around the booth until an invisible sphere of mage-energy surrounded them.

"I'm sure your father was just trying to protect you," Kirk said once he was satisfied the enchantment would hold.

"I don't care. It was *my* choice to make, an' he took it away from me!"

Tarquin all but screamed the words, but this time, no one paid the young lord any heed. He slumped down in the booth, arms sprawled on the table with his forehead resting atop them. For a second, Kirk worried the young lord might have passed out, but then he heard Tarquin's meek voice.

"My father's changed. He's not the same man he used to be. He's scared, like he thinks the world's coming to an end. He speaks in support of Neetra. I even caught him holding a meeting with Liro Adelwijn."

One of Otho's eyebrows quirked. "Really? Odd company for Joaquin."

Tarquin raised his reddened face. "I wasn't supposed to overhear. I came home late one night, and they were talking in the parlor. I shouldn't have snooped—it's bad form—but I was angry at Father, so I listened from the window."

"What were they talking about?"

Tarquin hesitated. "I—I shouldn't be repeating any of this."

Kirk gave Tarquin an encouraging smile. "It can't be that bad."

"Oh, it's bad!" Tarquin laughed madly.

"Go on," Otho said. "Tell us."

"All right, I s'pose," Tarquin relented. "Liro was saying Father needed to think long an' hard about where he wanted to place his allegiance when 'the truth' came out. I don't know what Liro meant by that, but anyway, he went on to say that soon, anyone found supporting the Radeks will be considered traitors an' if the councilors don't pledge themselves to the new ruler, their families could be endangered. He was openly threatening Father—an' then I heard Father say he'd do whatever was needed. I think that's why he's been supporting Neetra. I think that's why he's so scared. They've got him trapped. I don't know what to do."

Kirk's stomach twisted painfully. So it was true. Neetra *was* using terror to manipulate Joaquin, and probably other councilors as well. But if no one would come forward, how could it ever be proven?

Tarquin lowered his face again and blatted into his sleeve. He looked as hopeless as Kirk felt. Had Arden already slipped over the cusp? Was darkness all that remained? Maybe Marc *had* been right.

No. We can't give up.

For some time, the only sounds were Tarquin's muffled sobs. His shoulders quaked. It seemed he'd lost himself, whether to the remedy or his own despair. Or maybe both.

And then he sighed and grew suddenly still.

Alarmed, Kirk reached out to shake the young lord's limp arm. "Tarquin—"

"Don't," Otho said.

"But he could be—"

"He's not dead. Listen, he's snoring. He's just passed out. I might have been a little too generous with the dosage."

Kirk glared. "What?"

"It's nothing he can't sleep off. He probably won't even remember this conversation in the morning—which is just as well. C'mon, let's get out of here."

"We can't just *leave* the poor man in this state."

"Someone will scrape him off the table and make sure he gets home. C'mon."

Otho strode toward the door, and Kirk jumped to his feet in pursuit. Hastily, he dispelled the dampening magic.

"This is completely uncouth behavior," Kirk hissed as he followed through the door. "Haven't you any morals?"

Otho slowed his pace when they were out of the light of the tavern. He turned around slowly, spearing Kirk with narrowed eyes. His face was grim. "Does Neetra? How about Liro Adelwijn? It's time to stop playing nice. Nice will only get you so far, and it won't solve anything. It's probably too late as it is. You heard the Aldino loon. The High Council is a lost cause."

Kirk shook his head. He couldn't accept that. He'd never accept it was too late. Not while he still had breath in his body. "No matter how insurmountable the wall appears, there has to be a way over it."

Pulling his cloak tighter around his shoulders, Otho glared into the shadowed alley. "Then you best prepare for the climb of your life. There's a battle brewing. And I'm not talking about the one in Shiraz. Neetra's got all his pieces aligned. I'm not sure if there's time for the opposition to rally theirs."

CHAPTER FOURTEEN

A hundred glowing pinpricks flickered in the far distance. As the last rays of sun faded from the eventide sky, the alabaster city darkened, casting the illusion that the torches along the parapets were unbound and floating freely in the darkness.

Tahir's great outer wall rose out of the sand like the Gods themselves had willed it. Its shadowy outline loomed on the horizon, so high only the topmost peaks of the temples within the city were visible.

Hasain could feel bleakness festering in his guts and crawling its way up the back of his throat. Tahir's fortifications were higher than Silver City's. Even though the Ardenian army outnumbered Shiraz's a hundred to one, how would they ever breach the city? They'd starve before the enemy came out from behind their stone walls.

The nighttime air was hot, with no breeze to bring relief. Lifting a wineskin to his parched lips, Hasain drank earnestly. Maybe if he drowned his fears with ale, he'd be able to sleep tonight. It might very well be the last sleep he ever got.

He corked the canteen and turned his back to the distant city. He couldn't stand the sight of it anymore.

The eve of battle leeched into Hasain's bones like poison in the vein. All around him, soldiers hastened, inspecting their armor and sharpening their weapons. Some were doing drills on the outskirts of the camp, practicing over and over until their limbs shook with exertion and they finally wandered back to their sleeping mats to rest. Others merely sat around their fires, eating what could be their last meal and talking in muted voices to their comrades. They spoke of their families, the miserable heat, and the journey home but little of the impending battle. No one wanted to talk about that.

Hasain took another swig from the wineskin and glanced over his shoulder. The door flaps of the command tent were still drawn tight, offering relative privacy while the war council strategized for the morrow. Koal had been in there for marks now. Morathi, too.

Tular and Deegan stood outside. Tular was adjusting the prince's armor while they waited for the fire to roast a wild hare Nawaz had brought them earlier. It had been a lucky catch. Normally the sounds of the army scared the wildlife off, making hunting nearly impossible.

Hasain's stomach gurgled as the scent of the broiling meat reached him. Hunger tore at his insides. Like a faithful companion, it never left him these days. Even with the army pillaging, there was still too little food to go around. Three days ago, Koal had ordered two of the oxen be slain. They'd already lost a dozen or more horses. Rations had been cut in half *twice*. They couldn't survive much longer without food. They needed to take Tahir or perish.

Hasain brought the wineskin to his lips again, watching as Deegan unsheathed his sword and practiced swinging it. The image was chilling: a reminder of what could no longer be avoided.

Somehow, throughout the journey here—despite ambushes, skirmishes, and pilfering—the prince and his guardians had remained removed from the worst of the trouble. They'd been granted relative safety by staying near Koal.

Tomorrow though, there would be no avoiding battle. Deegan would ride with the rest of the army, and *all* of their fates would be decided. They'd survive, or they wouldn't.

The command tent flaps rustled, and men made their way outside. Their faces were grim as they dispersed into the camp. Hasain watched them, trying to get his choppy breaths under control. Time was moving too fast. The meeting was already over. If he even closed his eyes but for a moment, dawn might break across the horizon. He wasn't ready for this.

"Not having second thoughts, are you?"

Hasain whirled around, eyes impossibly wide as he searched fruitlessly for the demon. Where was it? Why couldn't he see it?

"You might want to stop flailing before someone thinks you've gone mad."

"Where are you?" he asked faintly. His heart hammered so hard he feared his ribs might crack.

"Hasain, you should know by now I'm always with you. I'm in your feeble heart and your treacherous mind. Don't tell me you can't feel me."

Clutching his head in his hands, Hasain staggered over to a supply crate and sank down onto it. He couldn't catch his breath. He couldn't make the world cease its spinning.

Leviticus was right. Hasain felt the demon inside, like a shadow creeping over his heart. He was never truly alone anymore. The realization gripped him tightly, making him gasp in terror. Is this what his father had dealt with his entire life? How had Rishi not gone mad?

"Go away!" he choked. Desperation added unintended volume to his words.

"You might lower your voice as well, unless you want everyone to suspect your insanity. Though, I suppose you could use that as an excuse to stay safely behind the lines of battle tomorrow."

Hasain slammed his eyes shut as if doing so could somehow hold the demon at bay. "Stop talking."

Leviticus cackled. *"Oh, you're such a pathetic thing. You know, I could help you. You wouldn't have to be brave with me to do your bidding. There's still a chance to avoid war."*

Hasain shook his head. Impossible. Morathi had seen to that. Nearly all the soldiers who marched now did so willingly. They *wanted* to face the Shirites in battle.

"The general is a fallible man, Hasain. He's not invincible."

Locking his jaw, Hasain did his best to ignore the demon's invitation, but his resolve was dangerously close to crumbling. How had Rishi disregarded Leviticus for so many years? How could *any* man ignore such sweet promises?

"Had he not rejected my help the last time I came to him, Rishi Radek would still be alive today. Will you make the same choice, Hasain? Will you turn me away tonight and allow Deegan to meet his doom tomorrow?"

Lies. His father had said never to listen to the demon's lies. But what if Leviticus really could help?

Hasain's jaw tightened further. If he lived to see the end of this damned war, he'd have to break down and talk to someone. But who?

Not Koal. Hasain was afraid to talk to Koal. Despite being Rishi's most trusted friend and confidant, the seneschal had never forged such a bond with Hasain.

"Koal Adelwijn is as soft as your sire. He'll never take the necessary path."

Marc was hardly a viable option. King Rishi had trusted the dean perhaps too much.

"A clown. Is this the best you have?"

Aodan! Aodan would know what to do—if he wasn't banished before the army returned, that was. Aodan knew firsthand about the legacy of the red stone. He must know how to stop the demon.

"Don't be so sure about that. I still don't know why that mongrel's given so much credit."

Hasain bit the inside of his cheek, eyes swooping around the clearing. He so desperately wanted to call for help. He could feel his resolution slipping away, like sand through the fingers.

Tular and Deegan edged around the campfire, engaged in a battle drill. Soft grunts lifted around them as each tried to best the other. Nearby, Joel's robes stood out against the dark backdrop of tents. He shuffled through a satchel of runestones, meticulously checking each to make certain they were charged. Natori sat beside him, donned in plate armor. Her head was down as she sharpened her sword. Hasain could hear the slide of the whetstone running along the ethereal blade from where he sat.

None of them noticed his distress. Even Natori didn't glance up. He held back the urge to scream at her. Could she not hear the demon? She was a Blessed Mage, for Daya's sake! How could she not feel its presence?

"No one can hear me but you. And the bitch Mage can't sense me so long as I

act through you. This is perfection, Hasain. Anything you desire, just ask it of me and it will be done. No one even needs be any the wiser. You can prove them all wrong. You can be the hero: the brave, noble son of the dead king, just like you always wanted."

A feeble gasp escaped Hasain's throat. It was true; all he'd ever wanted was to make his father proud, yet even now, Hasain felt like he'd failed. His father was dead. The rest of the royal family lay in shambles, broken beyond repair. And his little brother, Deegan—Arden's Crown Prince and only heir—would be thrown into combat tomorrow. His very *life* hung in the balance. He could be dead by the following nightfall.

I promised Deegan I would keep him safe. I swore to him I'd protect him.

Again, Leviticus laughed. *"Now Hasain, didn't your father ever teach you not to make promises you cannot keep?"*

Hasain clenched his hair in either hand, pulling so hard his skull burned. He'd do just about anything to protect his family, but what if he alone wasn't enough? Rishi had never called upon the demon for aid, but Hasain was not his father. He wasn't strong or wise or noble. He couldn't be relied on to keep Deegan safe.

Shadows engulfed Hasain's racing heart as if the demon were squeezing it. He could feel Leviticus' aura shift, growing darker yet.

"Deegan does not have to go into battle. No one does. You can end this war right now. Look. The general is away from his sentries. He's going alone to his tent. Now, Hasain. Unleash me. End this."

Hasain froze, watching as Morathi sauntered away from the command tent and toward his own, raised some distance away from the others.

He *was* oddly alone. Where were his servants? Where were the hand-picked scum who usually followed him everywhere? Why was not even one guard posted beside his tent?

A fire that had nothing to do with the demon trickled through Hasain's veins, a vengeful fury that consumed all rational thoughts. But who could blame him for his rage? Anyone allied with Neetra was an enemy. And Morathi was doing all he could to ensure Deegan didn't make it back to Arden alive.

Hasain's hands twitched restlessly at his sides. Would anyone really care if the general died? He wasn't a young man. It wouldn't be unreasonable to assume he'd perished from sunstroke. Or perhaps a bad heart.

"That can be managed. Just go to him. I can do the rest."

With no general to lead them, Koal would seize control of the army. He wouldn't wage war against Tahir. He'd find a way for peace between Arden and Shiraz. He'd find a way for all of them to make it back to Silver. There would be no battle in the morning if Morathi were disposed of tonight. Desperate times called for desperate measures.

"There it is. The only scrap of your father's conviction I've yet seen within you. For once in your life, take charge. Free me so we may end this."

209

Hasain licked his lips and climbed to his feet. No one paid any attention as he slunk toward Morathi's tent. He had a clear path inside. He was only steps away from ending the war.

"Tular, stop! Unhand me this instant!"

Hasain hesitated, looking over his shoulder at the sound of Deegan's bubbling laughter.

Tular had both of Deegan's arms pulled behind his back. The prince was stomping and twisting, trying to free himself.

"I'm the Crown Prince!" he squawked between fits of giggles. "I could have you arrested!"

Tular only snickered and lifted higher, forcing Deegan to stand on the tips of his toes.

Koal's voice rose from the depths of the command tent. He snarled a reprimand, but Tular didn't immediately concede.

"Yeah, you heard Koal," Tular teased. "Act your age."

Deegan balked. "Act *my* age? What about *you*?"

Koal shouted, louder this time, and both Tular and Deegan finally untangled their limbs from one another. Sharing a hearty laugh, they went to sit by the fire.

The shadow around Hasain's heart loosened its clench. Suddenly, he could breathe again. He could reason again.

Slowly, he backed away from the general's tent. What had he been thinking? What had he almost done? His eyes searched the clearing, and he searched within himself. Where had the demon gone?

It didn't matter.

Hasain made his way back to his brothers—his family. They'd get through this battle together. Hasain would keep Deegan safe without the demon's help. Maybe then Leviticus would realize he couldn't win. He'd learn that no matter how many sweet lies he whispered into Hasain's head, the Radek lord wouldn't be swayed. After tomorrow, perhaps the demon would leave Hasain alone for good.

It was probably a fool's mission to hope for such a thing, but tonight at least, Hasain could rest assured, knowing his honor remained intact.

Gib stared down at the tiny painted stones: black for the infantry, blue for the Healers, white for the mages, yellow for the archers, and red for the cavalry. They were set upon the table—which was really just two overturned barrels with a slab of hardwood thrown over top—and were strategically placed into organized clusters, like pawns in a game of Senet. This was no game, however.

The war council had dispersed moments before, and now only Gib and Koal remained inside the command tent. The seneschal paced back and forth across the space with hands behind his back, only unclutching them now and then to rub at his temples. Face lined with stress, Koal hadn't uttered more than a few words since the meeting had ended.

Tomorrow's strategy was laid out on the hardwood before their eyes. Morathi had appeared confident, even arrogant, when he called the meeting to an end, but Gib's stomach churned anyway. A single night's restless sleep was all that stood between him and the battle.

"What do you think will happen tomorrow, sir?" Gib asked. "Will it be as Morathi claims? If the Shirites refuse to come out and fight, will our mages really be able to breach Tahir's wall?"

"If it comes down to that, yes," Koal replied at length. "The army can't afford to lay siege. Our bones would be turned to dust long before the Shirites began to starve. Our mages are crucial."

Gib supposed he shouldn't question such things. Even if he never understood magic, he *had* witnessed the destruction on the riverbank—at the hands of a *single* enemy Firestarter. It wasn't inconceivable for a group of mages to have the ability to reduce a stone wall to rubble.

"It's not too late for them to surrender. We don't *have* to tear down their wall. We don't *have* to battle."

Koal slowed his pace but didn't stop entirely. "Our forces outnumber theirs ten to one. It would be in their best interest to surrender peacefully. Though the Dhaki regime will, in all likelihood, sacrifice every last man, woman, and child before they ever submit to foreign conquerors."

Gib's heart sank. "Then there really is no hope for peace, even at this late hour."

Koal glared down at the painted stones. "It was never in Neetra and Morathi's plan to find peace."

The tent flaps stirred then, drawing both men's attention, and Joel peeked between the folds. "Father? Nawaz is here to see you. May we come inside?"

Koal waved for them to enter. "You should be trying to sleep. Both of you."

Joel twisted the sleeves of his robe as he stepped through the threshold. Gib tried not to look. He hated seeing his former companion consumed by worry. "I'm afraid my unruly mind won't allow for sleep." His eyes fluttered over to the table, studying the stones. "Did the meeting fare well? Did they make a decision concerning our prince?"

Koal sighed. "Deegan will remain at the rear of the army. There will be less chance he'll have to engage in the battle there. I will do my best to negotiate a truce with the Dhaki princes, but Morathi's demands are—absolutely uncompromising. I don't believe they will lay their weapons down willingly. If battle is inevitable, I pray the fight doesn't make it to Deegan. I can't be there with him."

211

"I'll protect him, Father. With my life, if necessary."

"No. I'm leaving Natori and Tular with Deegan. I need you near the front. We'll need our mages there. We must keep the battle on the Shiraz side of the field."

"You think there's a chance they'll break through our lines when we outnumber them in such great numbers?"

Koal stared down at the minuscule stone army, his mouth set harshly. "I think the Shirites have had plenty of time to strategize. They've known for moonturns we were coming. I think underestimating them would be foolish."

The muscles in Joel's throat compressed as he swallowed. "We'll be ready for anything. Don't worry."

Koal nodded and turned his attention toward Nawaz. "I was hoping for good news from the pavilion, but the reports earlier were grim. Just how depleted are our medicine stores?"

The Healer didn't immediately respond. Veiled within the shadows, Gib hadn't noticed until this moment how pale and out of sorts Nawaz appeared. Gib's stomach flopped. What had gotten into him?

"Very," Nawaz uttered in a voice heavy with burden. "We're running low on just about everything, from salves to fresh bandages."

He wrung his clammy hands together and sagged his shoulders. Something was definitely wrong. The Healer's eyelids were brimming with tears. Was the fear of tomorrow's battle too much for him to bear? Gib had never taken Nawaz for a coward, but something had him completely distraught.

"Well, there's nothing to be done about that, I suppose," Koal said, more to himself than any of the others. "We'll have to manage with what we have. And pray to The Two injuries are light—"

"Koal," Nawaz croaked. "I–I have something I need to tell you. I might never get a chance to say it again, so—I need to confess now." He squeezed his leaking eyes shut, and his head dropped. "I did something terrible."

No one seemed to know what to say. Joel and Koal exchanged glances, eyebrows elevated on their foreheads. Gib dampened his lips nervously. What burden could possibly be weighing so heavily to have Nawaz this out of sorts?

The seneschal floundered for a moment. "What's this about? I don't understand."

"At the ambush by the river, I did something I shouldn't have, but— I can't undo it now."

"This is war," Koal said. The uncertainty in his voice suggested he was still puzzled. "Soldiers die every day. While we should never take that sacrifice lightly, know there's no fault in doing what you must to survive."

"That's not it," Nawaz gasped. "It's nothing to do with the war. It's something far worse."

212

Gib placed a hand on the Healer's back, fearing the young lord might collapse. His chest heaved like he couldn't catch a breath. "Come on. It can't be that bad—"

Nawaz came alive, whirling around so fast Gib drew back in surprise. "You have to apologize to her for me! She'll listen to you!"

Gib stared, dumbfounded. "She who? What are you talking about?"

Nawaz choked as he grabbed Gib's hands. "Kezra! There's no way in hell she will talk to me now. She wouldn't even look at me after—"

After what? The battle?

Koal's face hardened. "Nawaz, should this be a private conversation? Joel and Gib can leave."

Nawaz cringed, like he might be expecting a blow, but he blustered on. "I shouldn't have—I knew better. I shouldn't have done it. It's just—in the moment, I—"

Gib was still at a loss, but beside him, Joel had narrowed his eyes.

"You knew better than to *what*?" he demanded. The cold words were like ice down the spine.

Nawaz didn't even try to meet Joel's furious glare. His shoulders quaked as tears gushed down his face.

Dread settled in Gib's gut like a stone. This couldn't possibly be what it sounded like, could it? Nawaz and Kezra hadn't—had they? How? *When?*

"What did you *do*?" Joel snarled, sounding nothing like the soft-spoken lordling Gib had first met.

Nawaz gagged on a sob. "I'm sorry."

"What about Heidi? What about the baby? Did you even think of *them*?"

Pain shot up Gib's fingers when Nawaz clutched the hand tighter, but Gib couldn't bring himself to voice his complaint aloud. He held the Healer's hand and kept a watchful eye on Joel.

Already upset before, the mage was just about beside himself now. His contorted face was possibly even redder than Nawaz's. "How could you do this? *How?* You dog—"

"Quiet." Koal's unyielding voice filled the room. "Everyone calm down."

Gib winced.

Koal. Oh gods, what is Koal going to say?

Silence swelled, engulfing the space. A feather could have floated by, and Gib would have heard it touch the ground. He didn't want to look at his mentor—he didn't want to know what the seneschal might be thinking or, Goddesses save them, preparing to say—but Gib couldn't resist the impulse to glimpse up.

He lifted his eyes and almost couldn't comprehend what he was seeing. He would have expected to behold rage, despair, confusion, or sharp accusation—but not this. Never this. Koal's aged face was weary, grave, and—sympathetic? Was that empathy that lingered in his solemn gaze?

Koal trudged across the tent and stood with his back to all of them. He had both palms pressed to the makeshift table, as though he needed its support to stay upright. "Nawaz, explain yourself."

Nawaz's bulging eyes darted to Gib, desperate for help. The Healer's grip was so tight around Gib's wrists he worried his hands might actually be crushed. He shook his head, just once, to let Nawaz know not to run. Or lie. Or act upon whatever other insane ideas might be rattling inside his skull in this moment of utter dread.

"It just—happened," Nawaz muttered at last, tears and exhaustion garbling his words.

Joel laughed incredulously. "Oh, indeed? The two of you 'just happened' to fall naked together?"

"I didn't plan it. Neither did Kezra. It was right after the ambush by the river. She found me. She was alive and so was I, and—I'm so sorry. I never intended for this. You have to believe me."

An eternity passed while Gib tried to calm his pounding heart and Joel cried bitterly. Koal's shoulders drooped so low he didn't even look like himself. The distress inside the tent was so thick Gib could have reached out and grasped it between his fingers.

At long last, Koal's weary voice rose out of the shadows. "Nawaz, do you love Heidi?"

Nawaz hesitated, wiping at his downcast eyes.

"*Can* you love her?" Koal pressed.

A stab of indignation touched even Gib's heart. What sort of question was that?

Nawaz nodded his head earnestly. "Yes. It's getting easier. And this is the only time anything like this has happened. I've never even considered it before, I swear."

Joel couldn't seem to take it anymore, and he threw his hands into the air. "Da, are you hearing this? He talks like what he did is all right because he didn't plan it."

"That's not what I said!" Nawaz protested. "It's not right, and I am sorry. Joel, you *know* me. You *know* I've tried to do right by Heidi—"

"Yes, and you've *certainly* done an excellent job thus far!"

Koal's hand cut through the air, leaving no room for contest. Everyone fell silent, even Joel.

The seneschal waited until the silence began to fester before he craned his head, regarding Nawaz over one shoulder. "You can keep your promise then?"

"Promise?" Joel asked. "What promise?"

Nawaz and Koal exchanged knowing glances, some shared secret weighing heavily between them. Gib's legs were beginning to lose their feeling. He wished he could leave. He didn't know if he could bear any more secrets.

"Yes," Nawaz finally said through gritted teeth. "I can keep the promise."

Joel's determination, however, wouldn't be quelled so easily. He stormed over to his father, glaring at Koal's back. Gib worried for a moment Joel might wrench the seneschal's arm, but the son smartly kept his hands balled at his sides.

"*What* promise?" Joel demanded. "This is Heidi we're talking about—your own *daughter*."

Koal spun around so fast Joel nearly toppled over in his haste to jump back. "I *know* this is about Heidi. The reason I called for a promise from Nawaz was to protect *her* future. You're not stupid, Joel. None of us are. No one here really thought Nawaz to be in love with Heidi when they wed. We all knew what was going on between him and the Malin-Rai girl. And we all knew what Neetra was doing by forcing Nawaz into the marriage."

Gib closed his eyes. The tent and everything contained within it whirled in a blur of confusion.

Joel's voice spiked again. "What Neetra did was wrong, but so was *knowingly* marrying Heidi off to someone who didn't love her—who never had the best intentions at heart. Where's the justice in that? She's not some random highborn lady. She's your daughter. Father, why would you do that?"

"You're not giving your sister enough credit. Do you really think she's clueless? She knew. She knew Nawaz loved another."

"So you made Nawaz promise what? To keep his disloyalty secret? To not *openly* break her heart?"

"No," Koal said. "I made him promise not to marry her if he truly believed he couldn't *grow* to love her. His heart pined for someone he couldn't have. A person can't simply turn that emotion off, Joel. You can't just stop loving someone because your head tells you it's wrong. It takes time."

Gib held his breath. Was Koal talking about *him*? Did his mentor somehow know about Gib's conflicted emotions concerning Joel and Zandi? Guilt spread to his cheeks in a rosy flush.

Joel quieted as well, and his eyes grew misty. When he raised his voice again, it was with less ferocity. "You've never been one to indulge in fantasies, Father. Certain betrayals cannot be forgiven."

"People make blunders, Joel. This was a mistake, and it's not yours to forgive."

Joel glared over at Nawaz, who looked as if he wished the sand beneath his boots would swallow him whole. "*Who* could *ever* forgive something like this? Who, Father? *Who?*"

Koal slammed a fist onto the tabletop. The little stones representing the Ardenian army scattered everywhere. "Your *mother*! That's who!"

215

The ground seemed to tumble out from under Gib's feet. He lurched, barely managing to catch himself by grabbing Nawaz's shoulder. What? What was Koal saying?

Joel's handsome features were twisted with horror and frozen in place upon his pale face. "Y–you? *You* did this to Mother?"

"It was a long time ago. Another life, almost."

"How—how could you?"

"Mrifa and I were intended from a young age. I knew she'd one day be my wife, but I—loved someone else. Even after we married, I couldn't let go of that first love. What I did was wrong. My head knew as much, but my heart—"

Koal dropped his chin to his chest. If Gib lived to be a hundred years old, he would never be able to forget the shame engraved on the seneschal's face.

"How could you do something so awful? You're as bad as *him*." Joel waved feebly toward Nawaz.

Koal shook his head. "If you want to pass judgment on me so thoroughly, then you need to know the severity of my crimes."

Gib resisted the urge to cover his ears. He didn't want to hear any more. He didn't want to tarnish the longstanding ideals he held about his heroes. He'd once believed Lord and Lady Adelwijn's marriage to be perfect, as if the two of them had come straight out of a fantastical *Tale of Fae*. How could he have been so wrong?

Koal met Joel's critical eyes. "You'd banish Nawaz for taking a single misstep. What would you do with me then? For the better part of a wheelturn, I was disloyal to our new marriage. Every time I told myself I was better than what I'd become. Every time I'd vow to stop. And every time, I'd fail. Joel, I was lost. I made a horrible mistake. I was ashamed to tell Mrifa, but in the end, I had no choice. Your mother had every right to request a divorce—I even expected her to—but she didn't. She forgave me, whether she should have or not. She took me back and even accepted my—burden."

"Why did you marry Mother if your heart belonged to another? What about this other woman?"

Koal stared into the gloom. A great remorse, like nothing Gib had ever seen before, clouded his eyes. "I couldn't have her. She was above me and completely outside my reach."

Joel must have witnessed it too. His fair complexion grew even paler. "Do you love Mother now?"

Koal cleared his throat, or it might have been an abomination of a laugh. "Yes. Now, and for a great many years. But in the beginning, no. I had to work at it. *We* had to work at it. Mrifa and I, our love didn't blossom on its own. We had to nurture it, convince it to grow. As will Nawaz and Heidi."

216

"If Heidi can forgive what he's done."

"Yes, of course. But that is her decision to make, Joel. Not yours."

Gib didn't know when he'd sunk to the ground, but there he was, sitting dumbfounded in the dirt. His lungs screamed for air, but he couldn't breathe. The tension in the tent was far too dense. He needed to go outside. He needed space to clear his spinning mind.

"I'll speak no more of this," Koal said. He turned his back once again, and the silence encompassed the tent, creeping into the very fibers of the canvas. "Go now, all of you. Find sleep if you can. Dawn comes early in the south."

Joel wiped away a tear but didn't utter another word as he swept outside. Nawaz's own tears had dried; the only remnants were red tracks on his cheeks. He offered a shaky hand. Gib took hold of it and was pulled upright. He blinked, expecting to wake at any moment. This entire conversation seemed so incredulous that it *must* be a dream.

As he shuffled toward the threshold, he cast one final glance at the back of his mentor's tipped head. Gib's heart sank. Who *was* this other woman for the seneschal of Arden to be disloyal to Lady Mrifa? Who could possibly have competed against her for the heart of Koal Adelwijn?

Liro stood motionless in the palace hall, utterly transfixed by the portrait of Queen Jorja Viran. One trembling hand stretched up, touching the gilded metal frame, caressing the painted canvas like it was a lover. When finally the hand came to a rest, Liro's palm lay against the Queen's pregnant stomach.

Back to the wall and just barely concealed by shadow, Diddy could feel himself shake from head to toe. He lifted his eyes, looking to Aodan for guidance, but the bodyguard only shook his head and put a finger to his lips. Diddy understood. It would be impossible for them to leave now without being caught. They'd only just managed to tuck themselves into the hollow when Aodan heard footsteps approaching. If they moved, Liro would see them.

It was preposterous that Aodan had to sneak around. The palace had been his home for some thirty years. But Neetra was convinced Aodan somehow meant to deal harm to Arden. If he was caught outside the suite without an escort, there could be trouble. Diddy bit his lip. The royal family needed no more trouble.

Uttering a choppy gasp, Liro brought his hand back to himself, cradling it against his chest. He stepped away, as though he were contemplating taking his leave, though his tormented eyes never once abandoned the portrait hanging above.

Diddy watched, both mystified and frightened. He couldn't recall a time he'd ever seen Liro appear so forlorn. What was he doing here? And why was he so captivated by the image of Queen Jorja?

Suddenly Gudrin's high squeal could be heard all the way from within the royal suite. Diddy winced, glancing back over his shoulder. Something must have upset her. She might even have sensed Liro. Diddy hugged his back to the wall, wishing he could somehow escape by falling through it. Liro would surely notice them now. Gudrin's shriek had caught his attention.

The shadows in which they stood weren't nearly deep enough for either of them to actually hide, and Aodan didn't bother trying any longer. Arms folded over his chest, he stepped into the dimly lit corridor as Liro's eyes flicked in their direction.

The young lord drew back. *"You."*

Diddy's heart pounded in his chest, but Aodan remained as stoic and unmoving as the portraits surrounding them. "Aye. Me. What brings ya skulking 'round like some beaten dog?"

"How *dare* you speak to me like that. I've come on behalf of the steward to deliver a message."

Aodan nodded toward the Queen's portrait. "To her? Don't think she heard ya."

If looks could kill, Diddy knew for sure he and Aodan would have perished on sight. Liro had always been cold and unreachable. It was his nature. But the fury twisting his features was unlike anything Diddy could have imagined.

"You've overstepped your bounds, Derr," Liro lashed out. "Don't you *ever* speak so lightly of the late Queen in *my* presence! You're not fit to tread the same halls she once did."

"Ha. So you're the product of higher learning, are ya? A lot of good that education's done. The late Queen—Queen Jorja Viran to *you*—was the one who gave me my job. So really, it's her authority you undermine by tryin' to be rid of me."

"Shut your mouth! She had no way of knowing how you'd poison Arden."

"I served the Queen for a good many years before she was betrayed by snakes like you. I'd say she knew exactly who I was."

"Queen Jorja was forced to marry an idealistic fool—a traitor to his own country. *He* was the one who sent Arden plunging to the pits of hell—"

"Now *you've* overstepped," Aodan warned. "Make no mistake, Liro Adelwijn, if you speak ill of my king to me, no power in the world will be able to save ya."

Diddy shivered, wanting to flee. He sought to grab Aodan's arm and force him to retreat. They could run back to the suite. Yes, it was a cage, but at least it was safe. It was the only safe place they had left.

218

"Your king is *dead*," Liro hissed. "And if there were any justice in this world, his lineage would go by the same way."

"Careful."

Liro stabbed a finger toward the painting. "Queen Jorja's heir should sit on the throne. The Viran lineage ruled before the likes of Rishi Radek stole the crown away."

Head spinning, Diddy took a breathless step back. Had Liro completely lost his mind? What was he talking about? Everyone knew Queen Jorja had no living kin.

Aodan snorted. "Is that what this is about? Well, Jorja's daughter, Princess Nikki, is dead."

"There was another child."

Aodan's single eye narrowed dangerously. "*That* child's dead, too."

"That child deserved better. This kingdom deserved better."

Diddy reached for Aodan but was too late. Sufficiently baited, the bodyguard took a step closer to Liro.

"Jorja was a wise ruler. She chose her king and council well. It was she who laid the foundation to bring Arden to where it is now. Rishi only continued the path she'd set. It's liars an' cowards like you and yer steward who weaken this land." Aodan nodded toward the portrait. "That child could have had nothing better than to be born into the kingdom Jorja and Rishi built."

Liro's face was so red he might burst. "That child *should* have been born!"

Aodan came within an arm's reach of Liro. The bodyguard didn't seem to care the other man stood head and shoulders taller. "Not from where I stand. I'd even venture ta say it's a damn good thing it never was. Just *look* at the *lunatic* we could've been saddled with."

Liro's fury boiled over. He threw his head back and screamed. The piercing sound surged through the entire length of the corridor and resounded off the high stone arches.

Diddy winced. The Royal Guard would hear that. They'd arrive at any moment.

He called to Aodan, "We should go—"

"*No!*" Liro bellowed. He pointed savagely at the bodyguard. "You shouldn't even be out of your cage, monster. I'm going to see to it that you and every other trace of the dead king's *failed* rule are wiped from the slate. If anyone remembers Rishi Radek when I'm done, it will be as the *worst* misstep this kingdom ever took—"

Aodan swung without warning. His closed fist crashed into Liro's jaw and sent him sprawling back. The slam of the young lord's hind end on the marble floor echoed almost as loudly as the racing footfalls of the guardsmen who'd just appeared around the corner.

Liro scrambled to his feet, his cheeks blotchy with rage and humiliation. *"Get out!"*

The guards retreated so fast Diddy wasn't sure they'd actually been there at all.

Aodan grabbed Diddy's elbow and pushed him in the direction of the suite.

"What were you thinking?" Diddy asked as they hurried down the corridor. "Neetra will have your head."

"I couldn't listen to it anymore," Aodan said, glaring at the marble floor. "I couldn't listen to what he was sayin' about Rishi."

Liro's furious voice rang after them. "Stop where you are! Both of you!"

Aodan's arm tucked around Diddy's shoulders. "Keep goin'."

"Stop or *I'll* stop you!"

Diddy hastened his footfalls. The doorway of the suite was within sight. "Stay with me. We're almost there."

The steady hand slipped from his shoulder. Glancing back, a horrified gasp escaped the prince's mouth. Aodan had turned to face Liro. Time slowed to a halt as Diddy's mind scrambled through all of the terrible outcomes which might lie ahead. Would Aodan forsake his secret? Would he engage Liro? This could be the end of their family.

Blue magic arced between Liro's fingers as he stormed closer. He wasn't stopping, and Aodan wasn't backing down. The bodyguard bared his teeth. Magic sizzled in the static air, but he didn't budge.

"Aodan!" Diddy screamed.

Liro lifted one glowing hand, preparing to swipe.

"Liro Adelwijn, stand down."

Diddy swung around so fast he nearly toppled over.

NezReth stood within the threshold of the suite, his own hands flickering with magic. His eyes were squalling globes, narrowed and glaring intently at the intruder.

"I said *stand down*." NezReth's deep voice swelled, filling the entire corridor.

Diddy put both hands to his mouth. Would Liro listen? Would he obey the command?

Liro was a great many things, but he wasn't stupid. Pausing in his approach, the electricity surrounding them vanished as Liro retracted his magic. He scowled at Aodan for a moment before turning his nose into the air. "I've done as you asked, mage. Now it would only be polite for you to disarm yourself as well."

A feather-light smile touched NezReth's lips. "With all due respect, Lord Adelwijn, it will be a cold day in hell before I take lessons in etiquette from you."

Liro sneered. "Stand aside. I'm here to deliver a message to my aunt."

He pushed his way into the royal suite. NezReth didn't try to stop Liro but followed behind him, fingers pooling with magic. Aodan let out a growl, and he and Diddy hurried inside as well.

Dahlia already waited in the receiving room, holding Gudrin's hand in a vice-like grip. The young princess eyed Liro with predatory intent that made even Diddy uncomfortable.

Liro glared down at the little girl. "What do *you* want?"

"Mama says all people reap what they sow," Gudrin replied. Her eyes were all pupil, absorbing his every move. "I want you to get exactly what you deserve."

Liro drew back, growing paler. "Are you *threatening* me?"

Dahlia tugged the princess' hand. "Gudrin, enough."

"He shouldn't talk to us like that," Gudrin said. "Papa wouldn't have let him."

"Well, Papa is *dead*," taunted Liro.

Aodan balled his hands. "Watch yer mouth."

Smiling smugly, Liro turned his attention to Dahlia. "Forgive me, aunt. I'm here to deliver news."

"I see. And what news would you bring me?"

"An update on the army's progress in Shiraz, of course. Any day now they will battle outside the gates of Tahir."

"So you've come to gloat about the dire situation my son has been thrown into."

Liro laughed. "Well, had courage been a common trait in the Radek bloodline, perhaps he wouldn't have needed to be thrown."

Aodan came at Liro so fast that everyone in the suite uttered a collective gasp. "You lyin' sack of shit! I told you to keep yer venom to yourself!"

Liro instinctively raised a hand to shield his already bruising jaw. "Get away from me!"

Diddy watched in horror as Aodan crashed into Liro. They toppled back, both screaming and clawing at one another. Glass shattered around them as they struggled through the room and finally teetered out onto the balcony.

"You father's not here ta save yer rotten arse this time!"

Liro tore at Aodan's rusty hair. "Get your filthy hands off me! I'm going to purge Arden of you and every one of your little bastard monsters!"

Aodan screeched, the pitch reminiscent of a wild cat, and his hands grabbed for Liro's neck.

Diddy clutched his own throat as he watched them stumble closer to the balcony's edge. "NezReth, can you stop this?"

"As soon as Aodan steps clear," the Blessed Mage replied.

Aodan had Liro pinioned against the balustrade. The lord thrashed, clawing at the bodyguard's bare back. Magic seared into his skin, raising welts on Aodan's shoulders. He flailed and shouted some indiscernible insult about goats and Liro's preference for them. His grip around Liro's throat momentarily loosened.

It was all Liro needed to gain the upper hand. Grabbing Aodan beneath the arms, Liro lifted the smaller man off his feet, holding him precariously over the railing.

"Liro!" Dahlia screamed. "Stop this now, or I'll call for your arrest!"

Liro sneered around Aodan's dangling limbs. "A risk I'm willing to take. I *will* know the truth. What better way for the birdie to show me his wings?"

Aodan's boots scrabbled to find solid ground, to no avail. "Ya buffoon! What in hell do ya think yer doin'?"

"Last chance, monster. Fly."

Aodan's lone eye widened. "Are ya *mad?*"

A crazed, victorious grin flicked across Liro's face, and then he dumped Aodan over the edge of the balcony.

Gudrin shrieked as the bodyguard's floundering form disappeared from view. Diddy slammed his eyes shut. He couldn't look. He couldn't watch the chaos unfold. He couldn't watch his family shatter.

But nothing happened.

Diddy opened his eyes in time to see Gudrin bound over to the balustrade. She let out a whimper and stretched her arm as if she could reach the courtyard below. "*No!* Da!"

Oh gods, is he—?

Shaking himself free of his stupor, Diddy lurched to the ledge. He clutched the railing and dared to peer over.

Down below, Aodan sat in the grass, stunned and cradling his left arm against his heaving chest. Startled cries lifted around the courtyard. Servants were already running to his aid and calling for a Healer to be summoned.

Liro stood perfectly still, watching the scene below. "Why—why didn't he fly?"

Gudrin whirled around. A feral growl resonated from within her chest. "Why don't *you?*"

She sprang at Liro, crashing into his torso and sending him sprawling backward. He was only just able to right himself before *he* toppled over the balcony, too.

Diddy reacted without thought, grabbing for his sister's hand. "Gudrin, no! Stop."

Gudrin roiled and howled as she was torn away from Liro. "I hate you! I hate you, Liro! You deserve to be hanged! Leave my family alone!"

Liro's blanched features twisted from fear to rage. Snarling a curse, he lunged forward with a raised hand. "You tried to *kill* me! You miserable little *bitch!*"

Not even NezReth could react faster than Dahlia. In the blink of an eye, she swept between Liro and her children. Her own hand crashed across Liro's face with a sharp crack. "Don't you *dare* raise your hand to the princess of Arden. Have you completely forgotten your place?"

Eyes wide with shock, Liro fell silent, touching a hand to his reddened cheek.

Rage frothed in Dahlia's dark eyes as she took Gudrin into her arms. "Liro Adelwijn, you are under arrest—and you're lucky I haven't the power to call for your immediate death. You will be taken into custody, tried, and no doubt found innocent by Neetra's saving grace—but make no mistake, you are *dead* to me, as you already are to the kingdom."

Liro's shoulders sagged, and his foggy eyes shifted to the floor. The lord's stillness was unsettling. Diddy would have expected rage, indignation, or even cold laughter but never this hollow mist. Liro had fought for the last word for so long his silence now was unnerving.

Diddy watched, feeling oddly displaced, as royal guardsmen poured onto the balcony and led Liro away in shackles. Where was the joy of victory? Where was the warm rush of euphoria? Diddy couldn't feel either. In his heart, he knew this tiny win would be short lived. Neetra would see to that.

Diddy glanced over the balcony. The servants had helped Aodan to his feet and were leading him along the path, back into the palace. He limped along, never uttering a word.

A tear slipped down Diddy's cheek. How many more days could they go on like this? How much longer could the secret be contained? Liro had been foiled today, but he would try again. He'd keep trying until Aodan slipped. And then what?

Diddy took Gudrin's hand, small despite its strength, and wondered how many more times he'd be able to do so. "He wasn't badly hurt. Let's go to him."

The princess raised her face. Her teary eyes spoke the words in Diddy's heart. She knew as well as he did: their family stood on sword's edge. It was only a matter of time before they would be pushed onto the blade entirely.

CHAPTER FIFTEEN

The crimson sun loomed just below the farthest dune in Kezra's line of sight, its tendrils staining the sky in a garish premonition of the day to come. She watched from where she sat atop her sleeping mat, unable to tear her gaze away.

Around her, soldiers adjusted their armor and collected their weapons. Some knelt in various forms of prayer. Others saddled and tended their horses. Frantic remnants of life skittered around her as the camp goers made their final preparations. At a glance, it could have been any other morning on this long journey—except for many, this would be the last. This morning was the last promised to *any* of them.

Zandi fidgeted nearby, gathering their things. He was unable to stop the tremble in his hands as he wrapped a sash around his slender waist and tucked loose strands of raven hair beneath his turban. Kezra frowned as she watched him slip an ornamental dagger into one of his boots. She wished he would carry a sword, even if he'd never been trained to wield one. Relying on magic alone seemed a fool's mission.

Dwelling on such a thing at this late hour was futile, however. Her brother's magic had always been considerable. He would be fine. Kezra wouldn't allow herself to think otherwise.

Exhaling deeply, she slid a leather bracer onto her forearm. It took her even longer to don the other. The leather pauldrons she'd worn a thousand times suddenly felt like rocks atop her shoulders, and the brigandine wrapped around her trunk threatened to crack her ribs. She still hadn't mustered the strength to retrieve her boots. Would she ever be ready for this battle?

Zandi's shadow fell across her just before he took a seat. A familiar jar and pouch rested in his hands. "Ready?"

Nodding, Kezra sat still while Zandi applied the paint to her forehead. She couldn't quite meet his eyes. Never before had the mark felt so heavy on her brow. She'd always been confident in her ability to use her head and to think critically. The mark had always been a comforting reminder that she possessed a higher wisdom—that she wasn't a mindless animal, nor a fool, and that if she trusted herself, she could conquer any problem.

How had she failed so miserably with Nawaz then? When had she

224

stopped thinking clearly? When had she allowed her emotions to cloud her better judgement? If this was what thinking with her heart did to her, then perhaps the only rational thing to do was lock it away entirely.

Zandi's smile was timid as he handed Kezra the jar, awaiting his own adornment. "Tell me you're all right. No matter how tightly I hold you, you keep drifting further and further away."

Kezra dabbed a bit of wax between his eyebrows and then dipped a finger into the cinnabar powder. "The tighter you clench your fist, the quicker the sand escapes. So maybe I'm sand."

"Please don't mock me." Zandi looked away, tears in his eyes. "I'm being serious. Promise you'll be careful out there today."

Kezra's temper flared. She should have been worried for her own safety, but instead her mind kept fluttering back to their mother, imprisoned inside Anders' house, and to her siblings. Harper had only just managed to escape their father. Kezra's younger brothers were still trapped with him. And Tamil—she could lose her husband in battle today. So many people in Kezra's life needed help, and she was powerless to do anything for them. She couldn't even help herself.

"I'm to be stationed on the front line," Zandi muttered, still staring hopelessly into the distance. "Is it wrong of me to be afraid?"

Kezra touched his white sleeve. "No."

"I'm not even afraid for myself so much as the others. Mostly you and Gib. He'll be with the prince and Blessed Mage, at least."

Kezra's eyes grew large.

Gib.

She hadn't gotten to speak to her friend today. How could she have forgotten?

"I'll be right back," Kezra said, jumping to her feet, bare as they were. "Get the horses saddled, will you?"

Zandi might have called after her, but she was on a mission. Wax and cinnabar in hand, she tiptoed over sleeping mats and past soldiers in various states of dress. She had to find Gib.

Thank the Goddesses, he wasn't difficult to locate. As soon as the seneschal's tent came into view, so did Gib.

He sat on a crate, clothed but not yet in his armor. His sword rested across his lap, but his focus was on the sky. Indeed, Kezra was nearly able to reach out and touch him before he noticed her.

"What are you doing here?" he asked. "Shouldn't you be getting ready?"

"I could say the same to you."

Gib stared blankly at her. "At least I have my boots on."

She felt a smile curling one corner of her mouth, but given the circumstances, it hardly seemed an appropriate time for foolery. "Look, we have to leave soon, so I'm going to say this fast. Do you remember me telling you about the heritage mark on my brow? The one from my mother's homeland?"

"Yeah. It makes you wise or something of the sort, doesn't it?"

The smile might have won this time. "Well, that's stretching it." Kneeling in the sand, Kezra set down the pot and pouch so she could take Gib's hands. "You've been my friend from the first day of sentinel training. All the people who told me I couldn't do this because I'm a woman, all the people who hated me when I excelled, all the people who *still* won't listen to me when I give a command on the streets—*none* of them matter because of you and the others like you. You accepted me for who I am, Gib. You protected me. I always swore I'd do the same for you. But today—"

Gib squeezed her fingers. "We only have just so much control over today. Don't worry yourself over what may or may not happen to me, Kezra. Keep yourself safe."

Every beat of Kezra's heart was agony in her core. Why did love have to hurt so much?

"I will," she replied. "But I can't be by your side the entire time we're out there. Nor by Zandi's."

Gib squirmed at the mention of her brother's name, and Kezra worried whether or not she'd ever get to tell Gib precisely what she thought of him *settling.*

Later. That would have to wait until later. There *would* be a later.

"I'll do my best," Gib said. "And Zandi's a good mage—great even. We've as good a chance as anybody."

"I know. But I protect what I love. It's what I do. And I can't promise I'll be able to protect either of you today. So I have something for you."

Gib watched as she opened the pot and pouch. He laughed. "Did you bring me a snack?"

Kezra couldn't help but chuckle alongside him—and *damn*, it felt good. "Mark my words, Nemesio. You're going to be a fat politician one day. No, this isn't food."

Kezra's hands trembled as she gazed down at the wax jar and cinnabar dust. Her mother had taught her how to apply the mark. It was one of the only traditions Odessa had been allowed to keep when she'd married Anders, one of the last traces of Shantar she still possessed. But this wasn't about Kezra's mother or her homeland. This was about what the mark meant—to Kezra and to all else who bore it.

She took a deep breath and dipped her finger into the pot. "We all observe the world around us. We see with our eyes. Listen with our ears. Taste with our tongue. Feel with our hands. Smell with our nose. But there's more than that. We sense when something's amiss. We feel when someone's watching us. We judge what's safe, what's good, what's dangerous, and what's wrong."

Kezra pressed the wax to Gib's forehead. He didn't flinch and never let his attention wander.

226

"This is our higher awareness, guiding us and keeping us safe. I can't promise to stay with you today, but I *can* give you the mark. You might not need it—the ultimate truth seems to show itself to you often already—but just in case."

She dabbed one final crimson drop for that day and leaned back. It looked all right, she supposed. He may never need it, but she felt better, knowing he had it.

In the faint morning light, Gib's cheeks glistened. "Thank you, Kezra."

Kezra winced. Damn. She'd made him cry—and not miniscule teardrops that could be blamed on the dust, but rivulets pouring down his face.

She tried to apologize. "I'm sorry—"

Gib set his sword aside and dropped to his knees beside her. His arms were around Kezra's shoulders before she knew what was happening. He clutched her, shaking as he sobbed against her neck.

Kezra pulled him tight and wept with him. She cried for her mother and siblings, for her friends, for Nawaz and her own stupidity, and for Gib, who'd already lost so much and might be lost himself. She cried until there were no more tears to spare and her throat was raw from strain.

"How did we get here?" Gib asked, his frail voice muffled by Kezra's armor. "How did we ever end up so far from home?"

Kezra stroked his hair. "We're here *because* of home. We're here to protect it, and those we love. Remember your brothers. They still need you. Survive this so you can return to them."

"You survive as well." Gib raised his reddened eyes, imploring her to look at him. "And remember that no matter what happens today, no matter what we have to do to keep ourselves alive, neither of us are monsters."

Her heart might well have torn into pieces, blinded by images of terrible blue eyes and the glimmer of Nawaz's wedding band. "I may be a monster already, Gib."

"You're not."

"You don't know. You don't know what I did."

Gib's hands clamped down on her shoulders. "*Look* at me. You are *not* a monster. Everyone makes mistakes. You and he are no exception."

Kezra slammed her eyes shut. Gib knew. Somehow, he knew. "I–I didn't mean for it to happen."

"It's over. It's done. That was the night. Today is a new dawn. Fight for today."

She sucked in a mouthful of air, and it felt like the first real breath she'd gotten in sennights. She'd been certain there would be no forgiveness for her crime, but Gib knew the truth and he still didn't think her a monster. He forgave her. Perhaps in time, she would forgive herself.

227

Kezra rose, pulling Gib to his feet. Hands clasped, they stared at one another in silence. If this was the last she'd ever see of her friend, she wanted to remember every detail, from the mousy curls crowning his head to the modest smile playing upon his lips, always so genuine and compassionate.

She remembered when he was but a youth, dressed in peasant drab, half-starved, and bumbling through the Academy halls in bewilderment. He couldn't read back then and had no idea how to hold a sword. Had so much time really passed, to bring them here, to this very moment?

Her eyes lingered on the red mark upon Gib's brow, and it suddenly reminded Kezra of her own. She raised a hand, fingers grazing her forehead, as she recalled the wisdom of her mother: the mind could conquer all, if only it was trusted.

Today, she would trust it. Today, she would believe in herself.

Smiling, Kezra squeezed Gib's hand. "You're a brother to me. You always will be. The night *is* over. Let us ride together, as brave warriors, into the battle dawn."

Joel could feel the scratch of the falcon pendant against his skin. He reached down, taking hold of the silver cord, and repositioned the trinket so it sat atop his battle robes. Kirk claimed the pendant would keep Joel safe. Today, more than ever, he hoped the Imperial mage was right.

Ivory shifted her weight, making Joel's saddle creak. He reached down absently and curled his fingers through her coarse, silver mane. The filly pawed at the dirt, as restless as Joel. He patted her neck.

Almost time. Almost.

The morning sun had only just crested over the temple roofs. Joel squinted his eyes against the brilliance. The distant dunes shimmered in the crisp light, each grain sparkling like stars sprinkled across a banner of white sand.

Tahir's wall loomed ahead. Closer to it now than he'd ever been, Joel could make out each block of limestone, stacked with precision atop the next and reaching toward the sky. The wall cast a long shadow across the land, nearly reaching the place where Joel waited on the front line. Behind him, Arden's army stood motionless. They waited the same as he. They waited for their fates to be divined.

Just down the line, Koal sat upon his horse. Ardenian banners flapped in the breeze around his unmoving form. Clad in full mail and plate armor, he was barely recognizable and brought to mind the stories Joel had been told about his father's campaign in the Northern War. Was this but a glimpse of what Koal had looked like in his youth, before weariness and burden lined his face?

Before he'd settled into a loveless marriage?

Joel swallowed against the bitter taste in his mouth. Now was no time to dwell on that. If he survived the battle, he'd have all the time in the world to be angry at his father and Nawaz both. But not today. He couldn't be angry today.

Koal's steady gaze hadn't wavered from the wall in some time, but his head turned briefly then, and he locked eyes with Joel.

Joel nodded, hoping his father would understand.

I'm ready.

He closed a trembling hand around the pendant, sending a silent prayer to the Goddesses for Daya's intuition and Chhaya's strength. He didn't want to die, but if it was his fate to meet the Gatekeeper today, he begged his demise would come swiftly and without pain. He pleaded for the lives of his family and friends, even the few he might never be able to forgive.

By the grace of The Two, may they all be safe.

The groan of metal on metal sliced through the parched air. Joel's head shot toward the sound, his heart pounding in both chest and ears. The gates! The gates were opening.

Iron cuirasses gleamed beneath the rising sun as a procession of Shirite riders trotted forth. Each of the twelve white horses pranced lively in perfect unison, their golden hooves kicking up snowy granules of sand. Little bells chimed on their reins, and when they swished their tails, the gold lace woven into the fine hair shimmered.

The men atop the horses carried olive-colored banner flags that snaked in the wind as wildly as the sleeves beneath their chest armor. Indigo feathers, no doubt plucked from some exotic pheasant, fanned from the crevasses of plated helms like cresting waves. As the riders paraded closer, Joel could make out celestial depictions sewn onto their tabards: the sun and stars of Shiraz.

The riders halted, still a respectable distance away. They faced the Ardenian army, a dozen men against ten thousand, and waited, as motionless as the great wall at their backs.

Joel's breath caught in his throat. What now?

Without saying a word, Koal gave his horse a nudge and went out to meet them. The spell broke. Morathi's grey stallion lumbered after the seneschal, with a handful of guards and mages trailing just behind. Joel hesitated for only a moment before coaxing Ivory forward. He had followed his father all the way to the Northern Empire and back. He wasn't about to stop now.

Ivory's swift gait brought him to Koal's side just as one of the Shirite riders separated himself from the others. Joel thought the broad-shouldered man looked familiar, but it was difficult to judge, dressed from head to foot in regalia as he was. The quilted cuirass encasing his torso and wispy jeweled hilt hanging at his hip seemed more apt for a royal coronation than a battle, but then again, Joel had never proclaimed to be a scholar on such matters.

"Gods greet you, Seneschal Koal Adelwijn of Arden," the man said in broken Ardenian. "I am Rami Dhaki, Prince of Shiraz, Voice of Seven Holy Pillars of Tahir."

Oh, Joel thought. *He was one of the diplomats sent to the Northern Empire. No wonder I recognized him.*

His stomach rolled as he recalled how poorly things had gone the last time Arden and Shiraz met.

Koal bowed his head. "I remember you well, Prince Rami, from our first meeting in Teivel. I do regret our reunion could not fall under more— agreeable circumstances."

The Dhaki prince's long, braided beard moved with the rest of his face when he frowned. "You are long way from home, Seneschal."

"I am here to negotiate a truce."

"We wanted truce in Teivel, yet you fled like dogs with tucked tails."

Koal's face tightened. "We were betrayed by our host. We had no choice but to leave or be slaughtered by Emperor Sarpedon's army."

Prince Rami's sharp gaze swept across the army line. "And now you bring great sea of soldiers to our gates to do the same."

"No blood needs to be spilt today. There is still a chance for peace. If the Seven will hear Arden's terms."

Prince Rami shot a hand into the air and turned to one of the riders by his side. They exchanged terse words in their native tongue. Finally, the Dhaki prince looked back at Koal.

"Terms?" Rami said cautiously. "You spoke of negotiations moments ago, Seneschal."

Koal hesitated. "I'm sure we can agree that none of us *want* to resort to violence. Arden has demands, it's true, but I believe it would be in the best interest of both sides if we're willing to compromise."

The Shirites shifted in their saddles, muttering indiscernible words to each other. Joel could feel his father losing control over the situation.

Morathi must have sensed it too. His hulk of a stallion pushed ahead of Koal's, bearing down on the Dhaki prince. Morathi kept one hand on his sheathed sword, ready to slice down his adversaries at a moment's notice. The other hand reined in his horse. The beast reared and pawed the air, as if it too were challenging the Shirites.

"There will be no compromises," the general spat. "Conquerors do not make deals with the conquered."

The other riders closed protectively around their prince, but Rami, sitting tall in his saddle, didn't flinch. "Who speaks so boldly to one of the Holy Seven, chosen by the Gods?"

Morathi curled his nose, sneering as though he were addressing a vagrant. "Lord Morathi Adeben, Commander and General of this army. You will submit to Arden's demands—or die. The choice is yours."

"A mountain does not bend to wind, no matter how furious the gusts may blow."

"Do not mock the man who wields the power to destroy you," the general growled, his red cape flaring in the breeze. "With one word, my army can reduce Tahir to a crumbling tomb. You would do well to fear me."

Rami raised his chin. The telltale curl of a smile twitched on his thin lips. "Dhaki do not fear men. Dhaki fear only the Gods."

Morathi's horse snorted, and the general might have done the same. He whipped his head around, glaring at Koal. "Tell them, Seneschal Koal. Tell them our demands, so we can get on with this."

Koal set his jaw defiantly. "This is your war, General. You may have that 'honor.'"

For a harrowing moment, Joel feared Morathi might pull his sword and attack *Koal*. The general's hand fisted around the rawhide-bound hilt, but he didn't draw the weapon. He speared the seneschal with slate-grey eyes that were colder than deep winter and made Joel's blood freeze inside his veins.

"The Commander may voice his demands," Prince Rami said above the whispers of his riders.

Joel breathed a sigh of relief. Did this mean the Shirites were willing to listen? Was there still a chance for peace?

Morathi scowled down the bridge of his gnarled nose at the Dhaki prince. "Very well. First, we will collect our spoils of war. Tahir will empty her vaults, down to the last golden coin. Your livestock pens and grain stores will also be purged. My soldiers need nourishment for the long journey home. Wars cost resources, and it's only fair the conquered pay the price."

"We are not yet conquered people, Commander."

Rage darkened Morathi's face to deep crimson, but he snarled and went on. "Perhaps not yet, but soon. Next, the matter of the raiders who've taken refuge within your walls. They are responsible for the destruction of Ashvale and the slaughtering of countless Ardenian innocents. You will agree to turn them over to us so their treachery may be brought to an end. The lost souls of Arden deserve justice."

"What of justice for people of Shiraz? Our northern trade routes are stained with blood—blood spilled by Ardenian soldiers who attack our convoys and leave heads of traders on stakes along the path."

"The northern trade routes are no longer yours to worry over. As part of the terms of Shiraz's surrender, the Dhaki will hand over *all* land north and east of Winterdell."

Prince Rami drew back, like he'd just received a blow across the face.

"Impossible. We will not abandon a *third* of Shiraz holy lands—our most bountiful territories. We will not hand trade routes and mountain passes to godless foreigners."

"You *will*." Morathi growled. "You will empty the settlements in the north, or mark my words, we'll throw the bloated corpses of your people over the new border ourselves."

One of the Shirite riders shouted angrily, waving a cutlass in the air, and the guards surrounding Morathi grabbed their swords as well. Joel was certain the battle would break out right then and there, but Prince Rami motioned for the rider to stand down, and the man reluctantly lowered his weapon.

The Shirites spoke in low voices among themselves. Joel wished he understood what was being said. He'd only bothered to learn a few basic words of the Shirite tongue.

"We have heard Arden's demands," Prince Rami finally said. "Now you will hear ours."

Morathi's cold laughter made Joel shudder. "Foolish savages. You are in no position to make demands. *Look* in front of you. *Look* at *my* army—"

The Dhaki prince spoke over the threat. "You will turn your seneschal and crown prince over to Shiraz."

Joel gasped.

What?

He pressed closer to his father.

"If you do so willingly," Prince Rami continued, "your army is free to leave. No further drops of blood will fall. You can see the sun arise anew, Commander, and return to your home. If you refuse, if you do not give them to us, *all will perish*."

Koal had gone rigid, his facial features contorted by shock and dread. Joel raised his hands protectively, shielding his father with body and magic alike.

No! They can't have them! I'll die first!

Wide-eyed, Joel glanced over at Morathi. The general sat deathly still in his saddle. His face was a mask, unreadable yet terrifying. Oh gods, he wasn't actually *considering* it, was he? He couldn't throw Koal and Deegan to the enemy! He wouldn't *dare*!

"General," Koal said in a thick voice. "What is your decision?"

Joel could barely hear over his own jagged breaths.

Not my father. I won't let him. I'll strike that traitorous snake down myself.

Morathi finally blinked, and the haze of uncertainty left his eyes. He straightened to his full, towering height and sneered at the Dhaki prince. "Who are *you* to threaten me? Do you take me for a fool? Or a coward? How many men are hiding behind your walls? Five hundred? A thousand? It matters not! We have *ten thousand* men!"

Prince Rami only smiled. "Then ten thousand men will die before the sun reaches peak in the sky."

Morathi's sword flew out of its sheath. "I didn't march for three god-damned moonturns to listen to idle threats or to bargain with heathens! And I certainly didn't march all this way to go back to Arden empty-handed! Consider this your last chance, savage. *Yield.*"

"Shiraz will never yield."

"So be it. We will take our demands by *force*! You can't hide behind your walls. We will tear them down, and then we will slaughter every man, woman, and child inside that wretched city!"

Morathi flung his stallion around and cantered back toward the front line, bellowing orders to prepare for battle. Joel swayed, feeling like he might faint.

Oh gods, is this really happening?

It all felt surreal, like a dream. Or nightmare.

One by one, the Shirite riders rode back toward the gate, until only the Dhaki prince remained behind.

"Prince Rami," Koal implored. "Think of your people. Perhaps you should consider surrendering, for the sake of all Tahir."

Rami shook his head slowly, and Joel could see a remorseful gleam in the prince's dark eyes. "I am sorry, Seneschal Koal. May you make safe across The Veil. And may the Gods forgive my people for what we must do." He took hold of the reins, the tiny bells on the bridle ringing softly, and prodded his horse into a gentle trot.

"General Morathi *will* give the order to kill," Koal called after him. "It is *your* people who will die."

Prince Rami looked over his shoulder, just long enough to say, "No. We will not. The great golden dragon protects us now. Farewell, Seneschal."

In a flurry of silver horsehair and lace, the Dhaki prince galloped back into the city, and Joel could hear metal grinding as the gilded gate closed.

"So, this is it," Joel whispered, trying to keep control over his wavering voice. "Now we battle—"

Koal's arm shot out and seized Joel's forearm. "Go to Deegan. *Now.*"

Joel cringed at the sight of his father's white face. The terror in Koal's eyes was like nothing Joel had ever witnessed before. "B–but I thought you said I was needed on the front—"

"Listen to me," Koal growled, yanking so hard on Joel's arm it almost came clear out of its socket. "Find Deegan and the others. Take them and run. Run as fast and as far as your horses will take you."

"Father, I don't understand—"

The words died on Joel's tongue when the earth began to shudder.

"What you think they're gonna talk about?"

"Tea," Kezra grunted, watching General Morathi and Seneschal Koal ride out to meet the Shirites. Honestly, if not for their red capes, she wouldn't have been able to distinguish *anything* from this distance.

Nage raised a brow but didn't take his eyes from the wall. "Tea?"

"Yes," Kezra replied. "Tea. And who pours for whom when foreign dignitaries meet."

Nage grinned at that, but Gara seemed unwilling to join in their humor. The reedy girl fidgeted atop her ashen mare. "I hope the Shirites surrender. Can't they see we have the upper hand?"

Kezra scanned the army, looking from one white mage-robe to the next, searching for one with a red turban. Where was Zandi? She had hoped she'd be able to keep an eye on him, but she couldn't find her brother anywhere. "No. They'll never surrender. They will protect their city with all they have."

Nage huffed, shaking his head. "They'll die doin' that."

"Wouldn't you?" Kezra fired back harder than she meant to. She lowered her voice and added, "Wouldn't any of us do the same to protect Silver?"

Nage and Gara stared guilty into the distance, but neither replied.

They waited in silence, watching and waiting for something to happen. Morathi's cape fluttered in the breeze as he spoke, but Kezra couldn't make out the general's words. She shifted restlessly in Epona's saddle, frustration clawing at her insides. She hated waiting. It was quite possibly worse than engaging in battle. At least if she was swinging a blade, she wouldn't have time to worry.

"Gara's right though," Nage sighed. "They're too few. They don't got a chance unless they can summon up an army out of the sand an' surround our arses—"

Nage's mouth sank into a severe frown, and he turned, quite deliberately, to stare at Kezra. She scowled back at him, refusing to humor such a ridiculous notion. They held each other's gaze for an eternity before Kezra groaned and finally relented. In unison, she and Nage craned their necks, looking into the distance behind the army.

Nothing. Just an endless sea of sand stretching into the distance.

It would have been a lie to say Kezra wasn't relieved, as unfounded as her fear might have been. Nage's lopsided grin made her chuckle, and Kezra rolled her eyes at her own silliness. Were they children now, trying to scare each other with ghost stories? Armies were not conjured out of the sand.

"Look!" Gara exclaimed, pointing ahead. "The Shirites are retreating."

Kezra watched as the golden riders disappeared inside the city and the gates slid shut. She could barely hear the metal hinges grinding as the heavy door settled into place against the wall, and then—nothing.

234

Nage let out a snort. "Well, *now* what? I'm gonna be an old man before I ever get to see Nia again."

Kezra opened her mouth, meaning to jest with him, but paused when she felt a strange vibration stirring beneath Epona's hooves. Slight at first, it surged to a thundering tremor, rattling Kezra to her core. Startled gasps rippled through the ranks as the trembling wave rolled past, reaching the outskirts of the army in a matter of seconds.

Chhaya's bane!

"What in the two worlds was *that*?" Gara asked.

Nage pulled his reins tighter, trying to quiet his balking gelding. "An earthquake, maybe? Hell of a time for one."

Kezra's guts roiled as a second tremor struck so violently it made her teeth clank. In her heart, she knew this was no act of nature. This was something *much* worse.

She barely had time to grab for her sword before all hell broke loose.

A boundless rumble gurgled up from the depths. The sound was everywhere and nowhere at once, above and below, and all around. It was louder than a thousand marching feet and deeper than the roll of distant thunder. Never in Joel's life had he heard something more terrifying. And the ground! The ground was shaking!

Ivory whickered in alarm and threw her head, stumbling from side to side, unable to regain stable footing atop the shifting sand.

"Go!" Koal screamed. He reached out and gave Ivory's rump a smack. "Go to Deegan!"

Ivory took off like a bolt, lumbering back toward the army. Joel clung to her neck, praying the filly didn't go down. Soldiers shouted along the front, trying to steady their panicking mounts. Some men were even looking for a way to escape, but there was nowhere to go. The tremors were all around them.

Ivory broke through the line. Joel looked around wildly, trying to orient himself amid the chaos. Koal's voice still rang in his ears.

Deegan! I have to find Deegan!

"Ivory!" he yelled. "To the back—"

Joel's breath was ripped away from him as the first wave of dark power surged past. He barely had time to fling up a shield around himself, and even then, the magic still breached his barrier spell. It hit him like a gust of glass shards to the face, and he cried out and doubled over in his saddle. His skin burned in agony. Oh gods, it hurt! It hurt so badly! What *was* this? What could possibly feel so *evil*?

Joel fortified his shields, wrapping the magic bonds over and over again until the darkness pressing onto his body and soul was lessened to a dull ache. But he could still feel it. Oh gods, he could feel it in his bones.

"Look out!" screamed a nearby soldier. "The ground! The ground is opening!"

Joel managed to lift his head, and all color drained from his face.

Just ahead, the earth buckled, and a jagged fissure sliced through the crust. Sand poured into the widening gap. The larger the crevasse grew, the more quickly the powder rushed to fill it. Men were scrambling back, pushing and shoving each other in their haste to get away from the rift. One soldier was too slow. The ground gave out beneath his feet, and he tumbled down.

His fingers dug into the sand as he tried to climb to safety. His legs dangled precariously over the edge of the chasm. "Help! Help me—"

The man's eyes bulged with shock. The scream that tore from his gaping mouth a moment later was nothing short of blood-curdling. Joel could only watch, frozen in terror, as the thrashing soldier was lifted from the ground, his lower torso hopelessly trapped within a maw of razor-sharp teeth.

CHAPTER SIXTEEN

Over the rumble of sand and his own rushing pulse, Gib could hear nothing else. He teetered on the unsteady ground, watching as rubble and dust skittered around his boots as if the world itself were tilting. Astora and the other horses, tethered together in a nearby circle, pranced in place and nickered nervously. What was going on up there to make the ground shake so? Not even the march of the entire Shirite army could cause such a roar.

Hasain's panic-stricken voice reached Gib's ears above the noise. "What *is* that?"

"Earth tremor?" Gib replied, uncertain. He'd never experienced one himself, but his Pa had told stories about the one he'd lived through as a boy. He said the entire cottage had shaken like it was a ragdoll.

Deegan clung to Tular's arm. "A quake could swallow our army whole!"

Gib widened his stance as the ground jostled him. Was that true? Could the desert really drop out from beneath their feet and send them to Eternity? He sent a silent prayer to The Two.

Natori stood amid Deegan's Royal Guardsmen, her ethereal blade aflame. The guards were as unsteady on their feet as Gib, but the Blessed Mage barely moved. Every muscle in her lissome body was pulled taut.

"This is no quake," she said in a hollow voice.

The fine hairs on the back of Gib's neck and arms stood on end. The air grew static, like the stirrings of a fierce midsummer storm. The swell of magic was so strong even he could feel the tinge.

Hasain stumbled back, clutching his dark hair in his hands. "The magic—it's massive! It's *everywhere*! Natori, what is this?"

Gib tightened his hands around Oathbinder and looked to the Blessed Mage for guidance. Cold dread barred his heart.

Natori stood frozen, white as death. Her irises clouded over until they disappeared entirely and the whole of her eyes became lanterns of violet light. She said nothing as she stared ahead, her sole focus locked onto a dune, rising in the distance.

Gib's breaths hitched.

Rising. The dune was *rising*.

"Chhaya's bane," one of Morathi's thugs exclaimed. He cowered with bulging eyes behind Deegan.

The second of the pair jabbed a meaty finger, terror lining his face. "Look!"

But everyone was already looking. Gib stared, gaping in horror, as a creature straight from the darkest *Tale of Fae* imaginable broke free of the sand.

At the peak of its back, the creature stood taller than any two men. Scaly white plates covered the massive body, from the wedge-shaped head to a whip-like tail topped with sharp barbs. The dirt crunched beneath the weight of four limbs thicker than they were long. Dusky claws jutted out from the tips, each talon the length of a dagger.

A tear rolled down Gib's cheek. He might have even screamed. Never in his deepest nightmares could his mind conjure something so terrifying. What was this? What was this terrible monster? His knees knocked together, and he wavered. Gloom lined the edges of his vision.

No. He couldn't pass out. Not here and not now. He would stay awake and fight for this world. Gib lifted Oathbinder and pressed closer to Deegan. Hasain and Tular flanked the prince's opposite side. Blue fire swirled around Hasain's hands, and Tular stood with sword drawn high. Live or die, they were in this together.

Gib turned bravely to face the monster of nightmares.

The creature shook itself free of sand. A cloud of dust flew into the sky and blotted out the sunlight. The beast's bulky head moved from side to side, slowly and intently, fire in the beady eyes sitting low on the creature's snout. Its gaze passed over rows of scrambling soldiers until the black orbs settled solely onto Deegan's party. Slitted nostrils flared, the only warning, and then the beast sprang forward.

"Shield the prince!" Natori yelled, her sapphire blade a beacon for all. "Royal soldiers with me!"

In all his life—in all the books he'd read and all the places he'd been—never before had Joel seen something like *this*. This was something from beyond the world Joel knew.

The creature climbed out of the ground, each jagged row of teeth crunching down on the soldier's midriff, ripping through armor and flesh like both were made of parchment. The man's gurgled screams filled the air. He flailed his arms and clawed at the beast's scales, but the creature didn't release its hold.

Most of the nearby soldiers fled in terror, but a precious few stayed behind, shooting arrows that bounced harmlessly off the creature's thick hide. Others slashed at its limbs. They fought desperately to save their comrade, but their efforts seemed to further infuriate the creature.

The beast tossed its first victim aside, the body mangled and bloodied beyond recognition. A dreadful hiss rose over dying heaves as lidless black eyes searched for new prey.

Joel screamed along with the other soldiers when the monster's massive head jutted forward. Jaws snapped around the neck of a second soldier, his cries snuffed in an instant. Claws raked down another who couldn't jump away in time. Two more lives, taken in the blink of an eye. Blood smeared the sand.

Ivory's nostrils flared. She'd caught the death scent. Before Joel could reach to soothe her, she reared and jerked forward. Letting out a startled cry, Joel toppled from the filly's saddle.

He landed hard on his stomach, the impact so great it pushed the air from his lungs with an audible *whoosh*. For a moment he couldn't breathe. He lay there, stunned, until a horrible shriek reached his ears and woke him from his daze.

Ivory!

Joel could do nothing to save her. By the time he'd pulled himself upright, the monster already held the filly in its clutches. Ivory kicked and thrashed to no avail. Blade-sharp talons sank into her silver coat, slicing a gorge across the exposed underbelly. The horse slumped into the sand, wide eyes already glazing over as blood pooled around her broken body.

No! Ivory!

Caught somewhere between shock and rage, Joel called magic to his hands. The energy pooled in an instant, anger stoking the magic into a blazing sphere. Setting furious eyes on the monster, Joel hurled the flaming orb.

The sphere crashed into a magic barrier just before it touched the beast. Joel cried out in frustration.

The creature whirled about, searching for its attacker. Saliva dripped from its open maw. The roar that rumbled from within made tears form in Joel's eyes.

He stumbled back, putting more distance between himself and the beast. Another bolt of magic lashed from his hands, and again, it faltered. He couldn't break through! He couldn't reach the monster!

"Joel, don't!" a shrill voice called, and Joel raised his face in time to see Zandi riding closer. The mage's turban was twisted to one side and bits of onyx hair breezed out from beneath the crimson fabric, but he didn't care or notice. His eyes were wide; the whites of them were nearly the same color as his drained face. Zandi's horse pawed the air as he pulled the gelding to a stop.

"Get on!" Zandi leaned over the side of his saddle and offered a trembling hand. "Come with me!"

Joel reached for the offered hand without thinking and was hoisted up. He fell into place behind Zandi on the saddle. All Joel could do was hold on for dear life as the gelding took off running.

"You mustn't use magic," Zandi said over his shoulder. "It absorbs the magic! It takes the energy into itself! Magic will only make it stronger!"

Joel squeezed his eyes shut. The world was whirling too fast. "What *is* it?"

"They are *Zhal'mohr*, demonspawn from the Otherealm. I read about them in a tome in the Royal Archives. Daya, help us! They are *here*!"

"They?" Joel gasped. "There is more than one?"

Zandi's shoulders quivered even before Joel opened his eyes and saw the horrible truth for himself.

Dozens of them towered above the broken ranks, ashen scales gleaming like snowdrifts beneath a late afternoon sun. Despite their colossal size, the creature's movements were swift, catlike. Talons and teeth cut bloody paths through the army, leaving lumps of mauled flesh in their wake.

A desperate whimper pushed its way out of Joel's mouth. "There are so many of them."

"I don't understand," Zandi said, shaking his head in disbelief. "Legend says The Two imprisoned them in the Otherealm after the Great War. Their magic was too destructive for the human realm. They were wreaking havoc—"

A serpentine tail whipped into their path. Zandi jerked the reins to one side, and his gelding barely dodged the devastating blow. Another mounted soldier wasn't so lucky. Sickle-shaped barbs glistened scarlet as the horse came crashing down on top of its rider.

"They're wreaking havoc *now*! They're killing our soldiers!" Joel cried. "We have to stop them!"

Tears poured down Zandi's cheeks. "We can't."

"Hasain!"

Someone shouted his name, but Hasain wasn't listening. He could only stare, transfixed by horror, as the monstrous creature lumbered closer. It barreled through sentinels like they were insects, tearing into armor and smashing bodies against the ground. Swords and arrows alike barely left a mark on the beast's scaly hide.

Natori and six Royal Guardsmen strode bravely toward the thing, the Blessed Mage's sword a streak of brilliance against the white sand. Her footsteps seemed unhurried, but that could have been because time had slowed to an uncanny crawl. Each shifting muscle in Natori's face, every granule of dust gusting in the air, the sharp sheen of sunlight on the guardsmen's blades—Hasain saw all of it in intricate detail, as if he were a god, looking down upon the world.

His racing heart sputtered. If he were a god, he'd have the power to end this madness. But he wasn't. He couldn't stop this.

"But you can," the demon hissed in his head. *"All you need do is ask."*

Hasain shuddered, unable to tear his gaze from the massacre. Is this what it felt like to stare death in the face?

Selfishly, in the moment Hasain could think only of himself. He reflected on the life he'd lived so far and mourned the one he would leave behind, should he die. He thought of his fine belongings, his elegant estate, and even the girl he was promised to wed. Would he never see any of it again? Would every last scrap of who he was be washed away—erased— just like that? Had his father feared the same while *his* essence wilted away upon the deathbed?

No. Rishi's bravery was as steadfast as Hasain's cowardice. The dying king's thoughts hadn't included himself—only the loved ones he was forced to leave behind.

"You're weak," said Leviticus.

"Hasain!" Tular's snarl reached Hasain this time.

He blinked, and his thoughts finally leapt to where they should have been all along—to his brothers.

Deegan! Tular! I have to protect them!

Time resumed its normal pace.

The ground thundered as the beast bore down on Natori. Rivulets of hot saliva dripped from its maw, tinged red by the blood of fallen soldiers. Natori issued a fierce challenge and swung her ethereal sword high. The creature's eyes followed the sapphire flash as if mesmerized. Closer and closer it prowled, hissing madly, the sound like a pit of angry vipers.

"We should get Deegan out of here," Hasain gasped. "Let's take the horses and run—"

Tular's ruddy hair flew around his eyes. "The horses are *gone*! They scattered when the beast came up!"

"Then we can escape on foot—"

Tular grabbed the front of Hasain's robe. "If Natori falls, we won't get ten steps before we're cut down. We have to stand together! You're a mage, now *help*!"

"We have to fight," Deegan said in a brittle voice. "We don't have any choice."

Standing next to Deegan, Gib nodded. "For Arden," he whispered.

Hasain didn't know how he heard the words above Natori's war cry.

Kezra thought she'd been ready. Before she'd defied her father and joined the sentinels, before she'd broken her mother's heart by choosing to go to war, before she'd packed her rucksack and left behind the only home she knew, Kezra thought she'd been ready to face whatever foe stood in her way. When the ambush along the river struck, she'd been one of the first to answer the call. She fought knowing she could die, yet she hadn't been afraid.

But now, she was afraid. She was *terrified*. She'd been prepared to face mortal men, not creatures straight from her darkest nightmares.

Kezra watched breathlessly as the monsters slaughtered their way through Arden's army. Chunks of flesh and hair littered the ground. Soldiers missing entire limbs dragged themselves across the sand. Horses lay motionless with their entrails fanned out around their ruined corpses.

Kezra retched, but nothing came up. This *was* a nightmare. It had to be. She closed her eyes briefly, but when she opened them nothing had changed. The nightmare still engulfed her.

"What in hell are those?" Nage asked, swaying back and forth as his petrified gelding pranced in circles.

Kezra didn't know. She wished her brother were here. Zandi could likely identify the beast.

Zandi.

Her eyes fell desperately over the scattered army, but her heart already knew the chances of spotting him were remote.

"Look out!" Gara cried.

A barbed tail whipped past them, so close Kezra felt wind gust against her face. Nearby, a group of soldiers had rallied against one of the creatures. They closed around it, hacking with their blades, but for all their efforts, Kezra could see only shallow slashes rising on the beast's legs and belly.

The tail lashed back again, and dust flew into Kezra's eyes. The monster swiped a bloody claw, raking down a good number of men who stood ahead of it. Another lost soul writhed in the beast's splinter-sharp teeth. The sentinels kept fighting, but for every tiny wound they inflicted, the creature was butchering *tens* of them.

Gara pulled the bow from her back and nocked an arrow. Kezra wished to the damn Gods she had a ranged weapon, too. Taking aim, Gara let the arrow fly. The shaft sailed true, but Gara cried out in dismay when the arrow bounced harmlessly off the beast's scaly hide. It didn't even leave a mark.

"How're we supposed to fight them?" Nage asked frantically. "Nothing's slowing them down!"

Gara pointed a stiff finger. "Look, a mage is coming!"

Kezra's heartbeat quickened. Was it Zandi? She craned her neck.

It wasn't Zandi, but an elder with grey hair. Even though it wasn't the mage she'd hoped to see, at least a mage had arrived at all. If swords weren't touching the beasts, surely magic could fell them.

The mage lifted his arms, and Kezra saw a swirl of grey massing against the heavens. One moment there had been only blue sky, and in the next, clouds blotted out the sun. Thunder rolled over the dunes, and static forced Kezra's hair on end.

The mage plunged his arms down, and a bolt of lightning shot from the roiling clouds. It lashed the monster with a shattering crackle.

Yes!

Nage whooped in victory, only to have his merriment quelled seconds later. Kezra's mouth fell open.

Chhaya's bane!

The creature still stood. The lightning hadn't harmed it at all.

The monster let out a furious hiss and lunged at this newest attacker. A magic shield flared around the mage, but his eyes bulged a moment later when the barrier faltered—and then vanished completely. Terrified, he tried to run away, but the creature snatched him up before he could take a second step. The crunch of bones made Kezra shudder just as much as the sight of tattered white robes dangling from the beast's teeth.

It didn't touch the beast. The magic didn't touch it. Chhaya's bane! Zandi! I have to find Zandi!

"No magic!"

Seneschal Koal's cape billowed as he marched into view. He strode on foot, favoring one leg slightly over the other. His golden breastplate was dented beyond repair, and the longsword clutched in his large hands dripped with dark blood. Fire raged in his eyes.

"Magic makes them stronger!" Koal roared. "They absorb it! It heals them!"

Kezra flung herself around in her saddle and saw he spoke the truth. The little gashes on the beast's underbelly and legs were mending themselves, sealing as though the wounds had never been inflicted in the first place.

Impossible, Kezra lamented. *What is this? What is this dark magic?*

Koal waved his blade, rallying the soldiers. "To me, sentinels! To me!"

Frightened yells arose as the soldiers rushed to their commander.

"How do we kill them?"

"They are immortal!"

"We're no match against demonspawn!"

Koal's voice remained unflappable, a fixed boulder within rapids. "Aim for the maw! Their hide is weakest beneath the jaw. Listen, we will attack in unison—"

"*Look out!*"

Blood sizzled in Kezra's ears.

Oh no.

The swell of Koal's ruby cape had caught the beast's attention. Without warning, it screeched and barreled toward the seneschal.

Kezra reacted without thinking. Sword at the ready, she spurred Epona into a canter and charged the monster. Nage's alarmed shout followed at her back, but Kezra didn't care. For years, Seneschal Koal had been fighting in the council room for people like her. How could she not aid him now?

The beast's focus was still on Koal, so it didn't see Kezra ride up beside it. She was so close the monster's stench wafted into her nostrils. She gagged. The smell was putrid, like decaying flesh.

"Stand with me!" Koal said, squaring his broad shoulders and pointing his blade at the oncoming adversary. A handful of soldiers turned and fled, but many stayed with him. They raised their weapons next to his. "If we die, we die for Arden!"

Kezra straightened her legs, standing upright in the stirrups. They *were* going to die. The monster would cut through them like butter. They needed a distraction, and Kezra needed a chance to prove her valor—to them *and* herself. If she died, what better way than by defending Arden's seneschal?

Letting out a shrill war cry, Kezra pushed away from Epona's saddle and jumped at the creature's side. Elevated as she was, she still couldn't reach the ridged back. One hand grasped feebly at the bony knobs, but she felt herself slipping. She held on long enough to swipe her sword across the beast's shoulder before she was tossed to the ground.

The monster hissed and slammed a massive claw against the sand, barely missing Kezra's face. Breathless, she jabbed at the limb. The beast's wedge-shaped head whipped around, the little beady eyes searching for her. Kezra rolled farther beneath its girth. Her blade raked across pearly scales as she went, but the monster's belly was as armored as its back. Kezra cried out in frustration. She was swinging with all the strength she possessed, yet she wasn't inflicting more than superficial wounds.

Rows of teeth clinked together, so close Kezra could feel the blazing scorch of the monster's breath. The scaly body twisted, and Kezra rolled again, trying to stay under the belly. But this time the monster moved too swiftly. Light blinded her as she was left sprawled upon her back, staring into the sun. And then the monster's face appeared overhead, looming above her like the shadow of Death.

A flurry of boots and hooves moved around her. Kezra could hear Nage and Gara screaming, trying to draw the beast's attention. But it wanted only her. Kezra heaved her blade one last time before the weapon was knocked out of her hands. The flesh around the monster's maw peeled back, revealing rows of jagged teeth and remnants of Kezra's fallen comrades. And here she was, soon to join them.

Daya, let Zandi live. Let my mother and siblings be safe.

The beast's black eyes bore into hers. Kezra peered into the abyssal depths and saw her own hollowed face staring back. It wasn't the face of a warrior, but one of a foolish child. She looked closer and could see the path of devastation left in the creature's wake: the bloodied, unmoving shadows of horses and men alike. She saw Nage and Gara, their faces contorted in fear, and the flicker of Seneschal Koal's cape. She even saw Nawaz—surely an illusion summoned by her dazed mind—standing with his crossbow notched and ready to sail free.

Nawaz—whose life she had ruined in a moment of utter selfishness.

Kezra choked on the bile in her throat. She wasn't a warrior. She wasn't a hero. She was just as much a monster as the thing about to kill her. And she deserved this.

In her reflection, a red dot gleamed upon her brow, and Kezra's eyes widened with sudden recognition. The heritage mark!

Gib's gentle voice echoed in her ears. *"Look at me. You are not a monster. That was the night. Today is a new day. Fight for it."*

Kezra touched her forehead. The mind could conquer all, if only it was trusted.

She gasped.

No! I'm not a monster! And I'm not ready to give up fighting! I can do this! I trust myself!

Her hand grasped for the sword, just out of her reach. The monster's teeth grazed her neck. She just needed another moment—

Something small whizzed past Kezra's ear, and the monster howled so deafeningly that Kezra feared her ears might explode. The massive head recoiled, and from Kezra's prone position, she could see clearly that the underside of the jaw was free of scales. It was soft—penetrable. Kezra's spirit soared as her hand brushed over her sword. She grabbed it, curling her fingers around the familiar shagreen hilt. Letting out a savage cry, she thrust the weapon upward, driving the blade into the monster's jaw.

The beast screeched and collapsed into a mass of thrashing limbs and claws. Kezra scrambled back. Her sword was lodged hilt-deep through the jaws and roof of its mouth. Her heart pounded as she watched the beast convulse. Would it be enough? Was the blow fatal? The spasms lessened to feeble jerks, and at last they tapered to weak twitches. Finally, the monster gave one final heave and its body went limp.

Kezra crawled back over to the creature, and sitting on her knees, she yanked on the buried sword. It came free with a wet slide. Thick, black ooze covered the blade.

A wave of nausea washed over her. She sat back in the sand, uncertain if she could rise. Her legs were as heavy as stone pillars. More foul ooze seeped from within the monster's maw. Kezra stared in disbelief. Had she really killed it?

It was then she noticed a small protrusion above the beast's snout.

She squinted, investigating more closely. An arrow! An arrow shaft was wedged into one of the creature's lifeless eyes. So *that's* why the thing had reeled back in pain. But who had made such an expert shot—?

Firm hands hooked under Kezra's armpits and lifted her to her feet. She knew who it was even before he spoke. She'd never forget the feel of those hands…

"Kezra?" Nawaz asked. "Are you hurt?"

She turned to face him. Her chest heaved from so much more than the fatigue of battle. She wanted to scream at him to leave her alone—that it was for his own damn good—but instead, she uttered a meek "You saved me."

A crooked smile tugged at his mouth. "No. You saved us. You're a warrior, Kezra."

Kezra could have stared into those haunted blue eyes forever, but Koal was nearby, and he was calling to Nawaz.

The Healer's hands slipped away, and he dropped his eyes. "I gotta go. Morathi's given the order to retreat. Koal and I have to get to Deegan." He repositioned the crossbow across his back. When he managed to lift his chin, his eyes were imploring. "Come with us? We're securing the prince—and leaving."

Kezra shook her head. A part of her wanted to, but she couldn't. She couldn't go with Nawaz, now—or ever.

"No," she said. "I can't leave without Zandi." Kezra looked over at Nage and Gara, who waited in their saddles. "You two should go with Nawaz—"

Nage snorted. "Not a chance you're getting rid of us that easy."

"We're staying with you," Gara agreed.

Kezra bit her tongue.

Fools, both of them. Brave fools.

"All right," Nawaz said. He cast a final glance at Kezra, but he didn't beg her to stay with him. Instead, he simply said, "Be safe."

So she left. And so did he.

CHAPTER SEVENTEEN

"We have to find Deegan! My father ordered me to go to him!"

Onyx locks lashed Joel's face. He wasn't able to tell if it was his own hair or that belonging to the other mage. The ground whirled by so fast it blurred. Joel couldn't stare down at it without growing dizzy. But he didn't want to look up either. He didn't want to see the *Zhal'mohr* tearing Ardenian soldiers to shreds. Their screams of agony were enough to make him faint. All he could do was slam his eyes closed and cling to Zandi's back as the horse dashed through the scattered army.

Joel's terrified mind jumped to Deegan again. Koal had made certain the Crown Prince was well-protected. He was under the watch of the Blessed Mage. Hasain and Tular were there, both warriors in their own right—and Gib. Gib had the most common sense of anyone Joel knew.

But would they be enough? No one had expected an army of demonspawn to rise from the sand. What if Deegan and his protectors couldn't escape? They might already be dead. And what of Koal? Nawaz? Joel hadn't seen either of them since the attack began. Had they perished? Was it too late for Joel to say he forgave them?

No. There's still hope! They're alive! I have to get to Deegan!

Joel dared to open his eyes. Tahir's outer wall loomed ahead, so tall it shrouded the rising sun from view. Close as they were, Joel could almost reach out and touch the limestone bricks.

"We need to get to the rear of the army!" Joel yelled. "Turn us around!"

"I *can't!*" came Zandi's exasperated reply. "There are too many beasts behind us! They're pinning us in!"

Joel looked over his shoulder—and paled. The army stretched across the sand, a blanket woven from iron, leather, and blood—but the outer cusps were starting to buckle beneath the onslaught of *Zhal'mohr*. The soldiers were being pushed inward, toward the wall.

They're ensnaring us. They're herding us together to make it easier to slaughter us.

"We have to keep moving—" Joel's words gave way to a surprised inhale when a blurred object hummed past his head, nearly grazing his cheek.

"Shirite archers!" Zandi cried in warning. "On the wall!"

Joel let out a snarl and turned his eyes skyward as another arrow skittered to the ground.

Oh no you don't.

Magic surged to his hands. He might not be able to protect himself against the *Zhal'mohr*, but the enemy archers were mortal men. *They* were fallible.

He hurled a searing bolt of mage-fire at the enemy, and one of the archers screamed as he was knocked back. He disappeared over the far edge. Another bolt. Another hit. This time the victim plunged forward, tumbling into the sand.

Zandi wrapped a mage-shield around them, desperately trying to ward off the arrows, but the dark aura of the massing *Zhal'mohr* was sapping his magic. The barrier flickered unsteadily. Joel could feel his own energy waning even as he helped reinforce the shield.

"We can't stay here!" Joel screamed, watching as arrows rained down around them.

But they were surrounded. The army pressed from behind, and the wall stood in front of them. To either side, *Zhal'mohr* lurked in the shadows, picking off soldiers who were trying to make a run for the open desert. They were hopelessly trapped.

"Any great ideas?" Zandi said.

Joel shot off another blast of offensive magic. More archers plummeted to their deaths. "I need to think—"

"No time," Zandi replied. His shield was in grave danger of complete collapse.

Joel cried out in frustration and hurled another bolt. The Shirites jumped back this time, and his mage-fire slammed against the parapet instead. A chunk of mortar and stone came crumbling down. Joel stared at the rubble as it rolled across the sand and came to rest by the gelding's hooves.

And then he *did* have an idea. A crazy, reckless idea. But an idea nonetheless.

He grabbed Zandi's arm. "The beasts *can* be killed, right?"

"Y–yes," Zandi whimpered. "But our magic is useless—"

"We're not going to use magic." Joel ripped open the satchel tied to his belt, revealing the cache of runestones within. He reached inside and pulled out a fistful.

Daya, please let this work.

The *Zhal'mohr*'s gloom leeched Joel's energy, but power anew surged from the runestones to replace it. He took the magic into himself, hungrily, until it flooded his veins and he could hold no more. And then he set his sights on the nearest beast, the one crouching between them and a clear path to freedom.

Zandi must have sensed the swell of energy. He paled further. "What are you doing? It will only make the beast stronger! You can't—"

"Hold us steady," Joel hissed, and then he launched a well-controlled zap at the *Zhal'mohr*. The magic exploded against the beast's shield. With an incensed shriek, the *Zhal'mohr* whipped its head toward them.

"*Hey!* Over here, demon scum!" Joel shouted angrily. He flared his magic, hoping the monster would be drawn to the power, like a month to the flame. "Come and get us!"

Zandi gasped. "What are you—"

"*Don't* run," Joel demanded through gritted teeth. He drew the power of the runestones to his hands. Sapphire flames roiled in his upturned palms.

The *Zhal'mohr* lumbered at them with open jaws and spittle dripping from its teeth. Joel thought he might faint. Every bit of sense he possessed screamed at him to flee, but he didn't.

Closer. It needs to be closer.

Magic scorched Joel's hands. He could feel the *Zhal'mohr* trying to rip the power away, but he clung to it, refusing to relent.

Almost.

Zandi's scream was lost beneath the howl of the beast. Joel could see the reflection of blue flames in its eyes. It was right in front of them.

Now!

With all his might, Joel flung the magic at the wall.

Limestone shattered everywhere. The entire wall shook, buckling against the force of the blow. Enemy archers hollered in panic as the walkway shuddered beneath their feet. Even the *Zhal'mohr* paused and turned its head toward the commotion.

And then the wall caved and came crashing down.

"*Go!*" Joel yelled.

Zandi spurred the gelding, and the horse took off running. Joel could feel debris pelting him, stabs of agony against his back and shoulders. His ears roared with the sound of falling stone. He tucked his head and held on for dear life.

If this is our end, let it be the end for the beast as well.

He slammed his eyes shut. Whatever happened now was beyond his control.

The ground stopped shaking. The rumble ceased. The air grew deathly silent.

Zandi gave the reins a pull, and the gelding lurched to a stop.

"Daya!" he exclaimed. "Look!"

Chest heaving, Joel opened one eye and then the other. He dared peer over his shoulder.

A cloud of dust reached into the sky where there had been stone only moments before. Sunlight filtered through the haze, illuminating the ruins left behind. A large section of the wall was gone completely—crumbled into a vast heap. And one of the *Zhal'mohr*'s limbs protruded from within the rubble, limp and unmoving.

"It's—it's dead," Zandi whispered.

Someone began cheering.

Zandi's eyes widened. He cried joyously. A smile broke across his parched lips even as a tear slipped down his cheek. Joel squinted against the clearing dust, and then he smiled too. There, standing next to the wreckage, were Kezra, Nage, and Gara.

Gib took an unwilling step back as he watched Natori face the monster. He wanted to run. He wanted to run and never stop, but the firm press of Oathbinder's handle against his palm reminded him why he must stay.

Natori let out a vicious war cry. The sound rattled Gib to the bones. The Blessed Mage was usually so reserved. But now she held nothing back as her ethereal sword swung through the air. Flanked by the loyal guardsmen, she ran straight at the beast. Fire blazed in her violet eyes as fiercely as the runes along the enchanted blade. She gripped the steel hilt with both hands. Tensed her shoulders. Heaved the sword overhead.

And then the blade went dark.

Natori's face twisted with surprise as the weapon's magic failed, leaving her with a metal husk.

The monster swiped a claw. Natori recovered from her shock in time to swerve aside, but the nearest guardsman was knocked off his feet. Gib heard the clang of sharp talons bashing against the man's breastplate. A massive limb slammed the guardsman into the dirt, and the crack of shattering bones hissed in Gib's ears.

"Hasain!" Tular snarled. "Use your magic!"

Hasain seemed to be in some kind of panic-induced stupor, but at the sound of his brother's command, the Radek lord narrowed his eyes. Tendrils of lightning crackled from his outstretched hands and lashed at the beast. The magic sizzled and died before it even touched the monster's scaly hide.

Hasain wailed. "It leeched my magic! The monster's shield absorbs it!"

Gib's heart felt like it might pound straight out of his chest. Leeching magic? An absorption shield? Did that mean Natori's magic was useless as well?

Natori slammed her blade against the beast's bony skull, leaving a gash along the snout. The monster growled, but the blow did nothing to discourage it. Powerful jaws snapped the air. Natori jumped back, already preparing another strike.

A second guardsman moaned as dagger-length teeth closed over his arm. The monster thrashed its head from side to side until the limb ripped free of the man's torso in a gush of blood and shredded flesh.

Deegan cried in horror. "We have to help—"

Gib started to lurch forward, but Natori commanded them back. "No, Prince! Stay with your protectors!"

Another sentinel fell. And another.

Daya, help us!

Natori and the two remaining guardsmen formed a circle around their adversary. Their footsteps were light as they darted in a lethal dance with death. The beast shifted this way and that, seeming unsure which target to attack. A serpentine tail whipped across the sand with agitation.

"Aim for the eyes and throat!" Natori hissed. "We work together!"

For a precious reprieve, neither monster nor men moved. But then one of the guardsmen locked eyes with Natori. She gave him a knowing nod. Saying nothing, the sentinel rushed the monster, slashing at its throat with his broadsword. The beast's head tilted down as it closed over the guard's helm—and that's when Natori struck.

She thrust forward, a flash of deadly silver armor, and her blade sunk deep into the beast's eye socket. With a final roar, the monster slumped to the ground, limbs twitching as death shrouded its one enduring eye.

Natori pulled her blade free with a huff. A deranged noise—something between a sob and a cheer—escaped Deegan's gaping mouth. Hasain and Tular both sighed collectively, and some of the tension rolled off their shoulders. Even Morathi's two dogs whooped. Gib felt like he might vomit at the sight of so much blood and the mangled bodies of the royal guardsmen. But the monster was dead. Natori had slain the beast even without her magic. Perhaps the rumors at court held some truth to them after all: the Blessed Mages really were immortal.

Natori turned a victorious smile onto Deegan's party—

—and was slammed from behind by a second beast.

"No!" Gib screamed as he watched Natori's limp form crash to the ground. Her sword flew from her hands and skidded across the sand. She lay motionless, dazed from the savage blow to her head. The monster hissed and lumbered toward her.

Get up! Gib screeched silently. *Please get up!*

The last remaining guardsman jumped to Natori's defense, clanging sword against shield to draw the beast's attention and give the Blessed Mage precious moments to wake.

Readying his weapon, Tular pointed angrily at Morathi's men. "We must help the mage! You two distract the beast from the left, I'll attack from—"

"We didn't sign up for this!" one of them gasped. Before Tular could finish giving the command, they both threw down their shields and bolted.

"*Cowards!*" Tular spat.

The beast had the royal guardsman pinned on his back. He bashed the blunt edge of his shield against the monster's muzzle and aimed his sword at the closest eye. But the beast's claws pressed down on his silver chest plate, squeezing the life out of him. He screamed in agony as talons sunk into the weak points between his armor.

Tular shucked his cuirass off even as he marched forward.

"W–what are you doing?" Deegan asked, grabbing for Tular's arm. "She told us to stay—"

"Run, Deegan. Get as far away from here as you can."

Gib gaped as Tular discarded his breastplate. Why was he stripping off his armor? Had he lost his mind?

"No," Deegan stammered. "I'll stand with you!"

Tular shook Deegan's hand away. "Listen, I'll buy you some time. Hasain and Gib will stay with you."

"Tular, no," Hasain pleaded, face white as death. "The cloaking magic will fail. You'll be revealed—"

"It doesn't matter now! There's no one left alive to see, and Deegan must survive!"

Natori had risen to her knees and was crawling toward her sword. The monster was ripping strings of flesh from the guardsman's corpse, but its lidless eyes were already trained on the Blessed Mage. It was going to attack any moment—

"*Go!*" Tular growled, shoving Deegan at Gib. "Get the prince out of here!"

Natori stumbled to her feet. Blood trailed from a gash on her forehead and into her eyes. She reached for her blade—

The beast's tail whipped around, catching her thighs, and sent her spiraling for a second time. Her head jerked back as it cracked against the hard ground, and this time she didn't get up.

Tular howled and sprang toward the struggle.

Gib started to give chase—despite the order he'd been given to flee—but stopped dead in his tracks when Tular leapt off the ground and—*flew.*

Oh gods.

He flew.

Scarlet wings burst free from beneath Tular's tunic, fanning wide as he sailed into the air. Whetted talons capped the ends of each digit on his hands and feet alike, and a long, feathered tail spanned behind him like a rudder, sending dust scattering in every direction.

Gib's heart clambered to his throat. He gasped and stumbled back, unable to comprehend what he was seeing. Chhaya's bane, what *was* he?

"Tular, *no!*" Deegan screamed as he pushed past Gib. The prince ran into the clearing, clutching his rapier in one hand and waving his other wildly. "*Tular!* Tular, come back!"

Tular wasn't listening. He gave his—wings—a handful of powerful thrusts, rapidly gaining altitude, only to pin them tight to his body a moment later. And then he plummeted from the sky—no, dove. He swooped with dangerous intent. Tall horns nestled just above his brow gleamed in the morning light, and feathered hackles fanned around his twisted face. Letting out a shriek of fury, he plunged onto the beast's back.

This was a nightmare. It had to be.

A wave of panic rolled over Hasain as the magic Tular relied upon to shroud his identity was sapped by the beast's leeching shield, leaving his true self exposed and bare.

"*Shit*," Hasain spat to the wind. Dread reared in his chest, seizing him by the throat. He couldn't breathe. This wasn't happening! He *had* to be trapped inside a terrible nightmare. None of this could actually be real.

Yet there it was. The devastation spread before his eyes, and it wasn't going away, no matter how many times he closed and reopened his eyes.

"*You should have called on me sooner,*" Leviticus crooned. "*Just look at this mess that could have been prevented.*"

Hasain rallied enough strength to shout a warning at his brother. "Tular! Get back! Your cloaking spell—"

But Tular seemed beyond caring. Hasain knew the look in his brother's crazed eyes. He was prepared to defend the royal family—at any cost.

In a flurry of crimson feathers, Tular launched himself onto the beast's back, goring his claws into the thick hide. The beast howled with rage and whipped back and forth, trying to dislodge its attacker. Jagged teeth snapped shut just shy of Tular's tail feathers. His wings beat frantically as he struggled to stay balanced atop the thrashing creature.

Deegan's hysterical voice rose above the fray. He was screaming Tular's name—and running at the beast. Gib gave chase, yelling for Hasain to help, but Hasain couldn't follow. He couldn't even lift his feet. His legs were stone pillars, frozen by fear.

In desperation, Hasain held out a trembling hand, as if he could call his brothers back with the gesture alone.

"Deegan, no…" he whimpered.

The demon's hideous cackle echoed inside Hasain's head. "*Pathetic.*"

The monster shrieked, or it might have been Tular. Hasain wasn't sure. He sobbed as Tular was knocked to the ground, his wings pinned uselessly beneath him. One of the monster's giant claws slammed over Tular's chest.

"*No!*" Deegan screamed, lunging with his rapier. Within the beast's shadow, the young prince had never looked so small.

"*You really are going to let them die, aren't you?*"

Tears streamed down Hasain's face.

I can't. I can't. Father said not to listen—

253

Saliva trickled from the beast's open maw as blood-stained teeth came within an inch of Tular's face. He writhed to no avail. Sunlight gleamed in his watering eyes. The monster's claw pressed against Tular's heaving chest, and he screeched in agony as his body was slowly crushed.

Hasain's resolve shattered.

"No!" he gasped. "Don't let them die! Leviticus, save my family!"

Gib squared his shoulders, preparing to swing Oathbinder, and preparing to die. He deserved as much for not fulfilling his promise. He'd sworn to keep Deegan safe and failed. Once the beast was done with Tular, it would certainly turn next onto Arden's heir. And then Hasain. The Radek bloodline was finished. They were all doomed.

Gib flung his blade high. At least he could find some comfort knowing he would die fighting for what he believed in.

For Arden. I'm sorry I couldn't serve you better. I'm sorry I failed. Goddesses, keep my brothers safe.

The beast lurched back before Oathbinder could strike. Tular inhaled sharply, gasping for air as the massive weight lifted off his torso, and Gib's mouth fell open in shock. The monster was reeling *away* from them. It was retreating!

An infuriated roar rippled out from between the monster's splayed jaws as it raked talons across its own snout and eyes. It scratched so savagely droplets of black blood were pooling on its hide. The hisses and snarls it elicited were desperate, as though the beast were under attack. But it wasn't. No one was left alive to attack it.

The ground thundered as the monster lumbered across the clearing. Grabbing Deegan by the arm, Gib threw both the prince and himself to the ground to avoid getting swiped by the beast's thrashing tail. Deegan let out a soft whimper and closed his eyes. Gib refused to shut his own, even as gritty sand lashed his cheeks. His heart pounded within his chest.

The monster let out one final, mournful howl before it skulked away, fleeing toward Tahir's distant wall and trampling over the dead as it went.

Corpses. The bodies of fallen Ardenian soldiers.

The dead *littered* the sand. And Gib could see scores of beasts still attacking the army. A horn blared from within the mass of soldiers and monsters. Someone was sounding a retreat. Bile bubbled in Gib's throat. They had to get Deegan to safety—somehow. But where was there to go?

Deegan disentangled himself from Gib's arms and ran to where Tular lay sprawled in a heap of red feathers. The prince collapsed onto his knees beside the fallen warrior and helped him sit up. Gib's guts twisted, but he tried not to gawk openly at Tular. What *was* he? Some kind of Otherfolk? A changeling? Gib edged closer, keeping a cautious grip on his sword.

254

"What happened to it?" Tular snarled, his eyes darting around, no doubt in search of the beast. The long feathers crowning his skull stood on end.

Deegan's voice quivered. "Something must have scared it off."

"Scared it off? What the *hell* could scare *that* thing off?"

"I don't know, but it doesn't matter. It's gone for now. Tular, you have to shift."

Tular groaned groggily, touching the outside of his tattered tunic. "My ribs—it hurts to breathe."

"You're injured. You might have broken something."

"You don't say?"

"You have to shift," Deegan pleaded, glancing up at Gib. "Before anyone else sees you. Hurry, I can hear the retreat horn blowing. *Please*, Tular."

Tular's pale face was still racked with pain, but he gave a weak nod. And then—just like that—the wings and tail vanished, the horns and claws disappeared, and the long tufts of feathers capping his head yielded to tresses of sunset hair. The Tular Gib knew had returned.

Gib's eyes were so wide they might pop out of their sockets. Never in his life had he seen something so bewildering.

Tular clutched his sides as Deegan helped him stand. "Never a word, Nemesio. Not to anyone."

Gib tried to contain his ragged breaths. "What's one more secret, right?"

For a tense moment, Tular speared Gib with shrewd eyes, but then his somber gaze moved elsewhere. He exhaled sharply, and his frown deepened. "Natori."

Oh no.

Gib craned his head, following Tular's scrutiny to a nearby dune. There, at the sandy base, slumped the Blessed Mage's unmoving form. Hasain already knelt beside her, checking for signs of life. His face was grim and blanched of all color.

Deegan gasped, gripping Tular's arm. "Is—is she—?"

Gib thought he might retch.

Please don't be dead. Please don't be dead.

"Hasain?" Tular asked. "Is she—dead?"

Hasain didn't reply as he took up one of Natori's hands, but as Gib stumbled closer, he saw her eyes fluttering. Relief tempered the dread in Gib's heart. "She's alive. Just unconscious." He noted the gash on her face. "She's injured. She needs a Healer, fast."

A tear slipped down Deegan's cheek. "*Why?* Why did she and the guardsmen and—all of you—why do you risk your lives for *me*?"

Tular squeezed the prince's forearm. The simple movement made Tular cringe, but he didn't retract his hand. "Because some things are worth dying for, Deegan. That's why."

"My *father* was worth dying for," Deegan replied, hastily wiping his tears. "I'm just a spoiled brat who was lucky enough to be born a prince."

Hasain hadn't said anything in such a long time Gib had almost forgotten the Radek lord was there at all. He spoke now, in a voice so hollow it didn't even sound like himself. "You're my brother. You're worth *any* sacrifice."

No sooner had Hasain finished the sentence did the entire world begin to shake under their feet.

"Kezra!"

Kezra had never been more grateful to hear her brother's voice nor felt such sweet relief to see him, alive and riding toward her.

Zandi slipped from the saddle even before the horse stopped moving and came running at her on foot. Tangled strands of hair flew around his ears and neck, and his turban was missing entirely. Dust was enfolded in his tousled robes, yet somehow the fabric retained its pristine glow.

Mages and their trickery—

Kezra shook her head. It didn't matter. He was unharmed. *That* was all she cared about in this moment.

Jumping from Epona's back, Kezra clambered over the rubble of Tahir's wall. She met her brother with open arms. "I swear, *some* damn deity must be watching out for your sorry arse."

"Kezra." Zandi gasped again, as if he didn't quite believe she was actually standing there. "You're alive."

"Aye," Nage snorted. "An' it's a wonder, after the stunt she pulled."

Kezra hauled her brother into an embrace before he could raise a question. "We were looking all over for you. And then I saw Joel bring the wall down onto the beast and—do you know how close *you* were to being crushed?"

Joel, still perched atop Zandi's gelding, stared into the wreckage. One of the monster's claws was just visible amid the shattered alabaster. He gawped at the limb like he was afraid the beast might arise anew. "It was the only thing I could think to do. They're immune to magic."

"Yeah," Nage replied, shuddering. "We figured that out."

Kezra touched Zandi's damp cheek. "I'm glad you're safe."

"You as well, sister." Zandi wiped a sleeve across his eyes. "When the attack began, I feared the worst—"

Kezra could tell by the tremble in his voice that he was struggling to maintain control over himself. She squeezed his arm. "It's going to be all right. *We're* going to be all right."

Gara cleared her throat. She shifted restlessly in her saddle, eyes darting every which way. "Hey, guys, I don't mean to break up the heartfelt reunion and all, but we best keep moving. Those things are getting closer."

"The order to retreat's been given," Nage agreed. "Looks like we're gonna have to make a run for it."

"But—" Joel protested. "What about the rest of the army? And Deegan! I was supposed to protect him."

"Seneschal Koal was on his way to the prince last we saw him," Gara reassured.

"You saw my father? He was alive?"

"Yes, and you know damned well that if *anyone* can keep Deegan safe, it's the seneschal. We will find them later, Joel. For now, you must come with us. Kezra, Zandi, back in your saddles. Hurry."

Kezra sought the hilt of her sword as she stepped away from Zandi. The shouts at her back were growing louder and even more panicked. The smell of sweat and blood hung thickly in the air. She pivoted, peering through the haze. She couldn't stop herself. She had to see the destruction with her own eyes. Only the hatred surging through her veins—seeping into her very bones—held Kezra's tears at bay.

So many soldiers lay dead or dying. So many countless others were trying to flee but were hopelessly encircled by the beasts. Kezra thought *she* might die from the anger pressing onto her heart. So much loss of life. So many broken families and friendships—all for the sake of Neetra Adelwijn's contrived war. This was all *his* fault. She'd never loathed anyone so much.

Her fingers twitched around the shagreen handle. She knew the command to retreat had been given, and yet—she hesitated.

"Come on," Gara called again. "We have to leave."

Revulsion gushed into every corner of Kezra's mind until she could think of nothing else but revenge. Revenge on Neetra Adelwijn. Revenge on the High Council. Revenge on her father. Revenge on the beasts that had slain so many of her comrades—were *still* slaying them even as she stood by and did nothing.

Kezra began to slide the blade free of its sheath. The fallen deserved to be avenged. She deserved vengeance. And she would have it—

"Kezra?" One of Zandi's slender hands slipped over hers, breaking Kezra from her trance. She blinked and looked up at him. His imploring eyes were nothing short of devastating. "Whatever you're thinking of doing—don't. Live to fight another day. This battle is lost, but the war has barely begun." His bottom lip quivered. "Please. I need you."

Heat pooled on Kezra's cheeks. Damn. He knew her too well. Swallowing, she pulled her hand off the hilt. "Fine. Let's go."

Zandi gave a brief nod before navigating his way back to his horse. "We should ride close to the wall. Once we're clear, we can make a run for the open desert." He reached for Joel's offered hand. "We can follow the river. Hopefully the other survivors will go there—"

A violent shockwave rippled across the sand. Zandi staggered where he stood. He might have toppled over had Joel not grabbed Zandi's arm and pulled him into the saddle. The ground heaved as some unknown force bubbled up from the depths. Kezra stared breathlessly at the tiny rivulets of powdered mortar cascading around her boots. Was the entire world slanting? Chhaya's bane, what new horror was about to be thrown at them?

Gara's face drained of all color. "Is that—is that more beasts?"

Epona threw her head and whickered in terror. Kezra had to dive for the reins to prevent the mare from bolting.

Joel whimpered. He looked like he might be ill. "The dark magic is massing again. Zandi, do you—?"

"I feel it, too," Zandi said shakily. "Oh gods—it's everywhere."

"It must be *hundreds* more of them comin' up!" Nage hollered.

Epona was so unsteady on her feet Kezra had to crawl into the saddle. White-knuckled, she clung to the pommel for dear life.

"*Look!*" Gara cried. "Look at the ground!"

The earth ruptured beneath Epona's hooves. Kezra could only gape in horror as the dirt tore apart, like a garment being ripped at the seams. The jagged rift snaked through the sand, spreading rapidly from Tahir's wall and cutting a path all the way to the center of the battleground. Soldiers shouted and shoved one another aside in an effort to get away from the chasm. The shuddering ground caught the attention of the beasts, who ceased their carnage as scaly maws lifted into the air. The monsters hissed and flared their nostrils.

"Something has them scared," Joel said breathlessly.

The earth buckled.

Kezra braced herself as Epona reared, but nothing could have prepared her or anyone else for what happened next.

The ground simply gave out beneath the army, opening into a black pit—no, a pit would have been *something*—this was an abyss. *Nothing.* No bottom. No end. No *anything.* Just a void. It was as if the world itself had fallen away.

Hundreds of terrified screams lifted in unison as men plunged into oblivion. The monsters tried to flee, but too slowly. They were swept away alongside the Ardenian army. The beasts shrieked as they plummeted to their doom. The devastating timbre pierced Kezra's ears and left her frozen in terror.

Move! You have to move!

Kezra managed to tear her eyes from the battlefield. The sand below was sifting into the fissure. She could feel the earth dipping. A strangled squeak ripped free from her throat.

Daya, the ground is going to cave here too!

"Go!" she screamed. "Go now!"

With a snap of the reins, Epona bolted forward at a full gallop. Kezra crouched low on the saddle. Wind whipped around her face. Sand lashed her eyes. Her ears brimmed with the sounds of screaming men and the rumble of falling dirt. She refused to look back.

She rode hard and furiously along the wall. Alabaster stone whizzed past in a blur. The entire structure seemed to be moving—or maybe only she was. To her other side, Kezra caught the flash of white robes. Joel and Zandi were only a few paces behind. And Nage and Gara? She couldn't risk a glance over her shoulder but hoped they were there too.

The world narrowed to a single, desperate objective. Ride to safety. Don't stop. Don't look back. Just ride.

But then Kezra heard her brother cry out in surprise.

Zandi! No!

She pivoted in her saddle in time to see the gelding carrying the two mages stumble over the upheaved sand. Joel, who'd been sitting to the front, went flying overhead. Zandi was thrown off the side. He tried to scramble away as the horse crashed to the ground, but he didn't move fast enough. The gelding bowled over, pinning one of Zandi's legs against the sand.

Kezra didn't think. She simply reacted. Yanking on Epona's reins so hard the mare was forced into a lurching halt, she jumped from the saddle. A cloud of dust swelled before her like Death's shadow. The ground splintered. Entire plates of crust broke off and disappeared into the void, just paces from where Zandi lay helplessly bound. She didn't care. She raced back toward her brother.

"Kezra, no!" Zandi cried, struggling to free his leg. "Don't!"

Kezra only ran faster. She had to reach him.

Another chunk of earth bowed and broke away. Zandi's horse elicited a terrified squeal and rolled into the ravine. The gelding's kicking hooves were the last part of its body to disappear from view. The squealing ceased.

Zandi crawled desperately for safety, but the earth was disintegrating around him. His fingers dug into the sand but found nothing to grip. He slipped farther away.

No!

Kezra dove, grabbing for Zandi's hands. She managed to catch his wrists just as the dirt collapsed beneath his body. Zandi let out a shrill wail as he was left dangling helplessly above the abyss.

Kezra jolted forward with a gasp, nearly tumbling over the edge herself. Pain shot up her arms. Both limbs felt like they were about to pop out of their sockets. Her shoulders burned in agony, and her grip wavered.

Oh gods, I can't hold his weight!

"Kezra," Zandi sobbed wetly. His boots flailed for solid ground, but there was nothing below him. He couldn't pull himself up. He stopped thrashing. His tear-filled eyes met hers. "You have to save yourself."

Digging her knees into the sand, Kezra gritted her teeth. She wouldn't drop him. If he fell, she was going with him. "I'm *not* letting go."

The whites of Zandi's eyes shone against the shadowed void. Droplets rolled down his cheeks in waves. "There's no other way. I—I love you."

"No!" Kezra screamed, even as her grip slipped further.

"You have to."

"I *won't* let you die!"

Zandi's mouth dropped open, but any words he might have uttered died on his tongue. His gaze shifted beyond Kezra. A shadow splashed across his pale face, and hope rekindled in his eyes.

Kezra's head shot up. Her heart skipped a beat at the sight of Joel Adelwijn standing beside her. He might as well have been a gift sent by The Two.

"Help me!" she gasped.

Without hesitation, Joel went down on his knees, stretching a hand over the ledge. He clutched Zandi's forearm. "Grab his other arm. Don't worry. I have him. Good. Okay, at the same time now—*pull!*"

Together, they lurched to their feet. Kezra slammed her eyes shut, yanking with every ounce of strength left in her body. She could hear Joel's strained grunt above the rumble of falling sand as he, too, heaved.

One step backward. Two. Another—

Yes! YES!

Kezra's eyes popped open as Zandi tumbled onto solid ground in a heap of white robes.

They pulled the mage a safe distance from the ledge, propping him against a dune. Kezra's chest heaved with weariness. Her knees buckled, and a moment later, she collapsed beside her brother, too exhausted to go on. If the Gatekeeper wanted her soul that badly, then so be it. Let Him take her. She didn't care anymore.

But the chasm didn't widen. The ground had stopped trembling, and the rumble of falling earth ceased. Kezra held her breath, waiting—but nothing happened. The world had gone silent: stiller than Death itself. Chhaya's bane, was the madness over?

Zandi sobbed hysterically into the crook of Kezra's neck. "I thought—I thought we were both going to fall to our deaths."

Kezra was beyond the ability to form coherent words, so she squeezed Zandi closer and let him weep himself dry.

The chasm sprawled before them like a bone-dry lake. A thick haze rose from the bottomless depths, dampening the sunlight and making it difficult to gauge how immense the rift truly was. Kezra peered through the dust, hoping to catch a glimpse of fellow survivors, but she could see nothing on the far side of the gorge.

Joel's hands gripped his raven locks as he stared across the void in disbelief. His eyes misted with tears, and then he, too, wilted to the ground. "The army—*our* army—it's—they're all dead. Father, Deegan, Nawaz, Hasain, and—oh, gods, what if Gib—"

Zandi raised his soggy face at that, glaring angrily. "*Don't* say that. We can't be the only survivors. They might have made it."

Joel cupped his hands over his face. "Goddesses, be just to our loved ones."

Wretched sobs filled Kezra's ears. At first, she thought they belonged to Joel or Zandi, but no—the grief-stricken cries were drifting from farther away. She glanced in the direction of the sound. Her heart sank to the pit of her stomach. Daya, how had she forgotten?

Gara knelt at the edge of the chasm, reaching with outstretched hands into the dusty air. The scout's rigid body quivered as she wept. "I—I had just looked back."

A nauseating lump formed in Kezra's throat. Her eyes darted back and forth, searching frantically for the last member of their party. Where was he? Where was Nage?

"He was right behind me," Gara rambled on. Her choked words were nearly incoherent. "*Right* behind me. And then—" Her hands fell limply to the ground. "I promised Nia. I promised her."

Oh, no. No. Not him. Not Nage.

Kezra staggered to her feet. The truth already twisted like a dagger in the gut, but she refused to believe it. She *couldn't* believe it. Even now, as hope dwindled, her blurry eyes searched for him. "Gara, where is he? Where's Nage?"

The scout's anguished cry shook Kezra to the core. "Nage fell. He's gone."

CHAPTER EIGHTEEN

Gib stared vacantly into the chasm, unaware of the passing time. He could have been sitting there a quarter-mark or an entire day. His muddled mind and heavy heart didn't care. What was left to care about?

When the cataclysm struck, *nothing* near the center of the battlefield escaped its wrath. Men, monsters, horses—they were *all* lost. In the blink of an eye, thousands of soldiers had been thrown to the shadowy abyss. Gone in a single heartbeat. *Dead.*

Gib absently wiped a blood-stained sleeve across his eyes. The sun soared high in the sky. Angry, blistering rays beat down onto his cheeks. The heat dried Gib's tears almost faster than the droplets could fall. Not that it mattered. He wasn't making any effort to hide his grief. And he wasn't the only one weeping for Arden's great loss.

Behind him, the broken remnants of the Ardenian army were setting up crude tents and tending to the wounded. They worked in complete silence, their spirits surely as broken as Gib's own. The survivors—those scant few who'd been lucky enough to be fighting farther out when the earth shattered—roamed into the makeshift camp a handful at a time. Their eyes were all dull, lost to unthinkable sorrow. Many of them chose to keep walking around the outskirts of the war camp, too bewildered and disillusioned to sit. No one had imagined things would end this way. *No one.*

"Gibben?" Deegan called gingerly from beneath the shade of a nearby awning. The prince hovered beside Natori, who perched unwillingly on a cot while Nawaz attempted to bandage the gash across the Blessed Mage's brow. Tular and Hasain sat farther inside the tent, both mute.

"Let me be," Natori groaned. "The other survivors need your help. I'm fine."

Nawaz frowned as he attended to his reluctant patient. "With all due respect, Blessed Mage, I'm the Healer here. Be quiet and let me work."

Deegan was paying little attention to their banter. Wringing his hands, he sought out Gib's gaze. "Perhaps it's best if you come away from the ledge. It could crumble."

"Yes, Highness," Gib replied distantly, yet he made no effort to move. Did it matter if he tumbled to his death? What was the loss of one more soul after the *thousands* who'd just perished? After Gib's own friends had fallen? He set his face against his knees and wept silently.

He would go to Kezra and Zandi's mother as soon as he returned to Silver. He needed to see Lady Odessa in person. His apologies for failing to keep the two eldest Malin-Rai children safe would never be enough to ease her pain, but he felt it was his duty to offer condolences. Both Zandi and Kezra would have done the same for Gib.

He'd have to make the same trek to the Leal estate, to Nia, who'd barely had time to mourn the loss of her father. Would she ever fully recover when she discovered both her sister and fiancé had crossed The Veil as well?

Gib shuddered. Lady Mrifa. He didn't know if he could face her…

Joel, I failed you most of all. I'm sorry. I'm so sorry.

Gnashing his teeth against the urge to sob aloud, Gib focused his attention on the distant city. Fragments of plaster still crumbled from Tahir's battered wall. Much of the fortification was absent entirely, swallowed by the void. Inside the city, houses had been reduced to piles of rubble. Temples lay in ruins. Some buildings had sunk into the rift, while others had toppled during the quake. The damage was unspeakable. There were no winners this day.

A shadow fell across the sand. Gib raised his chin, staring up with blurry eyes at his mentor.

"On your feet, Gib," Koal said in a hollow voice. He set a hand on Gib's shoulder, squeezing feebly. "Come sit in the shade, before you get sunstroke."

That was what he was worried about? Gib coming down with sunstroke?

"Joel," Gib gasped, unable to prevent the forbidden name from escaping his lips. "Your son—"

"I know," Koal whispered and turned his face away.

Gib wiped away his tears as he stood, but it was a losing battle. Fresh rivulets flowed anew. "We should say the death rite. The fallen deserve as much."

"We will. When all the survivors are accounted for, we'll say the rite together."

After a brief lapse of silence, Koal looked over at Gib once again. The sight of the seneschal's haggard features and bloodshot eyes was almost too heartbreaking to behold. Gib could recall witnessing such defeat upon Koal's face only one other time: the evening King Rishi lay on his deathbed.

Gib choked on a sob. "I'm sorry for your loss."

"*Our* loss. Arden's loss."

A group of survivors limped into the camp then, and Koal excused himself to check on their well-being. Gib wandered over to the prince's tent, feeling lost and useless.

Deegan offered a wineskin. "Here, Gibben, have some water."

Gib accepted the canteen only because he couldn't think of any excuse not to. Lukewarm water touched his lips and trickled down his throat. It tasted like nothing, as empty as his heart. Gib corked the vessel, wondering if he'd ever again be able to enjoy life's simple pleasures. Perhaps the soul could bear only so much sorrow before it shut down entirely.

"Pass it here, Gib," Tular said from his position on the ground. He waved a hand. Even the slight gesture caused him to wince and clutch his side.

Gib tensed his shoulders. He couldn't help but stare warily as he handed Tular the wineskin. Gib knew he was being foolish. Tular might not be—what Gib had believed, but the other man sure as hell wasn't an enemy. His loyalty to Deegan was undeniable—and he'd risked his own life to save them.

Tular raised the canteen to his mouth with a groan. He was trying to downplay the severity of his injuries, but Gib could see the young lord was in pain. His face twisted into a grimace every time he moved.

Deegan jumped to help. "Here, let me hold it."

"I'm fine," Tular replied, taking a jagged breath.

Deegan motioned toward the Blessed Mage. "You're as stubborn as she."

Shrugging, Tular tried to pass the wineskin to Hasain, but the Radek lord shook his head. He sat rigidly atop a crate, hands clenched together. Gib could see they were shaking.

"Take it," Tular demanded.

Hasain's shoulders quivered along with his hands. "I'm not thirsty."

"You haven't drunk anything since sunrise. You'll become delirious."

"Worry about yourself. You're the one who's injured."

Tular raised a fist, like he might want to clobber Hasain. "You're damn lucky I'm injured."

"And *you're* lucky no one else besides Gib saw you," Hasain shot back in a low hiss. "You acted recklessly."

Deegan placed a hand on Tular's shoulder. "Don't be so harsh, Hasain. He did what he had to do to distract the beast. He saved Natori—and all of us."

Hasain glared at the ground, saying nothing more.

"What happened?" Nawaz asked without glancing up. He worked tirelessly to wrap a clean linen strip around Natori's head. "How was Tular hurt?"

Deegan hesitated, sharing a somber look with Tular, but finally replied, "One of the beasts pinned him to the ground. He would have been crushed if the monster hadn't suddenly been scared off."

Nawaz's eyebrows ticked higher. "Scared off by what?"

Tular scowled as he repositioned himself, with no small effort. "No idea. It stopped attacking us—just like that—and ran away."

"Maybe it knew the ground was going to cave. Maybe that had it frightened."

"I don't think so. It ran back toward the other beasts, right into the worst of it."

"Huh. Odd."

Gib swallowed. They might never know the reason the beast had fled nor what caused the ground to cave. And what did it matter? It wouldn't change anything. It wouldn't bring back the fallen.

Nawaz smiled tightly as he finished bandaging Natori's wound. "There. Good as new, m'lady." The Blessed Mage grunted under her breath, but Nawaz had already turned to face Tular. "All right, your turn. Let me have a look at you."

Tular recoiled. "No."

"This is serious, Tular. You could have broken ribs—or worse, a punctured lung. Even if you're only bruised, I can hasten the healing and numb some of the pain."

"You—can't—" Tular gasped, backing away from Nawaz as the Healer knelt.

"Look at you! You can't even issue a full sentence!"

Tular glanced around with wide eyes, pleading silently for help. "Marc is my Healer."

"Yeah, well, *Marc's* not here. You're gonna have to settle for me."

Deegan sucked his lower lip into his mouth. "Tular, let him Heal you."

"Prince," Natori cautioned. "I must advise against—"

"There's no other choice," Deegan said, his conflicted eyes darting back and forth. "Tular needs a Healer. Nawaz has been a loyal friend for years. We have to trust him now."

Gib cleared his throat, adding tentatively, "For what it's worth, Tular did take a hard hit. I think Prince Deegan is right."

"Then he must swear himself to secrecy," Natori said. "On his own *life*." Her attention shifted to Nawaz. She narrowed her eyes. "Nawaz Arrio, I want to hear your promise. Anything you should learn beneath this awning *stays* here. Do you understand?"

Nawaz's brows knitted as he looked from face to face. Gib understood. He'd been asked to make the same vow of secrecy. Never in his wildest dreams could he have imagined *this* was what he'd been agreeing to.

"Hasain's been my best friend since we were children," Nawaz said quietly, "Tular, too. I'd never betray them, nor their families. Whatever secrets you ask me to conceal, I'll do so without hesitation. You have my word."

Natori folded her arms, a scowl hardening her face. "Koal won't like this. Too many people know already, Deegan. All it takes is one slipup—accidental or not—and your claim to the crown could be jeopardized."

"I know," Deegan replied. "But we have to trust our allies. We have so few remaining…" Wringing his hands, he nodded for Nawaz to proceed.

The Healer crouched beside Tular, who was still wide-eyed and fidgeting. "All right. Sit still and relax." Nawaz gave no further warning before he closed his eyes and slipped a hand onto Tular's forearm.

Gib watched in tense silence. He recalled when his wrist had been broken during his first year at Academy and Nawaz had performed this same magic. Using the Healing Gift, he'd been able to See Gib's ailment straight through his flesh.

Gib held his breath. Everyone else seemed to be doing the same. Would Nawaz See more than he should? Gib didn't pretend to know anything about magic or how it worked to conceal Tular's true identity, but he could only assume the guise was vulnerable to exposure when scrutinized so intimately. Why else would Marc be Tular's only Healer?

At first, Nawaz's expression remained serene. But that changed in an instant. His brows hiked higher on his forehead, and then his entire face pinched. Another moment passed before the Healer uttered a startled gasp and his eyes popped open. He sat back, gaping first at Tular, and then at everyone else. No one said anything. What *could* they say?

After the shock of discovery had a few moments to settle, Nawaz cleared his throat pointedly. "Any other surprises I should know about before I continue?"

"We couldn't tell you," Hasain whispered, glaring angrily. "You have to keep your mouth shut."

All of Nawaz's typical wit seemed to have abandoned him. "Will do." He raised his hand again but hesitated before making contact with Tular's arm.

Tular looked like he wanted to crawl into a hole. "It's still me, Nawaz. You don't have to be afraid."

Nodding tightly, Nawaz shut his eyes and went back to work. "It looks like you do have one fractured rib, as well as some significant bruising."

"Will he be all right?" Deegan asked, hovering above. "You can help him, can't you?"

"For now, I can block some of the pain. But you have to take it easy, Tular. No sudden movements. Riding is probably going to be hell for a good moonturn or more."

Tular sighed. "Fantastic."

They fell into silence as Nawaz focused all his attention on the task at hand.

Gib's eyes wandered restlessly around the encampment. Another cluster of survivors had arrived, and Koal was taking quick steps across the clearing to greet them. Gib craned his head, trying to get a better look. His heart fluttered. Dare he hope? Could it be—Joel?

No. Gib's spirit came crashing down when he recognized Morathi's grey stallion. The general swung from his saddle in a flurry of crimson silk and gleaming armor, barking orders for someone to fetch water for his horse. Koal approached, and the two men exchanged terse words spoken too low for Gib to overhear.

Deegan's nose curled with revulsion. "Of course *he* survived."

"He's not the only one," Tular sneered. "Look."

Gib balled his hands as Morathi's two traitorous dogs separated from the crowd and raced over to meet the general. So, the cowards who'd abandoned their charge *had* lived after all.

"Traitors," Hasain said darkly. "They left Deegan to die after swearing to protect him."

"They deserve to be hanged," Gib heard himself growl. Rash anger gushed through his veins, only to be usurped by terrible apprehension moments later. "You—don't think they saw anything, do you?"

Deegan's eyes widened with uncertainty. "They'd already run off when Tular—saved us."

"Are you *sure*?" Gib pressed. "Did anyone turn and look?"

Tular snorted. "I don't think looking for Morathi's henchmen was on any of our minds with that monster bearing down on us."

"I'm serious. We need to make sure neither of them saw you."

"If they had," Tular replied. "I'd probably already be shot dead."

Deegan gave the young lord a swat on the back. "Don't say such things."

Tular shrugged. His shrewd gaze trailed the general's every move. Still shouting orders, Morathi trudged across the sand and disappeared inside a tent. His two dogs followed at his heels. Gib's skin crawled. He had half a mind to sneak over and attempt to eavesdrop on their conversation, but the open desert offered few places to hide.

Uttering an exhausted sigh, Gib stepped out from beneath the awning before anyone could tell him otherwise. He needed to tell the seneschal what had happened and that Morathi's men might be trouble. Gib scanned the place he'd last spotted his mentor—but Koal was no longer there.

Where—?

A wisp of the seneschal's red cape caught Gib's eye. Koal's long strides were carrying him toward the edge of the encampment. His arms were held out, almost as if in surrender, but no—he was reaching for someone.

The sight of a weary but radiant smile and misty eyes made Gib's knees weak. No. His mind must be playing tricks. He blinked, but the image of silky raven hair didn't fade away. There was no way—it couldn't be. But—it was. It *was*!

White mage robes shimmered in the sunlight, and a tender voice lifted above the din, calling for his father. A pitiful squeak leapt from Gib's throat as he watched Koal throw his arms around his son's shoulders. Joel! He'd survived! He was *alive*!

Gib stumbled over without thinking. "Joel! *Joel!*"

The mage had his eyes squeezed shut, but he must have heard Gib's voice. Still embracing his father, Joel raised his chin and locked his gaze onto Gib. Joel's mouth dropped open, and then he burst into tears.

"You're alive," he cried, sobbing against Koal's neck. "Daya, you're all alive."

Gib's heart was racing so swiftly he barely registered the sound of boots crunching in the sand, approaching from behind. He jumped when a small hand ghosted over his back.

"Damn good thing I had the insight to paint that mark on your forehead this morning, Nemesio."

Gib gasped. He *knew* that voice. He whirled around and gaped, dumbfounded. "Kezra!"

Kezra smiled back at him sadly. Sweat glistened on her cheeks and flattened her dark tresses against her skin. Her tabard was bloodied and ripped beyond repair, but the armor beneath remained intact. Gib took that for a good sign. At least she wasn't seriously injured.

Kezra took Gib's hands. Her clasp was frail, and her own hands wobbled beyond control. Gib was certain he'd never seen Kezra's eyes look quite so lost before. She was safe though. In that moment, that's all he cared about. Another day—together—there would be time to heal emotional wounds.

Gib squeezed her fingers. "Thank The Two you're okay."

"I saved a couple of mages for you," Kezra replied. She nodded over her shoulder.

The air deflated from Gib's chest for a third time when he noticed Kezra wasn't alone. He shook his head in disbelief. Surely this had to be a dream. The Goddesses were never so merciful.

Zandi lingered only a few paces away, holding Epona's reins. His hair fell in tousled waves around his face. The cinnabar paint on his brow was hopelessly smeared across his forehead. His robes were filthy. Nevertheless, his emerald eyes blazed. The smile that curled both corners of his mouth was bright. He came forward with arms spread wide, and Gib rushed to greet him.

"I was sure you'd fallen," Zandi choked. "When the ground opened up, I feared the worst."

Gib uttered a startled gasp when he was embraced with so much vigor that his feet lifted right off the ground. "Me too. I thought you were all dead."

"If it wasn't for Kezra and Joel, I would be." Zandi loosened his grip around Gib's shoulders but didn't let go entirely. "They saved my life."

That didn't surprise Gib, not one bit. He touched his companion's cheek, wiping away a stray tear. "Are you hurt? Nawaz is beneath the awning if you need to see a Healer."

Zandi shook his head. "I'm fine. Just in shock. The army—"

"I know." Gib wished he could offer something more, but speech failed him. How would Arden ever come back from this loss? There were so few survivors.

Koal passed by without a word, leading his son into the shade. Tears continued to stream down Joel's lovely face. Gib's heart twisted. There had been a time when he would have willingly wiped the droplets away. He *still* would, Gib admitted to himself, if only Joel asked. But he didn't say a word, and shameful heat seared Gib's cheeks when he had to remind himself that *Zandi* was the one standing at his side now.

Deegan didn't even wait for Joel to reach the awning. Throwing formalities to the wind, the prince greeted his elder cousin with a fierce hug. Even Hasain seemed to come out of his stupor long enough to grip Joel's shoulder. Gib's gaze lingered longingly on his former companion. He stared, perhaps too long, but if Zandi noticed, he didn't say anything.

Swallowing the hard lump that had formed in the base of his throat, Gib finally tore his treacherous eyes away. He still had friends who were unaccounted for. He glanced around the encampment. "Have either of you seen Nage and Gara?"

Kezra's hands found their way to Gib's forearms. The sight of her damp face, warped by sorrow and guilt, sent shudders racing down Gib's spine. He braced himself even as Kezra and Zandi rushed to do the same.

"There's something you need to know—" Kezra choked over the words. Chest heaving, she lowered her face. Tears clung to her lashes. One by one, they dripped into the sand. "Nage didn't make it."

Gib would have slumped to the ground if Zandi hadn't been there to hold him upright.

No. Not Nage. Not my friend.

Gib slammed his eyes shut, but the tears fell anyway. He could see Nage's crooked grin shining through the darkness. His boisterous laughter rang as clearly as if the sentinel were standing there even now. But he wasn't. Like Liza and so many other brave warriors, he was gone—lost to senseless war.

A cloudless autumn day brightened the gloom in Gib's mind. All at once, he was young again, a boy of thirteen. He stood alone in a sea of sentinel trainees, terrified for the young brothers he'd been ripped away from, and even more frightened by the strange new world surrounding him. He'd never known such hopelessness before.

But then a scrawny boy—clad in rags, shoeless, with absolutely *nothing*

269

to his name—had introduced himself. He'd accepted Gib with open arms and no questions asked. And just like that, Gib was no longer left to feel alone or scared. Nage had been Gib's first true friend. They'd gotten through that first day, first moonturn, and first year together. They'd grown up together. They'd shared laughter, love, and sorrow together. Nage had been a part of Gib's life for so long Gib couldn't imagine a world without his friend. In Gib's soul, he knew things would never be the same. Another life had been stolen too soon. Another unfillable void was left to fester in Gib's heart.

"He died a hero," Zandi whispered, stroking long fingers through Gib's curls. "He'll always be remembered as a warrior."

Gib leaned into the touch. "And as a dear and loyal friend." Somehow, he managed to hold himself together long enough to ask, "What about Gara?"

Kezra's voice wavered. "Gara's there—at the edge of the rift. She wanted a moment to be alone."

Gib nodded absently. He still refused to open his eyes. Maybe if he kept his memories trapped inside, Nage's infectious grin wouldn't fade away. Already Liza's face blurred in his mind. His father's kind smile had been shrouded for years. He was losing them all, piece by broken piece. Soon there would be nothing left to remember.

"We should go to Gara," Gib said at long last. "We should say our final farewells together." He bowed his weary head. A single teardrop slipped down his cheek. "Chhaya, keep vigil, for one of your children comes."

The last traces of color still clung to the eventide sky, bands of deep orange and ruby against a navy backdrop. Stars scattered across the heavens in perfect disarray and moonlight trickled through a hazy veil of clouds. The pale tendrils stretched over the sand, enticing each individual granule to twinkle. The sight was hauntingly beautiful. Perhaps the Goddesses Themselves had woven such an exquisite evening in tribute to the fallen.

Somewhere in the distance, Tahir's ruins still stood, though darkness had long since shrouded the city from view. No lanterns shone along the remnants of the alabaster wall on this night, only impenetrable gloom. The people of Shiraz had lost nearly as much as Arden. There were precious few survivors.

With a forlorn sigh, Joel turned away from the open desert. He didn't want to look at it anymore. He didn't want to see sand everywhere he glanced. How long had it been since he'd tasted fresh, mountain-chilled water? How long had it been since he'd stepped on grass that wasn't shriveled and brown? He couldn't recall.

Tinder crackled within a nearby fire. The flames burned low, bathing the faces of those gathered in golden light. Joel stared at the embers. The warmth made his eyelids heavy, but sleep was still far beyond him. People moved about, mostly silent as they finished meager meals and prepared their sleeping mats. Some were too exhausted for even that and lay sprawled upon the sand in their armor. A scant few soldiers walked the camp perimeter, keeping vigil, but most rested, preparing for the morrow, when the survivors would begin the long trek home.

Home. Joel's heart ached for it. He missed those left behind dearly—and more so, he worried for them. How was his mother coping after so many moonturns alone? And Joel's sisters? Were Heidi and her unborn babe in good health? What of his aunt, Dahlia, and cousins, Didier and Gudrin, trapped inside the palace, with Neetra and his councilors surely plotting the royal family's demise? Joel prayed they were faring better than the army. It made him sick not knowing.

Joel's fingers entwined around the cold metal trinket resting against his throat—Kirk's falcon pendant. Kirk, also left behind in Silver City, who was risking his very life to help the Radek loyalists. Was the Imperial mage safe and well? Had he and Marc found any sort of information to hold against the steward—or had their efforts been fruitless? What if they'd been caught?

Joel squeezed his eyes shut.

Daya, please don't let Kirk be harmed. I asked too much of him. I took advantage of his kindness. He'd send himself straight to the gallows if I commanded it. His emotions have blinded him. He thinks he—loves me.

And therein lay the problem.

When I get back, I have to tell him that I'm not—we're not—we're just friends…aren't we? Gods, where does friendship end and more begin?

Joel didn't know. He'd used the war as an excuse to push his own troubles aside, but Kirk deserved an answer. Joel just wasn't sure what his answer would be—or if it would be the one the Imperial mage hoped to hear. Joel frowned and opened his eyes.

Across the fire, Gib dozed within the drowsy heat. He sat propped against a barrel, still wearing his gambeson, with his sword sprawled over his legs. His lashes fluttered, like he might be enjoying a pleasant dream. Joel hoped so. After all Gib had been through—losing his sister, saying goodbye to Nage—he deserved a moment's reprieve.

I can't begin to fathom the pain he's in. I wish there was more I could do to help him.

Joel's heart ached. He longed to offer comfort—a gentle embrace, whispered reassurances, a light kiss—but it wasn't his place anymore. Even now, Zandi lay sleeping by Gib's side. Letting out a bitter sigh, Joel averted his gaze.

I did this. I pushed Gib away. I have only myself to blame now that he's found a new companion. Now that he's moved on...

Again, Joel's thoughts flitted back to Kirk—gentle, kind, *sweet* Kirk—who would walk to the ends of the earth and back again if it pleased Joel. Kirk, whose only mishap had been to devote himself to someone so *unworthy*.

Joel rubbed at his face, feeling more lost than ever.

Gods, I still love Gib. I don't know if I'll ever be able to love someone else that way again. But—if I don't let go, my heart will never truly be given a chance to heal. Kirk's a good person. Perhaps he deserves a chance...I don't know. I just don't know.

Light footfalls scuffed through the sand, drawing closer. Joel raised his chin only when a shadow fell over him. His stomach knotted at the sight of Nawaz's bloodstained jerkin. Joel hadn't seen the Healer since earlier in the day, when he'd been tending to Tular's and Natori's wounds.

"May I sit?" Nawaz asked, his voice weary.

Joel replied without hesitation. "Of course you may."

Nawaz's broad shoulders sagged with fatigue. He all but crumbled to the ground. "I just need to rest for a short while. They banned me from the pavilion. I wanted to stay—"

"You're exhausted." Joel touched the Healer's sleeve, noting his pallid complexion. "You should sleep."

Nawaz shook his head. "I can't. Not while there are still soldiers barely clinging to life. Morathi says it's a lost cause, but I won't give up. They were ready to die protecting Arden. They deserve a fighting chance."

"You'll do all you can. Everyone who matters knows that. Just remember to take care of yourself too."

"I know, but—we've already lost so many. We'll probably lose even more once infection sets in."

Joel squeezed the Healer's arm. "Is there anything I can do to help?"

"I don't know." Nawaz raised his hands to his face, gripping fistfuls of hair. "Most of our salves were destroyed during the raid. Those of us with the Gift are already exhausted. You know better than most that magic isn't infinite. The price of healing such severe injuries has drained us. It doesn't help that half of our Healers were lost during the cave-in."

Joel winced. "I wish to The Two that I had the Healing Gift. I know it's not the same, but—tomorrow, I'll be somewhat rested. If you can utilize my mage-energy in *any* way, I'll give whatever I can to help heal the wounded. I'm sure the other mages would gladly volunteer as well."

Nawaz laughed brokenly. "Drain our mages of their magic and leave us completely vulnerable to attack? What if the Shirites decide to come out from behind their wall? Nothing will stop them from slaying the rest of us now that two-thirds of our troops are gone."

"The Shirites are just as bad off as we are. You saw what happened to their city. By the time they recover enough to send their militia, we'll be crossing our eastern border. We need to save as many lives as we can. It's a risk worth taking. Our brave soldiers deserve better than to slowly die from infection."

Nawaz folded his arms, his expression dubious at best. "I don't disagree with you, and of course we can use the help of the mages, but— Morathi won't be happy if he finds out."

"He doesn't need to know. And quite frankly, I couldn't care less about following his orders. He's one of the rats on the High Council who pushed so hard for war. His poor judgement has *ruined* our army. Father warned them something like this might happen, and they didn't take heed."

Nawaz cast a wary gaze around. "Careful. You shouldn't so openly voice your contempt. The general has eyes and ears everywhere."

Glaring at the ground, Joel clamped his teeth over his tongue to help rein in the anger. "I know. I'm just upset."

"We all are. This should never have happened."

They sat in silence for some time, watching as the flames consumed the last bits of charred tinder. The fire guttered, swiftly reduced to nothing more than pulsating embers. No one moved to add fuel, and soon shadows rolled in, enfolding the camp in darkness.

Joel's head was so full it might explode. Above the barrage of unanswered questions and churning emotions, all he really wanted was to speak with his father—about the attack and about making amends. Joel had been wrong to judge so quickly. He saw that now, after nearly losing all he held dear. Some things were just more important than harboring resentment. Koal wasn't infallible. He made mistakes, like everyone else. But he *was* a good man. Joel knew that to be true. And Nawaz—Nawaz was a decent person too. He also deserved an apology.

Risking a glance at the Healer, Joel bit his bottom lip. He considered his words carefully. "Nawaz? I know this may not be the best time, but since none of us are ever guaranteed a tomorrow, I need to tell you something. It's about what happened last night—"

Nawaz drew back, knitting his brows. He must have already known where this was going. "You don't have to do this, Joel."

"Yes, I do. I shouldn't have spoken to you about Heidi the way I did. I don't agree—never mind. What I want to say is, I love you. We grew up together. You're a dear friend as much as a family member. You stayed by my side when no one else would. When so many others turned on me, your loyalty never once wavered. I'm sorry for turning on you the way I did. Father was right. It's not my place to judge your mishaps. I *know* you're a good person. I've known all along. Please, forgive me."

Nawaz pressed a hand to his mouth, but that didn't stop a strained croak from slipping free. Tears spilled over his pale cheeks. He nodded long before he could find his voice. "Thank you. I'm sorry too. I promise I'm not going to waste this second chance. What happened between Kezra and me—it's done with. It's over. Heidi deserves better. *I'm* going to be better."

Joel reached out, and this time Nawaz didn't flinch away. They shared a prolonged embrace before Nawaz excused himself, stating that he needed to return to the pavilion. Joel thought the Healer might have only wanted a reason to go weep in private. A bittersweet smile spread across Joel's mouth. One small victory in the midst of disaster. He'd take it.

Heat continued to ascend from the fire pit, though the flames had long since died. The warmth made Joel's eyelids heavy, tried to lure him into sleep. He flirted with the idea, but his father's voice from within the nearby command tent drew Joel's attention. Casting one final gaze at Gib, Joel dragged himself to his feet. He still wanted to talk to Koal before taking rest.

Joel paused as he came within reach of the entrance flap, debating if he should continue on. His father wasn't alone. Other voices could be heard conversing inside.

"You spoke to the Healers just before sundown, Seneschal." General Morathi's words slithered like the viper they belonged to. "How many injured soldiers do we have?"

"Less than fifty," Koal replied at length.

"Only fifty? Well, I suppose that's a bit of good news."

"Not entirely. Most of those injured during the battle weren't able to escape in time when the ground caved. Of the survivors who did make it, the majority are suffering from life-threatening wounds—torn limbs, gashes straight to the bone—and the Healers have had losses in their own ranks. There isn't enough manpower to assist the wounded. And with our supplies running dry due to the raid, we're stretched incredibly thin."

The conversation lapsed into brittle silence. Through the split in the canvas, Joel could see his father's tall form pace closer. Joel took the opportunity to peek inside. He cleared his throat politely. "Sorry to interrupt, Da. May I come in?"

Koal beckoned with one hand for Joel to come forward. "Shouldn't you be resting?"

"I couldn't sleep," Joel replied, stepping through the threshold. "My mind refuses to settle."

Koal nodded. "Often times the senses remain heightened, even after the battle is over. That will soon pass." He gave Joel a thump on the back. "Go sit with Deegan and the others."

Joel did as he was told and crossed to the rear of the tent, where Deegan slouched on a cot, a frail youngling nestled between Hasain's and Tular's larger frames. Collectively, they looked like hell. The Crown Prince could barely sit upright without leaning against the other two. Tular winced with every movement and kept one hand splayed against his side. And Hasain—Hasain's haggard appearance was possibly the worst of all. Dark rings encompassed the Radek lord's lids. His complexion was frighteningly pale, bordering on transparent. When Joel took a seat beside Hasain, he didn't even raise his eyes in acknowledgment. He stared vacantly into the darkness. Lifeless, like a statue.

Natori stood behind the prince, her face dusted by shadows and jaw set firmly. Her violet eyes were as calculating as Hasain's were hollow. Despite the bandage coiled around her head, the Blessed Mage had never looked more intimidating. Her enchanted sword gleamed from within its holster.

"The Blessed Son must favor you, Seneschal," Morathi remarked darkly. The general sat some distance away on an overturned crate, his garb badly misused and dirty, and his cape tattered in several places. Dressed so raggedly, he almost seemed a common man, but the haughty quality of his voice spoke volumes about his true nature. "I see He has, against all odds, reunited you with your son. Good fortune continues to bless your bloodline. Now, regarding the wounded—"

Koal's fingers raked through his peppered hair. "Here's my thought. We still have a handful of healthy oxen, but few supplies for them to carry. Those soldiers who are too weak to walk or ride can be loaded into carts and pulled. The Healers can tend to them while on the move, as is needed."

"The oxen are too slow. They'll impede our progress. We should slaughter them. At least the meat will be of good use."

"How, then, would you have us transport the men who cannot walk?"

Morathi met the seneschal's question with a cross countenance. "These are times of war. It's for the good of all that we make haste to the border. As difficult a decision as it is, in such a critical mark, we cannot afford—burdens."

Koal stepped back a pace, his face drawn tight. He made no effort to conceal his disgust. "*Burdens?* Is *that* what they are to you now? I won't leave them behind. Not while there is still breath in their bodies. These men risked their lives for our crown and country. To abandon them after the matter is not only unjust—it's despicable."

"Yes. Warfare *is* a despicable beast. And it knows no justice. Seneschal, you served as a captain during the Northern War. You of all people should remember. The wounded *will* slow us down. What will you say to the other survivors when the Shirites regain their strength and come riding over the hill to massacre us? Sometimes, for the good of the whole, sacrifices must be made."

An indignant gasp escaped Joel's throat. How could Morathi even suggest such a thing? Had he not a scrap of humanity in his soul?

Natori grunted, the first sound she'd made since Joel came inside. "What a notion, General—sacrificing even *more* of our army for the sake of this wretched 'war.'"

"Army? If you weren't aware, 'Blessed Mage,' we no longer *have* an army. We left Arden with ten *thousand* men. We're skulking back with fifteen *hundred*. Go on. Whine some more about injustice!"

Natori turned a fierce glare onto the general. "Morathi Adeben, were the choice mine, we'd be returning to Arden minus one more. So many lives were lost this day—not only from Arden, but Shiraz as well. And to what end? Whose ego was soothed here? Surely not yours, nor Neetra Adelwijn's. Both of you were so *certain* of victory. What will you say now to the countless widows? To the orphans and parents who will never see their loved ones again? Will you weave a lie of how they fell gallantly— that somehow their deaths were founded? Or will you slink into the shadows and lick your wounds like the beaten *dogs* you are?"

Joel drew his hands to his gaping mouth. Deegan did the same.

Morathi leapt to his feet with such force the crate below was knocked aside. He kicked it at Natori. "Damn you, *woman*, and your wicked tongue! Don't think I don't know the loss Arden suffered today. Don't think I can't feel the death of my army settling into my bones even as we speak here now. Don't think me unaware of the vulnerability our country faces. And don't *think* for a *moment* that the steward and I won't be having words upon my return to court—"

"Enough," Koal spat. "Both of you, stand down. I believe it's time we called this meeting to an end. We're starving, sleep-deprived, and heartsick. A thimbleful of compassion would go a long way right about now." His eyes wisped around the tent, passing from face to face. At last, his gaze settled narrowly on Morathi. "General, unless you're really so imprudent to risk certain *mutiny*, you best be sure every necessary effort is taken to save our wounded soldiers. Arden won't stand for it, and neither will I. Don't be a fool."

Morathi's hands were balled into massive fists at his side. He scowled so viciously it almost looked like a deranged grin. "The only fool I see is *you*, Koal Adelwijn. Just look at what you've become! There was a time when you were a reasonable man—before Rishi Radek warped your mind with lies and turned you against your own brethren. He softened your resolve, made you *weak*. He *ruined* you."

Koal's jaw tightened. Joel could only imagine how hard it must be for his father not to spit in the snake's face. "There was a time when I was naïve. I was *ignorant*. I didn't see the injustice in this world, even when laid beneath my nose. King Rishi didn't ruin me. He opened my eyes. He showed me there was more than one path to follow."

Morathi let out a snarl as he stomped toward the exit. "You'll follow that idealistic *idiot* straight to the grave if you don't watch yourself—"

The venomous words were cut short when a figure swept directly into Morathi's path, forcing him to a lurching halt.

Joel's eyes flew wide. He'd been so caught up in the argument that he'd failed to notice Tular jump to his feet. The young lord now stood boldly between the general and entryway.

"Step aside," Morathi growled, hand slipping over the hilt of his broadsword. He loomed above Tular like a great shadow over the moon.

A chill raced up Joel's spine.

Stand down. He's twice your size, Tular. Please stand down.

Tular refused to budge. Broken ribs or not, he squared his shoulders and glared with defiance up at Morathi. "If you consider someone like yourself—someone who threatens the seneschal, slanders women, and openly disrespects Arden's ruling family—to be 'reasonable,' I'll *gladly* choose to stand behind the 'weak' and 'foolish' without a trace of doubt in my heart."

The fingers grazing the metal hilt twitched, and for a moment, Joel feared the general might truly draw the weapon. But then Morathi smirked and withdrew his hand. A bout of cold laughter rumbled from within his chest. "I think there's a bit too much of your sire in you, Tular Galloway. A hard head and unyielding, blind loyalty."

"Some might consider those good qualities," Tular replied, so quiet Joel could barely make out the words.

"That depends on *where* the loyalty ultimately lies."

A clever smile tore across Tular's mouth. "Indeed. A hero is the villain's villain, after all."

Morathi's eyes narrowed dangerously. "Watch yourself. You might return to Arden a hero as it were, but victory is a fickle thing, boy."

Koal cleared his throat pointedly. "We're finished here. You may leave. Now."

Again came the sinister laughter that made Joel's skin crawl. "Finished? I think not, Seneschal. The true war's only just begun."

Flashing a haughty leer, Morathi stormed past Tular and disappeared into the night.

As soon as the general's footsteps faded, Koal slumped onto a crate. He rubbed his face, fatigue etched into the hard features. His mouth drooped so low his bottom lip touched the dip of his chin. Joel twisted his hands, waiting in silence for direction. He hated seeing his father like this, so hopeless and defeated.

At long last, Koal issued a sigh. "I suppose there's nothing more that can be done tonight. You should all try to get some rest. And may you find it. The sun rises early in the south."

"I'll stand watch," Hasain muttered, taking to his feet.

"No." Koal shook his head. "You need sleep. I'll keep vigil."

"I assure you that I *won't* find sleep tonight. I might as well make myself useful."

"Hasain, if you want to talk about the battle—"

The Radek lord's voice clipped. "I just want fresh air and to be alone." Without another word, Hasain pulled the canvas back and slipped outside.

Tular stared after his brother. "Should I follow? I can try to talk to him."

"No," Koal said. "Let him have his space for now. We all work through the horrors of the battlefield differently. He'll open up to us when he's ready."

Deegan tossed Joel and Natori each a sleeping mat before unrolling one for himself. "Tular, you take the cot. It's not good for you to lie on the ground."

Tular curled his nose. "Cots are for old men and…spoiled princes."

"That *wasn't* a suggestion."

Exhaustion sufficiently smothered any further complaints Tular might have had. Groaning, he lowered himself onto the cot and curled onto his side.

Silence swelled inside the tent as the others settled on their mats. Joel tossed for some time before finally rolling onto his back. He stared at the canvas above, bathed in cerulean moonlight. A gentle breeze rustled the fabric, causing it to buckle and lift, over and over again, as though it were a living entity. Joel watched, hoping the motion would lull him to sleep. It didn't.

More time passed. Deegan's breaths grew heavy and long, and soft snores rose from Tular's cot. Joel shut his eyes, tossing and turning so many times he soon lost count. He tried using his arm as a pillow and even shucked off his boots, yet still sleep evaded him. He couldn't get comfortable. His troubled mind was simply unable to find peace.

Finally, he could take no more and sat up. "Father?"

Koal rested on the ground, his back propped against a crate and legs stretched out before him. He'd been dozing, with his chin to his chest and eyes half closed, but he lifted his head when Joel called.

"What is it?" Koal asked.

Joel swallowed. His mouth was so dry the task took more effort than it should have. "May I ask you a question?"

"If I answer, will you go to sleep?"

Joel wanted to smile, but dark thoughts weighed heavily on his mind. He kept his voice low, so not to disturb the others. "When we were outside Tahir's gates, moments before the attack started, I saw the fear in your eyes. You told me to go to Deegan—to take him and flee. You *knew* something terrible was going to happen. How?"

Koal stared into the shadows for an eternity before he replied. "I had my suspicions when Prince Rami called for Deegan and myself to be handed over, but it wasn't until he mentioned the 'great golden dragon' that I knew our worst fears had come true."

A wave of nausea rolled over Joel. He closed his eyes against the delirium. He didn't want to ask—but he had to know. "The Empire unleashed those horrible creatures, didn't they?"

"Yes. Without a doubt."

Goddesses, help us.

278

Joel swallowed the bile bubbling at the back of his throat, fighting to keep his meager meal down. "This entire thing was a trap from the beginning, wasn't it? And we played right into their hand. Shiraz attacked Ashvale and our scouting troop to entice us across the border, but they never actually planned on facing us in open battle. Their militia feigned retreat—let us think we had the advantage—drawing us further in. Then they slowly weakened us. They cut off our supply train and raided our camp—demoralized us. They executed their plan perfectly, all so the Empire could have its way with us when we reached Tahir. Daya, how could this happen? We *knew*. We knew Sarpedon and the Dhaki princes had made an alliance. If those *fools* on the council would have listened—"

Koal hung his head. "The blame rests on my shoulders. I should have fought harder against the High Council. I should have forced them to see reason. All those lives—those thousands of soldiers—they could have been spared if I'd taken a stand against Neetra."

Joel was on his feet and by Koal's side before the seneschal could even raise his weary eyes. Joel knelt beside his father. "No, Da. This isn't your fault. You *did* try. Neetra's beyond reason, you know that. There's nothing you could have done to sway him."

"I promised Rishi I wouldn't let Arden fall into darkness, yet here we are."

Joel's hand sought out his father's. "The path may be encumbered by shadow, but we can still find our way to the light. We're alive, aren't we? We're on our way home. Deegan is safe. And don't forget about our allies in Silver. We'll be stronger when we're all together again. The High Council may even rebuke Neetra when they learn the outcome of the war. There's a good chance they'll turn to your leadership, Da. There's still hope for change."

It was hard to judge in the dim moonlight, but Joel was almost certain a smile momentarily lifted Koal's worn face. "You're wise beyond your years, son. And braver than you'll ever know. You're right. Even in the darkest hour, hope prevails. I shouldn't have despaired. Please forgive an old man for his lapse in faith."

"There's nothing to forgive, Da. Nothing. And know that every scrap of bravery—every bit of integrity and good inside my heart—it comes from *you*. You've spent your entire life courageously fighting for what's right. I'm honored to call you my father."

Koal's eyes grew misty, and then his arms went around Joel in a firm embrace. "I don't think a parent could ever be more proud of their child than I am of you."

Tears slipped freely down Joel's cheeks as he felt something raw and deep inside his soul finally start to heal. He rested his face against his father's shoulder and wept. "I love you, Da."

"And I you, son. Everything is going to be all right."

Joel returned to his mat with hope ignited inside him. The future remained shrouded—perhaps more unclear than ever before—but he *had* to believe things would get better. Evil couldn't reign forever—not when there was still so much good left in the world. The night was indeed dark, but he'd *never* stop fighting for a better tomorrow.

Joel laid down his head, a sense of great peace settling around him. A soft smile touched his lips. His eyes fluttered shut. And then sleep came, carrying him away.

EPILOGUE

Hasain stumbled through the thickening gloom, trying in vain to escape the guilt pressing down on his soul. He knew he should keep vigil outside the command tent, but he couldn't stay. He couldn't stand there and bear witness to their grief. He couldn't listen while they mourned the fallen.

This was entirely his fault. He'd *failed* in every way possible. He'd failed to keep his promise to his father. He'd failed to uphold his honor. He'd failed to protect his brothers without calling for the treacherous demon. He was a coward. A disgrace. A *murderer*.

Hasain lurched to a stop only when he reached the outskirts of the encampment. Coarse sand swallowed the soles of his boots. Choking on a gasp, he raised his eyes. The desert sprawled before him; powder-white dunes bathed in moonlight stretched into the vast distance. He wished nothing more than for the desert to devour him whole. He deserved such a fate after what he'd done. All those men. Those poor, brave soldiers. Hasain clenched his jaw so tightly his entire face hurt. The pain was nothing compared to the torment in his heart.

They're all dead. They're all dead because of me. Oh gods, what have I done? I killed them all—

"Hasain."

Hasain doubled over, shuddering with dread, as he felt the demon's presence creep over him in a sinister wave. Terror gripped his heart.

No, Hasain silently pleaded. *Go away!*

Darkness closed around him. He couldn't breathe.

"*Oh, Hasain.*" Leviticus's hiss was like a surge of blood searing through the ears. "*Perhaps if you hadn't waited so long to call for aid, such great sacrifices wouldn't have had to be made today. Regardless, what's done is done. You survived, and you'll only grow stronger with me by your side.*"

Hasain shivered. Lies. The demon told nothing but lies. His father had warned him—but he was weak. He was a *coward*. He'd succumbed to the monster's deceit. He had *failed*.

"*You should be thanking me,*" Leviticus jeered. "*Your brothers would have died if not for me. I kept them alive.*"

Hasain shook his head bitterly. At what cost? Arden's army was ruined. Gone. Lost to the sand. In a single, foolish moment, Hasain had destroyed it. He'd sent thousands of his own people to an early grave. Their screams would forever haunt his dreams. Their blood would forever stain his heart. If he'd known the demon's plan beforehand, he would never have agreed to accept help…would he?

Hasain wiped the tears from his eyes. He was no better than the vile creature that plagued him. *He* was a *monster*. His father would have been ashamed to see him now.

"Weep if you will, but you're alive and well. You're on your way home. The steward's disastrous war campaign will not sit well with the country. It will be the beginning of his downfall. Together, we'll tear him down entirely."

Lies. More lies.

Glaring into the night, Hasain reached into his pocket. His fingers brushed over the stone within. He couldn't risk any more harm. He had to be rid of the creature *now*. The demon's evil couldn't return to Arden.

He pulled the gem free, holding it at arm's length, cradling the polished crimson in the dip of his trembling palm. And then Hasain stumbled forward, venturing into the open desert.

"What are you doing?"

Shadows engulfed him, so like the shade over his heart that Hasain wondered if they were one and the same. With each footfall, his resolve ebbed, but he refused to turn back. This had to be done.

"Don't be a fool, Hasain. You still need me."

Hasain stopped when he was well outside the reach of the firelight. He was alone. No one would come out here. No one would discover what he had done. His fist tightened around the stone. Gritting his teeth, he clutched the forbidden gem, wishing he could squeeze the very essence out of it. He couldn't do that, of course, but he *could* cast it away. The demon didn't control him so wholly. And now it never would.

"You can never be rid of me. I'm in your feeble mind. I'm in your cowardly heart."

Hasain shook his head, refusing to believe the demon's words. He'd failed once. He wasn't going to make the same mistake again. This would end—now.

"Hasain—"

No. No more lies!

Hasain dropped the stone into the sand and walked away. He didn't glance back.

Kezra waited until Hasain had disappeared into the camp before she advanced. Her eyes narrowed at the sight of the glimmering ruby resting in the sand. Kneeling down, she took the gem into one hand. A frown pulled at the corner of her mouth. She'd never cared for the touch of magic energy. This focus stone must have been full of it, the way the static crackled along her fingertips.

A creeping unrest twisted inside, but she pushed the feeling from her mind. Why had Hasain discarded such a precious trinket? Was it because he thought himself weak? Didn't the fool know that a single mage could never have stopped what had happened outside Tahir?

The gem sat heavily in her hand, and she still didn't like the feel of it—but it was probably worth a small fortune. Once he'd had a chance to clear his head, Hasain might regret tossing it. With a sigh, Kezra slipped the stone into her satchel and went to sit by the fire.

FINAL WORD

Hope shattered. Arden's mighty army decimated. Lives forever changed. Nage, Liza—thousands of brave soldiers lost in a battle that should have been a sweeping victory but instead has left Arden dangerously vulnerable. Grief-stricken and weary, all Gib wants is a moment's rest and a chance to mend the broken fragments of his life. But the Silver City he returns to is anything but restful, and a dark plan has already been set into motion that may just destroy life as Gib knows it. *Exile: Book Four of the Chronicles of Arden*, is coming winter 2016!

If you would like to receive notifications regarding upcoming releases, please sign up for Shiriluna Nott's mailing list below.

If you enjoyed *Battle Dawn*, please consider leaving a review on Amazon.com. It would be very much appreciated.

Please sign up for the mailing list;
http://www.shirilunanott.com/mailinglist.html

Leave a review on Amazon

Shiriluna's Goodreads page;
https://www.goodreads.com/author/show/9757614.Shiriluna_Nott

'Like' us on Facebook;
Shiriluna Nott's Author Page;
https://www.facebook.com/authorshirilunanott
and
SaJa H.'s Author Page
https://www.facebook.com/pages/SaJa-H/794070493991829

Follow us on Twitter;
@ShirilunaNott and @SaJaH_ofArden

Official Website
http://www.shirilunanott.com

Printed in Great Britain
by Amazon